AS THE LILY GROWS

"There's an energy to a loving nature that makes a body shine,"
Ike said. "You got that shine, Lib."

Libby's jaw slackened at his kindness. She flushed and formed
words but could not speak them for the air trapped in her lungs.

Ike came to his feet and rubbed the back of his neck, a boyish
gesture she found oddly appealing. The grooves in his cheeks, so
pronounced when he smiled, were shadows in repose. Dappled sunlight gilded his eyelashes and the clean-shaven planes of his face.

The same feeling swept over her as had earlier when he'd smiled
at her from the audience. The other picnickers fell away like the background of a painting in which the focal point stood in bold relief.

Ike was the focal point.

Other Avon Books by
Susan Kirby

PRAIRIE ROSE

SUSAN KIRBY

As the Lily Grows

AVON BOOKS ◆ NEW YORK

This is a work of fiction. Names, characters, places, and incidents either are the product of the author's imagination or are used fictitiously. Any resemblance to actual events, locales, organizations, or persons, living or dead, is entirely coincidental and beyond the intent of either the author or the publisher.

AVON BOOKS
A division of
The Hearst Corporation
1350 Avenue of the Americas
New York, New York 10019

Copyright © 1997 by Susan Kirby
Cover art by Max Ginsburg
Published by arrangement with the author
Visit our website at **http://AvonBooks.com**
ISBN: 1-56865-328-X

Printed in the U.S.A.

1

The hissing gaslights spilled blue light over the crates and barrels and crowded shelves of Willie Blue's general store and onto the yellowed pages of the novel in Libby Watson's hands, which she was reading out loud. The clock ticked. The rocking chair whispered. The old beagle, Sugar, lifted her graying muzzle from her water dish and pricked her ears at the quiver in Libby's voice. The nail keg upon which Naomi McClure perched creaked as she shifted her lanky frame, straining closer so as not to miss a single word.

Recently estranged from her husband, Naomi shared not only a name with the protagonist in the story, but also her stoic character, acquired through suffering, heartache, and loss. Nor was Libby's widowed father, seated on a cracker barrel to the left of the cold stove, a stranger to trouble and tragedy. But as Libby glanced up from the blur of words, she saw that their eyes were damp, too. The knot in her throat thickened. Sugar whined and, toenails tapping against the plank floor, came to perch her paws on Libby's lap.

"Would ye have me take a wee turn, lass?" asked Libby's father, Thomas Watson.

She passed the book into her father's outstretched hand, then lowered her face to Sugar's, blinking back tears and fondling the dog's velvet ears.

Zerilda Payne, the dour, blunt-spoken mail carrier for one of Edgewood's two rural routes, muttered, "Don't know what ya want to read sech a sad old story for."

Yet Zerilda listened intently from Captain Boyd's rocking chair, her hard-bitten features inscrutable as Thomas read of Naomi, who had come through famine, separation from her homeland, the loss of her husband, the loss of her sons, and now wept bitterly as she bid her daughters-in-law good-bye. Thomas's Scottish diction imbued the tale with a haunting strain not unlike the lonely keening of a Highland bagpipe as the daughter-in-law Ruth emerged from the page with quiet courage to say she would go with Naomi. Based on the biblical account, the story was so skillfully written that Libby felt Naomi's seeping faith, her fear, and her helplessness, and Ruth's wrenching of heart as she turned on the road leading away from her country and watched her village, her family home, all that was familiar, shrink from view.

Libby caught a shallow breath, damp eyes fixed on Zerilda's crocheting. The thread shuttled around her coworker's stubby fifth finger, over cracked knuckles, between forefinger and thumb, and onto the hook, growing stitch by stitch into a thing of beauty incongruous with the woman's hard, homely hands. Like Ruth's character, grown through hardship and heartache, yet flowering with so fragrant a scent. *Oh, to write like that. Reflecting battered courage, anguish, loyalty, and the bloom of rare virtue with the stroke of a well-chosen word.*

Libby's nerves jumped at the bang of a fist on Willie Blue's back door. Jarred into the present reality of mail to be sorted and a route to be run, she brushed the dog hair from the lap of her blue-and-white-striped skirt, dried her eyes again, and read the time on the watch pinned to her shirtwaist. "He's early."

"Aweel, lass, 'tis a guid stoppin' place," said Thomas. He closed the book, passed it to Libby, and followed Sugar through the back section of Willie Blue's to let in Billy Young.

It was Billy's job to collect the first mail drop from the railway station each day at dawn. Soon, he was to take over Libby's route as well. A strapping dark-haired young man with a hat tilted rakishly over one blue eye, Billy flashed his infectious smile and flung the mail bag down on the sorting table. "Good morning, all. How's the book coming?"

"Too blamed much hurtin' in it fer my taste," muttered Zerilda. She put her crocheting away and lumbered over to her sorting case.

Naomi came to her feet as well. The nights had been too hot to sleep upstairs, where she and the children now lived. Her little girl, Opal, was still asleep on a mat in the front portion of the store. Her son, Frankie, was "camping out" in the buggy shed. Both would have to be stirred to their feet and fed by eight o'clock, the official opening time for Willie Blue's. The store, on the north side of the village square, doubled as the post office for the central Illinois farming community of Edgewood.

"Wish I'd shook 'em awake to hear the story. Cain't help thinkin' they'd profit from sech a book," said Naomi.

Her words touched a responsive chord in Libby. But Mr. Gruben, the editor of the town newspaper and Libby's mentor, had loaned her the novel. His wife's name was inscribed on the inside front cover, and Mrs. Gruben, who was a semi-invalid, was reclusive by nature and careful of her books. Wishing she could offer Naomi the use of it, yet knowing she dared not without asking, Libby said, "What this town needs is a library."

Naomi sighed in agreement and continued on her way to awaken the children. But Zerilda, true to her character, snorted and challenged, "Loafers thicker'n flies on a gummed strip right here in this store ever mornin', and you're wantin' to cultivate idleness?"

Sociable by nature, Libby looked forward to exchanging the news of the day with the old fellows who assembled at Willie Blue's each morning. Most of them had lived long, full lives. Although their hands might be idle, their minds certainly weren't. Whether they were arguing politics, talking crops, or sharpening their wit on one another, scarely a morning went by that Libby didn't learn something from them. Softening her reply with a smile, she said to Zerilda, "Slip a book in their hands, and they won't be idle."

Billy tipped his hat back and grinned. "Reading is a little tame for some of the boys."

"Swappin' lies and meddlin' in other folks' affairs, that's where their skill lies," claimed Zerilda.

Billy opened his mouth as if to defend the old boys, then shot Zerilda Payne a glance and shut it again. No point in getting on the wrong side of his soon-to-be coworker. Libby said no more about a library. She liked Edgewood, with its lush green park at the center of the town square and bustling shops and tree-lined streets and progressive attitude. Anyway, she had no heart for faultfinding when her life was so full, so brimming with possibilities, like a crisp white page waiting for the first mark of a pen.

Libby reached beneath the counter and took another peek at this week's *Gazette*. Her gaze skipped past the masthead, with its August 5, 1904, date, past the suspense-building headlines HOLD YOUR HORSES, THE CIRCUS IS COMING, below the article about the community dinner to be held while the circus was in town, to the very bottom of the page:

LOCAL MAN TO TAKE CAMPAIGN ON THE ROAD

by Elizabeth Watson

Attorney Angus Cearlock, Prohibition candidate for the legislature, is planning an autumn campaign tour of surrounding towns. The singing Berry Sisters, comprised of Miss Chloe Berry, Miss Dorene Berry, Miss Elizabeth Watson, and Mrs. Maddie Daniels, will be traveling with young Candidate Cearlock, entertaining the crowds. Family and friends including Mr. and Mrs. Chester Gentry,

Dr. and Mrs. Melville Harding, and Mrs. Madeline Dorrance plan to be a part of the entourage. But you needn't
wait until autumn to hear the Berry Sisters sing. They
will be performing at the union services to be held at
Spring Lake on Sunday.

Writing for the *Gazette* was a modest beginning for an aspiring novelist
like Libby, but an onward, upward stride all the same. This article was of
particular interest to her, as it marked the official debut of the singing Berry
Sisters, of which she was a member. Sweetening her anticipation over the
fall tour was Mr. Gruben's request that she cover Angus's campaign for the
newspaper.

Seeing Sugar's velvet ears come to attention, Libby got out of the beagle's
path to the door. The dog let out a yip and tore for the back door just as
Teddy Baker stepped over the threshold.

"W-e-ll, I was coming anyway, so I told him I didn't mind bringing it
along," said Teddy. He stuck out his hand, a telegram tucked between his
thumb and forefinger.

"For me or Father?" asked Libby.

"I don't know, he just said to bring it, that's all."

A gangly pale-eyed fellow in his early twenties, Teddy knew everyone in
town, knew their children and their dogs and their horses, too. But he never
referred to anyone by name, which made conversing with him confusing at
times.

"'Tis kind of you to be playin' messenger, laddie," said Thomas. He
crossed to the door to accept the telegram, a warmth in his smile and a vigor
to his step that belied his frail frame, sunken chest, and pasty complexion.

A billed cap shadowing his face, Teddy hunkered down on his heels to
meet Sugar's wags and wet kisses. A high fever in infancy had left Teddy
mentally impaired. But the old beagle, who had been passed from Uncle
Willie to Libby to the McClure children, loved Teddy better than any of her
masters. Teddy murmured and patted and returned the dog's affection with
a smile that exposed an abundance of pink gum and a row of teeth as square
and white as piano keys.

"Who's it from, Father?" Libby's gaze sought her father's.

"'Tis from yer brither Adam, askin' if his bonny Abigail might come for
a wee stay."

Libby's breath caught in her throat. Carefully, she asked, "For a few
days?"

"He doesn't say. Though I canna help thinkin' 'twill be"—Thomas cast the others a glance, dropped his voice, and for Libby's ears alone finished— "until her time of confinement be past."

Libby's heart plummeted. *Abigail was coming here to have her baby? What was Adam thinking?*

2

♨ The August sun beat down on the lid of Libby's mail buggy as she made her way over the fertile green countryside. A coal miner's daughter, Libby Watson had left school at the age of ten to care for the little brother her mother had died birthing. Leaving two older brothers in southern Illinois, where they held poverty at bay by working the mines amidst the turmoil of strikes, layoffs, and occasional outbursts of violence, she had, upon inheriting Uncle Willie's store, moved with her father and David to the heart of the state only three months ago. Mr. Gruben, the editor of the *Gazette*, learned of her interest in writing and gave her a few articles to write every week. Employed as a rural mail carrier, she honed her writing skills as her reliable buggy horse Proctor drew her along the dirt roads that crisscrossed the undulating countryside.

Fields pieced in golds and greens lay thirsting in the August sun. The birds are silent. Even the breeze is listless. The farmers are watching the skies in hopes of a good soaker. Libby scanned the brief paragraph Mr. Gruben might find useful for the column he called "Bits And Pieces." In the left-hand margin, she wrote in small letters: *Is this a drought?*

Knowing more about mining than agriculture, Libby relied on observation and asking questions to relate the tapestry of ever-changing crops and weather and season to a community who knew far better than she did what caused cornleaves to curl in the heat of the day, apples to grow lopsided, and hens to lay soft-shelled eggs. She jotted down questions as they came to her and sprung them on the old men who gathered at Willie Blue's for mail, tall tales and cracker-barrel repartee.

Preoccupation with her writing had momentarily crowded out misgivings over Adam's telegram. Libby was aware of the sweetness of clover and the thirsty scent of baked earth as the canvas-lidded mail buggy creaked along between a field of corn and a pasture of grazing cows. A red-tailed hawk hung in the air, defying gravity with the ripple of a wing while the section of land to the north called Old Kentucky shimmered, a cool, inviting patchwork of trees hugging the gentle contours of the earth like a quilt.

A quilt. Libby had planned to make one as a wedding gift for her brother Adam and his bride. Belated, albeit, but that couldn't be helped. It had been a "hurry-up" wedding, simple words spoken in front of the minister after Abigail found herself to be with child. Libby, having already moved to Edgewood, had learned of it after the fact. Quilts symbolized comfort to her, and she knew Abigail would need comfort when the baby came and the Thistle Down busybodies counted backward and came up with less than nine months. The baby was due in six weeks. Her condition was beyond hiding. *Was that what had prompted the telegram?* Libby thrust the intrusion from her mind. She bent her head and scribbled in the Memorandum notebook on her knee: "Cross-stitched fences and red barn appliqués."

Proctor dropped a wheel in a rut. Libby's pencil marred the carefully lettered page. "Bother," she muttered, and repaired the damage as best she could. It was too flowery for the *Gazette,* she decided, thinking of Mr. Gruben's previous editings. But if she could draw the pattern, it would make a pretty quilt.

"Easy, Proctor. Shoo, fly. Leave the poor fellow some hide." Libby scattered the bloodthirsty flies with a flick of the buggy whip. Eager for the cooler air of the grove, she closed her notebook, urged Proctor into a trot, and soon crossed Timber Creek amidst towering hardwoods. The trees formed a canopy, laying green shade over the narrow dirt road as it uncurled its way past the cemetery, Timber Creek Church, and the school. Following the curves and corners of the grove, Libby slowed Proctor as they reached the covered bridge and crossed Timber Creek a second time. Just over the bridge, hounds poured out from under the porch of Skiff's Store.

The bewhiskered storekeep stepped out on the porch. At his command, the wave of barking dogs receded. But Libby kept her eyes fixed straight ahead. It was said Carlon Skiff was a moonshiner. The rumor, to Libby's sharp regret, had not reached her ears until *after* she'd served as go-between, selling him canning jars on Sarah Jane Brignadello's behalf. The nail keggers at Willie Blue's knew what old Skiff had in mind for those jars, as did Angus Cearlock. Angus, who was courting Libby, was running for the Illinois legislature upon a Prohibition platform. His firm antiliquor stand enriched the old fellows' enjoyment of the incident, and though it had been weeks ago, they still liked to bring it up and wink and chortle.

A straight shot west, then a jog north and west again brought her to a wide space in the road where a pioneer settlement had once taken root. All that remained now was a deserted cabin that had until recently served as Naomi McClure's woodworking shop. Libby stopped at the mouth of wagon tracks across the road from the vacant shop. She reached under the seat for the matchbox present Opal McClure had asked her to deliver as a present to her father. The girl had decorated it with broken twigs and mismatched buttons. Libby climbed down. She couldn't put the child's gift in the mailbox as there was no postage affixed. But there was nothing in postal regulations to prevent her from leaving it at the foot of the mailbox. Nor would Decatur McClure miss seeing it there.

Her faithful white steed looked as if he could use a long drink, and she could stand to fill her water jar. So thinking, Libby urged Proctor across the road and pumped him a bucket from the pump behind the shop. She rolled up her sleeves and splashed away the gritty film of dust and perspiration. Cool rivulets ran down her neck, dampening her bodice as she drank from the pump.

Libby returned to her buggy and continued down the dusty road, over the Chicago and Alton train tracks at the Old Kentucky switch, then crossed yet another bridge over Timber Creek, a meandering tributary of Sugar Creek, so named for the proliferation of sugar maples growing along its banks. In a clearing skirted by heavy timber, Ike Galloway's maple camp had sprung from the ground over the summer. A horse harnessed to a slip scraper, a mechanical shovel-like device, rested alongside a dirt pile that butted up against the north side of the new structure.

At the beginning of summer, when Libby had inherited the Edgewood store that carried her Uncle Willie Blue's name, Ike had done some clerking for her. He was an independent, hardworking fellow who took initiative in a low-keyed way Libby found agreeable. Every third day, Libby passed his place carrying the mail. He had none today. But his name was the last on the list of contacts she'd been asked to make on behalf of the New Hope congregation's upcoming church social.

Libby ground-tied Proctor, followed a whistling rendition of ''The Animal Fair'' to the rear of the new building, and found Ike unloading firewood from a two-wheeled cart. He was working with his right side turned her way and didn't hear her coming. Injuries sustained during the war in Cuba had left him nearly deaf in that ear. Taking a piece of firewood off the cart, Libby added it to the pile he was making near the rear of his building and chimed in singing to his whistling accompaniment. ''And the old baboon by the light of the moon was combing her auburn hair.''

Ike swung around to greet her with a sheepish grin. ''Libby. Wasn't expectin' company.''

She smiled and teased, "My! We may just let you join the Berry Sisters. Go ahead! You were doing just fine."

He slapped his hat against his leg, a darker hue creeping over his sun-browned features. "Believe I'll leave it to the birds for now."

Libby laughed and waved a hand toward the woodpile. "It's awfully hot for splitting wood, isn't it?"

"I'm jest stacking some I hauled in from the woods a day or two ago. What brings you this away?"

"You're working too hard. You've lost track of the week."

His left eyelid drooped slightly lower than the right, fine lines creasing the corner as he did some mental calculations. "Thursday?"

"Saturday."

"Sure it is," he said as if he'd known all along. The crevices in his stubbled cheeks deepened at her laughter. "All the same, I wasn't expectin' you. Last I heard, Billy was takin' over yer route."

Libby nodded. "Starting Monday."

"Reckon he could use some reliable income. He's found it a struggle, gettin' that dray business off the ground."

"He hasn't given up on the venture altogether," said Libby.

"Takes time to establish yer own business," agreed Ike.

He and Billy Young had served together as part of the First U. S. Volunteer Cavalry. Billy relished his soldiering experience, whereas Ike never mentioned it at all. But their loyalty to each other was unmistakable.

She said, "People like Billy. He'll be all right."

"I reckon." Ike crossed to the chopping block for his discarded shirt.

Having grown up in a household of males, it wasn't his lack of a shirt so much as his reaching for it that drew Libby's attention to his muscled shoulders, lean torso, and narrow waist. His hair was longer than what she thought fashionable. It curled over his scarred ear and spiraled down his neck in sweat-soaked bark-colored ringlets. Dappled sunlight picked out the auburn on his unshaven cheeks and jaw. Long exposure to sun had gilded the tips of his curls and darkened his back.

Fixing her gaze on the north side of the building, Libby asked, "What are you digging?"

"Ain't so much diggin' as makin' a ramp for the team and sled to use bringin' in sap."

Libby's puzzled expression prompted further explanation.

"I'll need it to empty into an outdoor storage tank along the building. A pipe will run from the tank into the sap house. Gravity'll bring the sap into the evaporatin' pans."

"I see. So the tank must be higher than the pans indoors?" Thinking aloud, she added, "What's to keep the pipe from freezing?"

"I'm workin' on that."

Curiosity drew Libby around the side of the building for another look at the dirt ramp taking shape there. At length, she came back and found him still stacking wood.

"You could insulate the pipe in dirt, then make a fire pit under it. That way if the pipe freezes, you can thaw it out in short order."

He paused to wipe his brow with a faded shirtsleeve. "Careful there, you'll have me catchin' fire to the sap house."

Again, he rolled it off his tongue as one word in a prairie drawl as deep and rich and fertile as the soil beneath their feet. Libby wrinkled her nose. "Why don't you call it a sugar shanty? Doesn't that sound picturesque?"

Dimples came out of hiding as he thrust a piece of firewood her way. "Reckon you can get yer hands to movin' as quick as yer ideas?"

"I only stopped to ask you if you would like to come to services on Sunday."

"No point in standin' around idle while yer askin'."

Libby denied him the pleasure of looking pained and filled the gap between him and the woodpile. She established a smooth flow, thunking the pieces onto the pile as he gave them to her. "They'll be at Spring Lake. Pastor Shaw has a full day planned."

"You're talkin' about New Hope? I thought you'd thrown in with the Methodists."

"I didn't 'throw in' with anyone." She took issue with his careless phrasing. "Father and David have been going to New Hope. I thought I'd just as well go, too."

"Get over bein' mad at Mrs. Dorrance, did you?"

A vein throbbed at Libby's temple at the mention of Mrs. Dorrance. A couple of months ago, when Libby had been running the post office prior to Father's arrival in Edgewood, Mrs. Dorrance had stirred up a tempest in a teapot over their rural carrier, Captain Boyd, drinking on the job. Irritated that Ike should guess she was still giving Mrs. Dorrance a wide berth, Libby tilted her chin, and retorted, "I wasn't mad at her. I just thought she went too far, targeting Captain Boyd for reform. She would have gotten him fired from this route, you know, if he hadn't beaten her to the punch and retired first."

"How's the captain doin' anyway?" asked Ike.

"Just fine. He comes by the house a couple of times a week to study Scripture with Father. He asks some very thought-provoking questions."

"Still on the wagon, is he?"

"He is indeed."

"And you won't credit Mrs. Dorrance for that in the least?"

Libby's jaw tightened at the repressed laughter shining in his slate gray eyes. "Somehow or other, I got the idea it was a Higher Power than hers."

Ike conceded her point with an amiable smile.

"About Sunday," she continued. "It's a union service: New Hope, the Methodists and Timber Creek Church, all three."

"Takes deep pockets to put up a church building from scratch."

"I didn't invite you with the offering plate in mind."

"I wasn't sayin' . . . ." He laughed, tugged his hat down low over his eye, and remarked, "Yer awful touchy today. Must be the heat."

"Or the company."

"Careful, you'll hurt my feelin's."

Unrepentant, she countered, "I only took your name because I was timid about inviting someone I hardly know. And here you are making a chore of it."

"Sorry."

He didn't look sorry. He looked as if he was enjoying himself. And at her expense, too. Resolving to finish what she had begun and be on her way, Libby said, "There'll be a box lunch after services and the memory verse contest in the afternoon."

"You competin'?"

"I don't have the greatest memory in the world, but with a trip to the World's Fair in the offing, I may try. Or didn't you know that Mr. Gentry agreed to give the winner a trip to the fair?"

"Generous to a fault, Mr. Gentry," he said on a cryptic note.

"Mr. Brignadello, too. He's paying for accommodations." Libby gave credit where credit was due.

"Try one out on me."

Libby paused in stacking wood to look at him. "A verse, you mean?"

"Sure. Or cain't you think of one?"

"Remind me again: What is it I like about you?"

He laughed. "All right then. What time would you like me to pick you up for church?"

Heat flooded Libby's cheeks. "Ike Galloway! You know very well it wasn't that kind of invitation."

His smile lost a bit of its elasticity. "How is Angus anyway?"

"Come see for yourself. He's going to say a few words tomorrow."

"That so?" said Ike, crooking an eyebrow. He reached past her to chuck the last piece of wood onto the pile. "Seem to recollect the Master puttin' the money changers out on their ear. What do ya reckon he'll do to a politician who comes to the pulpit stumpin'?"

Libby could have told him it was a testimonial Angus was going to give, not a thing to do with the upcoming election. Instead, she said, "The choir from the Methodist Church is singing. An ensemble from Timber Creek Church, too. Not to mention Paulette Harding and the Berry girls and me.''

"Maybe I *will* come. What're you singing? Gospel songs?''

"No, Ike. We thought we'd drape ourselves in bunting and sing some campaign songs. Of course they're gospel songs! If you don't want to go, just say so.'' Libby dusted the bark from her hands and pushed damp tendrils away from her face.

"It ain't so much wantin' or not wantin','' he began.

The snap of a branch underfoot and the sight of Decatur McClure making his way around the side of the building distracted Libby from the rest of his excuse. McClure was long and lean with a rawhide face stretched over muscle and bone. He took off his sweat-stained hat to wipe his brow. The hair on the back of Libby's neck prickled as his riveting blue gaze lighted on her for a heartbeat before moving on to Ike.

"How's the ramp comin'?'' McClure asked.

"Uphill work, what with the heat.''

"Ain't much doin' over't home if ya need some help,'' McClure offered.

"Reckon if you was to run the slip scraper, I could make some headway with the hand shovelin'.''

"I'll get at it then.'' Decatur tugged his hat down low and ambled back the way he'd come.

"I should be going. I've got an article to write,'' said Libby. Offhandedly, she asked, "Have you heard anything about horses disappearing from private barns at night?''

"Stolen, ya mean?''

"Borrowed is more the word. Mr. Gruben is assuming it's boys up to mischief. On every occasion, the horses have been returned to their stalls before morning.''

"First I've heard of it, but thanks for the warning.''

"Let me know if you hear anything,'' said Libby. "Mr. Gruben wants me to cover it for the paper.''

Ike nodded as he fell in step beside her.

Libby's gaze strayed to the ramp in passing. The slip scraper resembled a giant scoop, sliding along the ground behind the horse, digging into the dirt. McClure had the lines to the horse draped around his neck, freeing his hands for the handles at the back of the mechanism.

"Got a way with horses, Decatur does. Takes skill to handle a team with yer hands tied up,'' said Ike, stopping to watch.

"I've heard the same thing about you,'' said Libby.

Ike grinned. "One runaway buggy, and they never let you live it down.''

"I wasn't thinking of that at all,'' Libby said quickly. "I was thinking about the Rough Riders. Folks in town never miss an opportunity to boast that you and Billy were part of that outfit.''

''And you're impressed, are you?''

''I don't know that I should be,'' she retorted. ''Didn't I read somewhere that your unit was unmounted the whole time?''

Unruffled, he returned in a bantering tone, ''You got a mean spirit, Lib, remindin' me like that.''

''Just paying you back for that buggy ride.''

''So you *haven't* forgot,'' he said, and laughed again.

Nor was she likely to. It had occurred on Decoration Day. The streets of Edgewood were crowded with folks watching the old soldiers parade past when Uncle Willie's funeral let out, and Ike, who was supposed to drive her out to the cemetery, lost control of the buggy horse. In all fairness, the noise and confusion and a well-aimed stone from the slingshot of Frankie McClure had contributed generously to the accident, which resulted in their being dragged down the street in the canvas lid of the buggy. Ike had been teasing her ever since, offering to take her for a buggy ride and prove he really could keep it upright.

Discomfited by the light dancing in Ike's eyes, Libby looked away and inadvertently caught a glimpse of McClure working the horses. He held the lines between his neck and his shoulder, sending unspoken instructions down their length with the inclination of his corded muscles. An involuntary shiver crept up her spine as she recalled a more recent narrow escape, and this one was no accident. McClure had raced his own team without mercy, wreaking havoc on his cornfield and garden and bearing down on his wife like a crazy man. Ike claimed McClure would have stopped short of hitting Naomi, but as far as Libby was concerned, it was Frankie's courageous leap in front of the barreling team that had spared his mother. After swerving to miss Frankie, McClure had shaken himself loose of the wagon wreckage and gone after his runaway team, but not before telling Libby to get off his land and to take Naomi and the boy with her, that he didn't want Willie Blue's castoffs.

Ike intruded upon her reverie, asking, ''How's Naomi and the kids gettin' along?''

''The gossip's been hard,'' said Libby, twigs snapping underfoot. She jumped as he touched her arm, then flushed at her skittishness as he drew her wide of a patch of poison ivy. ''But business is good at the store.''

''Glad to hear it.'' His hand fell away from her arm. He caught the branch of a young sapling to prevent it from snapping back on her. ''That was a good thing ya done, signing the store over to Frankie.''

''Uncle Willie would have done it himself if he hadn't been protecting Naomi.'' Libby hadn't seen that for a while. But after Decatur's drunken rage, she'd seen it well enough.

"Frankie helpin' her keep store?" Ike asked.

"If he can fit it in between playing marbles, smoking behind the lumber-yard, and making a general nuisance of himself."

"How's Opal doing?" he asked.

"Homesick, I'm afraid."

"Misses her daddy?"

Libby told him how seven-year-old Opal had made up a gift box for her father and asked her to deliver it.

"You give it to him yet?"

"I left it at his mailbox. I wasn't going to," Libby added, lest he think she'd softened her view of McClure. "But she started to cry, and I didn't have the heart to turn her down."

"I reckon the missin' goes two ways."

"Yes, well, he should have thought of that, shouldn't've he?"

"He's hurtin', too."

"If he isn't, he deserves to be."

"Where's the charity in that?"

The words, though gently spoken, brought Libby's chin up. Decatur's deeds spoke for themselves. She didn't feel the need to justify her sentiments. To Ike, least of all. He handed her into the buggy in silence, the strength in his callused palm not unlike that of his underlying nature. *Quiet but unyielding.* Shifting to a relaxed stance, one leg forward, the knee slightly bent, the other leg straight, bearing most of his weight, he lapped his arms across his chest, tucked his hands beneath his arms, and looked up at her on the buggy seat as if he had something more to say. But when it came down to things that they couldn't see eye to eye on, he wasn't one for wasting words.

"Take care of yerself, Libby. Goin' to miss seein' you pass while deliverin' the mail."

Libby could have told him she would still make it by now and then because she was Billy's substitute. Instead, she gripped the sun-warmed lines.

At length, he lifted his hand and moved away from the buggy.

Charity indeed. Slowly, she let her breath go.

3

Ike watched her pull away, her exasperation conspicuous in the stiff squaring of her shoulders. She had eyes like blue asters, a dusting of freckles across her pert nose, and a dimple in her right cheek. Her straw hat was slightly crooked, her hair a tangle of sunlight and curled copper. He sighed, aching a little as he watched her go and thinking maybe he should have kept his mouth shut.

But it bothered him how bent she was on kicking Decatur while he was down. Seemed out of character after she'd shown such sensitivity where the store was concerned. Willie Blue had bequeathed it to her, and everyone had expected her to keep it. Instead, she had seen a need greater than her own and passed it on to Frankie, with Naomi acting as proprietor until the boy came of age.

"Ya'd jest as well fall on a sharp stick as get yerself tangled up with that little gal," said Decatur as Ike returned to his work.

"Who, Libby?" He feigned minimal interest. "She's got herself a fella."

"Then what business she got lightin' here and sashayin' about?"

"Church doin's at the lake tomorrow. She was tellin' me about it."

Decatur snorted. "Wimmen. Ain't one in ten worth their salt."

"Yer startin' to sound like Hascal," Ike countered, referring to Decatur's father-in-law, Hascal Caton.

"Hack's an old fool, but he's right sometimes."

"He talks enough, he's bound to be right *sometime.*"

Old Hascal Caton had contributed generously to the trouble between Decatur and Naomi by his slipshod fathering. Hascal seldom complimented his daughter or came to her defense. So far as Ike could see, it wasn't deliberate meanness so much as ignorance. But that didn't help Naomi.

Decatur worked till he had a full load of dirt in the scraper. Presently, he ventured, "Read in that book the little red-haired gal's pa brought me that God got ta thinkin' man needed some company. Cut a rib clean out of man and made it into a woman. Reckon that's true?"

"Got no reason to doubt it."

Decatur grunted as he strained at the handles of the slip scraper, dumping the load of dirt on the ramp. He mopped his brow, and asked with a dark grin, "How do ya reckon a feller'd go about gettin' that rib back?"

Ike tucked his head and thrust the shovel into the mound of dirt. Wasn't any humor in it. Not after all that had happened since Willie Blue had died saving Frankie from a charging bull. It was a telling moment, Willie's death. Decatur had gone wild with the realization that Willie had lain with Naomi and fathered the boy he'd raised as his own son. Naomi, for her part, felt she'd dealt fairly with Decatur, for she had told him when he first came courting that she was carrying another man's child. What she had steadfastly refused to disclose over the years was that Willie Blue was the man.

Willie was a trusted friend. Not just to Ike, who'd been a boy at the time, but to Decatur, too. Looking back, Ike reckoned Willie hadn't been much of a role model. Not till he'd quit drinkin' anyway. And then he'd been about as fine a man as Ike had ever known. Libby was only half-right, saying Willie's silence was aimed at protecting Naomi. He'd also been protecting Decatur, fearing the truth would destroy him.

It very nearly had. He couldn't have festered any worse if he had rolled in that poison weed Libby had so gingerly sidestepped. Willie was dead, so there wasn't any way Decatur could avenge himself except by punishin' Naomi, which only worsened matters. Now they were split up, all of them hurtin': Decatur, Naomi, Frankie, and little Opal.

Decatur broke the silence. "Ya goin'?"

Ike leaned into his shovel, having lost the thread of conversation. "Goin' where?"

"To church."

"Don't look like it. Haven't got a clean shirt."

"Ain't worth the trouble, is that what yer sayin'?"

Paying closer heed, Ike asked, "Why? Was you wantin' to go?"

"I ain't keen on preachin', but I don't see no harm in stoppin' by to hear Opal recite." Decatur unfolded a paper from his pocket. "She sent me a matchbox with a note tucked inside. See here? Says there's a contest, and she's been memorizing some words to say, and if she was to win, she'll get a trip to St. Louis."

"To the World's Fair." Ike nodded. "Lots of folks interested in that."

"Opal ain't gonna win, she ain't that much for memory. Not like Frankie, anyways. He's clever, Frankie is. Still and all, the girl's wantin' me to come."

Ike couldn't recall Decatur ever going to any sort of program the children were in, school nor church. In the past, he had left all that up to Naomi.

"I ain't gonna cause no trouble, Ike," Decatur inserted into Ike's thoughtful silence. "Jest wanna see my kids, that's all."

In the sense of puttin' food on the table and clothes on their backs and seeing that they got schooling, Decatur had been as much a father to Frankie as he had been to Opal. Ike hated seeing that taken from the boy all because the truth had come out. On the surface, it seemed a good thing, Decatur including Frankie. But Ike was in no hurry to be relieved. He slapped a mosquito off his arm. "Skeeters are thick, ain't they?"

"Eat you up, this close to the creek," said Decatur. "Don't know why you ain't moved into the cabin. Told you b'fore you was welcome to it."

The cabin he spoke of had once belonged to Willie Blue. Ike had lived there for a while as a boy. More recently, Naomi had used it as a wood-working shop. He was reluctant to move in with her tools still there.

"Be a long sight easier'n cookin' over a wood fire and sleepin' in a tent," Decatur persisted.

"I ain't slept in that tent since I finished the sap house."

"When yer evaporator comes in and takes up all yer space, what're ya gonna do then? Tarnation, Ike! You cain't live in a sap house," said Decatur.

"Can for a while. Evaporator won't be shipped until fall," reasoned Ike.

"You ain't even got a stove to cook on nor a place for one neither."

"No point in building the firebox until the evaporator comes," said Ike. "Anyway, who needs fire this time of year?"

Decatur glowered at him. "If you won't do it fer yerself, then do it for me. I got a notion somebody been slippin' in the cabin at night."

Ike looked at him in surprise. "Since when?"

"Here lately. Found the door swinging open just this morning."

"I haven't seen anyone comin' nor goin'," said Ike.

"Me neither. But jest cause I ain't ketched 'em don't mean they ain't been there."

"What do ya make of it?" asked Ike carefully.

"Drifter maybe. Somebody hidin' out? I dunno."

"Reckon I could settle in for a few nights. Keep an eye out."

"Be obliged if ya did," said Decatur.

Ike nodded and went back to digging and thinking his own thoughts. The situation between Decatur and Naomi couldn't improve, not without changes in both of them. But anything less than mending would only produce more misery. So it seemed to him anyway.

Reconciliation. A tall word. He was glad it was God's work, not his. He had no plan, only faith. Scrawny at that. But then, there wasn't much size to a mustard seed. That, to his recollection, was all that God required.

4

Libby followed the Tile Factory Road back to Edgewood, passing her family's little yellow rental house on Fisher Street on the way into town. Mrs. Gruben, the wife of her friend and editor, Lucius Gruben, looked after Libby's little brother, David, while she and Father were working. The Grubens lived three houses down the street in a tree-shaded white bungalow. Spotting Florence Gruben working in her flower beds with a kitten pouncing on the weeds she tossed, Libby guided Proctor to the side of the road.

"Where's your little helper, Mrs. Gruben?"

Florence Gruben turned her head toward the street and called a greeting. Sprigs of damp gray hair clung to her perspiring brow beneath the shade of her gardening hat. She lifted the skirt of her apron, wiped her wrinkled face and soiled hands, and reached for her crutch.

"Stay where you are. I'm coming." Hastily, Libby climbed down and crossed the scorched grass.

Florence had lost a leg as a child. She got her crutch beneath her and was lumbering toward the house by the time Libby reached her. A lover of books, cats, and flowers, the editor's wife hoisted herself into the shade of the veranda, dropped heavily into a chair, and expelled a weary sigh. "It's too hot for weeding. Let me get my second wind, and I'll make some lemonade."

"No, no. I can't stay. Is David here?" asked Libby.

"He walked over the railroad tracks to the Mill Pond. I thought he'd be back by now."

"He's probably dangling his feet in the water."

"I sent Teddy Baker to see about him."

Touched by her carefulness, Libby said, "David isn't to be a worry to you, Mrs. Gruben."

"Oh, no!" Florence said quickly. "I wasn't worried. Teddy was cutting across my backyard and over the tracks anyway, so I thought there'd be no harm in his checking."

Libby smiled and patted her shoulder. "You aren't to give it another thought. I'll drive over by the Mill Pond and pick David up."

"I told him today that I hope he'll still come visit me even though you'll be home now that Billy is taking over your route. He promised to drop by on Monday."

"You aren't coming out to the lake tomorrow?"

Florence shook her head. "I believe I'll stay home and read. Lucius is disappointed in me, but I'm too old for hobbling over rough terrain on a crutch."

Libby had a feeling that even with two sound legs, Florence would have preferred a good book to a church social. She visited a moment longer, then climbed back in the buggy and hurried Proctor along. She crossed the tracks just ahead of a slow-moving freight train and turned north onto Mill Pond Road. The street ran parallel to the railroad tracks on its way through Edgewood, then veered to the west side of the pond. Proctor, steady of disposition and broad of back, was a reliable buggy horse. Even so, Libby kept a firm hand as the train came along. The heavy-laden cars shook the ground as the engine gradually picked up speed. The pond was in view, but there was no sign of David. Could she have missed him? He might have cut over the tracks and back to the Grubens' house as she followed the street to the crossing. Or maybe he had gone to Willie Blue's. Sometimes when business was slow, David idled away a little time behind the counter with Father or in the lot behind the store, playing with Opal McClure.

Libby was about to head Proctor toward the store when the shrill yips and yelps of children brought her head around. She thinned her lips at the sight of several boys leaping off the moving train. Frankie McClure was among them. He raced along, shouting and gesturing to a smaller boy who clung to the side of the swaying boxcar. All at once, something in the boy's posture grabbed at Libby's stomach. Good faith! It was David.

"Jump!" the boys shrieked. "Jump! Jump! You've got to jump!"

David clung all the tighter to the thin iron strips that climbed the side of the boxcar. Eyes wide with fear. Mouth a white line. Freckles dark stains on his blanched cheeks.

Libby bolted out of the buggy. She raced down the low-lying path skirting the east side of the water and struggled up the embankment, reaching the siding just as the boxcar carried her little brother past. The noise of clacking wheels and rushing blood filled her ears. David's face contorted at the sight of her. His lips shaped her name.

"Hold on, I'm coming!" Skirts hiked, Libby ran through the weeds, overtook the boxcar, and joined the boys' frantic urging. "Jump! Davie, you've got to jump!"

But fear held him in its tortured grip. Tears streamed down his face.

"Just close your eyes and jump!"

"Help me!" he wailed, his fear penetrating the roaring in her ears.

"Jump! David! It isn't going to stop; you have to jump!"

Libby's lungs burned, her legs, too, each step more painful than the last as the train picked up steam. Ahead lay the wooden fences of the stockyards. A loading chute stretched toward the siding. She couldn't keep up much longer. If she didn't talk him down before he reached the chute, he'd be out of town and out of reach. It was a terrifying thought, spurring her on. The boys, breathless from running, fell back. Libby struggled past them. All but Frankie McClure. He bounded along like a deer, so close to the boxcar, she feared he'd go under the wheels if he fell. Her blood went cold as he leaped and caught hold of the iron step on which David's feet were planted. Struggling to keep pace, she saw him claw at David's feet, trying to pull him free. He'd kill them both!

"Frankie, no! No! Get away!"

So intent was she on the boys' danger, Libby missed the rodent hole in the weed-choked siding. Her foot dropped in, sending her sprawling. Cinders chewed her hands. Weeds tangled around her ankles. She struggled up just as the boxcar approached the stock chute. She couldn't catch up! Mingled perspiration and despair stung her eyes, blurring her vision. But wait! Angus Cearlock was poised at the very brink of the chute. He stretched out his arms and plucked David off the side of the train. The momentum of the train and the weight of her seven-year-old brother threw them both on the ground at the far side of the chute. Frankie, dangling by a hand from the iron step, dropped off the train just beyond the chute. He hit the ground and rolled.

Libby rushed to the far side of the chute, where Angus was brushing off his jacket and trousers. Her little brother rose from the ground beside him. He was ashen, his shirt ripped, his lip bleeding. Libby gathered him in trembling arms. The other lads, all older than David, clamored around, a melee of discordant sound. Swifter to recover than she, David wiggled out of Libby's arms and wiped his eyes on his sleeve.

Frankie clapped him on the shoulder. "A little practice, and it ain't near so hard, gettin' shet of that train."

"Practice?" panted Libby, her lungs screaming for air. "Practice indeed! I could shake every one of you!"

"Hush, Lib, don't scold," pleaded David, his freckles standing out like pegs.

"One slip, and you could have both been killed! Frankie, too!"

"Shoot fire, it weren't no hill for a climber," claimed Frankie.

Libby glowered at his tittering friends. Hardly a day had passed since Frankie had moved to town that he hadn't instigated mischief of one kind or another. She took David's hand. "Let's go home and have a look at your lip."

Angus pressed the dent out of his straw skimmer and spoke up. "You have a more immediate concern. Proctor is finding his own way home."

Libby looked back the way she'd come to see her horse clipping along, pulling the empty buggy behind him.

One of the lads cried, "Come on, fellas, let's get him!"

"Whoa, there." Angus spread his arms to keep the lads from thundering after Libby's white horse. "No need in spooking poor Proctor. One is sufficient."

It was Frankie who trotted after the horse and buggy. Angus held the rest of the boys with a stern eye. "I advise you fellows to run along and tell your folks what you've been up to. Unless you'd welcome a visit from Sheriff Conklin."

"There's no need in vexin' the sheriff," one boy spoke up.

"What about the rest of you?"

They hung their heads and agreed it was their preference, too.

"Go on then. There's nothing to be gained by putting it off."

The boys started away, David with them, his lip beginning to swell. Libby didn't envy him telling Father how he'd split his lip and torn his trousers. Pity stirring, she was about to go after him when Angus intervened.

"Let him go, Libby."

"A sympathetic bystander is a comforting thing when Father gets that long look of his."

"Sympathy, I should think, would be counterproductive."

His tone caught Libby off guard. She lifted her chin in silent inquiry.

"Don't you see? He's got to learn that there are times when a fellow simply has to stand up and refuse to go along with the crowd."

Quickly, Libby retorted, "David isn't usually a follower. Truly, he isn't."

"Those boys are all a year or two older than David. It's understandable, him being anxious to prove he wasn't without nerve," said Angus soothingly.

He was right, of course. But Libby was so attached to David it was difficult to hear him being criticized. She tucked her head and battled mixed emotions.

"And from here on out, when my opinion is not solicited, I'll have the good grace to withhold it," Angus finished in an undertone.

His charm quenched Libby's irrational urge to defend David. Ashamed of herself for being so clannish, she said, "I can't thank you enough, Angus. Your quick thinking saved the day. How did you know David was in trouble?"

"Teddy was on the lookout. I just happened to be passing by. He flagged me down."

"Bless him," said Libby, for whether Teddy was picking up cans and bottles with Sugar at his heels, clearing the streets of horse droppings, idling about town listening to the old men's yarns, or initiating the rescue of foolhardy children, his unobtrusive acts of caretaking knit him to the hearts of the town. "Bless *you.*"

Angus's hazel gaze was as warm as the sun on his sandy hair as he reached for her hand and lifted it to his lips. "I'm happy I could be of service."

Frankie stopped beside them in her buggy. He clamored down, glowered at Angus, and tossed the buggy whip Libby's way. "Here you go."

Angus intervened, catching the whip in the air and tucking it under his arm. Together, they watched the boy lope away, red hair standing up like a cockscomb. "He's a daring lad but insolent," ventured Angus.

Frankie was indeed insolent. Irksome. Unpredictable. He could strike Libby's temper like a match. And yet, in rare moments he was so shot through with courage she felt pride in him and a love not unlike her love for David.

It was easier, however, to express love for a brother than for her Uncle Willie Blue's misbegotten son, who had accepted the inheritance she had surrendered as no more than his just due. Never mind that it had come at the cost of her dream of furthering her education in preparation for writing novels. No doubt, Frankie's ingratitude was Decatur's influence shining through.

Libby thanked Angus again as he handed her into the buggy. The sun was hot on the buggy lid, the flies were biting poor Proctor, and Angus had a meeting with his stepfather. Libby responded to Angus's inquiry as to what time she would like to be picked up for church services the following morning, then bid him good-bye and continued on her way.

The social was just one link of a fund-raising plan, the object of which was to construct a building on the New Hope congregation's recently purchased plot of ground at the north edge of town. They'd sold ice cream on the Fourth of July, had held several bake sales, and were busy organizing a community dinner to be held between the afternoon and evening performances of a circus Mr. Gentry was bringing to town at the end of August. He claimed it was a first-class circus, and he had received the permission of the New Hope congregation to let the troupe set up on the church lot.

"Giddy up there, Proctor. Good fellow."

Proctor drew her back along Mill Pond Road, then turned west toward the heart of town. Libby proceeded past the grain elevator and the jail and turned north at the Columbian, the handsome brick building where everything from graduations to community services to dramatic plays were held. Half a block further along, Libby turned Proctor up the alley past Angus's law office and in so doing saw Chester Gentry come striding out the back door of the *Gazette* and up the alley toward her. A rotund fellow with a handsome black moustache, he tipped his derby, greeted Libby in passing, and strode on to Angus's office.

Libby continued up the alley. Lucius Gruben emerged from the yawning back door of the newspaper office. A pencil was caught in his white hair and a cigar gripped between his teeth. Beckoning for her to stop, he strode out to meet her.

"Mr. Gentry stopped by. He wants a splashy article reminding folks that advance tickets for the Roth–Bigelow Circus are now available," he called as she rolled to a stop.

Libby reached for her notebook and pencil. "Where can the tickets be purchased?"

"The bank, the flour mill, the telephone company, the grain elevator, and every other business Gentry owns."

The proceeds, Libby knew, would go to Angus's political campaign. A shadow fell across her page as she began taking down the information. She looked up to find Captain Boyd standing on the other side of the buggy. He lifted his pillbox military-style cap and returned Libby's greeting.

"Mr. Gentry has style, using a circus as a political fund-raiser," Captain Boyd said. "Too bad the youngsters can't vote."

Mr. Gruben flicked the ash off his cigar. "It'll bring the country folk to town, which is good for the merchants, Gentry chief among them."

"It helps the New Hope Ladies Aid, too, guaranteeing us a good turnout for our community dinner," Libby put in.

"Absolutely. Pastor Shaw's wife was in my office this morning, asking if Florence would provide the flowers for the dinner tables."

"No one in town has any prettier flowers," said Libby.

"She's got the thumb for it," agreed Mr. Gruben. Abruptly, he got back to business, asking, "Have you finished the piece on the horse-borrowing pranks?"

"I'm working on it."

Captain Boyd drew himself tall, clicked his heels together, and saluted Libby. "Miss Willie's on the case. She'll get to the bottom of it."

Miss Willie. An endearment on the captain's tongue, likening her to Uncle Willie. They'd been good friends, her uncle and the captain. Libby angled the old dear a smile.

"How about a piece covering the social out at Spring Lake tomorrow as well?" Mr. Gruben said, flinging another assignment Libby's way.

"Yes, of course." She made several more notes before continuing to the buggy shed located directly across the alley from Willie Blue's back door. She was unhitching the mail buggy when her father strode out of the woodshed. Her heart constricted, for David followed on halting steps, his cheeks flushed and damp with tears.

"I canna help thinkin' yer sister would be pleased if ye were to relieve her of the duty o' seein' this old hayburner back to the livery," said Father, stretching a hand across David's back.

Dust and tears mingling as he dragged his hand over his face, David turned and came back for the horse. "I can do it by myself," he said, when Libby made as if to go with him.

"There now, if the laddie isn't just the man for the job," said Father.

David started away, chin up, dignity restored by Father's show of trust. Recovery was not so swift for Libby, for although she knew David had to be taught, her temper was stirred toward Frankie, whom she was sure had been the instigator.

"Did Frankie tell his mother what happened?" Libby asked.

"The lad hasna come hame," said Father.

"Isn't that typical?"

Father smiled at her tone. "Come now, lass. Wi' no fiery-haired sister threatenin' to carry the tale hame, 'twould be unnatural for the boy to lay his black deeds upon his mother's ears."

Libby thrust out her chin. "I'd like to paddle him myself."

" 'Tis a weak-kneed response, shufflin' off the blame," said Father. "David was a bigger man than that. He dinna complain o' Frankie coaxin' nor teasin' nor cajolin'."

"Nevertheless, you know that Frankie did."

"Aye, 'tis in the lad's nature," conceded Father.

"Then how is *he* to learn a lesson?" challenged Libby.

"I'll be leavin' that to the laddie's parents," said Father. He shot her a mild glance and changed the subject. "Will ye be trottin' over to Mr. Noonan's station and wirin' yer reply to Adam?"

"Adam's wire wasn't to me, it was to you," Libby replied, dodging the question.

Father gave her a long look. " 'Tis a great wonder the bonny lass isna staggerin' under her great load of grudges."

"Grudges? Against Abigail?" Libby widened her eyes. "Would I be planning a quilt for Abigail if I was bearing a grudge?"

" 'Tis not a quilt the lass be needin' " said Father quietly. At her failure to respond, he said, "Forgive me for thinkin' it, lass, but could ye be thinkin' this hurry-up wedding was of her own makin'? That she used her wiles and trapped yer brither? Are ye blamin' her for corruptin' yer big brither as ye blamed Frankie for corruptin' our bonny Davie?''

Heat flooded Libby's face. At times like this she missed having a mother, for how was she to speak frankly to her father on the subject of baby making? Not that she was *blaming* Abigail. No, she just didn't care to have her carting her troubles to Edgewood. Though if she were to say so, Father would think it unfeeling. Voice flat, she said, ''If she's set on coming, I guess we'll manage.''

'' 'Tis not a matter of managin'. 'Twould be a mortal pity if we were to open our hame but not our hearts.'' Father drew a deep breath and tried again. ''What is done is done, lass. 'Tis a forward view we'll be takin'. For Abigail's sake, for ye' brither's sake, too.''

Adam. The responsible brother. Jacob, who was older than Libby but younger than Adam, often referred to Adam that way. And indeed, until a couple of months ago, Adam had steadfastly put off Abigail's urgings to set a wedding date because of Father's frail health, thinking he might have to step into his shoes, becoming head of the household. Times at the mines were so hard these days. That, of course, had all changed when Abigail found herself with child. Resolutely, Libby said, ''I wouldn't hinder Adam's happiness for the world.''

''I dinna doubt but that ye mean it. But if the lad sends his wife to our hame, acherishin' the notion of her bein' held dear to our hearts, then I canna help thinkin' his happiness hinges on the quality of our love for the lass.''

''If he cherishes her so, why would he send her away?'' blurted Libby.

Father arched a sad little smile. ''To spare her the scandal, I'm thinkin'. 'Tis a hard thing for a lass to bear.''

And did he think it would be any different for her here if the matter became known? Libby pressed the thought down. Still, he wasn't fooled.

Gently, he said, ''If there be anything lingerin' in yer heart which would rumple the welcome mat beneath the lass's feet, then I would have ye speak of it now, Lib.''

She hesitated a long moment, then said, ''No, Father. There's nothing.''

''Be off to Mr. Noonan's station then and send Adam a wire.'' At Libby's mute nod, he touched her arm and added, ''If ye have no feelin' for it, than do it in faith, and in time, the feelin' will follow.''

Ashamed that he had seen through her, Libby set out for the station to send the telegram. But even as she went, she was praying Abigail would change her mind and stay home.

5

It was early evening by the time Ike and Decatur finished the dirt ramp and Decatur went home. Ike checked the bank lines he'd set earlier that day and found some bluegill and a catfish for his supper. He packed up what he thought he would need to get by, fed and watered his team, and turned them into the pasture just beyond the trees before trekking across the bridge and over the railroad tracks to Naomi's cabin. There was a breeze to his back as he let himself in. He left the door open in hopes of blowing the place clean of the odor of abandonment and decay.

Naomi's tools were strewn across the workbench. A badly gouged spindle was clamped in her lathe. There wasn't much in the way of furniture, and what there was was old and broken and awaiting repair. The only exceptions were a couple of chairs and a newly constructed oak table awaiting a final sanding and some linseed oil. Sawdust, curled shavings, wood chips, and other debris were strewn across a floor that sagged in some places and buckled in others.

Ordinarily, Ike took his wash to Widow Harpster in Edgewood, but it was too late in the day for that. He had no choice but to build a fire in the stove. The boiler and washtub his mother had once used were still in the shed behind the cabin. He put the boiler on the stove, shaved lye soap into the heating water, and washed what he would need for tomorrow. There was a piece of clothesline out back. He cut it down, strung it inside the cabin and hung up his wash, then warmed more water for bathing.

It was dark by the time he'd shaved, bathed, and cooked his supper. The heat drove him out of the cabin to eat. When he had finished, he laced his fingers over his stomach and sat with his back to the wall, watching the lightning bugs flit over the road and under the trees. The odor of drying fabric wafted out the cabin door, transporting him to wash days in his mother's steamy kitchen back in Missouri. At that time, Edgewood had been a distant place where his father's half brother lived. But when his father's death left them destitute, his mother, in an act of desperation, took Ike and his sister to Edgewood, hoping to find temporary shelter in the household of Chester Gentry, her husband's half brother.

As it turned out, Chester Gentry gave them a packet of food and directions to the poor farm. His mother took them by the hand and headed north, the direction Gentry had pointed. Ike recalled stopping to eat when they reached the trees of Old Kentucky. When every morsel was gone, his mother, having given the poor farm due consideration, put her arms around Ike and his sister, said she was going to pray, and they would wait right here until God answered.

Ike remembered looking up into the trees that blotted out the sky and feeling uneasy. He didn't put much stock in what he couldn't see or hear or touch, and this didn't look like a place he wanted to be when darkness fell and they were still waiting. His apprehension grew when a fellow with flaming red hair and bright blue eyes stumbled into their midst at dusk and introduced himself as Willie Blue. He looked like a drifter who had wandered down off the railroad, and he smelled like one, too. But despite soiled clothes, unshaven jowls, and unsteady feet, the man was sympathetic to their problem, which was more than Gentry had been. Mentioning a second home deeper in the woods, Willie Blue offered them the use of his cabin.

Ike's family's stay at the cabin stretched into a week and then two. By that time, he knew that Willie's second home was nothing more than a disabled boxcar abandoned by the railroad. His mother, seeing the goodness in Willie, came to trust him as a friend, and Willie, for all his weaknesses, never violated that trust. Summer came and went and came again, and his mother met the evangelist Clifton Jericho when he came to Old Kentucky to conduct a camp meeting. The nightly meetings went on for weeks, and when it was over, his mother had found a soul mate. She married Clifton Jericho and once again uprooted Ike and his sister. Ike had drawn close to Willie by then and hadn't wanted to go.

He had spent the next couple of years being a trial to his mother and stepfather, for he hadn't yet realized you couldn't shuttle loss to one side, that you had to talk to God about it and trust Him to work it out. That was something he had learned in Cuba.

Teddy Roosevelt might have had a capital time in that little war, but Ike hadn't. He had lost friends. Lost an ear, too. Been so sick with malaria he'd cursed God and hoped to die until he saw hell's fiery jaws yawning wide. Others said it was the fever and that he was delirious, but he knew it was more than that and he knew Who had delivered him. Sick, scarred, and tormented with dreams, he didn't go home to his family when he was mustered out. Instead, he sought out Willie Blue, and once again, Willie took him in.

Willie didn't ask questions. He didn't offer suggestions. He fed him from God's word. Nurtured his feeble faith and served as a living example of what God could do with brokenness when the spirit was yielded. Willie Blue was more of a father to Ike than his flesh and blood father had been. It was times like this when the owl called and crickets creaked and the moon climbed in the blue-black sky that he missed Willie the most.

Hearing a wagon approaching from the west, Ike came to his feet. The moon shed enough light through the trees he could see that it was Billy Young's dray wagon.

"Evenin', Billy," he called.

"Ike? Whoa, there." Surprise rang in Billy's reply. He stopped the wagon and climbed down. "I was planning to stop by your place before I headed back to town. What're you doing here?"

Ike explained Decatur's concerns over intruders and that he had agreed to spend a few nights.

"I've been all day hauling brick for the new barn out at the old Morefield place," said Billy, propping a hip on the hitching post. "I hope Thomas carted the outgoing mail over to the station for me."

The eldest son of a ranching family, Billy had grown up on the plains of Nebraska. Most folks didn't know he had been to college in the East, first as a student, then as a teacher, only to trade the suit-and-tie classroom for the tan battle fatigues of the First Volunteer Cavalry. He and Ike had become close friends that sultry disease-infested summer in Cuba. After the war, Billy chose Edgewood over returning to the ranch or to the academic world.

"How's the grammar book coming?" Billy asked.

"I've made it through the first chapter. Though it strikes me it ain . . . isn't so much studyin' it as it is hearin' which way's right and which way's wrong," said Ike. "Still and all, I appreciate yer loanin' it to me."

"Guess you know what you're doing," said Billy. "But if you ask me, it isn't verb tenses nor double negatives standing between you and Libby; it's Angus Cearlock."

"Nobody asked," said Ike, feeling touchy. "Though now that we're on the subject, a little self-improvement wouldn't hurt you none either."

"Any. Hurt you any."

"Any then," said Ike grudgingly.

Billy chuckled and clapped him on the back. "It's a sorry sight, seeing you fall so hard, buckaroo," he teased. "And while we're on the subject of women, how about coming to services at Spring Lake tomorrow and introducing me to Mrs. Daniels?''

"You mean Maddie?" It was Ike's turn to grin. "I'll warn ya, she's got strong views.''

"Prim and proper like her mother?''

Ike shook his head, wondering how Billy could have lived in Edgewood this long and not heard the whispers about Maddie. Or maybe the whispers were what had prompted the question. His grin grew. "Maddie don't think God has made the man she can't outthink, outsmart, outtalk, and outshine. Why, wouldn't surprise me a bit but what that doctor fella she was married to didn't die of pure intimidation.''

"She's a fine-looking woman," said Billy.

Ike couldn't argue with that. Time was, he'd been smitten with Maddie's lithe frame, smoldering dark eyes, and bold ways. Indeed, Billy must have heard as much, for he nudged Ike's shoulder, and teased, "If it weren't for Libby, I'd suspect you were carrying a torch for the young Widow Daniels yourself.''

"Not me. I took the cure on Maddie a long time ago. But I got no problem introducin' you," Ike offered.

"Then you're coming tomorrow?''

"Plannin' on it.''

Billy swatted a moth away with his hat. "Are you going to compete in the memory verse contest? You could win a trip to the fair.''

"So I heard.''

"You could dust off your uniform, saddle up, and parade with the rest of the First while you were down there.''

"Got too much to do right here," said Ike.

"Nothing that couldn't wait," argued Billy.

Several months earlier, members of the First Volunteer Cavalry had been invited to join the parade at the fair grounds for Illinois Day in September. Billy had been coaxing Ike all summer to go with him.

"Be good for you to face your demons," Billy added.

"What demons?" asked Ike. "You been listenin' to the old warhorses at Willie Blue's again?''

"How else is a man going to keep up on the news?" Billy grinned and added, "Say, Libby's brother sent a telegram this morning asking if his wife could come for a visit.''

Ike brushed a mosquito off his temple. "That so?''

"Struck me as curious that his bride would be wanting to go visiting so soon after their wedding. And that her husband would be willing to let her.''

"Let her?" echoed Ike. "See there, that's the sort of thing that'll get ya in trouble with Maddie.''

Billy grinned and stirred to go. "On second thought, maybe I'll hold off on that introduction until after the social. Dorene over at Baker's has been dropping hints all week about how her sister wouldn't be averse to sharing her box lunch with me."

"Who, Chloe? You won't go wrong there."

Billy climbed up to the wagon seat. "Are you bidding on Libby's?"

"Go home, Billy."

Billy laughed and waved his hat, then shook the lines over the backs of his team. Ike settled against the wall, thinking about Billy's jesting as darkness swallowed the wagon. Maybe he *was* being foolish. Being able to put words just right wouldn't change who he was inside. A full-grown man poring over a grammar book. Next thing, he'd be hangin' his head and shufflin' his feet like a schoolboy. Either the spark would catch or it wouldn't. And if it wouldn't, then he could read a whole library full of books, and it wasn't going to make any difference where Libby was concerned.

"What do you think? Should I keep it up, Lord? Or should I toss this ole book in the fire?"

A locust droned in the darkness. Ike didn't quite know when it was he'd started talking out loud to God. Maybe it came of spending so much time alone. But talk he did. About Libby. About Decatur and Naomi and the kids and the sirup camp, too.

After a while, he gave into a restlessness he couldn't explain, lit a lantern, and walked through the woods to Decatur's place to play cards. When he returned, it was still too hot to sleep in the cabin. He spread his bedroll on a pile of boards in the shed out back and thought once more of the grammar book. It seemed shiftless not to make the effort now that he was into it.

He yawned and tried to get comfortable. The shed was close enough to the creek that he could hear the water meandering over a fall of rocks. The trickling shifted as he slept, becoming in his dream the satiny whisper of Spring Lake lapping at the shore. Ike opened his eyes and saw a girl watching him from the water. He was pleased that she had noticed him but baffled by her request that he teach her to swim, for though she wore Maddie's face, she had fins and a tail and the body of a fish. He stroked the air with his arms and said, "Put your face in the water." But he was too late, for Angus called instructions to her from the middle of the lake, and she turned and swam toward the raft where he waited. Ike awoke, the sound of Maddie moving through the water still splashing in his ears.

As the dream faded, he looked back over the years to his sixteenth summer. Even then, the only thing he'd had in common with Angus Cearlock was an eye for the same girl. It'd been a vicarious sort of coming of age that summer evening when he had caught a fleeting glimpse of Angus and Maddie hastily donning their clothes in the tall grass at the edge of the lake. Young and reckless himself, Ike's initial reaction had been envy, wishing Maddie had given her heart and body to him instead of Angus. On the heels of that covetous thought came a contempt for Angus's lack of chivalry, for Angus, unaware Ike had already seen them, sneaked off, leaving Maddie to do the same. Maddie was fourteen, a couple of years younger than Angus. But her emotional makeup was as well developed as her form, and it wasn't in her nature to lie low, like a cast-off garment, or to slink away as Angus had done. Instead, she emerged from the shadows tying the ribbons on her swimming attire and called to Ike, just as unconcerned as if he'd discovered her picking berries.

Ike recalled with clarity the hurt that lingered in Maddie's eyes, betraying her true emotions concerning Angus's stealthy exit. He remembered his physical hankering fading to sympathy and a disillusionment he hadn't wanted to feel. Sensing as much, Maddie had tilted her chin and made a big show of recovering her spirit as she helped him bait bank poles. They swam awhile and built a fire and skinned the fish they caught. Ike cooked them over the fire. They were eating when Hascal Caton stumbled upon them, a jug tucked under his arm. He winked at Ike, dangled a silk stocking before Maddie's eyes, and said, "Ya lose somethin', miss?"

Maddie glowered as she snatched the silk stocking from his gnarled hands. Hascal chortled, clapped Ike on the back, and went on his way. Maddie soon ducked into the woods to gather her shoes, a dress, some other female gewgaws, and even a blanket. It was then Ike realized that the rendezvous had been carefully planned and that Maddie had had some romantic notion of spending the night there with Angus.

By the time Mrs. Dorrance, who had been out of town, returned home, the story of Maddie's escapade at the lake was all over town. Only it was Ike's, not Angus's, name that was linked with Maddie's. Ike made no denials. He had the callow notion that the more unsavory the rumor, the taller his stature in the eyes of his chums. As for those who might have discounted the story, Hascal dangled before their eyes the mate to Maddie's silk stocking. It might as well have been monogrammed, for only weeks ago, when Mrs. Dorrance had held a cotillion in celebration of Maddie's fourteenth birthday, every detail, right down to Maddie's imported silk stockings, had been hashed and rehashed on the streets and in the shops and around the supper tables of Edgewood.

Looking back, Ike wished for Maddie's sake that Mrs. Dorrance's reaction had been more forgiving and less fear driven. She had wealth and a flawless reputation, in both business and the manner in which she conducted herself within the community. She could have stood firm and protected her daughter with a shield of love and support that deflected the ugly spirit of it all. Together, they might have faced the gossips down. Instead, Mrs. Dorrance inadvertently fanned the flames by sending Maddie off to boarding school. It proved to be a failed attempt at taming her daughter's spirit, for Maddie returned even more careless of public opinion than when she had left. The next time she stumbled from grace, it was a long hard fall, causing a rift with her mother that by all appearances had yet to heal.

Ike swatted a mosquito that was buzzing around his ear, yawned, and prayed for dreamless sleep. But pleasant dreams were rare for Ike. Most of his were of a more violent nature.

Next time Billy took to pestering him, he ought to just up and tell him he didn't have to go all the way to St. Louis to be reminded of the war, that he revisited it all too often when he let his guard down in sleep.

6

Libby's house was located just across the railroad tracks from the Mill Pond at the edge of town. They had rented it a few weeks earlier after vacating the rooms over Willie Blue's for Naomi and the children. Naomi, in gratitude, had provided the furniture, which she'd made in her woodworking shop. They were solid pieces fashioned from the hardwoods of Old Kentucky and beautiful in their simplicity. The house would have been bare without them, for they had left all of their own furniture in their previous home in Thistle Down.

The house with its coat of yellow paint was cozy, the bed chambers and parlor were small. The kitchen, holding the heat of Libby's cooking, had a pump at the sink, a handsome black range, and a high, wide window that looked out over the backyard. Libby's father occupied the spot with razor, shaving mug, and mirror propped against the windowsill.

Libby poked the last piece of freshly fried chicken into the box lunch she'd be sharing with Angus, then goaded her father with a smile. "I'm taking no chances on you and your bidding. I've tucked in enough food for you and David, too."

"Courtin' 'tis dauntin' enough for a man of me age wi'oot these lunch-box shenanigans." Thomas Watson pulled his lathered jowl to one side with two fingers, leveling the peaks and raising the valleys of his parchment face to the whispering razor.

"Major Minor might outbid you just to get your goat. Hascal Caton, too, if he sniffs out Mrs. Baker's raisin pie."

" 'Tis an abnormal way of plantin' a house of worship, I'm thinkin'."

"Ye have only yerself to blame if ye have not figured on keen competition for Mrs. Baker's box,'' Libby teased in his own colorful tongue. "Why, ye must be askin' yerself, How ha' the old laddies become so stout and sturdy? 'Tis their everlastin' dinin' at Baker's on the square, Verna Baker bein' such a fine, fine cook.''

"Abnormal proceedin's,'' Father said with a sniff. " 'Tis not overpopular with any of the lads.''

"Is that so? Then why is it they're so full of monkeyshines once the bidding begins?''

"Mortal nuisance." Father made a final pass with the razor, splashed, dried his face, and turned away from the window. "What is it ye've done wi' my shirt and tie?''

"On the foot of your bed. And if my opinion counts for anything around here, there isn't a woman in all of Edgewood I'd rather see you court than Teddy Baker's mother.''

Her father dropped a soap-scented kiss on her cheek and replied, "Ye're a guid lass for all yer playful tormentin'.''

Libby smiled, her nerves over the Berry Sisters' debut abating as she counted her blessings. Father had nearly died of the lung ailment three months past, the sickness ending forever his labor as a coal miner. He was still painfully thin. But his eyes were clear and bright, and having secured the job of Edgewood postmaster had returned the spring to his step. It had been a gift from above following on the heels of Libby's decision concerning Willie Blue's. The salary was modest, but it was steady work, unlike mining, where in the best of times a man might be laid off as often as he worked.

Libby tied the lid on the box with a pink ribbon, humming with antici-patory pleasure of the day ahead. What with preparing Sunday clothes and cooking and scurrying around getting ready to go, she hadn't had much time to decorate her box. Last night, for want of paint, she'd dampened a scrap of wallpaper and used the lavender color to brush a small sprig of lilac in one corner of the lid. This morning, in a daring moment, she had adopted a similar trick, rubbing the pink wallpaper with a damp finger, then touching her lips.

"David? Are you combing your . . . Oops." Libby almost stepped on him backing away from the table. David's dark hair bore the path of the comb. His shirt was neatly tucked into his knickers, his tie neatly tied, his shoes blacked and polished to a shine. The only mark of yesterday's mishap was a swollen lip.

"You look very handsome," she told him.

"So do you, Lib.''

Libby swallowed a chuckle and thanked him for the compliment. She and Chloe and Dorene Berry had agreed in advance to wear white. Her blouse had bouffant sleeves that gathered below the elbow, an inset of tucks at the bodice, and a high collar adorned with lace and her mother's cameo. She took off her apron and smoothed her skirt. Close-fitting through the hips then flaring for ease of movement, her skirt fastened with a row of buttons off center and ended at the tops of her white kid leather shoes.

"I'll walk along with you to the store if you're ready to go."

"Isn't Mr. Cearlock coming for you?" asked David.

"Yes, but I have plenty of time. Anyway, I have to take my box lunch up. Billy is responsible for carting all the box lunches out to the grounds."

"You can't take your own lunch? Why not?"

"It's to be auctioned off. Angus will have to guess which lunch is mine and bid on it if he wants to share it with me."

"Can't you just tell him?"

Libby smiled at his male logic and smoothed down his collar. Her straw hat wore its age well, refurbished with new ribbons. She used Father's shaving mirror to pin it in place, picked up her gloves and box, and shooed David out the door ahead of her.

Birds twittered in the trees overhead as they made their way up Fisher Street and past the Grubens' home. Mr. Gruben was turning the corner half a block ahead and didn't see Libby. She waved to his wife, who leaned on her crutch as she tossed scraps to the cats gathered on the porch.

"Lovely morning, isn't it, Mrs. Gruben?" Libby greeted her.

Florence Gruben shifted her weight on the single crutch, and replied, "It is indeed. Heading out to the lake now?"

"In a while," said Libby.

"Lucius says Mrs. Shaw is wanting flowers for the community dinner. If you think of it, tell her I'd be happy to provide them." Mrs. Gruben smiled at David. "Hello, little neighbor. I found a story I think you'll like. We'll read it together in the morning, shall we?"

David smiled and agreed and waved as they walked on. Libby brushed a thread from his suit jacket. "Are you sure you won't ride out with Angus and me?"

"Just have to listen to a bunch of politickin' if I did," said David.

Libby laughed. "Davie Watson! You sound just like old Hascal Caton."

"That Mr. Caton can tell a yarn, can't he?"

Libby smiled, reminded of Zerilda Payne. Zerilda minced no words in saying that lies were old Hascal's native tongue.

"Anyway, Father said I could go in the wagon with Opal and Frankie," David said.

Billy Young had volunteered his dray wagon for transporting those who had no other way to the lake. "All right then if Billy has room. And try to get there with clean hands and your shirt tucked in. No horsing around, you hear?"

"Father already told me."

"Did you remember a clean handkerchief?"

David sighed and pulled his hand free and dashed ahead as they crossed the street just past the Columbian. Though it was early, folks were already gathering in front of the store. Opal McClure ran to meet them.

"See the dress Miz Brignadello stitched for me?" Clinging fast to her box lunch, the flaxen-haired child did a pirouette and pointed to one of the many circus lithographs posted around town. "Ain't I the spittin' image of that poster right there?"

"You're gorgeous, Opal," Libby assured her.

Opal beamed and with a sudden stroke of modesty claimed, "It ain't me, it's Miz Bee's magic needle. She can eye a picture and sew up something just like it!"

It was common knowledge that Sarah Jane Brignadello had run off with a traveling circus when she was sixteen. The circus wardrobe matron had taught her to sew, a talent that had served Mrs. Bee well in keeping up with her sister, Ida Gentry. Ida's husband could well afford her appetite for exquisite gowns, but Kersey Brignadello, on a traveling tinker's wage, could not.

Billy Young's wagon was parked alongside the store. Mr. Gruben and Mr. Lamb were loading benches into the back. Libby greeted them both and waved to Billy and Teddy Baker, who sat on the seat beside him. Teddy acknowledged the gesture with a customary tug of the hat and a jerk of the neck that reminded Libby of a duck bobbing its head.

"Good morning, Libby. My, just look at Miss Opal!" declared Billy with a wink.

Opal giggled as he swung down and came to them on his long stride. Billy flashed his infectious grin as he took Libby's box lunch in one hand and Opal's in the other. "It looks as if we're getting a good assortment here."

"Mama gave Frankie a dollar for mine. But he ain't gonna need it," said Opal.

"Got an admirer, do you?" teased Billy. "Suppose he'll punch my nose if I lift you into the wagon?"

Opal giggled. "Quit yer joshing, Mr. Young. I kin make it on my own."

Billy chuckled as the child skipped away to join her brother on the walk in front of the store. "Independent, these newfangled women. How about you, Libby? Hand up?"

"Thanks, Billy. But I have a ride."

"I'm looking forward to hearing the Berry Sisters today."

Libby braced her midriff with one gloved hand. "Keep in mind it's our first public appearance."

"You'll do just fine." Billy stored the boxes under the wagon seat.

Libby stepped out of the way as Madeline Dorrance, the widowed matron of the Dorrance Dairy family, approached Billy with two box lunches.

"Good morning, Mr. Young. Are you in charge of getting these to the grounds?"

"Yes, ma'am." Billy pointed out the block of ice and drinking water in the back of the wagon. "I'm going to park in the shade and keep things cool."

"Very well." Stern and straight and not much wider than the nearby porch column, though a good deal more elegant, Mrs. Dorrance acknowledged Libby with a curt nod. "How are you, Elizabeth?"

"Fine, thank you," said Libby.

A handsome woman despite her severe expression, Mrs. Dorrance was no wastrel of words. She had a keen mind for business and lent herself to the cause of Prohibition with the same tireless approach that had brought prosperity to the dairy. She was one of Angus's most ardent supporters but opinionated and dictatorial to a fault, which made Libby careful of her.

"Mind your feet, or you'll have them in someone's lunch," Libby heard her caution Teddy Baker.

Teddy scooted to the far edge of the seat as Billy leaned in with the box lunches. One was wrapped in white and tied in pink ribbon, and adorned with a fresh lily. Its similarity to Libby's box was striking, except for the lily.

Libby moved to the boardwalk where Opal was weaving her way down the hitching post. She asked, "Is your mama inside?"

"She went back to bed once she finished packin' my box lunch. Said she's plumb tuckered out."

Having spent her share of Saturday nights at the store, Libby knew what they took out of a person. "So she's not coming? She must be awfully disappointed."

"I reckon," said Opal, undaunted. She darted around to the back of the wagon, then turned back to ask, "Ain't ya comin', Miss Libby?"

"She's riding out with Mr. Cearlock," David answered for her.

Opal's eyes brightened. "Maybe if I was to run up and ask Mama, I could ride with ya."

"No, ya cain't, and you ain't askin'." Ten-year-old Frankie hoisted his little sister into the wagon and scrambled up after her. His red hair fell in his eyes as he reached down a hand and pulled David up behind him.

"I'll see you at the lake." Libby waved to the children and started home.

Mrs. Dorrance and her daughter, Maddie Daniels, passed in their fringed surrey as Libby waited to cross Mill Pond Street. The dark-eyed, ebony-haired young widow possessed her mother's classic features right down to her slim, alabaster throat. Bedecked in black silk, Maddie lifted a gloved hand in passing. Libby responded in kind, though in truth, she wasn't entirely comfortable with Maddie.

Maddie was as intelligent as she was beautiful, an independent thinker, outspoken, and a magnet for gossip. Libby had heard from more than one source that Maddie had lost her virtue to Ike Galloway when they were both in their teens, then had been sent off to boarding school only to return long enough to disgrace herself again with Dr. Daniels, who came to Edgewood with his medicine show. They left town together and were eventually married. Widowed less than a year, Maddie had returned to Edgewood last month.

As Libby continued down the walk, she thought Maddie seemed unperturbed by her blemished name. But people in Edgewood had long memories. So much so that people questioned the wisdom of Angus inviting Maddie to be a part of the singing group that was to go campaigning with him. But Maddie's family was a prominent one. She and Angus's sister, Catherine, had been childhood friends, and Angus was admirably loyal. Libby thought it spoke well of him that he refused to stoop to the level of the village gossips. She was striving for a similar noble spirit and made a concerted effort to cast no stones. Still, she wasn't altogether comfortable with Maddie or her liberal views.

Father was just leaving as Libby arrived home. He had to fetch Proctor from Woodmancy's Livery so that he could escort Mrs. Baker out to Spring Lake. Noting the jaunty angle of his hat and the scent of bay rum as they passed on the porch, Libby suspected he wasn't dreading the box lunch auction nearly so much as he pretended.

Angus arrived on time, dressed in a white suit, stiffly starched collar and cuffs, and a straw boater. They turned onto the Tile Factory Road just a block from Libby's home. The road was the familiar return leg on her mail route, paralleling the Chicago and Alton railroad tracks. The brisk pace of the team jostled a law book from beneath the seat of Angus's buggy. Libby picked it up, the idea of a town library flitting to mind.

"It would be an asset, the village board freely concedes as much," said Angus when she voiced the thought aloud. He squinted into the bright sunshine and added, "But something else always seems to eat up the budget."

"What about a subscription library? Or a fund drive?"

"Such as the church's building fund? Someone with good motivational skills might muster enthusiasm for the idea," said Angus.

"Maybe the Republican Club would be interested in getting it started. A strong show of citizenship and all that."

Angus crooked a sandy eyebrow and teased, "Hear, hear! We may make a politician out of you yet."

Smiling, Libby said, "Seriously, Angus, why don't you mention it to your stepfather? He knows how to get things done."

"Between planning strategy for my campaign and making preparations for the Roth–Bigelow Circus, Chester has his hands full. Make the rounds of ladies' clubs and see if you can muster some support there," he suggested.

"I wouldn't even know how to begin. Besides, I'm new in town. It should be someone well-known, someone whose judgment is well respected."

"Very well then: mention it to Mrs. Dorrance."

That was an idea with as much appeal as biting into a lemon.

Responding to her grimace, Angus smiled and pointed out, "Madeline Dorrance is tireless when inspired. I'd be happy to mention it to her if you'd like."

Without much enthusiasm, Libby said, "It would make more of an impression coming from you. She likes you."

"I can't take credit for that. Catherine and Maddie were such good friends, they would not have stood their families *not* liking one another," he said modestly.

Catherine, Angus's sister, was the first friend Libby had made upon moving to Edgewood. One week ago, Catherine had moved to St. Louis, where her husband Charlie was now working. Wistfully, Libby said, "Catherine would have been a good one for a library project. She always tucked a storybook into Tess's perambulator before coming to visit."

"I know all about Catherine and her books," Angus said. "I helped sort through a whole mountain of them when she moved, three-quarters of which she crated up and sent out to the farm to be stored in Mother's attic." He flung Libby a sidelong glance and abruptly changed the subject. "You're looking lovely today. New dress, is it?"

Libby shook her head. "Only the ribbons on my hat. They match the one on my box lunch."

He crooked a sandy brow. "Ah-hah! A clue. Do continue."

"White paper, pink ribbon, a sprig of lilac painted in one corner of the lid."

"White, pink, petals. I've got it."

The sorrel team gleamed in the sunlight as they cantered along. Libby settled back to enjoy green fields, golden corn silks, and the grove that glimmered like a green jewel on the horizon. Trotting hooves, creaking leather, and the links of chain dangling from the crossbar that linked the harness to the buggy made background music to the waltz of conversation.

By and by, they turned west just opposite the tile factory and rattled over the railroad tracks and onto the grassy clearing sloping down toward the spring-fed lake, a favorite gathering spot for picnics, boating, and fishing. Angus settled the team in a patch of shade beside Kersey Brignadello's tinker wagon.

"Good morning, Kersey. Aunt Sarah Jane," Angus called to his mother's sister.

A spry little lady with a lively interest in other folks' affairs, Sarah Jane Brignadello, or Mrs. Bee as she was known, jumped down unassisted, solicited a kiss from her nephew and a hug from Libby. "All ready for the big sing, my dear?"

"My stomach is performing stunts that would put stars in little Opal's eyes," confided Libby. "She's as proud as can be of that dress you made her."

"The pleasure was mine," said Mrs. Brignadello, her cheeks turning pink. She had no children of her own and had unofficially taken Opal under her wing.

"She thinks she's dressed as a circus lady. You *know* how enamored she is of the circus," Libby added.

Angus's aunt laughed, smoothed her sage green silk dress, and swept a distinguishing lock of white hair into the nest of black tresses fringing her hat. Despite nearing her forty-year mark, she looked like something straight out of the *Chicago Magazine of Fashion* as she lifted her chin and declared, "A pretty little thing like that should not be running around in her brother's hand-me-down knickers."

A good-humored fellow, Kersey Brignadello beckoned from the door of his enclosed tinker's wagon, calling to his wife, "Mrs. Bee? You want to mind your own *bees-ness* and give me a hand unloading these benches?"

Angus sprang to help. Libby visited with Mrs. Bee while she waited.

It was Libby's second visit to Spring Lake. She had accompanied Angus to the Republican Rally there on the Fourth of July, an event that drew thousands. The tranquil waters, the clearing known as Lake Pasture, and the beauty of the surrounding woodlands were no less enchanting today. She drew in a deep breath and asked, as Angus rejoined her, "Can you imagine anything lovelier?"

"The bustle of Springfield comes to mind." He laughed at her grimace.

Maddie Daniels stepped from beneath the shade of an oak and borrowing from Shakespeare said, " 'Upon what meat doth this our Angus feed that he has grown so great an ambition?' "

"Maddie! You've arrived in good time," Angus said, greeting her warmly.

"Your Aunt Paulette thought the Berry Sisters could use a practice warm-up. Hello again, Libby."

"Hello," Libby returned.

With a graceful swirl of black skirts, Maddie fell in step on Angus's left. "I hear you're giving a testimonial this morning."

"You've been going over the order of worship with the reverend, have you, Maddie?"

Maddie angled him a dark-eyed glance. "I applaud your initiative."

"Initiative?" he echoed.

"It's a conservative district you're hoping to represent. Angus Cearlock, devoted to God, country, and mother: Who would fail to trust such a fellow?"

Angus slanted her a look from twinkling eyes. "And that from a suffragette. Stop now. You'll have me blushing."

"Seriously, Angus, it never hurts to reaffirm where you stand."

"I'd best stand humbly lest I fall."

Maddie arched a satin black brow. She was not coquettish or flirtatious nor did she care much for teasing. But she had an ease with Angus that Libby sometimes lacked.

Pastor and Mrs. Shaw had arrived ahead of them. The pastor served both Timber Creek Church and the newly organized New Hope Church and had constantly promoted the idea of union services. Angus's mother, Ida, his stepfather, Chester Gentry, and the Berry family were already on hand as well as Dr. Melville Harding and his wife, Paulette.

Angus's mother, a fairer version of her dark-haired sister and several years older, had a cheery, fluttery way that put Libby in mind of a little canary. She greeted Libby, collected a perfunctory kiss from her son, and called to her sister who was helping arrange the benches, "Let the men get those, Sarah Jane. Melville, she'll listen to you." She solicited her brother's help when Mrs. Bee failed to drop the end of the bench she was carrying.

Dr. Harding greeted Libby and Angus, then excused himself to do his sister's bidding. It took only a glance from his wife to send Chester Gentry striding after him. In short order, Kersey Brignadello and his brothers-in-law had the benches arranged for the day's events.

Leaving Angus with his aunts and the Shaws, Libby accompanied Maddie to the hay-wagon stage where Chloe and Dorene Berry were waiting to practice while Martha Berry, several years their junior, stood looking on. Both Chloe and Dorene were sturdy, plain-spoken, hardworking, and unaffected. Both were good company, though Chloe, the eldest by eleven months, seemed of a steadier, more serious bent than the impressionable, fun-loving Dorene.

"Here we are, just like piano keys, playing in the key of F," said green-eyed Dorene, drawing attention to the color scheme of three white dresses and a black one. She giggled and added, "Three ivories, one ebony. Stand on the end, Mrs. Daniels. You're our B-flat."

"Maddie, remember?" said Maddie.

"Maddie then," said Dorene, eyeing Maddie's handsome dress with open admiration. Dorene had dropped out of school to wait tables at Baker's to help her large farm family make ends meet. Chloe, who kept house for Ida Gentry, had done the same. But while Dorene was won over by Maddie's democratic suggestion that they call themselves the Berry Sisters because Berrys were in the majority, Chloe wasn't so easily swayed. Libby suspected Chloe was concerned that Maddie's tainted reputation would rub off on her good name.

"We'll have to be quick about it if we're going to practice, ladies," said Paulette Harding, who accompanied the Berry Sisters on her accordion.

Though a decade and a half older than the rest of the group, the childless Paulette wore her years well. The satin sash of her white gown accentuated her tiny waist. Golden curls peeked from beneath her hat, framing a heart-shaped face. But despite her delicate appearance, she worked hard at organizing choirs, dramas, and other cultural functions for the community. Whether it was a simple choir session, a local drama production, or a full-blown traveling theatrical show on stage at the Columbian, Paulette was a stickler for presentation. She slipped her arms through the straps of her accordion, and called, "Get your hands away from your mouth, Dorene. Fold them in front of you. Don't you have a pair of white gloves? Never mind, I'll see to it myself. Shoulders back, Chloe. Libby, you're squinting. Ready now? Sing!"

Libby and the Berry sisters took Paulette's constructive criticism in the spirit it was given, and the practice, though brief, went well. Libby retired to the bench at the back of the stage, nerves continuing to build as the union gathering swelled three times and again the usual number for a New Hope Sunday morning. The lake was behind her, lapping gently at the shore, the pasture before her, strewn with men tugging at their ties, ladies stirring the air with Lamb's Mortuary fans, and children getting the last of the wiggles out before the service began.

The Methodist choir led into the service with a stirring rendition of "Joyful, Joyful, We Adore Thee." Beyond the gathered crowd, flowers and prairie grasses stretched toward Old Kentucky's towering trees, from which the song birds sang. The view was not lost on Reverend Shaw. Using Matthew as his text, he read of the tender attentions of a benevolent Father favorably disposed toward meeting the needs of His children.

Libby clasped her gloved hands together. The reading about the futility of worrying when God so graciously supplied food and clothing and all of life's necessities touched a nerve, for she liked a pretty dress as well as any girl. As for worrying, Abigail's pending visit hovered at the edge of her mind.

" '. . . for your heavenly Father knoweth that ye have need of all these things. But seek ye first the kingdom of God and His righteousness; and all these things shall be added unto you . . .' "

Reminded of the brevity of the lily and summer grass and life itself, Libby opened her eyes, seeking Angus in the crowd. But the gaze that met and held hers belonged not to Angus, but to Ike Galloway.

The warmth in his gray eyes brought a quickening within Libby. He had come! Ike acknowledged her look of pleased surprise with a smile so full of light, Libby's mouth curved of its own volition. A wave of heat followed as her thoughts flitted to the whispers linking his name to Maddie's all those summers ago. How much truth was there to the story? Quickly, she averted her gaze, lashes sweeping down, and did not look his way again.

7

Libby had no formal musical training beyond what she had learned from singing in church. But she was blessed with a reliable ear, good pitch, and a sweet tone. When the Berry Sisters came to their feet, she sang for love of singing, picking out notes between Maddie's earthy alto and Chloe's and Dorene's ringing sopranos in a medley of praise for all God's hand had made: "For the Beauty of the Earth," "Fairest Lord Jesus," "This Is My Father's World."

"Amen!" came the resounding affirmation as the fading notes lingered over the lake and pasture. And it was over. Libby followed the others off the stage to a bench reserved for them. The testimonies followed with Angus only one of several to speak. There was a confident flow to his words, his ease in front of a crowd impressive. Libby's heart stirred with pride as he left the stage and squeezed in beside her. The choir sang again, the sermon followed, then the congregation joined voices in the closing hymn and Reverend Shaw gave the benediction. Folks were quick to stir out of the sun, those who were not staying going to their conveyances, those who were, meandering to the shade of the trees where the box lunches awaited the bidding.

Billy Young's wagon became the dividing line between the men and ladies. Teddy Baker stood in the wagon, neck stretched out as he passed the first box lunch to Mr. Lamb, Edgewood's mortician. A mustachioed man with a twitching left eye, he called the proceedings to order.

"You know the rules, gentlemen. Highest bidder buys the box and the pleasure of lunch with the lady who prepared it."

"You aiming to sell 'em or bury 'em, Mr. Lamb?" called Hascal Caton, tugging at the grizzled whiskers on his jaw.

"Sell them, absolutely."

"Then get on with it. If the heat don't get us, my gnawing belly will."

"Hush up, Hack Caton, you're distracting Teddy. That's it, Teddy. Hold it up high." Mr. Lamb wiped his perspiring brow and, eye twitching, said, "My, now here's a glow-ri-us work of art. Do I hear five dolla, gentlemen? Five dolla . . . five dolla . . . one dolla? Who'll bid one dolla? Here! Have I got one-fifty? One-ten? One-twenty? One-fifty? Two? Here! Two-ten? Smells good, doesn't it, Teddy?" he inserted, and everyone laughed, for he'd caught Teddy with his nose pressed to the extravagantly decorated box. "Two-seventy-five?"

The bid ran surprisingly high before Mr. Lamb brought his gavel down. "Sold to Mr. Gruben's printer's devil. Now you be on your best behavior with that little angel, Earl," he said, coaxing a laugh from the crowd.

Those boxes belonging to the eligible young ladies were usually auctioned first, for it was here the money was to be made, the fun to be had. Some of the ladies, experienced in box-lunch proceedings, pretended dilatory interest. Others, like Libby, waited with a mixture of anxiety and anticipation for their own boxes to be held up.

Earl Morefield claimed Dorene Berry's box with a dauntless grin and found his way to her side. She blushed and tucked her head. The seesaw of bidding and pairing off continued briskly. The eating, however, would wait until the last box lunch was sold, the last picnic blanket spread, and thanks offered. Appetites ushered the proceedings along.

Libby found herself beside Mrs. Brignadello when Teddy held up a box wrapped in white, a lily tucked beneath the pink ribbon.

"One dolla. Do I hear a dolla? Who'll give me a dolla?" Mr. Lamb drilled away like a woodpecker.

"Right here."

Libby's pulse bolted as Angus made the opening bid.

Quick to note her reaction, Mrs. Brignadello whispered, "Don't tell me it isn't your box?"

Libby shook her head. "But similar enough. He may not realize. . . ."

Angus's aunt worried her bottom lip. "Whose is it? Do you know?"

"Mrs. Dorrance gave it to Billy." Libby kept her voice down, dismay mounting as the bidding climbed, Angus leading the way.

"Is it Madeline's lunch? Or Maddie's?" Mrs. Bee asked.

Libby shrugged. Hascal Caton, Mr. Minor (long ago dubbed Major Minor), and some of the other old fellows who gathered daily at Willie Blue's joined in the bidding.

"If we could catch his eye . . ."

"I can't even see him," said Libby, rising on tiptoe.

Mrs. Bee was no taller. She twisted her mouth to one side as Hascal called out in his booming voice, "Empty yer pocket, Minor. We'll tie together on this 'un."

"Reckon she's packed enuf vittles fer the both of us?" countered Minor, playing to a captive audience.

"I ain't even shore she can cook. Her daddy's awful skinny. What about it, Thomas? Kin yer girl cook as good as she sings?"

" 'Twould be unseemly to boast, wi' Reverend Shaw's fine words aringin' in me ears," said Libby's father, joining in on the fun.

"Lib's a good cook," blurted David. "She is!" he insisted, puzzled by the burst of laughter.

"Ten dollars!" called Angus.

Libby darted Maddie a glance. Her demure expression left little doubt but that it was her box Angus was bidding on. Libby's heart lurched.

"Going once, going twice . . ."

"Ten-ten," squeaked Hascal Caton. "Found a dime in my boot."

The laughter faded to expectant silence as they waited for Angus to up the bid. Mr. Lamb cleared his throat.

"Angus?"

"I'm sorry, gentlemen. I'm afraid . . . That is to say . . . My, this is embarrassing, but . . ."

"Aw-w-wwe-l-l. He's busted," Teddy Baker anticipated.

Guffaws resounded out over the pasture as Libby caught her breath and held it.

"Ten-ten going once, going twice. Sold! You've bought yourselves a lunch, gentlemen," called Mr. Lamb, and Libby ducked her head to hide her relief.

Major Minor came around the wagon, muttonchops framing a face lined by hard times, hard work, and hard drinking. Box lunch in hand, he said with a twinkling grin, "Seems we overbid our hand, Miss Libby. You ain't sore at us, is ya?"

"Of course not, Mr. Minor. I should tell you, though, that isn't my lunch."

His jaundiced jowls sagged. "Ain't yers? Then whose does it be?"

"It would be mine, Mr. Minor," Maddie Daniels spoke up.

Hascal Caton, following close on Major Minor's heels, nearly bolted. "Plumb slipped my mind, it was little Opal's lunch I was sent here to bid on. You won't hold it agin me if I bow out, will ya, miss?"

"Come now, Mr. Caton. You aren't afraid of me surely?" chided Maddie.

Her tone convulsed the crowd, their laughter ringing a flock of birds out of the trees.

Maddie, half a head taller than Mr. Caton, wasn't above a little grandstanding herself. She arched a black satiny brow. "The truth is, I find myself intrigued by what I've heard of your views. Perhaps we could discuss suffrage over lunch, Mr. Caton."

"Well now, I don't know's I'd go so far to call it sufferin'. I kin buck up and eat most anythin' set b'fore me."

Amidst the laughter, Maddie had the same look on her face as a cat giving the mouse just enough play to make the game entertaining. Meanwhile the men were congratulating Angus for his craftiness in pulling one over on the old codgers.

As the crowd shifted, Angus caught Libby's eye and smiled as the next box came up for bid.

"If you ask me, Mr. Caton is getting off easy," said Mrs. Bee to Libby. "It could have been Maddie's *mother's* lunch. My, wouldn't *that* have been rich!"

Over the summer, a war had been waged in editorials to the *Gazette* dealing with the subject of Prohibition. Madeline Dorrance's words drew blood. Hascal Caton fired back, though not nearly so eloquently. The controversy made for lively reading, which in turn sold papers. Mr. Gruben gave both sides of the issue plenty of ink, the result being that Mrs. Dorrance and Mr. Caton would sooner cross the street than risk coming face-to-face.

The bidding commenced once again, the boxes dwindling until only Libby's and little Opal's remained. The men had thinned out. Billy Young had bought Chloe Berry's box, but he sauntered back now to stand beside Ike. Libby's nerves twitched at the sight of him nudging Ike and reaching into his pocket. She braced herself for a repeat performance of the old men's antics. But Angus paid them no heed but simply waited, the fingers of one hand thrust into his vest pocket.

Opal slipped in beside Libby, her face shiny with heat, her mouth turned down.

"Are you hungry? Hold on, it won't be long now," said Libby, smoothing damp tendrils from the child's forehead.

"Don't matter. Grandpa done bought a lunch, and Frankie ain't around. Ain't nobody to bid on mine."

"Of course they will," said Libby.

"Ya sure he found it?" asked Opal.

Libby didn't understand. Puzzled, she looked into Opal's disappointed face. But before she could pursue it, Teddy held up Opal's box. Ike opened the bid. Angus upped it by a dollar. Spike Culbertson jumped in.

Opal shrank against Libby. "I ain't eatin' with *him.*"

Overhearing, Mrs. Bee cautioned, "There, there. You mustn't hurt his feelings, dear."

Mr. Culbertson was revered in Edgewood. Though the stick-legged, barrel-chested old dear couldn't find his way home, he could recite the Gettysburg Address with a pride and passion that drew tears. He'd committed a good number of other selections to memory, too, none of which impressed Opal in the least. But her worries were for naught—Ike bought her box.

Despite the dwindling field, Angus didn't win Libby's lunch cheaply nor painlessly. Those remaining recompensed him for the fun he'd had with Hascal Caton and Major Minor. By the time the whole thing was over, Libby was ready to side with Father: It did indeed seem "abnormal proceedin's" and "a mortal nuisance."

Reverend Shaw offered thanks, and lunch was officially under way. A line formed behind Billy Young's dray wagon. Chloe Berry climbed up beside Billy and helped him chip ice into the drinking water he'd brought from town. Friends, neighbors, and families converged in clumps, the better for visiting. But the courting couples sought a bit more privacy. Angus collected a Steiner jar, two glasses, and a picnic blanket from his trap. He spread the blanket at the fringe of the lake pasture in view of the others but not so close as to limit their conversation. He filled the glasses with a tilt of the jar.

"Lemonade?" exclaimed Libby.

"For the songbird. You ladies were marvelous. I'll be the proudest candidate on the stump this autumn with the Berry Sisters entertaining the crowds."

"How kind, Mr. Cearlock."

He joined in her playfulness, passing her a glass. "To Miss Elizabeth Watson upon the debut of her singing career. The United States Postal Department's loss is the music world's gain. Drink up!" he urged as she laughed at his toast.

The chilled drink felt like liquid heaven, gliding down Libby's parched throat. "Delicious! The crowning touch to a perfect picnic."

"I pride myself on being thorough."

"And clever, too," said Libby. She glanced over her shoulder to the north edge of the grounds, where Opal and Ike had joined Major Minor, Hascal Caton, and Maddie beneath the massive arms of an oak tree. Maddie was on her feet, box lunch in hand, poking at the contents. Turning back, Libby smiled over the rim of her uplifted glass. "You have to be clever to get one past Mr. Minor and Mr. Caton."

Angus chuckled. "Worried you, did I?"

"I was beginning to think you hadn't listened," Libby conceded.

"Of course I listened—white, pink, petals." Angus paused in untying the pink ribbon. His brow rippled above the wire rim of his glasses. "Lilac petals, did you say?"

Misunderstanding, Libby reached for the box. "Here. Let me." She dispensed with the ribbon with a flourish, lifted the lid, and gaped in confusion, looking for the chicken. "This isn't mine."

"Is it minced ham, lime pickles, deviled eggs, and cherry tarts?"

Libby swiveled on the blanket to find Maddie Daniels standing just over her shoulder. Major Minor was with her, box in one hand, pink ribbon in the other.

"This be what yer lookin' fer, Miss Libby?"

There was no mistaking the painted lilac on the lid nor the devilish gleam in Major Minor's eye. Libby conceded it was indeed her box.

"Now how do you suppose my lily got on your box?" asked Maddie.

"Reckon they's tokens among us?" ventured Major Minor, adopting Uncle Willie's word for *spirits.*

"That or a clever conniver." Angus darted a narrowed glance across the pasture. "The remedy is simple enough: We'll trade boxes."

"Oh, no. Not so fast. Could be a young whippersnapper like yerself ain't so well acquainted with the rules of box-lunch eddycut as Old Hack and me." Major Minor squatted down beside Libby. "Like Mr. Lamb said at the start, highest bidder buys the box and the pleasure of lunch with the gal what repaired it. Not that I ain't enjoyed yer company, Miss Maddie. I have, and that's a fact. But if it's Miss Libby's box I got holt of, then Miss Libby's honorbound to join us."

"He's right, you know." Determined to be no less a good sport than Maddie had been, Libby accepted Major Minor's hand up and smiled over her shoulder with feigned gaiety. But Maddie was already taking her place, her stylish black hat, lithe frame, and silken skirts a barrier between Libby and Angus.

Libby turned her smile on Major Minor instead. "Lead on, Mr. Minor."

The exchange had not gone unnoticed. Libby, crossing the pasture with Major Minor, turned more heads than Paulette Harding's sash popping off while she was pumping away on the accordion during the closing song.

Libby's father shot her an inquiring glance as she drew even with the blanket where he sat with David and Teddy, being served lunch by Mrs. Baker.

Libby shook her head, exchanged greetings with Mrs. Baker, and lifted her chin a little higher. "We're off to join Mr. Caton. It appears he and Mr. Minor bought my box after all."

"Good political material, Angus Cearlock," observed Mr. Gruben, who in the absence of his wife was sharing his lunch with the recently retired mail carrier, Captain Boyd. "Changing oars midstream without so much as a ripple. Now that takes skill."

"He can count on you two gentlemen's vote then, can he?" Libby volleyed back.

"Whatever you say, Miss Willie," said Captain Boyd. He smiled warmly and gave her a salute.

8

Hascal Caton, Ike, and little Opal waited in the shade of a burly oak tree. Ike, Libby noted on closer inspection, had rid himself of yesterday's whiskers. His suit jacket, draped over his knees, fell to one side as he started to his feet.

Libby waved him down. "Don't get up. Let's eat."

"Good to know the mix-up hasn't dulled yer appetite," remarked Ike, settling back again.

Major Minor cackled and rubbed his hands together. "Slide over, Hascal, and make room for the lady."

They had no more than opened the boxes when Frankie came out of the woods to drop between Opal and Ike.

"Not so fast." Ike intercepted Frankie's long reach for Opal's box. "Opal, you of a mind to share with your brother?"

"Ain't up to her. Mama packed mine in there with it," Frankie pointed out.

"Don't matter," said Opal. "You wasn't around to bid. It's Ike's now. Ike's and mine, and I ain't sharin'."

Frankie, flushed from playing, gave his sister a shove. Opal yelped and came back pinching.

"You young'uns simmer down," Mr. Caton thundered at his grandchildren, attracting the attention of those nearby. "Ain't gonna stand fer ya actin' like demons."

Short of crawling under the picnic blanket, there seemed no way to shirk the public eye today, Libby thought. Ike wasn't helping, setting the children at odds. Libby beckoned to Frankie. "Move over here, Frankie, and have a piece of chicken."

"Chicken? You got chicken?" Opal piped up. "Kin I have a piece, too?"

"You got a whole box, and ya want chicken, too? Yer greedy."

"I am not! I ain't greedy a'tall. I'll swap you some chicken, that's what I'll do."

"We ain't swappin', are we, Miss Lib?" challenged Frankie.

"Did you get yourself something to drink, Frankie?" Libby tried to distract them from their quarrel. "Opal, do you know how you could make that dress look even prettier? You could sit up straight like a little lady and lower your voice and not quarrel with your brother."

"What can Paw-paw and Mr. Major do?" Opal turned cooperative as Frankie trotted off to get himself a drink.

"They could give their permission for us to combine the contents of both boxes and share the meal." And Ike could quit smirking. What was there to relish? Not one amusing thing had transpired since she had joined him under this tree. Unless . . .

Angus's term *conniver* echoed in Libby's head. Suspicious suddenly, she tilted her chin and met Ike's gray gaze. "Is something wrong, Mr. Galloway?"

He grinned. "Nothin' at all. Had it in mind to suggest the same thing."

A light burned in those long-lashed eyes, but there wasn't a trace of guile. Nor could he have anticipated Angus's maneuvering. It was too convoluted to be anything but a comedy of errors. So why did her intuition insist that it was no accident that Angus was across the pasture in near seclusion, sipping chilled lemonade with Maddie Daniels while she sat amidst the din of bickering children, a pair of mischievous old men, and an inexplicably cheerful Ike Galloway?

Redoubling her efforts to endure it graciously, Libby took charge of combining the food, passing the napkins, and catching the deviled eggs as Opal tipped the box in an effort to beat her brother to them. "There now. Help yourselves."

Her chicken and Naomi's ham sandwiches vanished quickly. Major Minor smacked his lips and declared, "There ain't nobody kin cook ham like Miss Naomi."

Notorious for his stinginess toward complimenting women in general and his daughter Naomi in particular, Hascal tucked away another deviled egg and wiped his fingers on his trousers. "I'll allow she's got a way with it. Puts 'er on the stove and biles it and biles it till a body'd swear ain't gonna be nothin' left but the squeal."

"I'm mighty partial to pork. Mighty partial," claimed Major Minor. "Brings to mind a curiosity at the meat market . . . Oh, been a week or more,

I reckon. Ladies all in line, callin' orders to the cutter, when in from the street sashays this big ole porker.''

Hascal tugged at his chin whiskers. ''Thought they was an ordinance fer folks in town ta keep their livestock shet up.''

''There is, but this old feller had had his muzzle in the trough. Tell by the look of 'im, he ain't read up on council rules. Just stands thar, he does, and gets his eyes filled.''

Frankie paused in gnawing on a chicken bone to ask, ''Did the butcher throw a rope around him?''

''Why, no. He jest gawked he was that surprised. Weren't his hog anyways.''

''I'da got a rope iffin it was me,'' Hascal threw in.

''Well, it weren't.''

''So what happened?'' asked Opal.

''Why, the big old feller sauntered on up the street once he tired of lookin','' said Mr. Minor.

''Did he squeal?'' asked Opal.

''Not near so loud as Doc Harding over't the Columbian a few years back.'' Major Minor licked the grease off his fingers and bridged the gap between stories with a hoarse cackle. ''You was there, Hack. Dr. Daniels's Medicine Show and Hypnotic Vaudeville Combination?''

''Why, shore. The feller Maddie Dorrance run off with. A slick talker with a powerful physique, hypnotizin' eyes, and a gift for gab.''

''That'd be him all right, God rest his soul. Recollect how he asked fer volunteer subjects and tried out his hypnosis test? Yessir, got them folks under his control all right, even Doc Harding.''

Mr. Caton grunted. ''Put on if ya ask me.''

''Some of 'em maybe. Playin' the fool, catchin' fleas, and killin' snakes till the audience fell in stitches. But Doc now, he's a sofistycated feller. A scientific sort. I'll be danged if he didn't succumb, too, and commence to wallerin' on all fours and squealin' in the coal bucket.''

Ike grinned. ''I'd be careful tellin' that, Major. When ya find yerself stove up with rheumatism, Doc's liable to put to practice what he learned from that professor fella.''

Hascal wheezed and slapped his knee. ''You'll be wakin' up on the cutter's block lookin' fer yer squeal.''

''Speaking of cutter's block, ya see Kersey's shiner?'' said Major, helping himself to a piece of cake.

''Yep. Says he got it choppin' stove kindlin'.''

''That'll learn him,'' Major said sagely, to which Hascal grunted agreement.

''Learn him what?'' asked Opal.

"Why, ta let Miz Bee split the kindlin'."

"You two," exclaimed Libby, reminded of long mornings at Willie Blue's and the cracker barrel repartee. "Cover your ears, children. That's bad advice they're giving."

The old gentlemen cackled, delighting in her reaction. The children settled down to eating, their interest in stories in no way interfering with their food grabbing. Libby saw how they favored their mother's sour-cream cake and let them have her piece. Noticing, Ike broke his piece in half, intending to share it.

"It's all right. I've had plenty to eat," Libby said, declining. But he insisted. She sampled a bite, then wrapped the rest in one of the napkins she had packed into her box.

Stomach full, Frankie headed for the woods. Opal darted off to play circus with some other children, and the old men sauntered over to visit with Captain Boyd and Mr. Gruben. Relaxed by the food and the warm day, Libby turned her face up to sunlight that had found a hole in the leaves and waited for Angus to come claim her. Her hat slipped off her head.

"Catchin' freckles?" asked Ike.

"I hope not."

He grinned at the speed with which she retrieved her hat and ducked out of the sun. Propped against the spine of the tree, an elbow resting on a bent knee, he patted the ground beside him and invited, "Plenty of backrest here. Or maybe it's your head needin' a rest b'fore you start rattlin' off all those verses yer so set on takin' you down to the fair."

"I'd take a good snooze if I thought it'd do the trick," said Libby. But her smile faded as she glanced across the pasture to see Angus helping Maddie to her feet. Though his hand did not linger, the lassitude that had stolen over her suddenly fled.

"Do you think she's pretty?" she asked.

"Who, Maddie?" Ike cocked his head to one side, looking past Libby. He snagged a piece of foxtail grass between his fingers. "She's tolerable, I reckon."

Angus was folding up the picnic blanket while Maddie fed bread crusts to the ducks. She was tall for a woman, nearly as tall as Angus. Yet her carriage was exquisite. Graceful, self-possessed. Hating herself for making comparisons, Libby said flatly, "She's more than pretty, she's beautiful."

"Quit lookin' if it hurts."

"Who asked you?"

"You did. You said, Was she pretty?"

"And you said, Tolerable. But your eyes said something else."

"Don't think it's *my* eyes worryin' you," said Ike.

Intent on watching Angus join Maddie at the edge of the lake, Libby nearly stepped on Ike's hand as she came to stand with her back to the tree trunk. Distracted by a tug at the hem of her skirt, she glanced down to find him peering up at her.

"There's an energy to a loving nature makes a body shine. You got that shine, Lib. I wouldn't worry too much about Maddie."

Libby's jaw slackened at his kindness. She flushed and formed words but could not speak them for the air trapped in her lungs.

He came to his feet and rubbed the back of his neck, a boyish gesture she found oddly appealing. The grooves in his cheeks, so pronounced when he smiled, were shadows in repose as he stood with his hat in his hand and his feet spread. Dappled sunlight gilded his eyelashes and the clean-shaven planes of his face. The same feeling swept over her as it had earlier when he'd smiled at her from the audience. The other picnickers, Angus and Maddie, the lake itself, fell away like the background of a painting in which the focal point stood in bold relief. Incredibly, Ike was the point.

What a crazy notion! The piece of cake was crumbling in her hands. Seeking emotional footing, Libby harrumphed, tilted her chin, and replied, "No need in sweet-talking me, Ike Galloway. You gave me this cake, and you aren't getting it back." She stuffed the remaining chunk in her mouth, dusted the crumbs from her hands, and licked a speck of frosting from her thumb.

Ike smiled at her childish ploy. But it was a ragged smile, the light gone out of it. The toccata of an unseen woodpecker punctuated the silence. His gaze shifted to the hat in his hand. Libby's face grew hot, her hands sticky, her mouth dry. She turned to look across the pasture but couldn't crowd out the awareness of rushing blood and pounding pulse. Her heart bumped at the light touch of fingers between her shoulder blades.

"Caterpillar," Ike explained as she wheeled around to face him again. "Hold still. I brushed him onto yer skirt."

"Get him then."

Ike matter-of-factly brushed the woolly worm off her derriere, then winced, and said, "Durned if it don't look like ya sat on a bug."

"You didn't!" Hastily Libby pulled at her skirt, arched her neck back over her shoulder, then flushed as he chuckled over having made her look. "Very funny," she muttered with a narrowed eye.

"Yer welcome, Lib." Ike grinned, then turned as Major Minor and Hascal came stumping back, Captain Boyd between them.

"See here if the capt'in ain't got him some spectacles from a mail-order catalog," said Major. "They's dandy ones, too."

Libby's heart gave a leap as she looked past the old men to see Angus coming to reclaim her. Pained to find Maddie still with him, she pretended to be giving the old men her full attention as they passed the glasses back and forth.

Wire-rimmed spectacles perched on his nose, Major looked over the crowd. "Blamed if I ain't hankerin' fer a pair myself. Say, Hack, ya reckon Naomi could order some an' sell 'em at the store?"

"Thar's an idee," replied Hascal.

"Here, give 'em a try."

Hascal hooked the wire stems around his ears and blinked in owlish wonder. "Why, I declare! If it ain't like lookin' through a magniscope."

"You mean a telescope?" asked Maddie as she and Angus joined them under the tree.

The discomfort earlier when Hascal thought he'd mistakenly trapped himself into having lunch with Maddie resurfaced. Not only had Hascal and Maddie's mother had a running feud all summer, but he detested Angus and he had some things to say about Maddie, too. Nor did he like being corrected. So it came as no surprise to Libby when he stiffened his neck, dug in his heels, and declared, "No, ma'am. A magniscope."

"I see." Maddie traded smug glances with Angus.

Dander stirred, Hascal challenged, "Don't tell me ya ain't never heard tell of a magniscope?"

Maddie confessed that she hadn't.

"Don't only make things larger, makes 'em so's ya can see through 'em dimly. Ain't that right, Major?"

Out of the corner of her eye, Libby saw a grin tip the corners of Ike's mouth as he watched Major scratch his muttonchops and puff out his chest.

"Wondrous invention," declared Major. "They use 'em in scientific laboratories and medical explorations. Cain't jest everybody git one though."

Maddie took the bait. "Oh? Why is that?"

"If they was to fall into the wrong hands, think of the poor innocents out on the street, never knowin' they was transparent as glass."

"Now, now, Major," cautioned Captain Boyd. "There's ladies present." Major hushed.

But Hascal, slack on social graces, peered through Captain Boyd's glasses and picked right up where he'd left off, declaring, "Yessir, I'll allow a magniscope'd be jest the ticket for a poor man huntin' a wife. Why, he could spy out them silk stockin's from a block away and know right off thar weren't no way he could support a gal with sech fancy riggin's. Course some gals ain't all that shy about showing off their stockin's," he added with a glint in his eye.

Silence swallowed the old man's words. Confused, Libby's gaze skipped from Ike, alert but silent, to Maddie, haughty and hawklike, to Angus, flushed with anger. Suddenly it hit her. The silk stocking business! Ike and Maddie's long ago lakeside rendezvous! Good faith, what a wretched old fellow he was to remind them! She ducked her head, a scorching heat creeping up her collar.

Maddie, her demeanor as cool as porcelain, strode a step closer. Bringing her chin close to Hascal's face, she said, "You do know, don't you, sir, that women have keener vision than men? Yes, indeed! They can spot a knave without the aid of your so-called magniscope. It is his bombastic fabrications that unveil him."

Without another word, she turned on her heel and walked away.

Hascal's goading smirk faded. "Bombs and fabric . . . What the blazes was she jawin' about?"

"If you weren't such an ignorant cuss . . ."

Slipping her arm through Angus's, Libby cut him short, whispering, "Let it go, Angus. He's an old man."

"That's no excuse for bad manners," he growled. But he swung away from Hascal, Libby on his arm.

A few feet further on, Libby looked back over her shoulder and found Ike's gaze following her. Their eyes met for the briefest of seconds, his expression guileless. Quickly, she faced forward again, Hascal Caton's mean-spirited jab still burning her ears. Didn't the old coot realize the account reflected as badly on Ike as it did on Maddie? *And how, dear Lord, how could I have felt drawn to a fellow who would seduce a young woman, then be so bold as to stand there and meet my eye with no apparent shame?*

Durn that Hascal! Ike tramped through a patch of nettles, wishing he had stayed home. He hadn't fooled himself, saying he'd come on Decatur's account. He had come because Libby asked him to. To hear her sing. To talk a spell and let her smile stir over him like a breeze. He had gotten what he'd come for but only because of the mixed-up box lunches. Billy figured Teddy was responsible, inadvertently putting the lily on the wrong box when it fell off on the ride out. Teddy and maybe some Divine intervention.

The blessing proved to be as mixed as the boxes, which was about what he could expect from going to church for all the wrong reasons. But God had made him the way he was. He reckoned if anyone understood what made a man feel what he felt for Libby, his Maker did, and he sure didn't like old Hack talking that way. What had she heard about that night at the lake anyway? Nothing good, he was sure of that. He caught himself crushing things underfoot and deliberately slowed his steps . . . his thoughts, too.

There wasn't any use worrying about it. Nor fretting that a book-smart attorney with solid family behind him and a political career before him could satisfy Libby's ambitions better than he could. A low limb on a sapling snagged his hat and dropped it on the damp cushion of decaying leaves. He picked it up and saw the cake crumbs clinging to the brim and thought of her pushing cake into her mouth, then licking icing from her fingers. The image curled at his insides like a flame coiling a leaf before consuming it. Truth was, he wasn't much for settling for crumbs.

He drew a deep breath and let it go slowly. God wasn't hard of hearing. He'd heard, and there was an answer one way or another fitting snug to the prayer. He couldn't see it for what lay between, but it was there and knowing it was there lent strength to his patience. Ike swept his hat clean of crumbs and walked on to meet Decatur.

9

🕮 Angus suggested a walk around the lake. Libby, juggling mixed feelings over his defense of Maddie, made a conscious choice to define it as loyalty to his sister's friend, call it gallantry and forget it. Forget, too, that millisecond in which she had lifted her face to Ike's and felt as if she were careening headlong toward some unforeseen horizon.

Now the scales of her life had balanced themselves, and the world made sense again. They hadn't gone far when they overtook Maddie on a solitary stroll. Again, Libby fought a prickle of jealousy as Maddie fell in step with them with no thought that she might be intruding. Libby fully expected her to give Mr. Caton a verbal thrashing and was surprised when neither Maddie nor Angus mentioned the incident. Instead, the conversation flitted from the war between Russia and Japan to the gold standard to golf. Angus had learned the game in college, Maddie from her late husband, Dr. Daniels.

Not for the first time, Libby wondered what sort of man Maddie's husband had been. Angus's sister, Catherine, had confided that Mrs. Dorrance contended Daniels was a charlatan. If he was, then it seemed to Libby that Maddie would have needed her mother's emotional support all the more. But apparently she didn't feel she got it. Even when Maddie contacted her mother to say her husband had died in a hunting accident, Mrs. Dorrance had failed to rush to her side. Indeed, the man had been gone six months before Maddie came home.

For all her outspokenness, Maddie did not mention her husband and their short life together as they strolled beneath the warm August sun. Libby couldn't help thinking it would have made livelier conversation than war, politics, and golf. She hid a yawn and caught herself humming "The Animal

Fair.'' The silly tune had taken to loitering on the fringes of her conscious thought ever since she had heard Ike whistling it. Ike. She flushed at the thought of him, tightened her hand on Angus's arm, and stopped her humming.

At the end of their walk, Angus retrieved drinking glasses from the basket in his buggy. There were only two glasses. A pair. A duo. A couple. But, alas, the significance of it escaped Maddie. She lingered with them beneath the widespread maple shading Billy Young's now-deserted wagon.

"One could draw some interesting parallels between golf and politics.''

"Parallel, parallax, paraleipsis.'' Angus smiled at Maddie and vaulted up into the wagon to fill the glasses. "Do go on; don't keep me in suspense.''

Maddie lowered her parasol and clasped the handle with both hands. Turning to one side, she focused on some point out over the lake and simulated a golf stroke. "You study the shot, settle on what seems your best strategy, and swing.''

"And then?'' Angus crouched on the tailboard, a glass of water in each outstretched hand.

Taking one as Libby took the other, Maddie said, "You measure your success or lack of it, compensate for errors, and swing again.''

"Suppose you've had the misfortune of driving it into the pond? Maddie!'' Angus dropped to the ground and stepped away from the wagon. "Are you warning me that my expectations should be modest as this is my first time on the course?''

"Not at all.'' Maddie refused to be teased. "In politics, as in golf, it's the process. Persistence is rewarded with success.''

"And where does conviction enter in?''

"It's conviction that brings you to the game,'' Maddie told him. "Though, in my opinion, one ought to pick one's convictions carefully.''

Angus shook his head and contended, "You have it backward. A conviction picks you.''

"Not entirely. Those fighting the subjugation of women, for example, have picked up Prohibition as a tool to relieve the misery inflicted upon women and children at the hands of a certain class of men.''

"You do agree Prohibition would lessen the problem?'' asked Angus as Libby offered him a sip from her glass.

"The problem is much broader. Our political leaders have so little regard for women, they not only fail to fight for them, they also encourage them to become such weak sisters that they cannot or will not fight for themselves.''

Angus swallowed and passed the glass to Libby. But the intimacy of sharing was diluted by his good-natured responses to Maddie's observations.

"What about Miss Alice Roosevelt? You surely don't consider her a weak sister,'' said Angus.

"She may be unconventional, but it's ridiculous to suggest the president's daughter wields any influence," countered Maddie.

Angus feigned a worried frown. "You aren't going to put your views to campaign music and sing it on the road, are you? Need I tell you how *that* would go over?"

Libby smothered a giggle at his feigned look of horror. Maddie had a low threshold for frivolity. She flicked her an impatient glance. "It's unsporting of you to joke about it, Angus. My mother's rigid position on Prohibition has angered a lot of men, Mr. Caton among them. Wouldn't it be smarter to avoid drawing their ire over the alcohol issue? Rather, appeal to their sense of justice for the right to vote and with that vote, be heard at the ballot box concerning Prohibition?"

"You think they've put the cart before the horse?"

"Yes, exactly."

Libby stretched her hand toward the bright petal of a tall prairie flower and tried to coax a blue-fringed swallowtail butterfly onto her finger.

"What about you, Libby?" Maddie's swirling skirt frightened the velvet-winged beauty away. "Which issue do you feel deserves precedence? Prohibition or women's suffrage?"

Hers was not a studied opinion, rather a general feeling shaped by Uncle Willie and his intermittent appearances at her childhood home suffering the ravages of strong drink. She shrugged and ventured, "Father says alcohol enslaves."

"What do *you* say?"

"She says she'd like to think about it," Angus answered for her.

"That's what comes of letting a man think for you," countered Maddie.

Heat swept up Libby's neck as Angus again intervened, saying, "Come now, Maddie. It's not a matter of opinion so much as morality."

"And morally you find alcohol more offensive than the domination of half the adult population by the remaining half?"

"I've never thought of myself as being dominated," inserted Libby, lest Angus once again answer for her.

"Life has been kind then, has it?" countered Maddie. Softening her tone, she added, "Though from what I hear, Naomi McClure's suffering became real to you. Real enough that you were willing to sacrifice on her behalf."

Libby had no intention of discussing Naomi McClure with Maddie. Noticing Pastor Shaw, the Brignadellos, and the Gentrys with their heads together, she said, "It looks as if the memory contest is about to begin."

"I admire what you did," Maddie said, refusing to be diverted. "You've scored a point for sisterhood. I've been thinking of organizing a group of freethinkers to discuss how women might band together and take a more active hand in their own futures. Would you be interested?"

"No, she wouldn't," Angus said smoothly. "And I hope you won't act on that thought. Not before the election anyway."

"I have no intention of undermining your political endeavors, Angus. Now let her speak for herself. What do you say, Libby?"

"I'm sorry. I have so little free time . . ."

"For goodness sake! Don't wrap it in cotton batting. If you aren't interested, then be honest about it."

"All right then, I'm not interested."

"Why not if Angus will allow me to ask?" Maddie quelled Angus's protest with a narrowed eye.

Libby dodged the issue. "I have other interests occupying my time at the present."

"There's strength in diversity and room for many ideas. The vote is just the beginning. It opens the door for women who want and deserve some say over their own destiny."

The political embers that glowed in Angus's eyes were a mixture of firestorms and ice in Maddie's. Daunted by their intensity, Libby wondered if it was shallow of her to want to leave tedious social problems to those with a heart for it. As for her, she'd rather go for a walk in the sunshine. Teach David to skip rope. Read a book.

"The opportunity is before us to write a page of history," prompted Maddie.

Libby cooled her throat with another sip of water, passed the glass to Angus, and said, "I've been thinking Edgewood could use a library. But beyond that, I'll leave the social causes to you and Angus."

"Very well," said Maddie. "Let me know if you change your mind." At long last, she excused herself and walked away.

"You handled that well," said Angus, though Libby sensed he was not altogether happy with her. Before she could decipher the source of his displeasure, Pastor Shaw mounted the stage and called for the memory verse contestants to assemble.

Libby joined two dozen adults and at least that many children on benches facing the trees beneath which the audience convened. Frankie McClure squeezed in beside his sister to Libby's surprise. Had Naomi known that Frankie planned to compete? Libby doubted it. Though she remembered Naomi commenting on how helpful Frankie had been in tutoring Opal for the contest. Tutoring indeed! The scamp! He had been preparing for this moment all along. If only he had told her of his interest, she would have been glad to help him. Though no doubt he'd been afraid he would lose face in the eyes of his friends should he betray an interest in something constructive.

"If everyone is ready, let's go over the rules," Reverend Shaw began.

As he did so, Libby momentarily forgot Frankie, her thoughts reeling back to a Ladies Aid meeting three months earlier at which Angus's mother, Ida Gentry, had announced that her husband would award the winner of the New Hope memory verse contest with train and gate fare to the World's Fair in St. Louis. The trip was scheduled for the middle of September. However slim her chances, Libby knew the contest was her only hope of attending the fair.

The audience was in the shade, their backs to the woods, fans and hats and pawpaw leaves stirring the air. Pastor Shaw motioned for Opal. She lifted her white-gold head, thrust out her chin, and chirped her way through the Golden Rule, the twenty-third Psalm, John 3:16, and the Lord's Prayer. She was halfway through the Ten Commandments when her memory failed her.

Her cheeks turned pink at the polite applause as she sat down. Her monopolization of the best-known verses made it harder for the children who followed. Soon, only David and Frankie remained. David quoted a short psalm, named the fruits of the spirit, and sat down. But it was Frankie who astonished everyone. He began with the creation account and did not stop until God had made woman.

"You children have done an excellent job," praised Reverend Shaw. "If all of you will rise, I believe Mrs. Gentry has something for your efforts. Mrs. Gentry, if you'll come forward?"

Angus's mother gave Opal a red ribbon, David a white one, and the remaining children green ones, with the exception of Frankie.

"As the winner among the children, Frankie's verses will carry over to the adult division," Reverend Shaw explained.

Libby watched Opal race toward a man who stood slightly apart from the main crowd. Ike was back. With the sun's glare, she was slow to recognize the man at his side. Her jaw dropped at Opal's delighted cry.

"Daddy! Look! I won a red ribbon!"

Decatur McClure! Had Ike brought him here? But, wait. What was it Opal had said as she waited with a long face for her box lunch to be auctioned? *Ya sure he found it?* She had been expecting her father to be on hand to buy her box lunch, and when he hadn't shown, she had been disappointed.

But what had made her think he would come? The matchbox gift! Had there been an invitation inside? Had Naomi known? Of course she'd known. That's why she wasn't here. Naomi had denied herself the outing because of Decatur. Ike should have stopped Decatur. *But how could he stop him? Why would he? The purpose of the day is to draw people, not turn them away.*

Squirming at the clashing thoughts in her head, Libby averted her gaze. She tried to go over her memorized passages, but the sight of Decatur had fractured her concentration. She found herself looking for Angus in the milling crowd. They had started out this morning in a festive mood, delighting in one another's company. She couldn't have wanted for a more attentive escort until the box lunch mix-up paired him with Maddie. Educated, beautiful, articulate Maddie was well suited to Angus's interests.

Libby cast the unbidden thought aside and forced a smile as Sarah Jane Brignadello bustled over to her with a cup of water.

"I brought you a drink."

"Thank you, Mrs. Bee," said Libby.

As the cup changed hands, Mrs. Bee indicated Mr. Culbertson waiting a few yards down the bench. She leaned close, and whispered, "Now what do you suppose Cordelia is thinking, letting her father enter? Why, if the poor old dear were to win, he'd be so lost at that fair, he'd never be found again. And what would it mean to him anyway? The past is more real to him than the present."

It was indeed an oddity how the old man could recite lengthy pieces of speeches and prose and poetry learned so long ago and yet be so vague in the here and now. Libby poured the last drops of water in her hand and cooled her face and neck. "How is he at Bible verses?"

"Mr. Caton declares he has heard him recite letters of the New Testament word for word. I wouldn't be surprised if his daughter isn't planning to take the trip herself if he wins. It would be just like that Cordelia. It's nothing short of a scandal, the way she lets him wander." Mrs. Bee ran on about the negligent Cordelia Robins until Pastor Shaw asked the contestants to take their places again.

Frankie slipped in between Mr. Lamb, the mortician, and Mr. Culbertson, who was unaware of the concern he was causing. Libby wasn't long in seeing that consternation was warranted. When it came his turn, Mr. Culbertson rose on his short, spindly legs; thrust out his chest; and commenced to recite from the Book of Revelation. His voice trumpeted, then dropped to the whisper of a sputtering candle. It raised gooseflesh, crackling, fading, pealing like thunder.

The audience broke into spontaneous applause as he recited three chapters with his spellbinding dramatics.

"Perhaps we'd better impose a one-chapter limit per rotation," Pastor Shaw inserted when Mr. Culbertson sat down. "Mr. Lamb?"

"No point. Mr. Culbertson, I concede." A chuckle went over the spectators as the mortician, his left eye twitching, shook the old war veteran's hand, then joined his wife beneath the trees.

It served notice on the bench. And indeed, Mr. Culbertson proved an ominous competitor. In the early rounds, contestants fell away like buttons on an outgrown shirt. But the colorful portrayals of nature in Scripture stood Libby in good stead. She had memorized most as a child. It was from her father, who had been her only teacher from the time she was ten, that she had learned a love for words and the pictures they painted. No one did it better than God Himself, questioning Job out of the whirlwind with pointed reminders of who had made what and by what power it was held in place. It was to these verses Libby's mind turned when only she and Frankie and Mr. Culbertson remained in the running. She picked her way from passage to passage but in the end lost her way. The sight of Angus inclining his ear to his mother as if he were accepting compliments on her behalf insulated the sting of defeat. She felt partially vindicated, having shown him and Maddie, too, that although her head might be short on golf and politics, it wasn't altogether empty.

"Frankie?" Pastor Shaw called the boy to his feet.

It was clear by now that a trip to the fair had elicited Frankie's full attention. When had he learned all these verses? It must have taken a tremendous amount of work! Libby saw him glance toward the trees where Decatur stood with Opal and Ike before returning to the Book of Genesis, relating without a flaw the serpent's deception and man's expulsion from the garden.

"Mr. Culbertson?" summoned the reverend when Frankie was seated again.

The old soldier stood. "Yessir?"

"What passage will you be reciting?"

"What would you like to hear?"

Laughter rippled through the crowd.

"That is up to you, sir," said the reverend kindly.

The old man hesitated so long, someone from the front row prompted in a stage whisper, "Do the prodigal son."

" 'And he said, a certain man had two sons.' " Mr. Culbertson found his bearings and was off and running.

Libby slid Frankie a covert glance. A look of fierce concentration pleated his brow. He had been both troubled and troublesome since the breakup of his home. Yet this one thing he had disciplined himself to do. He must want to see the fair badly to work so hard, risk the opinions of his buddies, stand before all these people, fight down a nervousness that was only natural, and reel off verse after verse after verse. Libby grew increasingly anxious on his behalf, for defeat seemed inevitable.

"Frankie?" called the pastor.

"Saint Luke, Chapter Sixteen." Frankie scooped his red hair back with a fling of his hand and began to relate the account of the unfaithful steward who had wasted his master's goods. He spoke clearly, with an even cadence, coming eventually to, " 'Then said he to another, And how much owest thou? And he said, An hundred measures of wheat. And he said unto him ...' " Frankie hesitated. A hush went over the crowd as they waited, leaning forward, holding one collective breath, as he shifted to the other foot.

"Frankie?" prompted Reverend Shaw gently.

" 'Take thy bill,' " he began again, speaking slowly, each word standing out, " 'and write fourscore.' "

He turned as he spoke the last word, looked at Mr. Culbertson, and faded back to his seat. A light came on in the old war veteran's eyes. He needed no prompting. To his feet he came and with hat over his heart, lifted his eyes to the crowd, and proclaimed, " 'Fourscore and seven years ago our fathers brought forth on this continent a new nation, conceived in Liberty and dedicated to the proposition that all men are created equal.' "

"Mr. Culbertson," inserted Reverend Shaw, his face growing red.

But there was no stopping Mr. Culbertson. This was his lifeblood, his signature piece. Contest forgotten, he made the audience forget, too. Petty discomforts of heat and bloodthirsty mosquitoes and seats sore from long sitting fell away as he declared each line of Lincoln's Gettysburg Address. He touched in their hearts a common pride in themselves as a diverse people united by freedom, by blood, and by God.

It wasn't biblical, of course, and therefore disqualified him. But Libby saw more than one eye mist as the community came to its feet, clapping and cheering for Edgewood's "old dear." No one cheered any louder than Frankie. And why not? He had just won himself a trip to the World's Fair in St. Louis!

Cordelia Robins came forward to pat her father's arm and draw him into the crowd. Libby melted into the audience, too, and stood watching as Pastor Shaw quieted the crowd, then shook Frankie's hand and congratulated him on a victory that seemed nothing short of miraculous.

"Young man, you've done it. You've won the top prize. What do you have to say for yourself?"

Frankie kicked at a tuft of grass and replied, "I reckon I'm jest about talked out."

The minister's laughter mingled with that of the well-wishers waiting to congratulate Frankie. "In that case, we'll let Mrs. Gentry do the talking. But first, let me express my appreciation to her and to her husband as well as to the Brignadellos. Their generosity made this contest a success."

Libby found Angus just as his mother went forward to congratulate Frankie and present him with a blue ribbon and a bank draft to cover the trip. For the first time all day, Frankie looked timid. But his thank-you was respectable.

"Ah, ah." Ida Gentry intervened just as he was stuffing the draft into his trouser pocket. She wagged her finger under his nose in a matronly fashion. "That was hard work you did. You had better give it to your parents for safekeeping."

Libby saw consternation shape Frankie's features, saw too the blush on Mrs. Gentry's face as she realized the nerve she had inadvertently touched.

Frankie hesitated a long moment, then turned and looked to where Decatur stood with Ike and Opal and his grandfather, Mr. Caton.

Folks were stirring, mothers calling to their children as Mrs. Gentry gave Mr. Culbertson and Libby second and third place ribbons. Libby felt Angus's hand on her elbow but delayed a moment, watching the distance close between Frankie and Decatur. Their words were lost to her, but the awkwardness between the boy and the man as the bank draft changed hands was potent. Opal eased it some, ecstatic, proud, jumping up and down, tugging on her brother's arm. Hascal Caton was in the thick of it, too, relieving Decatur of the bank draft to have a long look. And Ike was congratulating the boy and clapping him on the back. Following his lead, Decatur shook Frankie's hand. Something in the gesture twisted at Libby's heart.

Where's the charity in that? Ike's words of yesterday echoed in her head.

Feeling unsettled, ribbon in hand, Libby accepted Angus's arm and let him lead her through the milling crowd to the fringe of trees where his buggy waited.

10

The trees cast long shadows as they sped south on Tile Factory Road. Libby's nose twitched at the whorls of dust lifting from the horses' iron-shod hooves. Unaccustomed to silence in Angus, she offered, "It's a fine thing your parents have done. Mr. and Mrs. Brignadello, too."

"Uncle Kersey may be wishing he had kept his money," said Angus, his eye trained on the road ahead. "The United States is entertaining the world in Missouri, and he would give his right arm to go."

"Wanting to go himself makes his gift all the lovelier. Though I think Mrs. Bee has a little surprise of her own in store."

"Her fair fund? Uncle Kersey may be surprised, but the secret is out where everyone else is concerned. The woman has been raising money by hawking everything from secondhand hats to crystal to garden vegetables."

"I'm the proud owner of one such hat, thanks to her creative fund-raising," said Libby. Angus made no comment. Her thoughts flitting to Frankie, Libby changed the subject. "I can't get over Frankie applying himself to learning all those verses. And then to come out ahead of Mr. Culbertson!"

"Everyone knows all you have to do is mention 'fourscore' and Mr. Culbertson's mind limps back to Gettysburg," said Angus. "It wasn't very sporting of young McClure setting him up that way."

"Had it been a court of law and the weight of judgment lain within the next breath, you'd admire the attorney smart enough to gain victory with one well-spoken phrase, wouldn't you?" reasoned Libby.

Angus arched a brow. "That's a clever comparison, Elizabeth, but totally irrelevant."

"Oh, I see. Shrewdness is commendable in lawyers but not in memory verse contestants.'' Wondering at the source of his uncustomary stodginess and why he had reverted to the formality of Elizabeth, Libby shot him a sidelong glance and added, "Mr. Culbertson couldn't have made the trip had he won. Not unless his daughter went along.''

"You're forgetting. Frankie will require a chaperon, too."

"Mrs. Bee thought of that possibility weeks ago. Someone suggested an alternate prize should a child win,'' said Libby. She braced her feet as the horses dashed along and added, "But your mother said that would take away from the contest, and if a child won, she and Mr. Gentry would chaperon.''

"Won't that be fun.''

"An Ivory City? Colored electric lights? Horseless carriages on the ground and airships overhead? People and animals from every nation and every new wonder of the world on display? Not only will it be fun, it will be the education of a lifetime. I'd love to go.''

"That isn't what I meant and you know it. Frankie McClure is a handful.''

"But your mother *likes* children. Why, she's grieved and grieved over Catherine and Charlie moving to St. Louis and depriving her of little Tess.''

"That's different. Tess is her granddaughter. Anyway, it isn't just Mother's concern. It's Chester's, too. And the other couples who are planning to go as a group, none of whom will be taking children,'' said Angus. "Frankie himself will feel out of place. Though, come to think of it, the way that boy behaves, the ratio of adults to Frankie may be their salvation. That boy has made mischief all over town. I'd bet my hat he's the one who has been sneaking horses out of private barns in the dead of night.''

Libby wasn't ignorant of the suspicions stirring, and although it touched a nerve to hear Frankie accused when evidence was lacking, she didn't risk a quarrel by saying so.

In the face of her silence, Angus softened his tone a bit. "Maybe it's the best you can expect out of the boy with Decatur as a role model. I wonder what got into him, showing up today.''

"I think Opal invited him.'' Libby related how the little girl had asked her to deliver the matchbox gift to her father the previous day.

"And you did it?''

"I didn't *hand*-deliver it. I left it beneath McClure's mailbox. I wasn't going to,'' she added, as his sandy brows beetled in disapproval. "But Opal started to cry.''

"Libby, you cannot go on forever trying to sort out other folks' problems.''

She plucked a bit of skirt between her fingers and weakly protested, "But I like the children. I like Naomi, too.''

"I've gathered as much. I hate to be the one to say it, but she hasn't the best reputation after everything that's happened.''

Libby knew that in the eyes of many, Naomi was a fallen woman. But if half the rumors that circulated concerning Maddie were true, then it seemed inconsistent of Angus to be digging up Naomi's past mistakes when he was so willing to bury Maddie's. So thinking, she defended Naomi, saying, "Naomi was young and made a mistake."

"I'm not judging her, Elizabeth," he said, his tone tart. "But it does puzzle me as to what you find in common with the woman."

"She once dreamed of writing poetry, did you know that? As for the children, Opal's a delight with her little circus antics. She and David are good friends. And Frankie . . ." Failing to find words to express her feelings for the boy, Libby borrowed some instead, saying, "Ike says he's not a bad boy, that he's just having a hard time."

"*Ike* says?" The edge to Angus's tone sharpened. "I saw him pat you on the behind."

Libby's jaw dropped. His words, toneless and hard-bitten, rang hot in her ears. "Pat me on the . . . Angus! Is that what you think? Good faith! He was brushing a caterpillar off my skirt, that's all."

"A caterpillar, is it?" He sniffed. "Blast his eyes! If he isn't a brazen piece of—"

"There *was* a caterpillar," Libby cut in, hanging on to her temper by a thread. "And there's no need to get into a shouting match over what you *think* you saw. I don't know why you waited until now to bring it up. Why didn't you ask me about it right away?"

"I'm not shouting," he countered in a tone she was certain served him well in court. "I've been admirably civil considering that from where I was sitting it looked as if the man was fondling you. And with half the town looking on, too!"

Flashing hot, Libby shot to her feet. "Angus Cearlock, that's enough! Stop the horses!"

"Sit down before you cause an accident!" His voice lifted another decibel.

"Stop them right now!"

Angus obliged with a jerk on the reins that nearly threw Libby over the dashboard. The dust was still swirling around the buggy as she bolted out and set off down the road, her shoulders thrown back, her white skirt whipping at her legs. She couldn't explain even to herself the emotions that had passed between herself and Ike under the tree. Particularly in light of the stories that lingered concerning him and Maddie. But when it came to the caterpillar incident, Angus was completely out of line.

"Confound it, Libby, you have a blind spot where that fellow is concerned," called Angus from the buggy seat. He matched his team's pace to hers. "I've warned you before, it's more than friendship he has in mind. How do you expect me to feel about that?"

She stopped short and swung around to face him. "Of all the self-centered, low-minded . . . You insult me and Ike as well, and I'm supposed to concern myself with what *you* feel? Frankly, Mr. Cearlock, I don't think your feelings for me are nearly so deep and abiding as your feelings for yourself, and I will thank you to whip up your horses and leave me to walk home unabused by your company or your crude remarks."

The spots of color drained from his face. His jaw slackened and the fire in his eyes died, replaced by swift remorse. He drew a long breath. "I'm sorry, Libby. I don't know what came over me. Perhaps I do know, but I don't think it sheds a favorable light on my character." He dragged one hand over his face and asked, "Could you be coaxed into riding with me if I asked very nicely? Or shall I climb down and we'll both walk?"

"You have a short memory," said Libby, for the last time he'd come after her in the heat of a disagreement, his horse had raced off without him.

Angus hauled a round, cast-iron anchor from beneath the seat, flung it to the ground, and climbed down. "Every quarrel we've had has been over Ike Galloway or the McClures. Why is that, I wonder?"

"I'll tell you why," she rounded on him. "It's because you take the liberty of assuming you know better than God Himself whom I should befriend and whom I shouldn't."

"So you prefer having your judgment go unchallenged?"

Wondering why he had even bothered apologizing, Libby caught her skirt in one hand and lengthened her stride. Angus's eyeglasses slipped down his nose as he snapped a line from the bridle ring of the left horse to the weight. He shoved his spectacles into his pocket.

"Forget the McClures. They aren't the real issue anyway. I've been irritated ever since you sat down to share your lunch with Galloway and the others, then lingered to talk with the fellow and let him touch your . . . skirt."

Flushed and defiant and growing more careless by the heartbeat, Libby met his nearsighted squint and retorted, "If you had come for me as soon as we finished eating instead of playing the jack-a-dandy with Maddie, we wouldn't be having this conversation! And, I might add, you were awfully quick to her defense when Mr. Caton got so ornery, digging into her past."

He talked right over her. "Irritated is too weak a word. I wanted to put my fist in his face."

Libby lifted her eyes and saw rivalry, passion, and desire play across his countenance. Her preconceived notions about men and the manageability of emotions seemed suddenly naive. Even her jealousy over Maddie was dwarfed by the magnitude of how little she knew of men. She lifted a hand, anxious to slow the progression of what she had awakened in him. It was a feeble shield, that upraised hand.

He sandwiched it between both of his and confessed, "I'm so smitten by you, Libby, I can hardly keep my mind on my law practice much less my political endeavors. I go to sleep with you in my head and wake up to find you still there, and the thought of Ike Galloway—of anyone—touching you in a familiar way scalds me so, I lose all reason. But that is no excuse for taking my bad humor out on you.''

The unwitting possessor of his swift-beating heart, she wanted to respond by reciprocating the gift but couldn't. There was that look, that one minuscule caught breath of a moment with Ike. The smaller she tried to make it, the larger it loomed. Against all reason, it was emblazoned in her mind. Clouds scuddled over the westering sun as Angus cupped her hand to his breast.

"I want to hold you as I'm holding your hand. But I want it to be right between us, Libby,'' he entreated. "A foundation upon which we can build a life together. I'd marry you tomorrow if I thought it fair to ask. But it isn't fair. Not with the election looming and no idea of what lies ahead. A man ought to know what sort of future he's offering a woman and whether it's a way of life she could be happy sharing.''

"Angus, please . . .''

"No, let me say it all while I've got my courage up,'' he pleaded. "I don't want to rush things. I want you to have the schooling you yearn for. I'd consider it an honor if you'd let me help make that a reality. And then, when you have your education and you feel the time is right, we can make plans to spend the rest of our lives together.''

Spots of color warmed his cheeks as his words dropped off into a silence as deep as the sky. With an anxious frown pleating his brow, he amended his plea: "You do understand, don't you, Libby? Or can't you find it in your heart to forgive this lovesick fool for behaving so badly?''

Sudden tears rose in Libby's throat and burned behind her eyelids, blurring his face. To think that she had accused him of caring only for himself when, in fact, he'd taken into account not only his own uncertain career, but also her unrealized goals and dreams and future happiness.

Moved by his gallantry, her temper melted away, replaced by a sweep of tender affection. Humbled, she said, "How can I, in view of your honesty, be any less candid? The truth is, what you felt about Ike, I felt about Maddie from the moment she took my place at your side and shared her box lunch with you.''

"You don't mean to say you were jealous of Maddie?''

"Is that so foolish? She is bright and pretty. She's your sister's best friend. She knows what subjects interest you and can talk endlessly of them.''

Relief flooded his face, chasing away the strain of their quarrel. "The subject that interests me most, Libby dear, is you.''

Heat rushed to her cheeks. "You are neither self-centered nor low-minded. It was my wretched temper talking. I'm sorry, Angus.''

He touched her lips with his finger to forestall further apology. "As far as I'm concerned, it's forgotten."

"As for school, I'm touched that you would offer. But beyond the propriety of the matter, there is David to consider. And Father. And now, it looks as if my sister-in-law may be coming to stay for a while. What I'm trying to say—"

"If you're saying no, then don't say it, Libby. Listen to me!" he insisted as her lips formed the word. "With my campaign heating up in the fall and your involvement with the Berry Sisters, it would be the first of the year before you could enter school anyway. Much can happen between now and then. At least promise me you'll mention it to your father, and after the election, we'll take it from there."

At length, Libby promised. But even as she did so, she kept her hopes on a tight leash lest they be dashed once again and she despair of ever getting the schooling she felt was necessary to progress as a writer.

11

✒ Libby arrived home ahead of her father. After Angus had gone, she lingered on the porch watching the colors in heaven's canvas and wondering how best to approach her father with Angus's offer to send her to school after the fall election. In one last flame of glory the setting sun threw light behind the ruffled clouds.

Father came whistling up the walk with David beside him. Libby stirred from the porch swing and called, "That was some fine reciting you did, Davie."

Father flung an arm over David's shoulder. "I canna help but wonder how a noodle wi' such a fearful horde o' words keeps from burstin' at the seams."

"Yes, well, he is no ordinary lad, our Davie." The sunbaked grass whispered beneath Libby's feet as she crossed the yard to meet them. She smoothed her little brother's rumpled shirt and tugged at the ribbon he had looped over his button. "Let's have a look. My, now isn't that a fine ribbon."

"I should hang it on the wall."

"An excellent idea! Let's pick out a choice spot tomorrow, shall we?" Libby slipped her arm through his. "And speaking of spots, what's this you've spilled on your shirt?"

"Lunch," he said.

She wrinkled her nose. "One more shirt for the collection heaped beneath your bed. Gather them all up after supper if you would please. I want to get an early start on the wash in the morning."

"Rubbin' and scrubbin'? Is that what ye plan to do with yerself, now that Billy is takin' over the mail route?" asked Father as he led the way inside.

"Rubbing and scrubbing and cleaning and cooking and everything else

I've let go while I was working. If I'm lucky, I'll have some time left over to practice with the Berry girls,'' said Libby.

"You sang good today," said David.

"Well. And thank you, Davie." She hugged him before adding, "But we have a lot of songs to work on before we go stumping with Angus."

"You aren't going tomorrow, are you?" asked David.

"No, no. Not until late in September." Libby took a twisted paper strip from the spill vase, touched it to the match Father struck, and lit the lamp.

David ran his tongue over his swollen lip and asked, "Who will cook for us while you're gone?"

Libby parked her hands on her hips and laughed. "Just listen to the lad, always thinking about his stomach. He's more like his big brothers each day. Very well then. Wash your hands while I set supper on the table."

David moved a short stool in front of the sink, stepped up on it, and made a quiet game of working the handle on the black sink pump. Libby put her hat out of harm's way, smoothed loose tendrils of hair away from her face, then took advantage of David's pumping to dash her hands under the stream of water flowing into the granite catch basin.

"I'm looking forward to having more time for my writing," said Libby as she tied on an apron. "Mr. Gruben wants a report on today's church social for the next issue and an article about the circus, too. Plus, I need to see if there have been any developments on the horse borrowings."

"Still workin' on that, are ye, lass?" Father sighed. "Mischief and pranksterin'! Ye can hardly fault the poor laddies for complainin' at comin' oot in the early morn to find their poor old hay burners breathin' hard and needin' a restie when there's work to be doon."

Libby thought fleetingly of Frankie and Angus's accusation but did not speak of it. She sliced some cheese and placed it on a tray beside buttered sandwiches while Father opened a can of peaches and David set the table. A search of the icebox yielded pickles and a jar of cranberry jelly that Sarah Jane Brignadello had given her. Setting the jar on the table, she exclaimed, "What am I thinking? I can't wash in the morning. I have a fitting with Mrs. Bee."

"Ah, yes. New gowns for the Berry Sisters."

"Dear Mrs. Bee. Stitching away like a Trojan. The least I can do is remember the fitting."

Father draped an arm over David's shoulder. "Would ye just look at the bonny lass? Jumpin' aboot the kitchen with star shine in her eyes, nary a thought to answerin' her poor little brither's inquiry as to who will be doin' the cookin' whilst she's skippin' away on her singsong this fall."

"There's always Baker's on the square," countered Libby. "Or was there something in that box lunch to make you change your mind about Mrs. Baker's cooking?''

Father feigned an injured sniff. ''Canna a fellow take a leddy picnickin' without his bairns goin' aspeculatin'?''

''He can if he's careful with his star-shine talk.''

Father artfully changed the subject, then held the chair for her to join them at the table. Libby bowed her head as he asked a blessing on the meal. The excitement of the day caught up with David. He nearly fell asleep in his plate. Libby offered no objections when Father dismissed him from dish-washing and sent him off to bed.

''I canna help thinkin' yer poor brither will be lost withoot ye this fall,'' said Father when he had gone.

''I don't know about that. He'll most likely enjoy the liberty. Like a little pup finding a hole in the fence and a big wide world beyond.''

Father laughed and followed her to the sink with the empty plates, teasing, ''I would not worry too greatly aboot the lad findin' his way into mischief and besmirchin' yer sterlin' reputation aboot town. Not so long as we hae Teddy keepin' an eye oot for him.''

''And Mrs. Baker: Who is she keeping an eye out for?'' Libby ventured with a mischievous smile.

Refusing to take the bait, Father stroked his chin. ''Mrs. Baker is a tireless, guid-hearted woman with a saintly patience aboot her. 'Tis a mortal puzzle how the dear leddy keeps from collidin' with her own shadow. Why, the runnin' of her boardin' and dinin' house and the welfare of Teddy to say nothin' of the caretakin' of her mother 'twould reduce a lesser leddy into a heap o' apron strings and tattered shoe leather!''

Resisting the playful urge to pry further, Libby asked, ''How *is* Gram Steadman anyway?''

''She grows more feeble wi' each passin' day. 'Tis all she can do to feed herself and not a thread of memory left. Mrs. Baker wilna say it to her sister, but she would welcome a bit of help wi' the poor soul.''

''Zerilda is busy herself,'' said Libby, who had grown accustomed to Zer-ilda's sparks, flames, and sullen moods. ''A full-time job, an invalid husband, and the temporary care of two grandchildren is no light load either.''

''Aye, that's true enough,'' said Father. He returned to the sink with the rest of the dirty dishes.

Methodically scrubbing each plate, Libby thought to broach the subject of Angus and college, then lost her courage and said instead, ''Like day and night, Mrs. Baker and Zerilda. Isn't it a puzzle that two sisters, born of the same parents and raised in the same house, could be so different?''

''Life is a journey, lass. Mrs. Baker, unlike Zerilda, has the Map. She travels the road lightly.''

"Lightly?" echoed Libby. "And just a breath ago, you were itemizing the weighty list of responsibilities on her shoulders."

"Aye, but the leddy isna packin' yesterday's burden, too. She' trustin' 'em to her Travelin' Companion."

Softly, Libby conceded his point, saying, "Zerilda's got an unrelenting memory, that's for sure."

"A mortal pity, limpin' through life draggin' a load o' grumbles and gripes and strife. Guid faith! Who could keep a sweet face with such a load o' bitter baggage?"

And jealousy. Libby's thoughts skipped from Mrs. Baker and Zerilda to the sisters Mrs. Bee and Mrs. Gentry to Angus himself and his careless words sparked by that very emotion. She remembered that she had not been immune to it either where Maddie was concerned. At least Angus had confessed his feelings of rivalry, for without that confession, she could never have been honest about her own feelings.

But had she been honest? Completely honest?

Ike's face drifted past the window of her thoughts. Libby crowded it out, took a deep breath, and plunged in, telling Father of Angus's offer to pay for her schooling. She saw clouds gather on his face, feared she was wasting her breath, but said in closing, "I would think of it as a loan, Father. I would insist he set it up in a businesslike fashion and that I repay him with interest."

"Sweetheartin' is a treacherous business, lass, withoot puttin' yerself in debt to the lad. See a banker if it's a loan yer needin'." Father rose from the table, kissed her cheek, bid her good night, and went off to his room.

A bank? Whoever heard of a bank lending a woman money for schooling?

Oh, well, had she not known in her heart of hearts that Father wouldn't hear of it? Still, it was dear of Angus to have offered.

Libby retreated to her room and battled her disappointment by looking to the week ahead. Angus would be in court in Bloomington all week. She lit a lamp and reached for her journal. She wrote of the Berry Sisters' first sing, the box lunch mix-up, and Angus's declared affections. She mentioned his offer to send her to school and Father's refusal to allow it. She wrote of her anticipation for the fall when the Berry Sisters would entertain in the little towns where Angus took his campaign and her eagerness to capture for Mr. Gruben's paper each step of the journey. She wrote of Opal's new red dress. Of the children's excitement over the circus coming to town. Of Naomi foregoing the church social so as not to run into Decatur. Of Frankie winning the contest and of the odd wrenching of heart she felt as Decatur congratulated him. Of Father's burgeoning friendship with Mrs. Baker and of Gram Steadman's deteriorating health. In closing, Libby penned a prayer concerning her trepidations about Abigail coming to visit.

Not one word did she write about Ike.

* * *

A thumping awakened Ike in the night. He had been dreaming of land crabs in Cuba and nearly dismissed the sound as part of the dream. But land crabs didn't thump. The creatures had left imprinted upon his mind the hideous clicking they made as they scuttled along on their nocturnal foragings. *Dead soldiers, eyes plucked away by the crabs.* He dragged his hand over his face as if to erase the unbidden image, then paused motionless, listening in the dark gloom of the cabin. The muffled thumping came again.

Wide-awake, Ike rolled to his feet. Decatur maybe? The doorknob rattled. The swollen wood creaked as Ike felt his way past the stove to the wall where he'd left his clothes. He was pulling his pants on when the door gave way. It was too dark to see the intruder, but his entrance was noisy with coughing and weary cursing. Ike retrieved a match from his pocket, struck it with a thumbnail, and cupped a protective hand about the flickering flame as the damp breeze blew through the open door.

"Something I can do for you, mister?" he called.

The fellow was so large of girth, he seemed to fill the whole doorway. Starting violently, he said, "Forgive the intrusion. I thought the place was abandoned."

"Now you see it ain't. What is it yer looking for?"

The man pushed the door shut and sagged against it, seized by another spasm of coughing. His cape dragged on the floor as he doubled over. His silk hat toppled off his head.

Poor devil looked too sick to be much of a threat, regardless of his size. Ike lit the lantern, got a grip on the fellow's arm, and helped him into a sturdy chair. The man muttered his gratitude. His eyes watered in the dancing lamp light as another fit of coughing seized him. At length, he sat with sagging shoulders, utterly spent and wheezing with each breath he drew.

"What's ailin' ya, mister?" asked Ike.

"A respiratory complaint, I fear. A dreadful pain in my head and a conflagration in my chest," he whispered weakly.

"You need a doctor?" asked Ike.

"No, no. If I could just rest here awhile, I'll be a new man."

"Ike Galloway's the name," said Ike and helped the man off with his cape.

"John Robinson," returned the fellow with the faintest hesitation.

Ike shook the man's fleshy hand. "Not much in the way of comforts here, but you're welcome to sleep here tonight."

"I thank you for your kindness," said Robinson.

Ike cleared off the bottom shelf of Naomi's workbench and spread a blanket from his bedroll there, turning the shelf into a makeshift bed. Meanwhile, with a good deal of huffing, panting, and wheezing, Robinson peeled off his frock coat, kicked off his boots, and shed his trousers and shirt. He shivered violently as he stretched out on the shelf dressed in his short union suit.

Ike gave him his last blanket and asked, "Have ya got a horse needs tending?"

"No. I was traveling by rail until the freight car I was riding in was sidetracked at the crossing." Robinson lifted himself on one elbow, coughing again. When he had finally stopped, he added, "A disagreeable brakeman prevented me from making a second choice. Lady Fortunate has been in a foul mood."

"What's yer line of work?" asked Ike.

"I was in the employment of a mud show for the last few months. They let me go last night."

"Wouldn't be the Roth–Bigelow Circus, would it?"

"You've seen the posters?"

"Yep. Comin' to a town up the road."

"We've been on a circuit of small towns all summer." Robinson battled another bout of coughing, and when he had his breath again, asked, "Where am I anyway? I dozed off on the train and lost track of progress."

"Three miles north of Edgewood." Seeing a sign of recognition flash in the man's feverish eyes, Ike asked, "You know of it?"

"I knew it was on the circuit."

Ike settled into a chair by the window, wondering what the man's role was with the circus. He had the look of a performer. Odd-colored eyes. Deep-set, darkly fringed, and beguiling. Made him think of a fellow he'd glimpsed on a street corner in Tampa while waiting to ship out to Cuba. He'd been advertising some bawdy backstreet show.

Much thinner fellow. Ike propped his feet on the windowsill, intending to stay alert and be on hand if the fellow worsened. But it had been a long day, and his need for sleep overpowered his good intentions.

It was daybreak when Robinson's intermittent coughing awakened Ike. He rubbed the sleep from his eyes, stood up to stretch the kinks from his back, and turned to find Robinson on his feet by the cold stove. His hands were in the air, his eyes glassy-looking. With a sweep of his hand, Robinson launched into words and phrases that made Ike think of a nursery rhyme gone awry.

"Glo-o-orious ladies in glittering array galloping . . . galloping . . . grasshoppers." Robinson scratched his furrowed brow and began afresh. "In ring one . . . ring-a-ding maiden Madeline . . . daring deeds of . . . heart-stopping feats . . . of . . . heroics of hypnotic proport . . ."

Robinson's knees crumpled beneath him. Ike leaped to catch him, but it was the stove that broke the man's fall. "Let's get a chair under you, mister."

"Conflaber . . . aggregation . . ." Robinson leaned forward, a rattling cough that ended in a mucky-sounding laugh. "It's a warm show, gentlemen. A lively girl. Sure to get your money's worth. Can't be, I wouldn't suggest . . . best leave the missus at home."

"See there," murmured Ike. "All that ballyhoo is makin' ya cough."

Robinson's eyes fluttered shut. Ike lowered him to the floor. Satisfied he was going to stay down, he got a basin of water from the pump out back and bathed the fellow's face. Robinson's eyes opened, but there was no comprehension, just fever burning in their muddy depths.

Ike had seen a lot of malaria in Cuba. It brought cycles of fever and chills and delirium. Nearly everyone caught it. The first two years after returning home, he had been plagued with reoccurring bouts of the disease in the spring. The remembered pattern of chills and fever made him wonder if the man had malaria. But he couldn't account for the racking cough.

Ike felt the man's fluttering pulse and murmured, "I ain't much at doctoring, Lord. Reckon it's time I was gettin' this fella some help?" Hearing the sound of a train whistle, he looked out the window to the east and saw the south-bound limited stopping at the Old Kentucky Crossing. The train would be faster than horseback. If he hurried, he could catch it into town and get Doc Harding.

12

🌹 Sarah Jane Brignadello kept office for her brother, Dr. Harding, on the west side of the square in Edgewood. She had just finished Chloe's and Dorene's fittings when Libby arrived.

"Put your dress on inside out, Libby. It's easier for me to mark and pin," Mrs. Bee instructed.

Libby cast aside the apron she had donned that morning and trekked back to the anteroom to change. Dr. Harding was out making house calls. But Opal McClure, self-appointed entertainment committee, was in and bent on keeping her captive audience.

"You ain't leavin' surely," she pleaded with Chloe and Dorene when they had changed back into their cotton skirts and shirtwaists. "See here? I got another trick." She stretched out her arms and tippytoed down the length of Mrs. Bee's outstretched measuring tape as if it were a tightrope. "Ta-da! How'd you like that un?"

The Berry sisters clapped on cue.

"A simple 'You're ravishing' will suffice," said Libby. She dropped a deep curtsy in her inside-out gown.

"They were clapping for me!" cried Opal.

Libby's crestfallen expression delighted fun-loving Dorene. But Opal, thinking her serious, showed her tender side and amended, "But ya *do* look purty, Miss Lib."

Mrs. Bee's laughter mingled with Libby's and the Berry sisters'. She hugged Opal and said, "You're priceless, Opal. Aren't we lucky to have you for a friend?"

Flushed with pleasure, Opal returned to her circus antics with renewed fervor. Libby held her bare arms away from her sides so Mrs. Bee could check the seams, the darts, the tucks. The sleeves had yet to be sewn in as well as a sheer bodice inset, lace trimmings, and other embellishments.

Down on her knees, talking around a pin, Mrs. Bee asked, "How does the waist feel? Too snug?"

"Like a hug," said Libby.

"Without any of the complications," inserted Dorene with an impish grin.

Chloe turned a narrowed eye on her younger sister. "If Dad sees you and Earl Morefield huggin', you'll think complications."

Brow puckering, Opal asked, "Don't you like huggin', Chloe?"

Dorene chortled. "How would she know? She's never tried it."

"So? That's the way I want it until I get married."

"Who's going to marry you if you don't do any hugging?" demanded Dorene.

Chloe sniffed and countered, "If you were as smart as you think you are, you'd have figured out that men don't want to marry a girl every fellow and his brother has snuggled up to. Am I right, Mrs. Bee?"

Mrs. Bee poured cold water on the tit-for-tat squabbling for which the Berry girls were so renowned, saying, "Girls, girls! It's warm enough in here without short words raising the temperature."

Libby wiped her perspiring brow. It *was* warm with the gaslights burning overhead and drawn curtains closing out any breeze that might have found its way through the windows. Dorene made a fan out of a folded *Gazette* and fanned Mrs. Bee and Libby with wild abandon. "Is that better?"

"A regular northerly." Libby rubbed her bare arms, feigning a shiver.

Mrs. Bee smiled at their playfulness, made a final adjustment on one of the bodice darts, leaned back on her heels, and surveyed the results. "How's that? Can you breathe comfortably?"

"Just fine," said Libby. She ran her fingers over the yellow voile fabric.

"I've left plenty of room in the side seams and darts if it needs to be let out."

"No, no. It's perfect," Libby insisted.

Mrs. Bee wiggled her finger in a circle. "Turn. Let's be certain the skirt flows the way it should. All the way around."

"Can ya be in a circus if ya cain't sew, Mrs. Bee?" asked Opal from an upside-down position. Her hands were on the floor, her knees bent and planted on her elbows.

"Certainly."

"That's good, 'cause I cain't sew a stitch." Opal popped up like a jack-in-the-box, took a flurry of steps, struck a pose, planted her hands on the floor, and kicked her dusty bare feet into the air. "Watch! I can walk on my hands."

"Don't brush against Libby's dress, dear," warned Mrs. Bee. She pushed a short-legged stool toward Libby. "The hem and then you can go. Chloe, hand me the pins, would you please? Climb up, Libby."

The pinning was proceeding smoothly when Mrs. Bee jabbed herself. "Fiddlesticks." She struggled up from her knees as a droplet of blood pooled at the end of her finger. "I'll be right back."

Opal watched her mentor hurry down the corridor sucking her pricked finger. She planted her hands on her shapeless hips, tossed her white-gold hair, and exclaimed with theatrical excess, "Beastly pins!"

Opal's words sent a tune chasing through Libby's head. Bending her knees, she poked her face up close to Opal's and sang, "The beast, the beast, the beastly pins. Oh, I went to the animal fair. The birds and beasts were there. Come on, Opal, sing!"

"I don't know the words."

"I'll teach you." Balanced on the footstool, Libby stretched out her arms and waved her arms like a choir director, swaying to the rhythm as she sang, "The old baboon by the light of the moon was combing her auburn hair. The monkey was scared of the skunk. He climbed up the elephant's trunk . . ."

Chloe and Dorene linked hands with Opal on the second time through, singing and dancing in a circle as Libby made up actions to fit the words. She flapped her arms. Mimed combing her hair. Flung one arm in the air, wrist hanging loose, curled the other behind her back like a primate tail, and pinched her nose on the word *skunk,* singing, "The monkey was scared of the skunk. He climbed up the elephant's trunk. The elephant sneezed and fell on his knees and what became of the monk, the monk, the monk?"

At Chloe's swift intake of breath, Libby swung around to find Ike Galloway standing in the doorway grinning.

"Jest waitin' for the commotion to fade," he said.

Chloe stammered, Opal giggled, Libby clambered off the stool and dashed for cover, and Dorene, laughing loudest of all, came galloping after her. In the examining room just off the lobby, Dorene offered between giggles, "Turn around and I'll help you out of that thing."

"Doesn't that man know how to knock?" exclaimed Libby, hot to the tips of her ears.

Pulling out the pins holding the back of the dress together, Dorene struck a listening pose. "Wait! Shh! Listen!" She cocked her head to one side. "It's Ike. He's wantin' an encore."

"Dorene, you ornery thing! I'm not stepping foot out of this room until he's gone!"

They both jumped at the sound of approaching footsteps. Snatching her clothes off the hook and shielding herself with them, Libby whirled around and all but bowled Mrs. Bee over. Mrs. Bee jumped back and dropped the towel with which she had been drying her hands.

"Land, you're jumpy! And what are you doing, changing?" she asked. "I haven't finished pinning the hem."

"Ike's out front asking for Doc," said Dorene.

"Is he sick or hurt?"

Dorene shot Libby a twinkling glance. "I think he came for dress rehearsal."

Libby flung her apron at her. Mrs. Bee scratched her furrowed brow, gave a shake of her head, and turned away to investigate. Dorene ducked out the door after her, Libby's new dress draped over her arm.

Her steaming skin making a struggle of the dive into her shirtwaist and skirt, Libby assuaged her dented dignity thinking, *Oh, so what? It was only Ike.* With a tilt of her chin, she buttoned her shirtwaist and jerked her skirt into place. All that stood between her and the lobby was one thin wall. She strained her ear to the continuing round of conversation led by Mrs. Bee:

"Hello, Ike. What can I do for you?"

" 'Morning, Mrs. Bee. I'm lookin' for Doc."

"He's out making calls. Why? Are you sick?"

"Not me. There's a fella stopped at my place last night. He's running a fever and coughin' pretty bad. I think Doc better have a look. Got any idea where I might find him?"

"Try Baker's. He was going over to check on Gram Steadman. An older gentleman, is it?"

"Nope. In his prime, I'd say. A big fella. Fancy frock coat and top hat. Says he'd been workin' for the circus."

"You don't mean the one that's scheduled to play here?"

"That's the one. Said his name was John Robinson."

"John Robinson?"

"Yes, ma'am. Does the name mean somethin'?"

"No, not really. Except in circus talk. John Robinson means anything cut short, which is neither here nor there," said Mrs. Bee. "If you think it's urgent, Ike, we can help you look for Melville."

"Thanks, but that ain't necessary. I'll find him. And if I don't, jest ask him to ride out to the grove. I'll be at Naomi's shop."

"All right, Ike. We'll send him."

Libby heard the door close behind Ike. She smoothed down her skirt placket, combed her fingers through her tousled hair, and returned to the lobby, where Mrs. Bee and the Berry sisters were speculating as to what might be ailing the circus fellow. Crossing to the window, Libby opened the curtains and gave the shade a tug. She watched Ike cross the park but quickly averted her gaze as Dorene joined her at the window.

Nudging her with her shoulder, Dorene teased, "Chloe said Ike wants to know if you're gonna do that number when Angus goes campaigning."

"What Ike *wants* is a poke in the nose," countered Libby.

Dorene laughed. But Mrs. Bee looked up from gathering her pins and scissors and other sewing widgets. Finding her thoughtful gaze unnerving, Libby flushed and turned away. "If we're finished here, I've got writing and washing waiting at home."

"I'd better go, too, and find Mrs. Gentry," said Chloe. "She's got some notion about washing windows this afternoon. I told her I could walk out to Erstwood, but she said she was coming to town anyway and didn't mind picking me up."

"When is our next fitting, Miss Bee?" asked Dorene.

"Depends on how quickly I progress. We can get together after one of your practice sessions next week," said Mrs. Bee.

"Here comes Maddie." Dorene tapped on the window glass and waved.

Libby turned to the window too just as Maddie Daniels set the brake on the Dorrance Dairy wagon and climbed down. Her black skirts rustled about her willowy frame as she strode into Dr. Harding's office to a flurry of greetings.

"What do you think? Grand enough for the singing Berry Sisters?" asked Mrs. Bee, displaying Libby's gown.

Maddie pinched the fabric. "Lovely material. And making up beautifully."

"Gonna be airish without no sleeves," observed Opal.

"I'm sure Mrs. Bee has them in mind." Maddie's smile was warm but fleeting. "I came in to pick up my niece at the station. The train is due in just a few minutes. Can you come out to the wagon, Libby? I have some books for your library."

"Library?" Mrs. Bee and Libby chorused.

"What's this about a library?" Paulette Harding asked, sweeping through the door, looking stylish in a handsome silk dress and plumed hat.

"Libby said she wanted to start one," said Maddie.

"Yes, but I didn't mean *today*," said Libby.

"There's no time like the present for getting books into the hands of readers. It occurs to me, too, that a library is a logical gathering spot for people to come together and share ideas and explore solutions to public concerns," reasoned Maddie.

"Such as women getting the vote?" piped up Dorene, who had apparently already been approached by Maddie concerning her group of freethinkers.

"It's an issue of great interest to a lot of women, myself included," said Maddie.

"Me, too," said Dorene. "If I'm supposed to abide by the laws of the land, shouldn't I have some say in electing those who make them?"

"Hush, Dorene. Studyin' who to vote for isn't as simple as crochetin' or cookin' or churnin' butter. You don't know anymore about law or leaders or politics than I do," chided Chloe.

Rebelling against Chloe's big-sister manner, Dorene retorted, "I could learn. You'd help me, wouldn't you, Maddie?"

"Bravo, Dorene! Of course I would!" Maddie beamed at her. "Your education doesn't stop the day you walk out of the classroom. Not so long as you continue to read and think and explore and grow. A group of progressive-thinking women coming together to learn from one another would serve this community well. You'd agree with that, wouldn't you, Chloe?"

"I'm not sayin' I do or I don't," Chloe answered, refusing to be crowded. "It doesn't matter anyway, 'cause I got no spare time to wheedle away."

"Well, it sounds terrific to me." Dorene ignored the silent warning her sister was sending her with puckered lips and added, "If you hold your meetings when I'm not working, I'll come."

"Not if Dad learns of it, you won't," muttered Chloe.

But Libby seemed to be the only one to hear her, for Maddie had turned to Mrs. Bee and Mrs. Harding, seeking their input regarding such a group. Both responded pleasantly enough, though Libby noted neither committed themselves to attending. Before Maddie could launch a full-fledged membership drive, Libby steered the conversation back on track.

"About the library . . ."

It was all the prompting Maddie needed. "I was thinking if everyone who has books they are no longer using donates them, we should be able to start it right away."

"Just a moment, Maddie. You're moving too fast for me," said Paulette. The feather on her hat fluttered as she whirled around to block Chloe and Dorene's path to the door, saying, "Before you two rush off . . ." Untying a parcel, she handed them each a pair of white gloves and instructed them to try them on before turning her attention back to Maddie. "A library requires a good deal more organization than filling shelves with books. You'll have to petition the city council, see if they have the budget. And if they don't—"

"You've tried this before?" Maddie interrupted.

"Yes. It's been discussed a number of times over the years."

"What happened?"

"So far, nothing."

"Then used books and a room to put them in is better than nothing, isn't it?" reasoned Maddie.

"Maddie's right, Paulette." Mrs. Bee panned the room, adding thoughtfully, "What do you think Melville would say about *this* room?"

"Sarah Jane!" Paulette's blue eyes widened. "You can't be serious!"

"Why not? It isn't as if he *needs* a lobby," said Mrs. Bee.

Indignant, Paulette replied, "But of course he needs a lobby. This is a doctor's office." Distracted by Chloe fending off Opal's bare feet, which were waving in the air like windmills, she inserted, "Don't get the gloves dirty fighting that child's feet, Chloe. How do they fit?"

While her sister-in-law saw to the Berry girls' gloves, Mrs. Bee paced from one end of the room to the other and then to the open door. Right elbow cupped in her left hand, she drummed her chin with her fingers. "Books in a waiting room. Think about it, Paulette. It might even be *good* for business."

"Exactly how?" demanded Paulette.

"A farmer comes in for a book, for example, and thinks that while he's here, he might as well have that pesky corn removed."

"What about someone who is ill or injured? He shouldn't have to pick a path through the books to find the doctor," countered Paulette.

"There's always the back door."

Maddie crooked her finger at Libby, then inclined her head to whisper, "Let's leave Mrs. Bee to her arm twisting, shall we?"

Reasoning it was petty to be miffed at Maddie for rushing forward with her idea, Libby brushed past Mrs. Bee and followed Maddie out to the dairy wagon. She peered over the painted side at the boxes of books. They made her fingers itch. It was always that way, the urge to touch and explore and lose herself in a good story.

"What have you got there?' she asked.

"Some children's stories. A few classics, a general assortment of fiction, and some nonfiction volumes on horticulture, dairy farming, and such. Ride over to the station with me," Maddie invited. "I'll pick up my niece, then we can drop these off."

"Drop them where?" asked Libby.

"You can store them at your house while Paulette lets herself be talked into an idea she's only sorry she didn't think of herself," said Maddie in that commanding way of hers that gave little thought to the convenience of others. She mounted the wagon, picked up the reins, and shot Libby an expectant glance. "Aren't you coming?"

Chiding herself for second-guessing Maddie's overture of friendship, Libby joined her on the seat. On the short ride to the station, she learned that Maddie's niece was nine, that her name was Sophronia, that she belonged to Maddie's brother, who was prospering as head of a manufacturing firm, and that Maddie hadn't seen her brother, sister-in-law, or niece in five years.

"I have no experience with children," Maddie conceded as they watched the train pull into the station. "But if Sophronia Kay has a single original idea, I'm committed to protecting it from Mother's inhibiting spirit."

Was that how Mrs. Dorrance had shaped Maddie? Trying to wring the originality out of her?

"Are you cross with me for adopting your library project?"

Surprised at Maddie's perception, Libby made a conscious choice not to yield to that deflated sense of having had her thunder stolen. "It isn't important who does it, just that it gets done."

"A new building with books still smelling of fresh ink would be nice, but this should work in the meantime."

Was she motivated by the books or by the idea of a public meeting place to assemble a group of suffragettes? Libby couldn't resist asking, "What if Dr. Harding refuses?"

"He won't. Not if both Mrs. Bee and Paulette go to work on him. He prizes his harmony too highly to hold out against a united front."

On first meeting Dr. Harding, Libby had seen right away that he was caught in a tug-of-war between Mrs. Bee, self-taught nurse and overzealous sister, and his wife Paulette, who enjoyed the social status of being a doctor's wife, but had little interest in the healing profession itself. Libby started at Maddie's nudge.

"Someone you know?" Maddie asked.

"Where?"

"With the tapestry valise. See there? She's waving."

Libby scanned the sparsely peopled platform. Her heart fell. It was Abigail stepping down from the train! A drab cloak enveloped her dress but failed to hide her condition. Her hair was parted in the center and drawn into hiding beneath her hat. Her dark eyes stood out like needlework on the muslin face of a rag doll. Even her smile seemed limp and in danger of unraveling.

I'm not ready for this, Lord. Libby lifted a wordless plea even as she moved on wooden legs to meet her brother's wife.

13

S "Hello, Libby," said Abigail, her soft tone in keeping with her pinched countenance. "I hope I haven't come at a bad time."

"Of course not." Libby responded to an inner urging and embraced Adam's wife. Abigail hugged her back, but the moment was made awkward by the mound of unborn humanity between them.

Resisting the urge to retreat nine yards, Libby took Abigail's valise, and asked, "Why didn't you wire us?"

Looking puzzled, Abigail left her question unanswered, saying, "If you didn't know I was coming, how is it that you're here?"

"I came with someone. She's meeting her niece."

"And just when I was thinking Jacob was right, that you *are* a mind reader."

Libby smiled. "No, though it would be helpful where Jacob is concerned. We have yet to get a letter from him. What's keeping him so busy that he can't jot his family a line?"

"Wooing all the girls in Thistle Down. Adam told him to find himself a wife and settle down, that he didn't take him on to raise," said Abigail, growing more at ease.

Missing her two older brothers and their good-natured camaraderie, Libby said, "It didn't take Adam long to become an advocate of marriage. How is he anyway?"

"He's fine."

A faint tremor reshaped Abigail's dimpled chin. Libby saw the glint of unshed tears and knew with a sinking heart that Adam was not fine and that Abigail wasn't either. But she had been the only female in the family for so long, sensitive to male pride and practiced at respecting no trespassing zones, that she averted her gaze and asked no questions.

Following her lead, Abigail held back her tears and regained her composure as she spoke of the house, the garden, the friends and neighbors Libby had left behind in Thistle Down.

"It's been slow at the mines. Adam got only two days of work last week. Jacob, too." Abigail wound to a close.

Libby knew all too well how marginal an existence the mining life could be. The intermittent labor unrest frequently resulted in lost days and lost wages. She drew a shallow breath. "You look tired, Abigail."

"I haven't slept well the last couple of nights," she conceded.

"I'll put fresh sheets on the bed when we get home and you can rest awhile."

"I don't want to make work for you, Libby."

"It's no work. I planned to do some wash today anyway."

"I'll help you then," said Abigail.

The conversation limped to a halt as Maddie returned with her niece in tow. The girl was about David's size. She had hair like winter-bleached grasses, tar-colored eyes, a chin as sharp as a possum's, and was exquisitely adorned in frills and ribbons and lace that accentuated her plainness. The girl asked, "Where is Grandmother?"

"She's waiting for us at home," said Maddie.

"Is she sick?"

"No, she isn't sick."

"Then why isn't she here?"

"Because I'm here," said Maddie in a tone that discouraged further discussion.

Linking her free arm through Abigail's, Libby said, "Maddie, I'd like you to meet my brother Adam's wife, Mrs. Abigail Watson. Abigail, this is Maddie Daniels and her niece, Sophronia."

"Sophronia Kay," said the little girl. Her inquisitive gaze traveled from Abigail's protruding belly to her face and on to Libby. "If we decide to be friends, you can call me Phronkay. Phron*kay*," she repeated, pronouncing it as if it were one word, the emphasis on the second syllable.

"Welcome to Edgewood, Sophronia," said Libby.

Maddie commandeered a porter to load her niece's trunk onto the back of the dairy wagon. Maddie paid the man and climbed onto the wagon seat. She picked up the reins, and called to Libby, "Aren't you coming?"

"We'll walk. You don't have room on the seat."

"Nonsense. Sophronia can ride in back with the trunk. Climb up."

Libby gave Abigail a hand up and clambered up after her, while Sophronia stood by as if rooted to the ground. Impatient, Maddie clapped her hands, and said, "Hurry up, Sophronia. The horse is getting hot and so are we."

Sophronia's eyebrows rose like the hair on the back of a hissing cat, but she did as she was bidden. The wagon rolled ahead. They had gone only a block when Libby saw the little girl fling a book out of the wagon. Looking back the way they had come and seeing another half-dozen books scattered along the street, she caught a sharp breath.

Maddie looked over her shoulder and stopped the wagon. "Sophronia Kay, what *are* you doing?"

"I'm leaving a trail for Mother."

"Sophronia," Maddie said, "your parents are on a ship headed for Europe."

Sophronia jutted out her pointed chin. "Mother will change her mind. She'll come for me. I *told* her I'd die if she left me behind."

"She isn't coming." Maddie's voice gentled a fraction. "You're here until school starts, and that's that, Phronie."

Her eyes glittered like chunks of coal. "Phron*kay.*"

"Phronkay, then," Maddie amended. "Now jump down and fetch those books if you please."

Sophronia climbed out of the wagon as sullen as a thunderhead. Once to the ground, she tipped her head back and shot Maddie a bullet-eyed glance. "You're wrong, you know. If I don't like it here, I can always go to my *other* grandmother."

"We'll keep that in mind," replied Maddie. The moment the child was out of earshot, she said for Libby's benefit, "Her nanny wouldn't be coaxed off the train. Claimed she was traveling on to St. Louis to visit her aging parents. St. Louis, huh! I know a runaway nanny when I see one."

Her thoughts full of Abigail, Libby managed a feeble grin.

With the books gathered, they continued on their way. David was stretched out on his back on Mrs. Gruben's front porch, with a book in his hands. He and Mrs. Gruben both took notice and waved as they passed. A block ahead, Libby recognized Dr. Harding's buggy leaving town by Tile Factory Road. Ike was in the buggy with him.

Maddie deposited the boxes of books on Libby's porch while Libby showed Abigail to her small room, which they would now be sharing. She found fresh sheets for the bed and would have made it up for her, but Abigail insisted that she would not be waited upon.

Libby returned to the porch to fetch Abigail's luggage. She was surprised to find Maddie in the swing, wiping the dust off the books her niece's antics had soiled.

"I didn't know you were still here. Where's Sophronia?"

"She marched up the street to introduce herself to your brother. Without asking, I might add.'' Looping her hands around one knee, Maddie said, ''I've been giving it consideration, and it occurs to me that a children's reading hour would be a desirable function of a library.''

''Just one hour?'' asked Libby.

Maddie shot her an unrepentant grin, and conceded, ''Eight would be better, but I suppose Mother would grow suspicious as to what I had done with the little mouse.''

''Leave her to your mother then.''

''Oh, no. I can't do that.''

''Why not?''

''Mother will ruin her.''

Libby, harboring no affection for Mrs. Dorrance, nonetheless found Maddie's bluntness harsh. Tactfully, she said, ''I have a feeling Phron*kay* has come complete with her own set of original ideas.''

''Phron*kay.''* Maddie shook her head, and said, with a humorless grin, ''I did imply that was a desirable thing, didn't I? I have a feeling I'm about to be recompensed.''

''Does this mean you're volunteering to be storyteller for the children's reading hour?''

''Oh no, not me. I've put myself on the book-collecting committee, and when that job is done, I plan to transfer my attention to promoting the library as a gathering place for community groups.''

''In other words, your club of freethinkers?''

''For goodness sake! To hear you, you'd think there was something subversive about ladies getting together to discuss issues of common interest.''

''All I said was—''

''It was the way you said it. Oh, never mind. About the library—Mrs. Bee and Paulette can be on building and grounds. And you—''

''Publicity,'' said Libby. ''I'm going inside right now to finish my articles for Mr. Gruben. I'll dash off a piece regarding the soon-to-be library while I'm at it.''

''You're turning down the opportunity to read to Edgewood's children? To introduce young minds to your favorite pieces of literature?''

''To occupy Phron*kay?''* Libby inserted.

''If I say please?''

Libby smiled in spite of herself. ''You're persuasive, Maddie. Let me think about it.''

As Maddie went on to share other ideas for the library, Libby tried once again to come to grips with her mixed feelings about Maddie. It had been six years since Maddie thumbed her nose at public opinion and ran away with the medicine-show man; the incident at the lake with Ike had been a couple of years prior to that. But while Angus's loyal support of his sister's childhood friend was admirable, ladies were measured by a different standard. How much of a risk was she willing to take where Maddie was concerned? Or had she filled her ears with gossip, leaving no room for God's small whisper? *What about it, Lord? What would you have me do about Maddie?*

"Isn't that Mrs. Gentry's rig?" Maddie asked, interrupting Libby's reverie.

Libby looked up Fisher Street to the buggy passing the Grubens' house where she could see David and Sophronia playing with the kittens on the grass. "Chloe said Mrs. Gentry would be giving her a ride home."

"Chloe is with her. But home is in the other direction," said Maddie. "She must be coming here."

Here? Libby's heart sank. She threw a glance over her shoulder, thinking of parlor rugs to be shaken, laundry heaped in the kitchen, and Abigail.

Maddie came to her feet and tugged at the pointed corners of her short black jacket. "Ida would be a good one to ask for books. Catherine left a ton of them behind when she moved."

"Angus mentioned as much," said Libby, her consternation growing as Mrs. Gentry's buggy drew nearer. *Why today of all days?* Clutching at straws, she shot Maddie an impulsive glance. "Would you mind taking Abigail's luggage in and telling her we're having company? She's had a long trip. I don't want her to feel obligated to—"

"—entertain callers in her condition?" finished Maddie, laying open Libby's pretense with the ease of a hot knife slicing butter. "Libby, Libby. What am I going to do with you? There's nothing shameful about being with child."

Carefully, Libby murmured, "I didn't say there was."

"So what *are* you saying?"

"Nothing. Never mind."

"You realize, don't you, that it is ridiculous to expect a woman to hide simply because she's carrying a human life inside her? Why, you don't see the man confined, do you?"

Leaving Maddie on the porch spouting her rhetoric, Libby went with dragging feet and a nervous heart to greet Mrs. Gentry.

Angus's mother was dressed in yellow from the crown of her hat to the tip of her satin slippers. She returned Libby's greeting, chirping, "Good morning, Elizabeth. Forgive me for dropping by unannounced, but I wanted to talk with you while I was in town. I hope I haven't come at an inconvenient time."

"No, of course not," said Libby.

Chloe clambered out of the buggy ahead of Mrs. Gentry. She dragged a cast-iron weight out from under the seat, dropped it on the ground beneath the horse's head, and called to Maddie, "I thought you were picking up your niece."

The horse arched his neck and danced a few steps.

"Merciful patience, Chloe!" cried Mrs. Gentry, grabbing for the lines with glove-clad hands.

Chloe looked back over her shoulder. "You said secure the horse, didn't you?"

"Yes. But I didn't tell you to panic him in the process," exclaimed Mrs. Gentry, all aflutter. "Would you please not shout in the poor brute's ear?"

"Sorry," said Chloe, though judging by her expression, she shook off the rebuke much as Prince shook off the flies.

Mrs. Bee had implied that her sister was a bit of a prima donna, and on occasion Libby detected shades of that. But for the most part, Libby found Mrs. Gentry to be democratic. Tireless, too, on behalf of the New Hope Ladies Aid and their effort to raise monies for a church building. The ongoing project had benefited a great deal from both of the Gentrys.

Thinking that it might be something of that nature that had prompted the call, Libby invited Mrs. Gentry inside. She declined, saying she would be staying only a moment.

"At least come into the shade of the porch," urged Libby. She hastened to dust the sun-faded padding of the black wicker chair with her apron before inviting Angus's mother to sit down.

Resembling a little goldfinch as she perched on the edge, her head pertly cocked, Mrs. Gentry flashed Maddie a smile. "I enjoyed visiting with your mother yesterday. She's excited about her granddaughter coming for a visit."

"Yes," said Maddie, but she didn't elaborate. Nor did she excuse herself to go collect her charge, rather she settled into the porch swing beside Chloe.

"I'd be happy to make tea," offered Libby.

"No, dear, that won't be necessary," said Mrs. Gentry. "I hope you won't think it terribly bold of me, but I've come to ask a favor."

"Certainly," said Libby.

Visibly curious, Chloe leaned forward in the swing. Noticing, Mrs. Gentry said, "Chester will huff and puff if I bring Prince home sunburned. Would you mind if Chloe moved him into the shade of the yard?" At Libby's word of permission, she called after Chloe, "Lead him onto the grass beside Maddie's wagon."

Maddie, quick to take the hint, came to her feet as well. "I'll take Abigail's baggage inside and leave you two to talk in private."

"Very well, dear," said Mrs. Gentry, then belatedly, "Who is Abigail?"

"My brother's wife. She's visiting," Dropping into the swing Chloe and Maddie had vacated, Libby forestalled the necessity of further explanations by asking, "You mentioned a favor, Mrs. Gentry?"

"It has to do with Franklin and his victory yesterday."

"Franklin? You mean Frankie McClure?" Libby smiled. "He did a splendid job, didn't he?"

"Indeed. I was impressed with the young man's proficiency. However, having a youngster win the contest does present the complication of an appropriate chaperon. Particularly since Franklin has made something of a reputation for himself by being—how shall I say it—mischievous?"

Employing careful tact, Libby said, "Frankie worked very hard for the honor of going. I'm sure he'll be on his best behavior while at the fair."

"Of course he will. That's the only reason that I dare ask if you would be so kind as to accompany us to the fair in September and take charge of Franklin. We would pay your way, of course, and compensate you for your services."

Breath driven from her lungs, Libby squeaked, "You want me to go with you?"

Misunderstanding her reaction, Mrs. Gentry said quickly, "If you don't care to do it, say so and we'll speak of it no further."

"Oh no! It isn't that. I'm just . . . overcome."

"Then the idea isn't entirely disagreeable?"

"No, not at all. I would love to go to the fair," cried Libby, barely refraining from leaping out of the swing and throwing her arms around Mrs. Gentry at the great gift she was so apologetically bestowing.

"Chester will speak to your father, of course." Mrs. Gentry tipped her hand as to her true eagerness to be relieved of responsibility for Frankie. "As you know, there are a number of people from Edgewood going. You and Franklin would stay at Catherine's house with us."

The opportunity to see Catherine again only sweetened the prospect. But belatedly, Libby realized that, as part of the Berry Sisters, her obligations to Angus's campaign might conflict with the scheduled trip. When she said as much, Mrs. Gentry brushed her concern aside, saying she didn't think his speaking engagements started that early in September, but if she was mistaken and they did, the singers could surely do without her for an engagement or two.

Chloe, hurrying back to catch the general drift of the conversation, said, "My sister Martha can fill in. She would love to be a part of it."

"Why, yes, of course!" said Mrs. Gentry, beaming. "I forgot about your limitless supply of musically talented sisters, Chloe."

Her mission accomplished, Mrs. Gentry didn't linger any longer. Libby waved to her as she pulled away, Chloe bouncing on the seat beside her. They'd no more than gone when Maddie came out on the porch.

"I've upset your sister-in-law," she said without preamble.

The hair on the back of Libby's neck lifted. She caught her breath, half afraid to ask. "What happened?"

"I mentioned our plans for a library and suggested she might like to help. She pleaded confinement, at which point I espoused my impatience with the prudishness of conventional thinking." She grimaced, and confessed, "She's in the bedroom crying."

"Good faith!" muttered Libby.

"You'd better go talk to her." Maddie stepped off the porch, then turned back to say, "Tell her I'm sorry, Libby. But just between you and me, I still think hiding a woman away because she's pregnant is an insult to her womanhood."

Pulse throbbing at her temples, Libby dropped her head back and squinted skyward. *Lord, make her go away.*

The tranquility of cotton-batting clouds drifting soundlessly in the blue heavens seemed by contrast to punctuate her agitation. Reluctant and faintly resentful, she turned inside, letting the screen door slam behind her. Abigail was seated on the bed. Her shapeless Mother Hubbard dress hung like a sheet from her quivering shoulders. At the sight of Libby standing there, she covered her face with her hands.

Libby sat down beside her, inept, silent, miserable with conflicting emotions. "What is it, Abigail? Are you sick?"

Face still covered, Abigail shook her head. Brokenly, tearfully, she struggled to explain. "Adam didn't want me to leave, but I th-thought it would be easier here. But it won't, will it? Th-the wondering glances, the whispers—they've followed me here."

Wondering glances? No one here in Edgewood knew Abigail and Adam had gotten the cart before the horse. Trying to soothe her, Libby said, "I wouldn't worry about Maddie. She's an independent thinker anyway."

"You haven't told her?"

"Told her what? That you were coming?"

Abigail's hands slid down her face, her fingertips touching. Fresh tears pooled in her eyes as she spoke through templed hands. "Th-that I'm eight months pregnant and only two wed."

"Of course not," said Libby, startled that Abigail could think she might have done so.

"And the others?"

"What others?"

"I heard voices."

"I haven't told anyone, Abigail. Nor will I," said Libby.

"But they'll find out. Folks always do somehow."

Libby offered no empty reassurances, for as much as she hated to face it, it was quite likely someone would stir up some tittle-tattle. Yet even as she sympathized with Abigail's feelings, she had a nagging sense that her distress was of a deeper vein than dread of being whispered about by people she didn't know and, in all likelihood, never would. Had she and Adam quarreled? She said he hadn't wanted her to come. He most likely didn't want to burden them.

There was a moment of clear choice. Did she accept Abigail as a burden to be borne? Or did she open her home, her arms, and her heart? Father's admonition rang in her ear: *If you have no feelin' for it, do it in faith and soon the feelin' will follow.*

Libby slipped her arm around her. "I don't think we should worry what anyone thinks. I've always wanted a sister, and now I have one, and if old Adam is cross, he'll get over it. He always does." Seeing Abigail's eyes fill again, she patted her hands, then slipped to the floor at her feet. "Here, let me help you off with your shoes. I'll bring you a basin of water, too, so you can freshen up. You'll feel better once you've rested."

14

Ike showed Dr. Harding into the cabin. He was relieved to find Robinson still breathing.

Dr. Harding's knees popped as he dropped down on the hard floor beside the fellow. "You didn't tell me he was such a big man."

"Didn't know it was important."

"It isn't." Opening his black bag, the doctor grimaced, and added, "This isn't much of a place for healing, Ike."

"Sorry, Doc. Maybe I should have hitched up the wagon and brought him to town. But, big as he is, I don't know how I'd have got him loaded by myself. Or how he'd of weathered the road in."

"By the look of him, it's a chance we're going to have to take." Dr. Harding put his hand to the side of the fellow's throat. "Why don't you wait outside while I have a look?"

Relieved, Ike let himself out. He got a cup of water at the pump and sat down on the brick well surround. A cardinal sang from a nearby bush. Admiring its bright plumage, he thought of Libby's hair coiling down the back of her inside-out dress as she sang and moved her slim arms and quick hands like comic poetry, bringing the critters to life. He hadn't seen anyone have that much fun with that little song since he'd crowded aboard the *Yucatan*, the ship that Roosevelt, through quick thinking and hot air, had commandeered for the First Volunteer Cavalry to transport them over to Cuba.

The First, many of them bowlegged cowboys, all wearing blue polka-dot bandannas and packing six-shooters, bullied the band of the Second Regulars, who had by good fortune made it aboard, into playing that tune over and over again. "De monk, de monk, de monk." They'd take up the chant and beat on their mess tins and make the deck ring with pounding boots. For six days, they steamed in the backwater stench of Port Tampa, hooting and hollering that song and waiting for orders to lift anchor and go.

His thoughts drifting ahead, Ike took a knife out of his pocket and whittled away at a finger-sized piece of elderberry. Come spring and his first official sirup season, elderberry spiles would serve to channel the flow of sap from the drilled hole in the tree to the bucket. They worked as well as any factory-made ones, though he'd hate to count up the hours he'd spent whittling them. Someday when the camp was turning a profit, he'd order manufactured spiles. He had finished one and was starting another by the time Doc came out the back door, rolling down his sleeves.

"This fellow didn't give you any personal information?"

"Nope. Just that his name is Robinson and he was with the circus until they let him go."

"He's got a little cash on him but no identification. I couldn't rouse him enough to get any answers."

"What do you want to know?"

"There's something familiar about him. I can't quite put my finger on it. Makes me wonder if he has family nearby. Someone to look after him. He's going to need care. If he pulls through, that is."

"That bad, is he?" At Doc's nod, Ike asked, "What's wrong with him?"

"By the looks of it, I'm saying he's got a severe case of influenza." Doc tunneled a hand through his thinning hair and came to a decision. "Guess the best thing to do is get him into my office. Sarah Jane can help me keep an eye on him. Better hitch up your wagon and find someone to help us lift him into it."

Ike sighed and gave up on the idea of getting any work done today. "I'll see if I can find Decatur."

Libby, with David in tow, trekked to Willie Blue's to tell her father of Abigail's arrival. The store was empty except for Father and Naomi. Tall and angular with her long auburn hair braided and coiled at the nape of her neck, Naomi called a warm welcome and untied her shopkeeper's apron.

" 'Lo, Libby. I was hopin' ya'd stop by. Reckon I could have a word with ya when ya git time?"

"Sure," said Libby, smiling. "Can I get some some butter while I'm here?"

"Help yerself." To David, Naomi said, "If yer lookin' fer Opal and Frankie, they's makin' a flyin' ginny out of an old tree stump back of the buggy shed. Better hurry, though. I'll be callin' 'em to eat in a few minutes."

David dashed out the back door while Naomi locked the front door for lunch, then climbed the stairs to the quarters she shared with her children.

Libby stood by as Father closed his postal cash drawer into the safe, locked the handle down, and gave the dial a twist.

"If ye had told me ye needed butter, I would hae saved ye the trip. What would ye be havin' for lunch?'' asked Father.

"Beans and tomatoes and cucumbers from Mrs. Gruben's garden. And butter sandwiches. Get the butter for me, will you, Father, while I sign the charge slip? Better bring some milk, too. We've got company,'' added Libby.

"Abigail,'' said Father.

"You knew?''

"Aye. Mr. Noonan brought a wire from yer brither sayin' to be expectin' the lass.'' Father fetched the milk and the butter from the icebox in the back pantry. "I was intendin' to be at the station and welcome her off the train, but ye know yerself how the laddies tramp in of a mornin' and wheedle away at me time. Between their partiality for gossipin' and a bit of lively business, if the hands on the clock dinna slip ahead o' me. By the time I reached the station, ye had already fetched the lass. How is she, Lib?''

"Pale and heavy with child and fragile-looking.''

"I winna say I'm surprised.''

"I gather Adam wasn't too happy with Abigail's decision to come here,'' said Libby. "She no more than made it home when she broke down and cried.''

"Ye wouldn't be withholding yer warm fellowship from the lass, would ye, Lib?'' asked Father with a searching glance.

"Father! I was the model of hospitality, truly I was.'' Realizing any ill feeling she had previously been nursing had melted away in the face of Abigail's shame and vulnerability, Libby added, "Abigail cried because she's worried that people in Edgewood might learn the truth and whisper about her. At least that's what she said. But I couldn't help wondering if something else is bothering her.''

" 'Twould seem to be an endless source of possibilities there.'' Father's troubled gaze gentled as he amended, "Forgive me, lass, for ever thinkin' ye might stoop to holdin' a grudge. Ye've an uncommonly handsome heart.''

" 'Tis not to me own credit, but to me faether's.''

He waived the compliment, mouth twitching at her parody of his colorful brogue. "Och, lass! 'Tis yer own dear mother ye favor, I'm thinkin'. Ye're growin' to be the verra vision o' her.''

Pleased at the comparison, Libby pecked him on the cheek and started away. "I'd better see what Naomi wants. Why don't you take the butter and milk and go on home? I'll be along with Davie just as soon as I can.''

She had taken only a few steps when Father called her back, saying, "Lib?'' He paused, his brow deeply pleated.

It was unlike him to look so ruffled. "What is it, Father?''

"'Twas a letter from Jacob this mornin' lendin' some insight as to why the lass has come. I winna willingly heap upon yer heart more hard news," he added with marked reluctance. "But if ye are to be on the mendin' side and a true help to yer brither and his bride, I'm thinkin' ye need to know the whole story." He hesitated a moment.

"Go on," urged Libby guardedly.

"Ye'll remember 'twas not so long ago Abigail and Adam were at odds wi' one another?"

She nodded. Adam and Abigail had a history of breakups in their courtship. To the best of Libby's knowledge, their quarrels were about Abigail wanting to marry and Adam wanting to wait. The livelihood of a miner was a precarious one, and the financial burden of providing for a wife wasn't to be taken lightly. Complicating the problem was Adam's concern over Father's fragile health. He knew if anything should happen to Father, it would fall to him to finish raising David.

"It seems some of the bickerin' was over another fellow havin' turned Abigail's head. A guileful common sort of a rascal, accordin' to yer brither Jacob," said Father. "The fellow daffed aboot, charmin' Abigail's virtue away, and when the damage was done and she was with child, he contrived to shy away from his responsibility."

Libby's jaw dropped at the weight of his words. Blood rushed to her face. Inanely she cried, "Surely it can't be!"

"'Tis a temptation sech is common to man," said Father. "Dinna I tell ye to be verra cautious when the lads come sweetheartin'?"

Her disbelief was not with the unnamed lecher, but with Abigail. Adam had had no other sweetheart, just Abigail. Libby struggled with a riot of emotions. "But if what Jacob writes is true, and Adam knew she had been unfaithful—*did* he know, Father? Did Adam know when he married her that the baby wasn't his?"

"Yes, lass. Accordin' to Jacob, he knew."

The budding compassion Libby had felt for Abigail at the house quickly withered. "When did Adam tell Jacob all of this? Before the wedding or after?"

"'Twas not from Adam that Jacob learned of it," said Father.

"Who then?"

"The verra one who seduced her. Amidst a crowd of lads, the fellow fell to boastin' shamelessly of his popularity with the lasses and of the liberties he had taken." Sagely, Father added, "I canna help thinkin' he repented of his foolishness when Jacob overheard his gallopin' tongue."

"Jacob gave him a thrashing, did he?" said Libby, for Jacob could make his feelings known when his temper gained the better of him. Fiercely, she said, "Good for him!"

"Whist, lass. Jacob's sound cuffin' only fanned the flames and set the tongues to clackin' afresh. 'Tis the reason Abigail came against Adam's wishes to seek sanctuary among us."

Abigail had betrayed her brother! Why had he married her? *Why,* at the expense of his own good name? "What did Adam say when Jacob confronted him?" At Father's silence, Libby persisted. "What did he say, Father? Did he offer some reason as to why he married her?"

"He dinna say, Lib."

Libby's anger spilled over. "How can she expect him to live with this? He shouldn't have married her. What was he thinking?"

"The lad took his time in weddin' the lass," reminded Father. "I winna be a stumblin' block to him with pesterin' sympathies."

"Pesterin' sympathies?" Bewildered by his outlook, Libby retorted, "What are we supposed to do? Pretend we don't know the child isn't his?"

"Secret keepin' is unnatural-like in a lovin' home, and for all that I have set my heart upon helpin' the lass and Adam, I canna force her into explainin', and I winna ha'e ye doin' so either. No, lass. We must wait for Adam to confide in us himself. Or Abigail. I would have ye to pray while we're waitin', pray for word of mendin'."

"But this changes everything! I'm not even sure I can be civil!"

"If ye love yer brither, ye must contrive to love Abigail, too," Father said firmly.

Love her? Knowing only the facts of baby making and none of the strong emotional drive leading to it, Libby couldn't conceive of Abigail wittingly or unwittingly getting herself into such a fix. *Love her?* To come to them and expect to be treated like . . . Libby's thoughts faltered. The image of Abigail's pinched face hovered in her mind's eye. What Abigail *expected,* what she feared, was the resentment, the indignation, the hard feelings that were swiftly mounting. Libby saw with stark clarity the cause of Abigail's breakdown in the bedroom. Guilt. Guilt at betraying Adam. Guilt at coming to his family for sanctuary. And fear that they would learn of her unfaithfulness.

Love her? How?

Perceiving Libby's hardening heart, Father said gently, "Ye winna wound the verra One who breathed the breath of life into the lass, surely. I canna help thinkin' He is mortal sensitized to her tears."

Libby winced at his words. "I can't help it, Father. It makes my blood boil!"

Steadily, Father said, "If ye stay in close company with God, ye will see how He pines for his lambs, and ye winna be so overly keen to judge."

He left by the back door, the milk and butter in hand. Though his admo-

nition clashed with her resentment toward Abigail, Libby felt her heart twist
as she watched him go, for he looked his years and then some.

She felt as if she had aged, too. Jarred from innocence. She couldn't conceive of Abigail being so careless with her body! The idea of letting a man
touch her that way. Who was the man? The whole degrading affair had to
have happened while she was still living in Thistle Down. But Libby hadn't
heard even a whisper of gossip linking Abigail's name to anyone except
Adam.

She circled to the back of the buggy shed and watched in silence as Frankie
pushed David and Opal around and around on the flying ginny. It was a
homemade device made of a tree stump and a board. Frankie had drilled a
hole through the knee-high stump and attached the board with a long bolt.
David and Opal straddled the board on opposite ends. The children squealed
in delight as Frankie pushed them ever faster. Libby's thoughts circled like
the pivoting board, but her mental squeals were cries of anguish. Adam,
Adam. Always striving to be responsible. To be dependable. To be just. He
didn't deserve this. Love, true love was painful only if unrequited. Wasn't
that the rule? *How, God? How could Abigail have done this?*

Libby didn't know how long she had stood watching the children when
Naomi came out to call the children in for lunch. "Yer welcome to stay too,
Davie," she added.

"Can I, Lib?"

"You don't mind, Naomi?"

" 'Course not. Davie's always welcome here."

The children washed their sweaty hands and faces at the pump and clamored across the back lot and into the back door of *Willie Blue's.*

"I heard from Miz Gentry that yer goin' to look after Frankie on the St.
Louis trip. I want to thank you and to ask ya somethin'. But it's hard, on
account you've already done so much," said Naomi, averting her green gaze.

Distracted from a dilemma she felt ill equipped to face, Libby cried,
"Thank me? I should be thanking Frankie! I'm thrilled to get to go!" Noting
Naomi's hesitant expression, she added, "We're friends, Naomi. Whatever
you want to ask, you ask."

"I been so busy with the store and all, I ain't had nary enough time to be
with the young'uns. I don't want them fallin' into mischief. Now that ya
ain't carryin' the mail, would ya be willin' to oversee 'em some?"

"They can play at the house anytime. They're always welcome."

Naomi entreated, "I ain't talkin' about sendin' 'em ta play. I'm talkin'
about ya lookin' after 'em while I'm workin'. I got no idea what I ought to
pay ya, so ya can jest as well name yer price."

"I can't take money from you."

Naomi started to protest, saw Libby meant it, and after further thought said, "How about groceries? You could take yer pay in staples, couldn't ya?"

Her head still reeling with the pain of Adam and Abigail, Libby could scarcely think. Lamely, she said, "I don't want it to be a hardship."

"You ain't." Naomi regarded her for a long moment, as if she had more on her mind. At length, she ventured, "Lib? Would ya hold it agin' me if I was to poke my nose whar it don't belong?"

Libby lifted her face in an unspoken question.

Naomi stopped beside the pump and rested her hand on the black handle. "The ceiling over the store is thin, and if that ain't enough, voices come drifting right up the iron grate. Couldn't help but overhear what yer pa said about the little gal who come to stay with you a spell."

"Abigail?" Libby's heart thumped at Naomi's solemn nod. Unbidden tears sprang to her eyes.

Naomi slipped an understanding arm around Libby's shoulder. "Ya want to talk about it?"

Her vision blurred, Libby dragged a hand across her eyes and gave vent to her raw emotions. "I'm not sure I'm allowed to. It's supposed to be a secret, you know. We wouldn't want to upset Abigail by letting on we're wise to her shenanigans."

"Aw, Lib. Don't take on like that. It's goin' to be hard enough for the gal as it is. Look at me and Decatur. I'm tellin' ya, it ain't no easy row to hoe, startin' yer life together under sech a cloud as this."

Belatedly recognizing the parallel between Abigail's situation and Naomi's, Libby averted her hot face. From the very beginning, her sympathies in Naomi's relationship with her estranged husband had been solidly behind Naomi. It was disturbing to catch a glimpse of the situation from Decatur's point of view. "It isn't the same," she blurted. "Decatur wasn't courting you when—"

"When I got pregnant? No, but that don't matter. A man likes to think he's the only one ever touched ya, and when he's faced with raising a child that ain't his, he's reminded each day that there was someone besides him. It'll eat away at him if he lets it."

Naomi swept a tendril of hair behind her ear with a work-roughened hand. "I'm thinkin' yer brother ain't goin' ta carry on the way Decatur did. I reckon he'll make the best of it. You Watsons are good at that."

"Father is. But me?" Libby shook her head, a bitter taste in her mouth. "I'm not so sure I even want to be."

"Ya tellin' me ya cain't do for kin what ya did for me?"

Libby ducked her head and made no response.

"He ain't jest yer brother, he's her husband now. Ya got ta treat her the way ya'd want ta be treated yerself iffen it was you in such a fix. Ain't that what the Good Book says?'' Naomi inserted a sigh into Libby's silence. "Why don't ya come on upstairs and eat with us? Do ya good.''

Libby declined, the thought of food holding no appeal.

"All right then if yer sure. But if you or that little gal, either one, needs someone to talk to, I'm here.''

Naomi started across the grass and had almost reached the door when Libby called after her, "Naomi? About the kids. We can start our arrangement this afternoon if you like.'' She swallowed salty tears, and added, "The way I'm feeling right now, I'd welcome having someone at the house besides just Abigail and me.''

"Ya want ta come by for them when ya feel up to it?''

Libby agreed and instructed her to send David home if he got underfoot before she returned.

Naomi hesitated a second longer, then asked, "Ya goin' to be all right, Lib?''

"I guess. It's just that I wish . . . Oh, never mind. It's a little late for wishing.''

Naomi shrugged as if to say she knew all about belated wishes.

Libby's eyes filled again. Loath to go home and face Abigail, she headed toward the north edge of town and followed the road into the country. It lay like a dusty ribbon between fields. The corn was tall and green and fragrant with tassels stretching toward the cloudless blue sky.

She stopped to watch a robin try to pull free a strand of hair from a horse's tail that was snagged in a fence post. The bird lifted into the air, the hair in his beak, but he couldn't tug the hair free of the splinters in the knotty post.

The robin's quandary seemed to parallel her own. Held earthbound by tangled emotions, by hard, fast loyalties and wounded trust. For she *had* trusted Abigail, not so much a conscious trust as an assumption that she meant Adam good, not harm. That she might shame or betray him had never even occurred to Libby. And yet Abigail had. It was difficult to fathom Adam's forgiveness.

Libby looked back to see the robin rising in the air. The horse's hair was still caught fast in the post. The bird had released what was holding him back. But could she? Such forgiveness seemed beyond her.

If ye have no feelin' for it, do it in faith and the feeling will follow, Father's words came echoing back. She had no feeling for it, and barely enough faith to lift her eyes to heaven, where the bird was now just a faint smudge in the sky.

15

David and Opal were digging in the railroad ditch at the edge of the backyard. The warm summer breeze carried their murmurings to Libby as she spread a quilt beneath the apple tree. She brushed a granddaddy longlegs off the faded patchwork quilt, stretched out on her stomach, with knees bent, and ankles locked, and opened her Memorandum book. Buried in the disorganized jumble of journal entries, story ideas, favorite Bible verses, noteworthy quotes, and idle thoughts was an article concerning the library. Pencil in hand, Libby withdrew into a world of words and phrases and did not lift her head until she had finished the article.

Aware once again of the heat, a hard green apple gouging her thigh from beneath the quilt, and Abigail stirring on the other side of the screened window, Libby rolled to her feet and called, "I thought you were taking a nap."

"I decided to write Adam instead," Abigail replied from inside the house.

"Don't you want to come out in the sunshine?"

"Thanks, Libby, but I like a table under me when I write," Abigail answered. "Anyway, your pencil flying so fast over the pages distracts me, and I can't think of a thing to tell Adam except that his sister sure can find a lot of news when Mr. Gruben pays by the word."

"I'm saving up to buy my little niece or nephew a toy or two."

Libby didn't notice Abigail moving away from the window, but when she looked again, Abigail was gone. Maybe she shouldn't have mentioned the baby, but it seemed pointless to skirt the little life that would soon be part of their family.

The baby. Libby sighed. The past week hadn't been an easy one. At times she felt like the world's greatest pretender in her dealings with Abigail. Father's phrase about overcoming feelings with faith had become her morning prayer. God had supplied the strength each day to plod along accordingly, though that was not to say ill feelings didn't well up inside her from time to time.

If Abigail was aware that she and Father knew the truth of the matter, she didn't let on. Father had written Adam but had had no personal word from him. Adam had written Abigail only once since her arrival last week.

Yet in spite of, or maybe *because* of, his devotion to his eldest son, Father was solicitous of Abigail, drawing her out in conversation, gentle of her feelings, and trying in every way to make her feel at home.

Abigail, in turn, was polite and considerate. She shared the cooking, laundry, and other chores. She respected Libby's need for privacy when she was writing. And she was patient with David as well as the McClure children, whom Libby now spent several hours a day overseeing.

So thinking, Libby looked across sunburned wisps of August grass to the steep railroad ditch where Frankie stood looking on while Opal, dressed in Frankie's hand-me-down overalls, held one end of a narrow board and David, the other.

"Pretend them weeds is the Nile River and that it's plumb full of gators and the board is my tightrope," said Opal.

"Say if you fall, the alligators eat you up." David waded through the weedy ditch to anchor his end of the board into the steep incline, making a bridge.

Opal lifted her hands over her head and struck a classic circus pose. " 'Nounce me, Davie."

David put a rolled newspaper to his lips. "In ring one, Miss Opal McClure will try to cross this thin rope over the Nile River."

"David Watson, you say it like you're counting rocks," exclaimed Sophronia, coming around the side of the house. She sprinted past Libby, all ribbons and lace right down to the bows on her dainty white shoes. "Say it like this: The daring, dauntless damsel, Miss Opal McClure! Death-defying attempt! Gossamer strand spanning the swampy alligator-infested danger-ridden Nile River!"

Opal whooped with delight. "I was afraid your granny wasn't going to let you come play, Phronky."

"Phron*kay*," corrected Sophronia, just as she had since the day she and Opal had first met. But whether in haste or stubbornness, or from a simple inability to get it right, Opal persisted in pronouncing her new friend's nickname so much like her brother's name that it was sometimes hard to tell whom she meant.

Maddie came around the side of the house, fanning her face in the noon heat. Libby smiled a welcome, for the situation with Abigail had clarified her thinking where Maddie was concerned. The bottom line for Libby seemed to be that God hadn't asked for her help in judging people. If He ever did, there were plenty of folks in Edgewood already in training for the job. Hascal Caton, intolerant of women in general, was chief among them.

"Sophronia was a model citizen all morning in hopes of being allowed to come play with David and Opal while we go to lunch at Baker's," said Maddie without preamble. "I'm going to treat all my library volunteers, and I won't take no for an answer."

Libby tucked her pencil between pages and closed her notebook. "What about the children?"

"I already talked to Abigail. She's going to watch them. I told her I'd bring lunch back to them. Hurry up and get your hat. Mrs. Bee and Paulette are going to meet us there. We'll stop by the store on our way and get Naomi, too. She closes up for lunch about this time every day, doesn't she?"

"Yes, but only to fix something for the children. She's invited David to eat lunch with them."

"Whatever she's planned for lunch will surely keep until suppertime. It'll do her good to go with us," said Maddie.

Libby couldn't argue with that. The breakup of Naomi's marriage hadn't been easy. Yet Naomi plodded along, filling her days with the store, her children, and lately with what had become known as "Maddie's library project." Reasoning that lunch out was a treat Naomi shouldn't miss, Libby said, "Just give me a minute to check with Abigail and grab my hat."

Abigail, who had become accustomed to Maddie's visits and outspoken ways, assured Libby it was no imposition and sent her on her way. Libby climbed into the buggy and waved to the children, who had raced around front to see them off.

"I'm counting on you to talk Naomi into joining us. You four are the nucleus of my group," said Maddie.

"Not your freethinking club again?"

"Society," corrected Maddie, unperturbed by the gentle gibe.

"I thought we were cataloging books and skipping paintbrushes over the shelves. I should have known better."

"Inviting ladies to meet and discuss issues relevant to their lives has met with little success. I'm trying a more circumspect approach."

Libby chuckled at Maddie's fortitude. She braced her feet as the horse clattered across the railroad tracks.

"I'm not saying everyone has to agree with my rhetoric, as you so disdainfully call it, just that there should be some discussion. Is that so terrifying?"

"No, Maddie. It isn't terrifying at all," Libby admitted. "Disdainful, by the way, is too strong a word."

"I'm glad to hear it, because I was hoping that when the library is finished, we could continue to get together for my 'rhetoric.' " At Libby's silence, Maddie arched a satin brow and challenged, "Unless you're afraid?"

Reminded of the times her brother Jacob had coaxed her into mischief with that very taunt, Libby grinned. "You're wasting your time on me, Maddie. Father weaned me of tantrums years ago."

"Tantrums?" cried Maddie. "Since when does demanding fair treatment equate with tantrums? Tantrums, indeed."

The buggy rolled to a stop in front of Willie Blue's. Leaving Maddie to her sputtering, Libby climbed down and went inside to fetch Naomi for their library luncheon.

Naomi seemed pleased by the invitation. She had flung herself wholeheartedly into helping turn Doc's waiting room into a library, her enthusiasm indicative of the high value she placed on education. Like Libby, Naomi's own school years had been cut short by the death of her mother. Dreams had died that day, too, dreams of someday writing poetry. Naomi took the surrender of them the same stoic way she endured all of life's disappointments. But she held hopes of better things for her children.

By the time they arrived at Baker's, Paulette Harding and Mrs. Bee were already there. Dorene Berry took their order. Mrs. Bee filled them in on John Robinson while they waited for their food to be served. The man's condition, she confided, had deteriorated since Dr. Harding had brought him in from the grove a week ago.

"It's too bad he hasn't been lucid enough to tell Doc if he has any family," said Libby.

"It's a shame really. I can't help thinking a familiar face at his bedside might motivate him to fight a little harder," said Paulette, the corners of her mouth drawing down.

Maddie hadn't met the man. Nor had Libby or Naomi, though they'd heard enough about his illness from Mrs. Bee to share her concern for his well-being.

The conversation turned to plans for the opening day of the library, just one week away. Naomi asked Libby, "Did ya git yer article for the paper turned in yet?"

"I've got it right here." Libby patted her Memorandum notebook on the table beside her. She took the tablet with her these days in order to be prepared should a news or social item come to her attention. She flipped the tablet to the proper page and passed it to Mrs. Bee, who promptly read the article aloud:

"BOOK A VACATION

Books, it has been said, can take you anywhere you want to go. Now you can explore the world without leaving Edgewood thanks to the generosity of Dr. Melville Harding, who has offered the lobby of his office as a village library. Thank you also to Edgewood Lumber for donating the boards for shelving, which C. Taylor and Sons, in a show of public spirit, have installed at no charge. Boxes of used books have been donated, and more are promised. The office of librarian will, for the time being, be filled by volunteers. The children of Edgewood are cordially invited to attend Children's Hour, to be held at two o'clock every weekday afternoon, beginning immediately and lasting until school begins in the autumn. If you would like to borrow a book or you have books you would be willing to donate, please drop by Dr. Harding's office and visit Edgewood's new library.''

Dorene Berry had stopped to refill their water glasses and caught most of the reading. She said, ''You sure do have a way with words, Libby.''

''She has a way with a paintbrush, too,'' said Mrs. Bee.

''Ya ain't no slouch with one yerself, Miz Bee,'' pointed out Naomi. ''And you, Miss Paulette. If ya ain't a whiz at that thar catalogin'. Miss Maddie's got the touch fer organizin'. Why, I kin scarce believe all we've got done.''

Mrs. Baker, who had paused to greet Lester Morefield's wife and daughters at the next table, called over, ''The town owes all of you ladies a debt of gratitude.'' To Mrs. Morefield, she added, ''I guess you know we're soon to have a library?''

''So I heard. Lester's been prodding me to donate some books,'' said Mrs. Morefield.

Encouraged by Fanny Morefield's polite response, Maddie suggested they all have lunch together. Oblivious to Mrs. Morefield's faint hesitation, she pushed their table over against the Morefields' and exchanged pleasantries with Mrs. Morefield's daughters, Maralee and Lyneer, who were near in age to Libby.

Mrs. Morefield's husband, Lester, owned the tile and brick factory north of town, which supplied the tiles for draining the rich, heavy soil of the central Illinois fields. He had built a home for his family made of bricks from his own factory. Encircled by a wrought-iron fence, it was spacious and handsome, an architectural rival to any modern house in Edgewood.

In the course of the conversation, Maddie offered to stop by Fanny Morefield's house and pick up the books she'd mentioned. Mrs. Morefield, who had been watching the door from the moment Maddie pushed their tables together, declined with a hasty excuse, saying she hadn't yet decided which books to give and which to keep.

Maddie dropped the subject and went on to mention her society of free-thinkers. She issued a general invitation. ''Would a week from tomorrow evening agree with everyone? What about you, Maralee? Lyneer? Are you free on Tuesdays?''

The Morefield girls deferred to their mother in a telling glance. Libby stirred uncomfortably as Mrs. Morefield murmured, ''Tuesday, Tuesday,'' and worried her bottom lip, as if trying to conjure a mental image of her social calendar.

Paulette, wise to Mrs. Morefield's unspoken concern, asked shrewdly, ''Will your mother be coming, Maddie?''

''I'm not sure,'' Maddie replied. ''What with the dairy to run and Sophronia here visiting and the time she devotes to the Women's Temperance Union, we haven't had much of an opportunity to discuss it.''

''Your mother *does* keep a busy schedule. I admire her stamina,'' Mrs. Morefield offered heartily. She patted her moist brow, darted a glance toward the door, and cried, ''My goodness! I believe that's her now.''

''Why, yes it is. How fortuitous,'' said Paulette, her tone so pleasant Libby wasn't certain whether she was sincere or subtly mocking the transparent Mrs. Morefield. Paulette came out of her chair and beckoned to Mrs. Dorrance. ''Madeline? Over here!''

Madeline Dorrance crossed the room, slim and straight and elegant of carriage. She returned the round of greetings but declined to join them, explaining she was seeking Sophronia. Maddie explained that they had left Abigail in charge of her and the other children and that she herself was planning to take lunch home to them.

''That won't be necessary where Sophronia is concerned. She can eat a late lunch with me in Bloomington.'' At Maddie's blank look, her mother prompted, ''The shopping trip I mentioned this morning?''

''I'm sorry, Mother. I'd forgot.''

''I assumed as much when you didn't come home.''

''Mrs. Morefield? Wasn't there something you wanted to ask Madeline?'' prompted Paulette.

''Ask? No, I don't believe so.'' Mrs. Morefield recouped her momentarily ruffled composure, and added with an ingratiating smile, ''Maddie was just telling us of her plans to organize a new women's society. That on the heels of the library. I say, Madeline! Aren't you proud of your daughter's interest in community affairs?''

''Women's society? Oh! That suffrage business,'' said Mrs. Dorrance, her tone dismissive.

''You said yourself that if women had the vote, Prohibition would become the law in short order,'' Maddie reminded her mother.

''I did,'' acknowledged Mrs. Dorrance. ''But I don't feel the cause is lost without the vote. Men of noble conscience and intellect can be trusted to take the right measures, men such as Angus Cearlock. I'm confident he'll be a voice for national sobriety.''

"I couldn't agree more! Angus has a promising future indeed,'' said Mrs. Morefield. Carefully avoiding eye contact with Paulette, she added, "So tell me, Madeline, will you be coming to Maddie's meeting next Tuesday?''

"I'm afraid not. With so many commitments demanding my attention, I simply can't justify the time,'' said Mrs. Dorrance. "If you'll excuse me, ladies, I need to collect Sophronia before we miss our train.''

Mrs. Morefield and her daughters rose to go as well. Maddie scraped her chair back from the table. "If you find you're free on Tuesday evening, the invitation is open, Mrs. Morefield.''

"Thank you, Maddie, but I wouldn't count on our making it. "Maralee was just this minute reminding me that she and Lyneer have dress fittings on Tuesday. If you'll excuse us.'' She beckoned to her daughters. "Come along, girls.''

Watching her go, Paulette said with little intonation, "I can't bear that woman. She's been walking around with her nose in the air ever since she was chosen chairman of the Thespian Club.''

"You were running for that seat, weren't you, Paulette?'' Mrs. Bee inserted mildly.

"Yes, I was, and I don't mind saying I was better qualified, too.''

"On your behalf, I do have to say you know the difference between acting and reality, which is more than poor Fanny Morefield understands,'' said Mrs. Bee. "I'm afraid she's so frightened of a bad performance, she doesn't know how to be herself.''

"Indeed,'' agreed Paulette. "I shouldn't be surprised to see her eating her peas with her hatpin, if she spied Madeline Dorrance doing it first.''

"Oh, forget it!'' said Maddie. "If she can't commit herself without being assured the social hierarchy will be in attendance, then what could she possibly have to contribute to a group of freethinkers?''

Suspecting it was Madeline Dorrance, not Mrs. Morefield, who had put the flint in Maddie's voice, Libby glanced at Naomi, who had been silent throughout the exchange. Admirably so, for Paulette and Mrs. Bee, though well intentioned, were only underscoring Mrs. Morefield's painfully obvious discomfort with Maddie.

"Would you like me to make some lemonade for Tuesday evening?'' Libby asked quietly.

"I thought you weren't interested,'' said Maddie in the same flinty voice. "I thought you were weary of my views.''

Knowing it was unwanted sympathy Maddie was guarding against, Libby countered, "So you're excluding me now?''

"I'm not excluding you. I just don't want you there unless your heart is in it."

"My *whole* heart?"

"I'm serious, Libby. Do you want to come or don't you?"

"Tiresomely serious," said Libby. "Do you want the lemonade or don't you?"

A grudging smile flickered a corner of Maddie's mouth. "All right, all right. I'll accept the lemonade, and you can kindly stop mimicking me."

Libby grinned over the rim of her coffee cup, relieved to see Maddie's intemperate mood lifting.

"I got some good peaches in from Michigan. Should be jest right for a cobbler by Tuesday," Naomi offered.

"I'll unlock for you, Maddie," Mrs. Bee chimed in. "I'll be at the doctor's anyway, sitting up with Mr. Robinson. If he's still with us, that is."

"What can I bring?" asked Paulette.

"Yourself," said Maddie. Her glance all-inclusive, she said, "I'll see you all at seven on Tuesday, and I promise to make it enlightening."

"You're very good at that," noted Libby.

"At what?"

"Making lightning."

Smiling, Maddie shook her head and excused herself. With shoulders squared, she strolled into the kitchen to see about food for Abigail and the children. Paulette and Mrs. Bee went on their way, leaving only Libby and Naomi at the table.

"I reckon goin' to her meetin' ain't goin' to hurt us none," Naomi said. "Might help cushion the disappointment of failin' to git what she's chasin' after."

Misunderstanding, Libby said, "You don't think the vote is a lost cause surely?"

"I was talkin' about her mama's respect."

"Oh. Well, *that* may be even harder." Libby brushed bread crumbs from the tablecloth and angled a backward glance before admitting, "I don't understand Mrs. Dorrance, do you? Maddie's cause is a legitimate one. I mean, who doesn't want to vote? Of course, I'm not always comfortable with her combativeness, but you don't have to look far to see whose example she's following."

"Miz Dorrance?" Naomi nodded. "That old gal shore enough knows the wheel that squeaks the loudest gets the oil, and she ain't shy of squeakin'."

"But not a peep when Mrs. Morefield praised Maddie's community spirit," said Libby.

"Too bad. Miss Maddie could use the support."

Thoughtfully, Libby said, "Makes me thankful for Father."

"Ya should be, Lib. He's a fine man."

Pleased, Libby flushed, then lifted her chin and smiled. "He is, isn't he?"

16

The library opened ahead of schedule on Friday, just a week and four days from the day Maddie had taken charge of the idea. Libby, wanting to reciprocate Maddie's generosity in treating them for lunch at Baker's on Monday, invited the ladies who had helped make the library a reality for a picnic lunch in her backyard.

Paulette had a luncheon meeting elsewhere and couldn't come. Nor could Mrs. Bee. She was doubling as volunteer librarian for the morning of their first day and keeping vigil on Mr. Robinson, who had yet to regain consciousness.

But Naomi was coming over during her noon lunch hour, and Maddie and Sophronia had promised to come as well. Libby had the picnic luncheon prepared and cookies in the oven when Opal and Frankie arrived just a few minutes before noon. She found a blanket and followed the children into the backyard.

"Hope Abigail will join us, 'cause Mama's bringin' her a present,'' said Opal.

"She's on her way then?''

"Yep,'' said Opal. "We ran ahead. Guess what Mama's bringin' her?''

"Ain't nothin' but ole baby clothes,'' said Frankie.

"Hush up, Frankie! Ya spoilt my surprise!''

Frankie grinned at Opal's sulky expression, then turned as David came running from the edge of the railroad ditch where he'd been playing.

"I found a snake hole! Come see,'' he urged.

Frankie and Opal went with David to investigate.

Libby's Memorandum book and a pencil fell to the ground as Libby gave her blanket a shake. "Ah-hah!" She had an article to turn in for the paper and had looked for the tablet earlier in the morning.

Libby extracted the article, then scanned the entry she had made yesterday afternoon while lazing on the grass. It began with a salutation to her mother, as did so many of her entries dealing with matters close to her heart. It helped strengthen her just to think of her mother, whom she had lost when she was ten.

Dearest Mother:

I believe Abigail has benefited from my keeping Frankie and Opal a few hours a day. She enjoys having them come, and she and Naomi hit it off from the first day Naomi came to walk her children home. I guess what applies to Mrs. Dorrance and Maddie applies to me, too: Abigail needs support. But before I can fully support Abigail, I guess I need to forgive her. I'm trying, Mother. I really am and so is she. We're very polite to each other, but it isn't the closeness I had hoped for in a sister-in-law. The truth is, Abigail's much closer to Naomi. That's only natural, I guess. Naomi understands far better than me what she's going through. Adam hasn't responded to Father's letter yet, so we can only imagine what he's feeling.

Libby leaned against the tree and started a new paragraph:

Opal says Naomi is bringing some baby clothes today. If Abigail has many, she's kept them packed away in her suitcase.

The aroma of baking cookies wafting out the kitchen window, Libby pushed away from the tree and dashed inside to find Abigail taking them out of the oven.

"I figured you'd forgotten them," said Abigail. Cheeks flushed, hair loose about her face, she crossed to the table on bare feet and slid the pan of cookies onto a wrought-iron trivet.

Thinking she could almost pass for a schoolgirl, Libby thanked her.

Abigail held on to the table and lowered herself into a chair. Propping her swollen feet on the rungs of the chair, she asked, "Are you working on something for Mr. Gruben?"

"No, just jotting."

"Mama's here!" cried Opal, dashing in the back door. She grabbed Abigail's hand and tried to haul her to her feet. "Come on out, Miss Abigail. She's brung ya a present."

Abigail accepted Libby's helping hand, then followed Opal out the back door to exchange greetings with Naomi.

Impatient for the gift giving, Opal tore the brown paper off the bundle in her mother's hands, crying, "Looky here what used ta be mine, Miss Abigail!"

Hand braced over her unborn child, Abigail caught a shallow breath and traded swift glances with Naomi as Opal unfolded a yellow baby gown.

Beaming proudly, Opal said, "Kin ya believe I was ever so tiny?"

"My, but you were, weren't you?" said Abigail. "You're so thoughtful! Thank you, Opal. You, too, Naomi." Accepting Naomi's loose hug, she added, "I'll give them back when I'm done with them."

Libby sent the children to the backyard pump to wash their hands.

"Don't seem like Maddie's got anything planned but talkin' for her meetin' Tuesday night," said Naomi while Libby picked her journal up and put it in the fork of the tree for safekeeping. "I was wonderin' if we was to take some fabric scraps along, if we could start piecin' a baby quilt. What do ya think about that, Abigail?"

"I'm not going to the meeting," Abigail said quickly.

" 'Course yer not. What I meant ta say, is thar a quilt pattern yer partial to?"

"That's thoughtful of you, Naomi, but I couldn't let a group of women who don't even know me do that for me," Abigail said firmly.

"Maddie and me know ya. Lib, too, of course. And ya met Mrs. Bee when she come by with Doc, didn't ya?"

"Yes, but . . . Please don't, Naomi. I wouldn't feel right." Abigail thanked her for the thought. Hugging the bundle of baby clothes close, she turned toward the house.

Following her inside, Libby said, "You're coming back out to eat with us, aren't you?"

Abigail's hand made a furtive pass over her eyes. "In a minute."

"Bring some plates when you come, will you?"

"All right."

Surprised to see tears standing in her eyes, Libby stopped in the door, undecided whether to acknowledge them or let them pass unnoted.

Abigail turned away. "I'll be there in a minute."

Respecting her bid for privacy, Libby backed out the door. *Is it the baby clothes? The quilt suggestion? Or something else?* Having no idea, Libby went out to greet Maddie and Sophronia, who had just arrived.

Decked out in her usual frilly garb, Sophronia snatched a scrap of newsprint off the ground and tried to read it. "What is it?" she asked as Libby reached for it.

"A quilt pattern," said Libby, taking it. "Must have fallen out of my journal."

Naomi turned from spreading the picnic lunch out on the laundry bench. Misunderstanding, she said, "Then ya thought of a baby quilt yerself, did ya?"

"No, not a baby quilt." Libby stuffed the pattern piece back into her journal, then returned the journal to the fork of the apple tree while describing the quilt idea she had gotten on the mail route.

"Cross-stitched fences? Appliquéd barns and patchwork fields?" mused Naomi. "Sounds purty."

"If I ever get it pieced and quilted, I'm going to give it to Adam and Abigail for . . . for Christmas." Libby caught herself just short of saying a wedding present.

"We was jest talkin' about a baby quilt," said Naomi for Maddie's benefit. "Thought maybe we could start piecin' it tomorrow night if ya wouldn't find it distractin' at yer meetin'. But Abigail didn't take to the idea."

"Actually, it would rather nicely reflect the spirit of sisterhood," mused Maddie. "Where'd she go anyway?"

"Who, Abigail? She's inside," said Naomi. "Carryin' that young'un kinda low, seems to me."

"You don't think she's about to deliver, do you?" asked Libby, alarmed.

"Cain't say about that, 'ceptin' it'll come when it's ready. Ain't no point in makin' her nervous with guesswork," said Naomi. "Abigail's bringin' plates, son," she added, distracted by Frankie's grab for a sandwich.

"Why are you always so piggish?" said Sophronia.

Frankie glowered at her, grabbed a cookie as well, and scaled the apple tree just as Abigail appeared with the plates. To Libby's relief, she was dry-eyed and composed. Abigail filled a plate for herself and joined them on the blanket. She even contributed a comment or two to the conversation.

Opal and David gobbled their food down, while Sophronia picked at hers. They finished their lunch and retrieved a board from the railroad bank. Libby heard the word *leaper* bandied about as they lugged the board around to the front yard,

Abigail excused herself to take a nap. With the store to run, Naomi didn't stay long either. She said something about Frankie going with her to help dust shelves, but when she left, Frankie was still up in the apple tree.

"How's Angus?" asked Maddie, lying on her back on the quilt, one arm flung over her eyes.

"Fine, I guess. He's been in court in Bloomington so much lately, I've hardly seen anything of him. He'll be home this evening, though. We've made plans to skate at the Columbian."

"Is it serious?"

"Is what serious?"

"You and Angus."

Deliberately evasive, Libby countered, "Ask Angus."

Maddie yawned and changed the subject. "How's Mrs. Baker's mother?"

"Not good. Father was over there last evening."

"Ouch!" Maddie rolled up on one elbow, then came to her feet all of a sudden and peered into the tree. "Frankie McClure, you should be at the store, helping your mother! Throw one more green apple at me, and I'll come up there and teach you some manners!"

Frankie took the punch from her threat by dropping out of the tree voluntarily. He snatched a cookie and shot around to the front of the house to join the other children.

"You aren't the boss, Frankie," Libby heard Sophronia squeal.

"Hesh up. Yer jest a piddlin' gal," Frankie shot back at her.

"If he isn't Hascal Caton all over, I'll eat my hat," said Maddie, rubbing the mark the hard green missile had left on her hand.

Libby grinned and carried the lunch leavings inside while Maddie shook the crumbs from the quilt and returned it to the house. Together, they circled to the front yard where Frankie and David were using a board and a nail keg as a seesaw.

"Where are the girls?" asked Libby.

Maddie smothered a laugh, nudged her, and beckoned her toward the front door just as Sophronia and Opal slipped out of the house. Libby lifted an eyebrow at the sight of them, for they had traded clothes.

"Opal, what have you done?"

"Oh, leave her alone. They're having fun," said Maddie, laughing as Opal pranced from one end of the porch to the other, preening like a peacock in all that ribbon and lace.

Sophronia came down the steps, her hands in the pockets of Opal's faded overalls. She fixed her gaze on Frankie, and ordered, "Get up on the porch, Red. I'm ready to leap."

Frankie hopped off the board so fast, David's end dropped with a thud that left him blinking hard. Frankie growled, "Who you callin' Red?"

"Your hair is red, isn't it?" said Sophronia with a haughty sniff.

"Yes, and them's my old overalls yer wearin', too, and if ya call me Red once more, I'm gonna shake you right out of 'em and take 'em home with me and that's a promise," Frankie retorted.

His ground-eating strides in her direction motivated Sophronia to employ a bit more caution. "All right. You've made your point. But if you want to play with us, there'll be no rough stuff."

Frankie was burning to the tips of his ears. His eyes narrowed to calculating slits. He moved toward the porch and away from Sophronia.

"Pretend I'm the last act," said Sophronia. "The grand finale." She placed both feet on the bottom end of the inclined board, curved her arms overhead like a diver poised to spring toward water, and lifted her nose as if inhaling the scent of the yellow roses spangling the trellis that climbed the front of the house. "Leapers leaping," she called.

Frankie clambered up on the porch railing. He fixed an eye on the raised end of the board and, with curled lip, drew his arms back and propelled himself toward it in less time than it took Libby to cry a warning.

He hit the board with both feet and enough momentum to catapult Sophronia into the air. She careened headlong toward the house with nothing but Frankie between her and the rose trellis. Frankie couldn't get out of the way fast enough. Sophronia crashed into him, carrying them both head over heels into the roses.

Opal rushed toward the pair screaming. Scratched and rose-scented, Frankie extricated himself from the melee. But Sophronia lay sprawled amid mangled roses and broken trellis, wide-eyed, dumbstruck, arms and legs curled like teacup handles.

Opal crouched down in her fancy dress and seized her friend's hand, imploring, "Kin yah hear me? Speak ta me, Phronky, speak to me!"

Sophronia blinked and let out a low moan. Her limbs began to stir and straighten. Letting out a caught breath, Libby joined Opal and helped Sophronia up out of the roses.

"In ring one, our friend Phron*kay*. Put your hands together for her brave effort, folks," David said through his fingers.

Frankie, undaunted, called from the porch, "You wanna try that again?"

Sophronia lifted her pointy chin. "I believe once will be enough."

"Dear me, if you're not a fright, Sophronia. We'd better . . ." Maddie trailed off, struggling not to laugh.

". . . get you cleaned up," Libby finished for her. The affronted expression on Sophronia's face combined with Maddie's laughter was her undoing. She escaped to the kitchen on the pretense of getting a basin of warm water from the stove reservoir.

Abigail, disturbed from her nap by all the commotion, lumbered into the kitchen. "What's going on out there?"

Libby told her. Abigail's laughter ended in a hissing noise, and she caught her breath. Alarmed, Libby cried, "What's the matter? Does something hurt? You're not going into—"

"No, no. It's not that. It's just that every once in a while, he pounces on my bladder."

"He?"

"He. She. Whichever." Her mood shifted abruptly, and sudden tears sprang to Abigail's eyes. Her voice dropped to a whisper. "Libby?"

Misgivings stirring, Libby waited as Adam's wife struggled for words. "What is it, Abigail?" she said finally.

"This baby is coming soon . . ."

"Yes?"

"But . . ."

Was she trying to tell her what she already knew? *Oh Lord.*

As if sensing Libby's apprehensions Abigail turned away, hiding the tears trembling on her lashes. "Never mind. It's nearly time for your Children's Hour anyway. You go on."

"If you want me to stay, Maddie can read to the children."

"No. You've looked forward to it all week. You go on. I'm going to lie back down. Go on, Libby," she urged. "Really! I'm fine."

Libby thought about doing away with the pretenses, thought about saying, *I know all about it, Abigail,* thought about it but didn't. For if pressed, she would have had to admit she didn't have the fortitude to put Abigail's betrayal behind her just yet. That God was still working on her, and until healing came, civilities were the best she could do.

Letting the moment pass, she took the basin of water and slipped back outside to find that Sophronia had retired beneath the porch, mad at them for laughing. She couldn't be coaxed out to have her scratches bathed.

Out of concern for her dress, Opal hadn't crawled under there with her. But Frankie must have joined her there, for Libby heard Opal warn him, "You best not, you'll git in trouble."

With Abigail on her mind, Libby didn't bother asking what sort of mischief Frankie was into now.

Maddie was ready to leave for the library and ordered Sophronia to come out and wash up. When the girl refused, Maddie said, "That's fine. You can come out whenever you like, Sophronia. But don't think I'm waiting around for you. Let's go, Libby. Opal. Davie. You can each have a turn driving the buggy."

"We're leaving, Frankie," Libby called. "If you aren't coming with us, you need to go to the store and check in with your mother."

He didn't bother replying.

17

Under Maddie's able guidance, David stopped the buggy in front of Willie Blue's.

"Brown paper," chimed Opal.

"And pencils," said David. "We'll get the stuff and be over." He passed the lines to Maddie, climbed down, and rushed into Willie Blue's. Opal broke stride to smooth her borrowed dress and wave to her grandfather and Captain Boyd, who were sitting in the shade of the storefront.

Libby climbed down, too. She had several articles to turn in at the newspaper office located next door. Mr. Gruben was out. She left her articles with his printer's devil, Earl Morefield, and strode back out into the sunshine, greeting Hascal Caton and Captain Boyd in passing.

Mr. Caton acknowledged Libby with a nod as the captain came to his feet and touched his fingers to his cap in his customary salute. "Afternoon, Miss Willie. Guess you heard about Gram Steadman passing on."

"No!" cried Libby, stopping. "When?"

"Just a bit ago," Hascal said. "Doc's still over t' Baker's. Mr. Lamb, too."

"Is Zerilda in off her route yet?" Libby asked, for Gram Steadman was Zerilda's mother as well as Mrs. Baker's.

"Not yet," said the captain. "But your father's expecting her anytime."

"Reckon it'll fall to him to tell her," said Mr. Caton. "Unless she stops off home first and hears it from her husband and the young'uns."

Libby had seen Zerilda's grandchildren around town, but she had never met Mr. Payne, who she understood was in poor health.

"Ya reckon Gram ketched whatever it is ailin' the feller over t' Doc's office?" asked Hascal.

"I don't think so. She's been failing for some time," said the captain.

"Still and all, I don't much cotton to Opal and Frankie goin' over to that thar whatchacallit?"

"Children's Hour?" inserted Libby. "You surely don't object to their hearing a story?"

"It ain't the story that worries me."

"They won't be anywhere near Dr. Harding's patient if that's your concern," said Maddie, who was listening to them from the wagon seat.

Libby added, "Opal's excited about the library. She's in the store right now getting paper to draw a circus mural. Naomi has painted and fixed furniture and helped us get ready, all so the children can enjoy good books."

"All I'm sayin' is it's a good place to ketch somethin'."

"At least it won't be ignorance," said Maddie, her words for Libby alone. Her impatience showed in her handling of the buggy whip as she urged the horse into the street, muttering, "Are you going to sit there and tell me you aren't affronted that that man can vote and we can't?"

Libby lowered her lashes and smiled, as much concession as she dared give Maddie without inviting a discourse on the inequality of the sexes. Maddie made another quarter turn around the town park and stopped the buggy in front of Dr. Harding's office on the west side of the square. Leaving her to secure the horse, Libby strode across the boardwalk and through the door with the newly lettered glass denoting Edgewood's library.

The transformation was still under way. Books lined only two of the five newly installed hardwood shelves that ran the full length of the south wall, hidden treasure waiting between leather-bound pages. A floral arrangement was flanked by a globe and a ship in a bottle on one bookless shelf. A mortarboard, Dr. Harding's medical degree, and a painting of a young scholar in a gilded frame adorned another.

"Mrs. Bee?" Libby called softly so as not to disturb the patient. She trekked down the corridor just as Mrs. Bee exited an alcove off to the left.

Mrs. Bee pressed a finger to her lips and pulled the door closed behind her. She led Libby back down the interior hall into the library, explaining as they went that she was waiting for Dr. Harding to return from Baker's and relieve her of her vigil over Mr. Robinson.

"How is he?" asked Libby.

"Gravely ill and getting worse all the time, I'm afraid." Mrs. Bee paused to greet Maddie, then mentioned the sad news concerning Gram Steadman. Learning they had already heard it, she said, "As long as you girls are going to be here, I don't think anyone would miss me if I ran home for a bite to eat."

"You haven't had lunch yet? Of course you should go," Libby urged. "About Mr. Robinson . . ."

"If you'd just look in on him once or twice. That's about all we can do," said Mrs. Bee. A careworn expression carved fine wrinkles about her eyes. As she pinned on her hat and reached for her wicker lunch basket, her distinctive white lock of hair, defying confinement beneath her hat, fell across her forehead. "I'll bring the fellow back some clear broth and see if I can't spoon a little down him. Should you need the doctor before I return, he's at Baker's."

Maddie offered to drive Mrs. Bee home and followed her out, leaving Libby alone. The silence was so deep, she could hear the mantel clock ticking. It was one-thirty. The children would begin arriving soon. The scent of Maddie's garden flowers and the underlying odor of freshly dried paint and oiled floors permeated the room. The chairs were arranged, and *Toby Tyler,* the book she planned to read, was on the footstool. It was a charming story relating the adventures of a young boy who ran away with the circus. They'd have to make good progress each day to finish it before school started. Libby thumbed through it a moment, then came to her feet and went down the hall to look in on Mr. Robinson.

It surprised her to find he was such a large fellow. On the young side of thirty, he had a full dark beard. Thick black curls spilled over his high brow. His mouth, though punished by fever, was well formed; his eyelids were transparently pale, yet handsomely fringed in dark lashes that nestled in the valley of deep shadows formed by exhaustion. Heavy though he was, his skin hung loose as if he had lost a good deal of weight; sapped and sallow and not cognitive of his surroundings, he was nonetheless striking. Libby listened to his labored breathing, then tiptoed out again, closed the door, and trekked down the short interior corridor to the library just as Zerilda Payne came through the door, leading her two grandchildren by the hand.

"Miz McClure said to fetch the young'uns over, that you was gonna read to 'em. Thought the company of other youngsters wouldn't hurt 'em none," Zerilda said, even as Libby grappled with the possibility that she was not yet privy to the news of her mother's death.

The girl and boy, no older than David, kept their chins tucked and their eyes downcast as Zerilda dropped to her knees. She licked her finger, scrubbed the jelly moustache off the little boy's face, smoothed the girl's hair back from her sweaty brow, and told them, "I'll be home scrubbin' floors so's Mr. Lamb can bring Ma overt' the house and get her laid out for the wake."

So she *did* know. "I heard she'd passed away. I'm sorry, Mrs. Payne," said Libby.

"I been expectin' it," said Zerilda in that stoic roughshod way of hers. "She ain't been well for some time."

"You say the wake will be at your house? Not at the restaurant?"

"Verna offered Baker's, but it don't seem fittin'. With rooms rented and boarders upstairs, there'd be all that comin' and goin' commotion. My place ain't fancy, but it'll do once I get things in order. Kinda hard keepin' house what with the mail to deliver and these two underfoot. Speaking of the mail, my substitute's gone down to the fair and won't be back for a week. I'd be obliged if ya'd run my route for me tomorrow and again on Monday."

"Of course," murmured Libby.

"I know ya ain't never run it b'fore, but I spoke to yer father about it, and he said since Billy knows the countryside better'n you, maybe he could run my route, and you could run Billy's."

"If Billy's willing, yes, that would be easier," said Libby.

Lifting one, then the other child onto a chair, Zerilda said, "You two sit quiet now. Don't fidget while Miss Libby's readin', and come straight home when it's done with, hear?"

The children nodded and followed their grandmother with their eyes as she stamped out the door in her man-sized shoes. She had no sooner gone when Maddie returned from taking Mrs. Bee home. Opal, David, and Sophronia trooped in after her.

"You two girls go into the back and trade clothes," Maddie instructed.

Opal tugged on Sophronia's hand. "Come on, Phrony." Sophronia started to protest, but Opal whispered something in her ear and Sophronia promptly acquiesced.

"Mother may come to town this afternoon and I don't believe she'd be amenable to Sophronia wearing overalls," Maddie explained when the girls were out of earshot. Her gaze skipped to the chairs where the two children huddled close like orphan pups, dangling their dusty bare feet toward the floor.

"Zerilda's grandchildren," whispered Libby.

Maddie crooked an eyebrow but asked no questions.

A cluster of children of varying ages flooded through the doors just as the clock struck two. Libby introduced herself, showed them the book she had chosen to read, and explained that all the books in the library could be checked out for two weeks at a time. Still waiting for Opal and Sophronia to return from trading clothes, she said, "If there are no questions, I'll allow you a little time to choose a book to take home."

"Has Dr. Harding come?" asked Maddie as the children pulled books from the bottom shelf.

"Not yet," said Libby.

"I had better warn the girls to be quiet and not bother his patient then," said Maddie.

Libby was helping one child pick out a book when Maddie screeched.

Libby shot to her feet and down the interior corridor just as Opal fled the left alcove.

"We was jest lookin'," Opal blurted as if to duck a scolding.

Sophronia's strident voice rose over hers, saying, "We didn't bother him. We didn't make a peep!"

Libby brushed past them both and turned into the room to find Maddie rooted at the foot of John Robinson's cot, staring at the man as if she'd been knocked senseless.

"What is it? What did they do?" cried Libby, certain the girls had in some way vexed the gravely ill Mr. Robinson. Her heart leaped to her throat at the sight of his wide-open eyes. Odd-colored, muddy-looking spheres, they fastened on Maddie. His lips, blistered and peeling, parted, then came together in a soundless word. His hand twitched but never made it off the bedsheet.

Her face ashen, Maddie staggered back. Her fist curled against her mouth as the light dimmed in the man's eyes. His mouth slackened, his breathing eroded, a final hiss leaking out of his lungs. *Dear God!* His life was ebbing away, his eyes glazing like stagnant water. Libby searched for a pulse and found none. "He's dying, Maddie! Get Dr. Harding."

Maddie stood stunned, as gray as the mantle of death passing over the man's features. Feeling twisted inside, as if by an unseen hand, Libby forced a calm to her voice and called Opal.

But even as she dispatched the child to bring Dr. Harding, she knew it was too late. *Dying alone among strangers.* Swept by emotion too obscure to define, she took the man's limp hand between both of hers and drew breath past the crushing weight on her chest. She thought of her father, of her own dear brothers. She prayed without words, a silent anguished plea to the One who gave life, who shielded His children from those darts that could be deflected and absorbed the pain of those that couldn't.

When she opened her eyes, Maddie was gone. A troop of wide-eyed faces peeked in from the corridor, Zerilda's grandchildren among them.

Libby singled out Sophronia, still dressed in Opal's coveralls, and tried to quiet the silent alarm in their faces. "I left a book on the footstool in the lobby," she said in a voice too calm to have come from her own throat. "Take it across the street to the park and read to the children until I can get there, Sophronia."

"Get in line, everyone. Let's go." Sophronia turned away, corralling the children and calling out orders in a strident voice. "No pushing. Put the book down, Jenny Lou, she told *me* to get it."

They had no sooner gone than Dr. Harding strode in and took Libby's place at the man's side. His confirmation of what Libby had already surmised rang in her ears. She watched him close the man's eyes, drew a shuddering breath, and made her way out of the building by way of the back door.

Maddie was huddled on the step overlooking the alley. Head down, arms hugging her knees. She lifted her face at the sound of the door closing. There was a sheen in the hollows beneath her eyes. Whether tears or perspiration, Libby couldn't tell. She saw Maddie's throat move as she swallowed and asked, "Is he . . . ?"

Feeling numb, Libby nodded.

Maddie rose, her jaw working. She moved to the end of the building and back, aimlessly at first, then gaining momentum until her feet punched the earth, raising miniature clouds of dust that turned her black hem gray. Her growing agitation watered the seed of suspicion that had been sown in Libby moments ago. She blurted, "You knew him, didn't you?"

"No!" The word erupted as if Maddie were spewing bitter poison. "No, I didn't know him. I didn't know him at all." She wheeled around and tramped away.

But the heat of her denial only heightened the question burning in Libby's mind. *Who is the man?*

Children's Hour. The reminder penetrated Libby's numbed senses. She circled the building and crossed the street to the park and relieved Sophronia.

Libby had read *Toby Tyler* as a child and again a few months ago to David. But today she had no sense of the story. She forgot the brown paper and her plans to help the children draw a circus mural. Nor did she notice when Frankie McClure slipped in among the other children. She just knew that he was there and listening with pretended detachment.

She did see Mr. Lamb cross the park with his undertaker's hat riding low on his brow. Heard his boots whisper in the sunburned grass as he passed on his way to tend business over the dead. Felt the dampness of her clinging camisole and the heat of the sun on her face as it shone through the ginger-bread trim of the bandstand where she sat with the children. Grappled with a fleeting verse, something about all things that were hidden coming to light.

What is Maddie hiding?

18

🌺 Maddie returned when Children's Hour ended but only long enough to ask if Libby would take charge of Sophronia while she attended to some business. Libby agreed, then stood looking after Maddie as she made her way across the street toward Dr. Harding's office. She resisted the temptation to follow on the pretense of returning *Toby Tyler* to the bookshelf, certain Maddie would resent the intrusion.

What did she know of her really? That she held modern ideas. Was politically inclined. Free with her opinions, yet guarded about her past. A past in which she had allegedly disgraced herself, first with Ike and then with Dr. Daniels, with whom she had run off and eventually married.

Seeing that Zerilda's grandchildren were standing at the edge of the park, each with a book in hand, reminded Libby that she hadn't checked out any of the books the children were taking with them as they dispersed toward their separate homes. But then she hadn't bargained on a man dying during Children's Hour.

Libby cringed at the thought of Hascal Caton hearing the news. She could hear him now, expounding in self-congratulatory glee: *Tried to tell 'em. Didn't I, Captain? Didn't I try to tell 'em?*

Seeing Frankie disappear into Willie Blue's, Libby collected Zerilda's grandchildren along with David, Opal, and Sophronia and walked the few short blocks to Zerilda's house. Once there, she offered to take the children home with her so that Zerilda and Mrs. Baker, who had come to help, could continue preparing the house for the wake.

"Be better'n havin' 'em underfoot," Zerilda said, accepting the offer with her usual lack of grace. She instructed the children to put their library books away first.

Mrs. Baker followed Libby outside. Anxious not to reveal to the children any more than they had already guessed, Libby told Mrs. Baker in hushed tones about Mr. Robinson's death. She had no opportunity to mention Maddie's odd behavior, for Zerilda's children came out the door and stood waiting.

Once home, Libby picked green beans to take to Zerilda's house. She snapped them, seasoned them with salt and onions and bacon fat, and left them to simmer on the stove in the washhouse while the children played circus in the backyard. The green beans were almost done when Maddie came to pick up Sophronia.

Naomi came for Opal just as Libby, Father and David, along with Zerilda's grandchildren, were sitting down for supper. Teddy Baker came for Zerilda's grandchildren shortly thereafter. Angus arrived just as Libby and Abigail were finishing the dishes. He covered her hands with his as she met him at the door. Looking every inch the smart young attorney in his handsome summer-weight suit, glistening shirt and collar, he greeted her warmly and pressed his lips to her hand.

Never failing to find it an awkward gesture, Libby pulled her hand away and asked, "How did you do in court?"

His mouth curved into a smile. "You make it sound like a sport."

"Well? Did you win or didn't you?"

He laughed and replied, "Justice was served, and yes, my client won."

"Good for your client's attorney." She stepped out onto the porch. "We've eaten, but I could warm something up for you if you'd like."

He declined, saying, "I'm going home to clean up. I'll be back around seven to pick you up for skating." His smile faltered, a reflection of what he saw on her face. "You are still planning on going, aren't you?"

"I can't, Angus. Gram Steadman died today."

"Yes, I heard. How is Mrs. Baker doing?"

"She's intent on helping everyone else cope and in so doing is coping herself."

"A remarkable woman, Mrs. Baker. Is the wake at Baker's then?"

"No, Zerilda's," said Libby, relieved he had brought it up, thereby making it easier to say, "Father and I are going over there in a little while."

His face fell. He turned his straw skimmer in his hand, smoothing the narrow band with a slender finger. "You're obligated to pay your respects, of course. But tomorrow would be soon enough, wouldn't it?"

"I'm carrying the mail for Zerilda tomorrow."

"Then she surely wouldn't begrudge you an evening with a man who has missed you all week."

His rationale, flattering though it was, made the decision more difficult. Libby dropped her gaze from his and wavered between her own wishes and how she might best be of service to Zerilda and Mrs. Baker. There was, too, the matter of Angus's feelings. Lashes sweeping up, she entreated, "I think wakes are dreadful, and if I had the option, I'd choose skating. You know that, don't you?"

"You're right, of course," he conceded. Struggling to balance social duty with his own plans, he tapped his hat against his leg. "Let's compromise, shall we? We'll stop by the wake, pay our respects, and *then* go to the Columbian for skating."

Libby hated to protest again and risk having him think she wasn't glad to see him, as eager as he for the evening he'd planned. But it seemed callous to trek from a wake to the Columbian for an evening of fun. "Do you think that's a good idea?"

"I don't see why not. Surely Zerilda doesn't expect you to stay the entire evening? After all, it isn't as if you are best friends."

"That's just it. Zerilda has no best friend."

He was the first to drop his gaze. Capitulating with a sigh, he said, "Very well then. We'll spend the evening at Zerilda's."

His vexation, though mild, was not lost on Libby. Nor did she fault him for it. Blunt, irascible, and gloomy, Zerilda hadn't endeared herself to many people, and Angus was no exception. Still, there was within Zerilda's character sprinkles of goodness, a sense of duty among them. Instinctively, Libby knew Zerilda would feel slighted if the wake were not well attended.

Libby needn't have worried. The community turned out at Zerilda's to show their respects. Some stayed only briefly. Others mingled in the kitchen and parlor and overflowed into the yard. It was an overcast evening, the clouds building in low, thick gray layers that allowed the heat and humidity no avenue of escape. It was even worse indoors. The flies were biting, a sure sign of rain. Or so the old ones said as they swatted, sweated, and shared memories of Gram.

Libby's father intended to remain with a group of family and friends who would keep vigil of the body overnight. Libby had arrived early with him and had been there for a while when Angus came in. Mrs. Baker, with Teddy at her side, thanked him for coming. Teddy shook his hand. Even Zerilda muttered a word or two, for which Libby was thankful. Angus mingled with the men for a while, then came to the corner where Libby was fanning air thick enough to serve with a spoon.

"Are you saving this chair for someone, Miss Watson?" he asked, the gravity of his voice relieved by the light in his eye.

Libby patted the empty chair by way of invitation. They shared in the small talk and ate the pie that Mrs. Baker brought and engaged Zerilda's husband in conversation.

Mr. Payne was so hard of hearing, he used an ear horn. His pink head was speckled with brown age spots and blue veins and small white tufts of hair just over his ears. He sat by the window with a lap robe draped over his knees and informed Angus in a loud voice that while he would like to vote for him in the upcoming election, he found his Prohibition view just a little too dry to swallow.

Smart and handsome, full of potential, and able to laugh at an old man's joke even when he was the target of it, Angus was a fellow any girl would be proud to claim as her beau. And yet later, as they exchanged all that had transpired in their separate lives that week, Libby felt oddly lonely.

It was a puzzling sensation, one she explained away as simple fatigue at the end of a long and trying day. Once home, she bid Angus good night, then slipped into the dark kitchen and felt along the shelf where she had been keeping her journal since sharing her bedroom with Abigail. Mrs. Baker had given her some information for Gram Steadman's obituary for the *Gazette*. She had taken notes on a scrap of brown paper and wanted to tuck it into her notebook for safekeeping. But the book was not there. What had she done with it?

Her mental backtracking stopped at the apple tree. She recalled putting the notebook in the fork of the tree, out of the way of their picnic lunch.

Distant thunder rumbled as Libby stepped out into the night. The sultry air intensified the fragrance of the roses as she brushed past them. A flash of lightning illuminated her path. Dry grass rustled underfoot. Fireflies took cover in advance of pending rain and blinked from the grass as she lifted on tiptoe and groped the fork of the tree with her hand. Feeling nothing but bark and a few broken twigs, Libby's nerves twitched. Had her notebook fallen to the ground?

She got down on her knees and patted her way around the base of the tree and found one small piece of the newspaper quilt pattern she had stuffed into the book but no sign of the book itself. Slapping a mosquito off her neck, she came to her feet thinking of Frankie. He'd been in the tree when she'd placed the journal there!

Tired as Libby was, it took only seconds for consternation to turn to panic, for that multipurpose Memorandum book contained candid thoughts, some of them about Frankie himself, about Naomi and Decatur and Angus and his family, about Maddie and Mrs. Dorrance. All the faces of Edgewood condensed in bits and pieces!

Father wouldn't be home from the wake until morning. Davie had gone to bed as had Abigail. Concern growing, Libby set out for Willie Blue's. The store was dark, nor was there a lamp burning on the second story. As hot as it was, Libby doubted Naomi and the children were sleeping up there. Many mornings, she had come to work to find Opal stretched out on a mat downstairs and Frankie in the buggy shed, using the seat of her mail buggy as a bed.

Let him be there, she prayed as she turned at the corner. There was a lamp burning in Angus's office. His buggy was parked in the alley. The horse whinnied recognition. Gliding quietly past, Libby continued up the alley to find the doors of the buggy shed standing open.

"Frankie?" Libby peered into the dark void, called him again, then strode in only to ram into one of the buggy shafts, jarring the buggy. Frankie bolted upright on the buggy seat at her smothered yelp of pain.

"Who's there?"

Catching his alarm, she said quickly, "It's me, Libby. I came for my tablet."

"Tablet?"

"Yes, my Memorandum notebook, the one I left in the apple tree this afternoon."

"Oh, that." The silt of disrupted sleep slurred his voice.

"You've got it then?"

"Why would I have it?"

"It isn't there, and you were the last one in the tree."

"That don't mean—"

"I'm not going to scold, I just want it back." Libby rubbed her stinging thigh and stretched her hands out so as not to blunder into some other hidden obstruction as she moved closer. "Would you get it for me please?"

"I'm tellin' ya I ain't got it."

The day had delivered more than its share of jolts. Weary, trying to be patient about it, she said, "I heard Opal warning you against something when you were under the porch this afternoon. 'You best not, Frankie. You'll get in trouble.' Something like that."

"She wasn't talking to me, she was talkin' to Sophronia."

"Frankie, do you want to tell me what you've done with it, or shall I wake Opal up and ask her?"

"Go ahead. She'll tell ya I ain't got it." Frankie climbed down on the other side of the buggy and stalked out into the night.

"Stop right there! I haven't finished talking to you!" Libby hurried to catch up with him, but he'd melted into the night. No book. No Frankie. What now? Knock on the door? Wake both Naomi and Opal? She started that way, then stopped. What if he was telling the truth?

As slim a possibility as it was, it still gave her pause. Thunder rumbled as she hesitated. The skies growled like dray wagons rumbling over ruts in the clouds. Fast running out of ideas, frustrated, fearful of what had become of her notebook, Libby turned to retrace her steps home.

A light still burned in Angus's office. She plodded toward the mouth of the alley, swept by a wave of affection. He had been so considerate, staying the whole evening at Zerilda's. It was a sacrifice deserving of better than her concern over the prick of loneliness. Who didn't brush against loneliness at a wake? Death touched the spirit in a way only Spirit could alleviate. It was unfair of her to have charged the emotion to his account. Chastised by her own thoughts, Libby's feet slowed, then ground to a halt at the sound of voices. One was female and familiar. Maddie!

Business, she told herself. At this time of night? What could be so urgent that it couldn't wait until tomorrow? The Memorandum book driven from her mind, Libby drew closer to the window. The wall held the heat of the day as she crowded against it, nerves stretched thin as she listened.

"You're not thinking clearly, Maddie," she heard Angus say. "You make it sound as simple as shipping a package home."

"It *is* a package."

"A package with a body in it."

"So what do you suggest?"

"Be open about it. Tell your mother the truth."

"And then what?"

"Accept the consequences, I suppose."

"Spoken like a man whose mother has championed his every cause. Even when you were in the wrong, she protected you."

"Blast it, Maddie, my mother has nothing to do with this. What I want to know is why you are bent on keeping this a secret? Can't you just bury him in the family plot?"

"My mother would never allow it."

"You haven't asked her."

"How can I ask her? She thinks he died months ago."

"Of course she does. You told her he had."

"What was I supposed to do? I had no money. I could barely eke out a living."

"Was life with Daniels so unbearable? Why did you leave him?"

"Because I was weary of him growing fat on my charms! There now, I've said it. Is that plain enough for you, Angus?" The words burst like infection from a wound. They echoed in the brief stunned silence, ringing with festering pain as Libby pieced together the incredible truth that John Robinson was in reality Maddie's Dr. Daniels!

"Egads! Maddie, I'm sorry," cried Angus. "I just naturally thought—"

"What? That it was all my fault? That we had some trifling disagreement and I stuck my nose in the air and came home to Mother?"

"I didn't mean it that way."

"Of course you did. How would you understand?"

"Maddie—"

Bitterly, she talked over him. "Damon with his silver tongue and his bottles of miracle elixir! Medicine Show and Hypnotic Vaudeville Combination, ha! White lightning colored blue was the medicine, con and swindle was the combination, and when he couldn't get a respectable audience, he'd pull into the seedy part of town and start hawking a 'really warm show.' Yes, Angus, put your eyes back in your head, I was the show. Oh, he did his part, playing the straight man to my off-color jokes, and the blushing swain to my tawdry song and dance, but it was me they came to see."

Angus was silent. A silence so taut, so deep, Libby feared her pounding heart would give her away.

"All I wanted to do was come home. But I was afraid Mother wouldn't let me if she knew Damon had not really died. I was afraid she'd say I'd made my bed. And she wasn't far from wrong." Maddie's voice, thin and reedy, finally broke.

Libby heard her sniff, envisioned her drawing her hand across her eyes before she continued.

"Even when she thought he was dead, that I was a widow on my own, she didn't write and invite me home. I had to swallow my pride and take the risk." Brokenly, she finished, "You can't know how often I envied you and Catherine. There's nothing either one of you could do that would make your mother disown you. Or your stepfather either."

"Your mother loves you. You don't see eye to eye, that's all," said Angus, inadvertently stirring some rudimentary passion in Maddie.

"What good is love that tramps all over the soul of a person? She caught her breath when I ran off with Damon and has been waiting ever since for the second shoe to fall. No, before Damon. That time at the lake—she has treated me like an outcast ever since—like a wanton woman and look at me now. I've very nearly lived up to her expectations."

"Maddie, don't," Angus pleaded softly.

"Forget it then. I didn't come here to cry on your shoulder," she said with a swift anger that left Libby wondering at all that had gone unsaid even as Angus tried to appease her.

"I didn't mean it that way," he said. "If it helps to spell it out, then go ahead—"

"There is no help! Men never understand that! They go after a woman as if she were a trinket at an amusement park, and when she's no longer fit for decent society, they cast her aside as if they had nothing to do with the tarnishing that has made her so contemptible. Of course you wouldn't know anything about that, would you, Angus?"

"No one is condemning you, Maddie."

"Would you open your eyes! The whole town condemns me without knowing the half of it. I know this town. I can hear them now: Why did she come home? Why did she lie? Why did she say he was dead? The more this unravels, the closer it comes to where I've been and what I've done and what will they think of me *then?*"

"Does it matter so much what they think?"

Emotions shredded, she cried, "Are you really that blind?"

"I don't know, maybe I have been blind. About you. About a lot of things. But at the moment, I'm seeing more clearly than you, and I'm telling you, Maddie, you can't do this."

"If it isn't against the law, why can't I? Who am I hurting?"

"I'm not talking to you as a lawyer, I'm talking to you as a friend. Look what came of saying he was dead when he wasn't."

"If he's buried in Indiana, how is anyone ever to know?"

"You're covering a lie with another deception."

"I have to! Even now, Mrs. Morefield doesn't want me coming to her door. Chloe Berry hovers over her sister like she's afraid I'm going to corrupt her. I invited every woman in town to a meeting next Tuesday night, and only seven say they'll come. Seven, Angus, and that's counting Libby, Mrs. Bee, Paulette, and Naomi. If this should get out, how many do you think would come then? I *have* to cover it up. Not just for me, but for Sophronia and Mother."

"It isn't about your mother," he reasoned.

"It's *always* about her. I'm telling you, Angus, I won't be treated like I've disgraced her again. I can't bear it. Help me to do it the easy way, and you have my word, I'll never ask anything of you again."

Maddie's pleas gave way to a storm of weeping that peeled away every pretense and revealed an anguish so deep, Libby's eyes filled. Of their own volition her feet carried her to Angus's door. She slipped in just as Angus folded his arms around Maddie. Slow to see her in the deep shadows, he was rocking Maddie, comforting her as one would a child, when their gaze locked over the top of Maddie's head. The swaying stopped. The flickering lamplight fell across his face and lit his startled thoughts.

"Libby, this isn't what you think."

"It's all right," said Libby, reassured in a way she wouldn't have been had he jumped away in guilt. He didn't. His arms stayed around Maddie even as Libby drew nearer. Though no explanation was requested, she nonetheless offered a lame, "I had to see Frankie. I was on my way home again when I heard voices and—"

"Then you know?"

"That John Robinson is Maddie's husband?" Libby nodded. "What is it she wants you to do?"

"Confirm that she is Dr. Daniels's wife so Mr. Lamb will release his body to her. She wants to take it back to Indiana where he's from, for burial without anyone but Mr. Lamb and Dr. Harding being any the wiser."

"But would they keep her secret?"

"If Angus asked them to . . ." said Maddie. She lifted her face from Angus's shoulder, turned imploring tear-swollen eyes on Libby. "Is that so much to ask?"

"Talk to her, Libby," urged Angus. "Tell her she isn't thinking straight."

Libby drew a step closer and laid a hand on Maddie's shoulder.

Maddie shrugged it off. Her chin came up. "This has nothing to do with you, Libby. Not unless you're going to be a true spirit sister and help me."

"Maddie, you're stronger than this. Smarter, too," said Angus.

Moved by Maddie's pain, fear, and crippled pride, Libby saw that for once being strong, being smart, wouldn't pull Maddie through. She was a vine growing wild, caught between the weeds and the pruner's shears.

"I'll be your spirit sister," Libby said. "Come home with me, Maddie, and we'll talk this through."

Maddie shook her head emphatically. "I won't be talked out of it, Libby. I'm handling this in my own way."

"Calm down and consider the possible consequences, that's all I'm suggesting," said Libby.

"Listen to her, Maddie. Stop trying to figure everything out for yourself and listen to someone else for a change."

Angus's impatience achieved what soothing words had not. Maddie agreed to go home with Libby.

19

Ike had awakened with a headache that worsened all day. By evening he found himself craving rest more than supper. He gave into the languor creeping over him and stretched his bedroll out on the cot he'd brought to Naomi's cabin. He slept the sleep of exhaustion, and when he opened his eyes again, he was on San Juan Heights, where battle raged in eerie, silent fury.

He ran from one wounded soldier to another, turning them over. They were weightless, a deck of cards in his hands, face cards, every one, but bodies still. Each looked like Spike Culbertson, pallid features contorted, eyes and lips eaten away by scavenging land crabs. A passing shadow like that of a hawk riding the currents drew Ike's attention to the sky where a balloon hovered, filled with flame yet not consumed. Cannon fire exploded, numbing his senses.

Ike bolted upright on the cot, heart pounding, nerves strung as tightly as the stretched canvas beneath him. Thunder, not cannon fire. He raked his hand through his hair. Weather moving in over the grove.

The wind came as a friend, blowing his head clean of nightmares and turning his attention to the storm unfolding beyond the wide, uncurtained windows of Naomi's woodworking shop. Jagged splinters of light burst across the sky like artillery fire, illuminating the quaking limbs of groaning trees in glistening flashes. Head throbbing, back aching, Ike lay down again, arms curled across his chest, shivering as the night rains sheeted off the roof. The dampness seeped into his bones and joints. He dozed and awakened and dozed and awakened and finally sat up, held his pounding head between his hands, and stopped denying the symptoms. He had quinine back at the sap house, though he had hoped never to need it again. Planning to go for the medicine at the first slackening in the rain, he closed his eyes and prayed for morning.

It was the rush of damp air and the sound of the door closing that awakened him from a fitful sleep. A lamp sputtered to life. Stars glittered before his eyes as he turned his aching head and found Frankie McClure, lantern swinging from his hand as he stared back at him.

Frankie was the first to overcome his surprise. "Didn't expect to find you here."

"Bad night to be out," observed Ike.

"Yep."

Frankie's bare wet feet made sucking sounds as he circled around behind Ike. A chair scraped against the wooden floor, sending slivers of pain shooting through his head as he watched Frankie climb up on the chair and hang the lantern from a hook. There was a neediness in the boy's eyes when he turned to face Ike again. It made him yearn for the dull oblivion of dreamless sleep. He stirred himself to ask, "Yer mama know yer here?"

Rainwater dripped off the boy's chin as he hung his head.

"Ya smell like wet horse."

"Proctor."

"Guess it'd be silly of me to ask if Libby knows ya got her horse."

Frankie pulled the chair around to the side of Ike's cot. He curled his feet around the legs of it, dropped his forearms onto his knees, and sat looking back at Ike. He asked, "Did ya ever get blamed for somethin' you didn't do?"

"Once," said Ike, thinking of that night at the lake when Hascal Caton found him and Maddie eating fish they'd caught by star shine.

"Make ya mad?" asked Frankie.

"Yep," said Ike, for it was the only time Willie had ever bawled him out. Sent him home to his mother, too. It had hurt Ike's feelings more than anything and him, just stubborn enough, he never had eased Willie's mind by telling him it was Angus who had been tumbling around in the grass with Maddie. "What makes ya ask?"

"Miss Libby thinks I took a book of hers and I didn't."

"What kind of book?"

"One she writes in."

"For the paper, you mean?"

"That and some other stuff, too."

"What kind of stuff?"

"I don't know, I ain't seen it. Jest stuff."

"But you didn't take it?"

"Nope. Sophronia did. Crawled under the porch and hid it in her overalls."

"Did you tell Libby that?"

"Nope. Wasn't no call for her to think I'd steal from her."

Aw, Lord. Ain't it enough I'm sick as a dog? Ike summoned the strength to sit up on the cot and found in so doing he could hold Frankie's eye without seeing blurred pinpricks of light like fireflies flashing over a black field. Measuring his words, he said, "You took her horse, didn't ya?"

Frankie flinched as if he'd been struck. "I ain't no thief, Ike. I'm takin' Proctor back soon as the rain lets up."

"You been helpin' yerself to other horses, too?"

Frankie dropped his chin. "Not ta keep. And I ain't gonna do it no more."

Uncertain he'd seen the connection, Ike tried again. "But you see, don't ya, how Libby might think you had her book? If you'd take a horse . . ."

"She don't know that."

"She may know more than you think. She's been writing about the horse borrowin's in the paper for the last few weeks. Anyway, you sit there sayin' ya aren't gonna do it anymore, and poor Proctor's standin' out in the rain."

"He ain't in the rain. I put him in the shed. Anyway, I reckon I got a right to Proctor, seein' as he belonged to my old man."

"If yer talkin' about Willie, then you're forgettin' he left the horse to Libby."

"He give her the store, too, but ya don't see her livin' there, do ya?" said Frankie.

"She had her reasons."

"I got mine, too."

Ike opened his mouth to put him in his place, then caught himself and gave it more study. His head wasn't so dull he couldn't see there was a lot going on behind Frankie's indignation and that some of it had to do with all he'd faced over the summer. Finding out Willie was his father. Knowing that had caused Decatur to turn him and his mother out. Being told it wasn't his fault, yet smart enough to see he was a reminder of what had happened all those years ago. It was a lot for a boy to handle. But where did Libby fit in?

At length, Ike said, "You go to Libby tomorrow and tell her Sophronia took the book. That'll set things straight."

"I ain't no tattletale." Frankie put his feet on the floor, dug one toe into a crack. "Besides, Sophronia ain't got it no more."

"How do you know?"

"I rode out there and bawled her out for gettin' me in trouble with Libby."

"That's why you took Proctor?"

Frankie nodded.

"So what became of the book?"

"Old smarty-pants let her granny get holt of it."

"Miz Dorrance?"

Frankie nodded.

Ike groaned. Libby had already tangled with that woman over Captain Boyd. Resolutely, he said, "Ya gotta tell her, Frankie."

Frankie jutted out his chin. "I don't know as I will. She was wrong about me."

Ike puzzled again over Libby's mistrust having hurt Frankie. Or was the answer so obvious he was lookin' right past it? He thought again about that long-ago night at the lake with Maddie and the chewing out Willie had given him, telling him he was ashamed of him, taking advantage of a girl that way. *Ashamed.*

That had stung worse than any scolding his mother had ever given him. He'd hated being diminished in Willie's eyes. Was that how it was with Frankie? He didn't want Libby thinking poorly of him? All of Edgewood maybe, but not Libby. *Why?*

Again he found the answer in his own relationship with Willie. Willie had been good to him without cause or reason or hope of anything in return. Simple grace from an unexpected source. Likewise, Libby had had no reason to give up the store and befriend Frankie. But she had. And even when she got mad at him, it wasn't because she didn't care; rather, it was because she *did.* After all that had happened, Frankie needed to know he was worth caring about. It lingered in his eyes, that neediness, like an orphan pup left to fend for itself.

Frankie tucked his feet on the chair rungs, his brows beetling. "You don't look so good. Ya got the ague?"

"Backwash of malaria."

"Want me to get Doc Harding?"

"Nothin' he can tell me I don't already know." Five-day fever, the army doctors called it. The affliction came in cycles of chills, fever, and wracking body pain. Ike had been recovering from his wounds the first time he caught it. The fever got so bad, he thought he was dead and they were burning up his corpse.

Ike watched Frankie pick at the mud on his trouser legs, saw a shadow cross his face.

"You ain't gonna die, are ya?" he asked.

"Don't plan on it."

"Neither did Willie," said Frankie.

"Willie now, is it? What happened to *my old man?*"

Frankie stirred sawdust with his bare toes and conceded without looking up, "Name don't seem to fit somehow."

"Fits Decatur better, does it?"

"Used to."

The lantern flickered. The rain was coming softer now. "Maybe it will again."

"Don't know as I care much one way or the other."

Ike winced at the belligerence in his tone. His head swam as he leaned forward. He braced his elbows on his knees and held Frankie's gaze. "Yer foolin' yerself, Frankie. It's carin' makes ya hurt. There's things come along that ain't yer fault. If ya cain't change 'em, ya jest gotta learn to live above 'em."

"How?"

"Can't do it by yerself. Wrap up the mad and the hurt, and jest give it to God and trust Him to fill ya up with somethin' better."

"I ain't sure about God. I been thinkin' maybe He don't like me too much."

"That ain't so, Frankie. He thought you was worth makin'. He'll stand by ya. Good Book says we can all be conquerors through Him."

"I know all them words," said Frankie. "Didn't I win me a trip sayin' 'em?"

Ike thought that over a minute. "Them words is like a train ticket. They's jest part of takin' the ride. See what I mean? There's a bigger purpose than sayin' 'em like you would the alphabet."

"I know."

"Do ya? Then how come you been takin' horses? How come you didn't think none about worryin' yer mama if she should come awake and find ya gone? How come ya ain't been helpin' her out at the store?"

"I like the woods. I ain't fitted to storekeepin'," said Frankie, jutting out his chin. "Anyways, I got enough folks tellin' me what to do without you startin' in."

"You think I don't know that? When I was yer size and my mama or my stepdaddy said do this or that, I got my back up jest like you."

Frankie's blue gaze swept over him. "I didn't know you had a stepdaddy."

"I still do. A good man. I didn't see it back then when he was tryin' to do right by me. No, sir, I'd jest light out for Old Kentucky and Willie, 'cause it was easy with Willie."

"How come?"

"He didn't keep after me the way a boy needs keepin' after if he's gonna be more than a pain in the neck. 'Course there was a quieter Presence. But I wasn't listenin'. All I could hear was my own clamorin' voice."

"What was it sayin'?"

"Reckon I oughtn't to say on account it mighta been sayin' some things you ain't thought of yet."

"Like what?"

"Don't matter, Frankie. You listen ta me now. A feller shouldn't hafta get his ear blowed off b'fore his own head grows quiet enough, he starts listenin' to his Maker.''

"God ain't said nothin' to me. I'd know if He had." Frankie's tone had turned argumentative.

Energy spent, Ike issued a warning: "If ya go on takin' horses that don't belong to you, you ain't going to the fair, Frankie. You're gonna be locked up in Sheriff Conklin's jail.''

Frankie was quiet so long, Ike lay back and rested his eyes. The chills were passing. He was hot now and wracked with fever pains. He needed the quinine. Maybe Frankie would fetch it for him once he got over feelin' sore. And the rain stopped. Growing drowsy, Ike closed his eyes and listened for the rain to let up.

But when Ike awoke again, it was daylight. The fire was out, the sun was shining, and Frankie was gone. He lay chilled in his own sweat, praying it was over but knowing it was not.

The train tracks, the creek, and the road—that was all that stood between him and the quinine. He struggled to his feet and made it to the door without falling. But pain and exhaustion distorted the world outside. Ike held his head in his hands to stop the spinning and stepped into a blurred green wilderness. By the time he reached the bridge, he had forgotten where he was going and the purpose of the journey.

He was lost in a feverish, pain-filled haze when dimly he saw the cool, gurgling water below and wondered if he could reach it in time to put out the flames.

20

Libby huddled with Maddie in Angus's buggy as the wind and rain and Angus's buggy whip spurred the horse on. Once inside, she shook the rain off her garments and made a light.

"I'll make some tea," Libby said and excused herself to do so, while Maddie, with Angus at her side, collapsed onto a fainting couch in the parlor.

Davie was sleeping soundly in the little room just off the kitchen. Normally, Father would be sleeping there, too, but he wouldn't be coming home from the wake until morning. Libby closed Davie's door, drew hot water off the stove reservoir, and put tea leaves to brewing. Suspecting Maddie hadn't eaten since their picnic at noon, she fixed a light snack and added some cookies to the tea tray.

Libby returned to the parlor to find Maddie growing calmer as Angus offered an alternative plan. It, too, smacked of secrecy, but it was far less complicated than shipping Daniels' body back to Indiana in the dead of night.

"Why not bury him out at the Brock Cemetery northeast of town?" he was saying. "It's isolated and rarely used anymore."

The teaspoons clattered as Libby set down the tray. Maddie, deep in thought, seemed not to notice. At length, she nodded.

"All right, Angus. But I want it done tomorrow."

"I don't know if the details can be worked out that soon. A grave will have to be dug. A casket built. But I'll ask," he added.

"Tomorrow afternoon at the very latest," said Maddie, fresh clouds surfacing in her demeanor. "I don't want a funeral either. Just a burial."

"Maddie," said Angus, his tone gently reproving, "that isn't decent."

"Neither was Damon," she said coldly. "No funeral, no obituary in the

paper. No stone either. And I don't want Damon's identity revealed to anyone. Be sure to caution Mr. Lamb to keep his mouth shut. I won't have this
getting all over town.''

"You're forgetting the death certificate," reminded Angus.

"I told you, Dr. Harding wrote his name as John Robinson.''

"That information is a matter of public record, Maddie. It has to be filed
at the courthouse.''

"What difference does it make? Damon wasn't known in Edgewood anyway," argued Maddie.

"That isn't the point. I won't ask Uncle Melville to do something uneth-
ical.''

"All right, all right. Do what you have to do, but do it discreetly, Angus.
Swear him to secrecy.''

"He's a doctor, Maddie. He knows how to keep a confidence.''

"Very well then," said Maddie. "No one will be any the wiser.''

If Angus had reservations, he kept them to himself. He drank his tea
quickly and departed to work out the details of Damon Daniels's burial.

He had just gone when Abigail opened the door to her bedchamber. Elbows
bent, hands bracing her back, her night shift draping the outthrust mound of
her belly, she regarded them in owlish silence.

Maddie glanced at her and away.

Hoping to avoid an explanation, Libby said hastily, "We woke you, didn't
we? I'm sorry, Abigail. We'll keep our voices down.''

Libby was about to suggest that Abigail go on back to bed when she heard
a knock at the door. They didn't normally lock doors at night, but with Father
gone, she had turned the key in the lock. Thinking it must be him coming
home earlier than he'd expected, Libby went to let him in. But it was Naomi
standing there on the rain-swept porch.

"Naomi!" Libby swung the door wide and urged her inside.

Naomi stamped her feet on the rug. "I ain't staying, Lib. I saw yer light
and thought maybe Frankie was here.''

"Frankie? You mean he hasn't come back?" Guilt-stricken at her worried
expression, Libby glanced back over her shoulder to see Maddie looking on
and Abigail standing in the dark doorway of the bedchamber beyond the
parlor. Lowering her voice, she explained how she'd questioned Frankie and
why and that he'd grown angry and run off into the night.

"So that's what brung ya over earlier. The windows was open, and I heard
ya talkin' to Frankie, but I couldn't make out what you was sayin'.'' Naomi
leaned her dripping umbrella against the lampstand. "When I went out to
check on him, and he weren't there, I got ta thinkin' maybe ya might know
where he got off to.''

"I'm sorry, Naomi, I'm afraid I don't. But let me grab a shawl, and I'll come help you look."

"Naw, there ain't no need in that. He'll come home when he's ready, I reckon." Peering beyond Libby, Naomi assessed Maddie's bedraggled state and frowned. "Yer lookin' poorly, Maddie. Somethin' wrong?

"It's kind of personal," Libby began.

But Maddie cut her short. "Oh, what's the use! If I can't trust my sisters, who can I trust? Come on in, Naomi. Sit down and I'll explain. You too, Abigail."

Libby saw Maddie's hand tremble as she raked it through her disheveled hair, but her voice was steady as she entrusted to them an abbreviated account of all that had transpired since noon when they had picnicked together. When she fell silent, Abigail didn't say a word, but Naomi urged Maddie to tell her mother the truth.

"Angus said the same thing. Libby, too, but I'm not sure I can."

"Sheddin' light on our dark corners ain't never easy," said Naomi. She clutched her work-hardened hands in her lap. "But I learned the hard way that sooner's better than later. Take me and Decatur. He knowed I was carryin' another man's child when he married me. Bedeviled me for years to tell him who it was, but I wouldn't."

"It wasn't any of his business," said Maddie, a spark of her usual spirit showing.

"Decatur didn't see it that way."

The rain dripped off the eaves outside and a cricket chirped from some hidden corner as Naomi lifted her eyes to Abigail. "All the while we was at odds on the subject, he was storin' up anger, and I was storin' up shame."

Discomfited by Naomi's steady gaze, Abigail ducked her head. But she remained in the doorway, arms crossed high over her chest. She gripped her upper arms so tightly her knuckles gleamed white in the flickering lamplight.

"When he finally learned the truth, it was awful fer both of us," Naomi continued quietly. "I come ta wish I'd told him the first time he asked b'fore we ever was wed."

Maddie looked doubtful but said nothing.

Abigail's hands whispered against the worn fabric of her night shift as she chafed her upper arms. It wasn't cold, yet she was shivering.

Naomi rose from her chair and went to her. "Ya've caught a draft sittin' thar by that window. Come on now, and I'll help ya off ta bed."

A moment later, Libby heard the rustle of the straw tick as Abigail stretched out on the bed. Heard Naomi's soothing voice, saying, "Ya rest now, Abigail. That young'un's goin' to make a journey one of these days soon, and ye're goin' ta need yer strength. Ain't no time to be takin' a cold."

Arrested by the sound of Abigail's hoarse whisper, Libby paused in clearing away the tea tray.

"The baby?" she heard Naomi reply. "Ya mean Frankie? Oh my, no, Abigail. Not for anything. Not even on his pesky days."

A moment later, Naomi crept out of the bedchamber and closed the door behind her. She thanked Libby for the tea and started for the door, then paused a moment in parting.

"We got plenty of room up over the store, Miss Maddie, if ya was to find livin' in town more to yer likin'."

Maddie's eyes misted as she assessed the offer, nodded, and thanked her. Naomi reached for her umbrella and let herself out.

Libby followed to ask, "What was it Abigail wanted to know?"

"She asked was I ever sorry 'bout keepin' Frankie."

"Good faith!" exclaimed Libby. "She really asked you that?"

"I reckon she's gettin' cold feet about this motherin' business," said Naomi. "Facin' the pain that lies ahead. Thinkin' what if he grows up ornery and teases his sister and sasses his mama and runs off on a stormy night, leavin' her to worry."

Was that what was worrying Abigail? The weight of responsibility for another human being? "Is that all?" asked Libby.

With a downcast glance, Naomi said, "Not railly." Shifting uncomfortably, she said, "She wanted to know, did I ever think he'd o' been better off if I *had* give him up."

Libby couldn't bring herself to ask what her response had been. Naomi strode out into the rain, shoulders hunched against the damp chill.

Libby shivered and stepped back inside and invited Maddie to stay the night rather than to venture back out in the weather. Exhausted, Maddie accepted. She borrowed a night shift and tiptoed into the room she was to share with Abigail, leaving Libby to try and get comfortable on the fainting couch in the parlor.

She awoke at dawn to a painful crick in her neck and the sound of Father coming in the front door.

The blended scents of overripe bananas, sweeping compound, and oiled leather hit Libby in the face as she let herself in the front door of Willie Blue's the next morning a little after eight. Father and Billy were on the other side of the counter, sorting mail. Major Minor, Captain Boyd, Mr. Lamb, and Teddy Baker were gathered around the cold stove. Uncle Willie's old dog Sugar was resting his head on Teddy's boots while Naomi, a few yards away, was stacking cans on a shelf. Limbs aching, eyes gritty from lack of sleep, Libby yawned and greeted them all and stooped to pat the old dog's head.

Teddy fingered the brass handle on the coffee wheel. The beagle wagged her tail in greeting.

"Fine morning, Miss Willie. Rain has washed everything clean." Captain Boyd, wearing his new eyeglasses, came to his feet, touched his fingers to his hat in his usual salute, and smiled.

Mr. Lamb and Major Minor went back to wrangling over a checkerboard.

Libby took off her hat, whisked loose hair over her shoulders, exchanged a glance with Naomi, and called a general greeting to the rest of them.

"Thought yer girl gave up stamp lickin', Thomas, and danged if she ain't back again," called Hascal Caton.

"And wantin' her pay docked, looks to me, comin' in this late," said Minor. He tipped his pocket watch to the light.

"Well now, wait a minute, boys. At least be sporting and give her a chance to think up a good excuse," said Billy. He turned from the wooden letter case on the other side of the counter and angled Libby a baiting grin.

Libby stopped the apology that leaped to her lips. Her head was dull this morning, too dull to field their teasing with her usual ease. "The boss said to take my time, isn't that right, Father?"

"Aye, lass. 'Make guid time.' Those be the verra words that fell from my lips as I was leavin' me hame and withoot a scrap of breakfast, too."

The old men chortled and shuffled their feet.

"Now that we've established that you've caught up on your beauty rest, are you here to help or are you picking out a cracker barrel to your liking?" Billy asked Libby.

Captain Boyd leaned back in the rocking chair that the community had presented to him upon his retirement earlier in the summer. "You take it from me and hold out for one of Mr. Lamb's chairs, Miss Willie. Mr. Lamb does fine work. Mighty fine work."

"Thank you, Captain." The mortician blushed with modest pleasure and paid Naomi for a keg of nails.

"I'll allow rockin' chairs is cheerier work than coffin building," ventured Minor. He shot a stream of tobacco toward the coal bucket and added, "Still and all, Mr. Lamb, I ain't too keen on ya comin' around me with a measurin' stick."

"Speakin' of measurin' sticks, hear tell that feller what died overt' Doc's is gonna take a couple extra slabs of lumber and some mighty strong nails," said Mr. Caton. He cradled his pipe and eyed Mr. Lamb.

"He's a sizable gentleman," agreed the mortician.

"Any luck locatin' next of kin?" asked Minor.

Libby's heart missed a beat. She pivoted and looked back across the counter just as Mr. Lamb swung the keg of nails up on his shoulder. He said,

"It isn't my job to identify him, just build the box and put him in the ground."

"Identify him?" said Caton. "Thought Doc already done that."

"Yes, he did, didn't he?" replied Mr. Lamb. "Good day, gentlemen."

Libby watched Mr. Caton stare after Mr. Lamb and prayed Mr. Lamb could be trusted to keep Maddie's secret.

"He actin' peculiar this mornin'?" Caton asked as the door closed behind Mr. Lamb.

Minor scratched his head. "Seemed to be an air of mystery 'bout him, sure enough."

Feet spread, forearms resting on his knees, Caton puffed on his pipe and squinted through the screen of smoke. "I tell ya, Minor, I been uneasy 'bout that Robinson feller ever since Doc fetched him to town. Guess ya know there's smallpox down in Lincoln."

"Now, Pa. Don't be startin' that," said Naomi. "Dr. Harding woulda said if the feller had somethin' ketchy."

"Then what the devil is Mr. Lamb actin' so tight-lipped about?"

"Two burials comin' up, he got no time for standin' around jawin', that's all," said Naomi.

Hascal glowered at his daughter. "Don't need no smallpox outbreak. And if I was you, gal, I'd keep them young'uns away from that there library until yer dang certain they've buried Robinson's sickness with him."

Libby stood a full minute, looking at her letter case without really seeing it. She stirred from her reverie, reached for a letter, and saw with a start that Billy had already cased her mail.

Billy ceased whistling off-key and grinned at her from the neighboring case. "Then again, I could be mistaken."

"About what?"

"You and your beauty rest. Sugar's eyes are open wider than yours, and that old dog sleeps twenty-three hours out of the day."

Chagrined, Libby swept a hand through her bangs. "I don't care what anyone says, you're a nice fellow, Billy Young." He chuckled. She smiled, and offered, "The least I can do is help you finish your casing."

"No need, I've nearly got it." He tapped a letter as he studied the names on the slots. "I brought Proctor over from Woodmancy's on my way. Thought I'd save you the trip."

Libby thanked him, bundled her mail, bought a new Memorandum book to take along with her on the mail route, and left by the back door. Naomi came out as she was stashing the mail in the buggy, an empty mail bag, and her lunch under the seat.

"Frankie show up yet?" Libby asked as she angled toward the pump to fill her water jar.

"About an hour before daylight." Naomi sighed and shook her head. "Wet clear through and asleep on his feet. I asked him about your notebook."

Libby swung around. "What did he say?"

"Says he ain't got it. Says Sophronia took it."

"Sophronia!"

"That ain't all. Frankie went out there to git it, but the little gal claimed her granny'd found it and took it away from her."

Libby whirled around, splashing water all down the skirt of her dress. *Oh, God, please! Not Mrs. Dorrance!* "Maybe Sophronia just told him that. Maybe it isn't true."

"All I know is what the boy told me."

Through her own dismal worry broke an awareness that Naomi looked worried herself. About Frankie, no doubt. "I'm sorry, Naomi. I shouldn't have come over here last night accusing Frankie. Falsely, at that. Then he takes off and worries you all night."

"Wasn't your fault."

"Yes, it was. I should have been more careful of his feelings. Where is he? I'll talk to him and apologize."

"Sleepin'. Anyways, I don't know as he needs you bein' sorry so much as he needs a switch to his backside." Dully, Naomi added, "Ain't the first time I've woke up and ketched him gone in the night. Ain't easy, havin' no man around to back me up."

Libby's thoughts skipped to the horse-borrowings. She didn't put words to it. She didn't have to. She could see the concern lining Naomi's face. But she didn't know how to reassure her, or even if it was honest to do so.

"Miss Maddie still at your house this morning?" Naomi asked.

Libby nodded. "She was stirring when I left."

"She ain't talked to her mama yet?"

"No. She was anticipating taking her husband's body back to Indiana, so she'd already told her mother some story about paying her in-laws a weekend visit."

"So Miz Dorrance ain't expectin' her home?"

"No. Not until Monday. Though I'd imagine Maddie'll go home as soon as she's fully awake. David was going up to read with Mrs. Gruben, and Abigail isn't much of a conversationalist early in the morning."

Libby rolled her head from side to side, trying to alleviate the kinks in her neck.

"You might oughta give Ike a holler whilst yer out at the grove," Naomi said. "Frankie was out there last night. Said Ike was sick."

"Sick?" Libby stopped the neck motion.

"Don't think it's got nothin' to do with the feller what died," Naomi said, as if anticipating her first fear.

"But it was Ike who had first contact with him. You don't suppose he *did* have something contractible?"

Naomi shot her a warning glance. "Ain't no point in givin' Pa somethin' more to put in his pipe—he been real touchy 'bout disease all his life. Lost his family to somethin' ketchy when he was a boy. Most likely, ain't nothin' serious wrong with Ike 'cept he pushes hisself too hard. Just thought it wouldn't hurt if you was to give him a holler, see if he needed Doc to come out."

"Of course," said Libby, Naomi's calm tone settling her alarm. "I'll check on him."

"He'll be at the cabin. Leastwise, that's where Frankie come across him last night."

Two hours down the mail route, Libby sat with her notebook in her lap, her head full of thoughts, yet hesitant to put pencil to paper when one journal of private reflections had fallen into Mrs. Dorrance's hands.

What am I going to do about that, Lord? The stillness was broken only by the rustle of grasshoppers in the roadside ditch, birds twittering in the trees, and Proctor's plodding steps. "I should just march up to her and tell her it's mine and ask her to hand it over," she said aloud.

Keep her eyes open and maybe she'd get the chance. Maddie had mentioned that her mother and some other ladies from the Women's Temperance Union had plans today to visit Skiff's Store to check out their long-held suspicion that he was actively involved in the moonshine trade. Libby could only hope that Mrs. Dorrance's preoccupation with plans for the temperance outing had kept her too busy to peruse her journal. She shifted on the seat, mortified at the thought of her private thoughts becoming public knowledge.

Body aching from too little sleep, she noted that Proctor wasn't stirring so well either. "Giddy-up there. You'd think you were towing a barge," she chided as the white horse dragged around a muddy tree-lined turn. He picked up his pace and drew her across the covered bridge and on past Skiff's Store. There was no sign of activity there. Even the dogs were caught in the grips of August lethargy and didn't come out from beneath the porch to bark as she passed.

She took a sip of tepid water from her jar and fought drowsiness all the way to Naomi's woodworking shop. The green gloss of tree-filtered sunshine spilled over the leaf-littered roof. It looked as if it had stormed in earnest here. Branches were scattered about the muddy road, and the front door was standing open. The wind? But if Ike was staying here, wouldn't he have closed it?

An uneasy feeling stirred along Libby's nerve endings. She called Ike's name and got no answer. Hesitantly, she poked her head in the door. There was a blanket and muslin sheet strewn in disarray over a straw tick–covered cot, but no sign of Ike. She circled to the backyard and checked inside the leaning outbuilding. No sign of life there, either.

Must have gone back to the sirup camp. Why had he been at the cabin, anyway? Naomi hadn't said. Libby delivered mail to the boxes at the end of the lane that led to homes deep in the woods, Decatur McClure's among them. She whisked the flies off Proctor's back and was under way again. As they rattled over the Chicago and Alton railroad tracks, a growing anxiety crowded out thoughts of Mrs. Dorrance and the journal, and even of Maddie's predicament.

Ike's sirup camp was straight ahead as she came off the bridge. Pulling over, she hailed the sap house, but got no answer. Reasoning she needed to water Proctor, she climbed down, walked past Ike's mailbox, and took his only piece of mail to the door of the sap house. The door was closed, as were the storm shutters he had installed for off-season, when the place would be closed up. She knocked, waited, knocked again, and finally let herself in, calling his name. The dirt floor was dry, the air stale—as if it hadn't been aired out in days.

Where was he? Cutting oats, cutting wood, cutting hay, hunting, fishing, hoeing corn? Libby enumerated the possibilities as she trekked through the building, out the back door, and across the back lot to where the trees opened to land that Ike was farming for old Maudie Morefield. Unable to reason away her disquietude, she hiked her skirts and started to cross the fence and check the barn where he kept his team. But it was like a game of hot and cold and instinctively, she knew she was growing colder. *He was here, somewhere.* The feeling was so strong, she stopped questioning it and asked for guidance. *Where, God? Show me where.*

A bucket was upended on the stone surround of an ancient-looking well. Libby moved toward it without conscious thought, turned the crank to lower the rope, then saw that it was broken. Her hands froze as a horrifying thought occurred. If God had led her here . . . *Not in the well!* She looked down, heart in her throat. "Ike?"

She flushed as one caught in some childish vagary, yet stubbornly called his name again and when no answer came floating up, swung full circle, possibilities conjuring ghost Ikes in her head. Ike striding out of the timber. Ike climbing down off the roof, hammer in hand. Ike stacking firewood. Ike following his team across the field. None materialized. The silence was deafening. She gripped the bucket with hands gone cold on a hot summer day, patted Proctor on the shoulder just for the comfort of another breathing creature, and continued on toward the creek, bucket swinging.

The bank was steeply pitched, spilling directly into the creek twenty feet below. The well-beaten path was narrow and slick from last night's rain. Blackberry bushes obstructed Libby's view of the near shore and caught at her skirt as she began her descent. She was halfway down, allaying her nerves with a breathless, reedy song, when she saw Ike. He was floating on the water, facedown, fully clothed and motionless.

21

Ike hunkered down between blood-splattered rocks and threw off his blanket roll and haversack. When the order came, he took his cartridge belt and canteen and crawled on his stomach through the matted grass on the thick jungle floor. Out of breath, back aching like it was broken. A sound like popping corks and humming wires filled the air. He recoiled at the chug of a Mauser slug tearing into the flesh of an unseen comrade.

He heard a wood dove coo, knew it was a human imitation and that he was not dreaming, for his war dreams were always silent. The conical hat of a Spanish soldier emerged from the tangled maze of vines. He sank lower in the tall wet grass and held his breath as the tropical rains soaked him to the skin. The soldier passed so close to where he lay, Ike could see the weave of his blue-and-white pin-striped trouser leg, hear his boots slush in the rain-sodden morass that had once been a road.

A small boot, yet heavy enough to make the ground shift beneath him. He felt for his rifle and realized he had left it down the valley between the blood-wet rocks. Cold sweat extinguished the flicker of fear and turned to tempered steel his determination to survive. Hearing again the sound that was his own name, he cursed the clever guile of the Spanish soldier who was disguising himself as a friend. He gripped the fellow's ankle with both hands, jerked and twisted and leaped upon the enemy even as he fell.

Libby plunged backwards into the creek, propelled by the upthrust of Ike's body. Even as her mind reeled from the shock of it, his arms were closing around her, pulling her deeper. They twisted to the bottom together in a slow, time-suspended dance of death, his feet tangled in her billowing skirt and petticoats. Hysteria racing full tilt, she swung and kicked, throwing elbows and knees, and sank her teeth into his jaw. She felt him flinch and loosen his grip. Then she twisted and was almost free when his shoulder clipped her chin. The cushion of water softened the blow, and still she tasted blood as her teeth gnashed into the soft underside of her lip. Pain shot like flaming arrows, burning straight to her screaming lungs. *Dear God, he'll drown us both!*

Stop fighting. It came upon her consciousness as clear as her own desperate prayer, yet it was a hard command to follow with the deprivation of oxygen building pressure behind her eyes, numbing her ears. Her blood surged in her veins like wind-driven flames. But the Voice was insistent. She ceased struggling, willed her body to relax until every muscle was limp. Abruptly, Ike's hold loosened.

Libby rolled free of him in the water, pushed off the sandy bottom, and, lungs bursting, arched up out of the brink to see her hat bobbing downstream and a stranger in Ike Galloway's skin surfacing beside her.

There was no sign of recognition in his feverish gaze. In a vertigo of coughing and sputtering and hoarse sucking of air, she stumbled backwards and went down again and came up to find him standing chest deep in the water between her and the shore. Shrinking from the hands he stretched toward her, she trod backwards in the water, crying, "Stop it, Ike. It's Libby! Would you stop it! I'm here to help!"

He stared at her, his gaze bright and glassy. Slowly, his hand drifted across his flushed face. He covered his eyes, kneaded them as a dreamer awakening to clear his head of distortions, and probed his scarred ear. Time hung suspended as water trailed from his hair, catching on his lashes, dripping off his chin.

Delirious. Peering at her from some nether world. Bewildered. Wary. At length, with the dazed uncertainty of a half-lucid moment, he mumbled, "Maddie?"

Close enough. Libby bobbed her head and let her breath go, for it was clear from the look of horror that came over his face that his feverish mind brushed close enough to reality to recoil at what had nearly happened. But in the next heartbeat, his attention had wandered. He threaded his fingers through the water and watched with childlike fascination the ripples it made, then turned his eyes to the green canopy overhead, staring as if he had never seen trees before.

Her compassion stirred, Libby eased up so as not to startle him, took the arm that had held her under only moments ago, and led him to the shore, saying, "Let's get out of here."

There was no beach, just the water cutting into the bank and the steep incline to the road above. Libby dragged herself out of the creek and half led, half pulled Ike out behind her. He was wilting before her eyes. He collapsed on his back, unmindful of the weeds and leaves and sticks that littered the steeply inclined bank beneath him.

Winded, exhausted, Libby rested beside him, staring at patches of blue between the leaves and waiting for the strength to flow back into her trembling limbs. After a moment, she sat up.

"Ike?" Her gaze skipped over his limp form. His eyes were closed, his lips parted. His head lolled to one side. Alarm flickered. Her hands fell away from her tangled hair. "Ike?"

Still, he didn't stir. Her heart constricting, Libby pressed her ear to his chest. The drumming fingers of panic slowed, for his breathing was unobstructed, his heart beat strongly. But his skin was so flushed, so hot. Since the death of her mother, she had been nurse to the family and was no stranger to burning brows. But never had she felt human flesh this hot. And his lips! Blistered, swollen. His whole *face* was swollen. *Like Robinson's.*

Was he dying? Fear renewed its drumbeat. Fiercely, she prayed. He wouldn't die. He wouldn't! She'd get help. But she couldn't leave him this close to the water.

Locking her hands under his arms, Libby pulled him a few feet up the steep bank, eased him down and sank to the ground to rest her aching arms and legs. She looked over her shoulder and measured the distance to the top, where the timber skirted the road, and, in so doing, lost her grip on him. His slack form began to slide.

Libby scrabbled after him, whimpering as a briar snagged his scarred ear and tangled in his hair. She grabbed his shirt in an effort to stop his slide. His feet were in the water by the time he came to a rest. Libby moved backwards up the incline, on her bottom, crablike, dragging him behind her. She strained and pulled, then rested, his head and shoulders propped against her bent knees, then strained and pulled and rested again without releasing her hold. Her muscles shrieked. Tears gathered in her throat and burned behind her eyes. She couldn't do it. Not without help. *Send help. Somebody. Anybody.*

The prayer was scarcely thought-borne when Libby heard the steady gait of an oncoming team on the road above. "Help me!" Clinging to Ike so as not to lose hard-won ground, she came to a half-standing position and still couldn't see the road or who was passing. Panicking, she cried all the louder for help.

The sound of slowing hooves and the babble of voices flowed over her in sweet relief. Falling back, she sat down again, her skirt draped over her spread knees like a rain-drenched tent. She kept her forearms locked beneath Ike's arms, bracing him against her shins. Creek water trickled down her face, mingling with sweat, burning her eyes and dripping off her chin. Her calves and shoulders ached. Her ankle throbbed. Her lip tasted of blood. Heedless of Ike's head half-buried in her ruined skirt, she twisted around to see feathered hats and bejeweled white dresses and astounded faces peering down at her from above. Mrs. Dorrance, Paulette Harding, and Mrs. Lamb. Libby's heart took an eternal slide to rock bottom.

Anybody. God had taken her at her word. Her damp, bedraggled hair curtained Ike's face as she dropped her head between her knees and wondered if drowning might not have been more merciful after all.

22

If Libby had ever entertained any doubts as to who was the commander in chief of the Women's Temperance Union, Mrs. Dorrance swiftly dispelled them. Ascertaining little more than Ike's need for medical attention, she postponed the investigative visit to Skiff's Store, then dispatched Mrs. Lamb to return to town for the doctor and Paulette Harding to the nearest neighbor for help hauling Ike up the bank.

"Release your hold on the fellow and come up here, Miss Watson," said Mrs. Dorrance, as Mrs. Lamb sped toward town and Paulette, in Libby's mail cart, rattled up the road and over the bridge.

"I can't. He'll slide into the water," said Libby.

"I'll come down."

Wishing she'd stay where she was, Libby tried to discourage her. "You'd better not. The path is slick and treacherous."

But Mrs. Dorrance had made up her mind. Using her folded umbrella as a walking stick, she steadied herself with the help of saplings that grew along the steep path and descended with the determination of a woman on a mission. Feet staggered on the sharp incline, she peered down at Ike's inert form. "It would seem your penchant for swimming with the ladies has landed you in trouble, Mr. Galloway."

"He can't hear you. He's lost consciousness and we weren't swimming," said Libby, offended in spite of her exhaustion. "If you would help me get him over to that tree . . ."

Mrs. Dorrance's dark gaze flitted over Libby's bedraggled form. There was no softening in her expression, just a tight-lipped acceptance of duty. Each taking one arm, they eased Ike off the path and laid him at the foot of a tree, the trunk of which would stop him, should he start to slip down the incline.

Libby sat between Ike and the tree, her quivering legs tucked under her. He looked terrible. She felt his forehead. Put fingers to the pulse that quivered at his temples. Lifted his translucent eyelids and saw no flicker of consciousness. She glanced toward the rise where the road ran. "If I thought we could get him the rest of the way up the bank . . ."

"We can't. He'll come to no harm where he is until help arrives."

Mrs. Dorrance's dispassionate reply, practical though it was, brought the sting of unbidden tears to Libby's eyes. Laying her sudden vulnerability at the doorstep of physical exhaustion, Libby tucked in her chin and tried to make Ike comfortable as she blinked her eyes dry.

Mrs. Dorrance upended the bucket Libby had abandoned on her skid down the path to Ike's aid and her own near-destruction. She sank one rim of the bucket into the soft earth to make it level for sitting, dusted it with a plain white handkerchief, and sat down with her folded umbrella across her knees. "While we're waiting, Miss Watson, you can tell me what happened here."

Libby beckoned toward the creek where a partially submerged log was anchored to the creek bank by jutting limbs. From this vantage point, it was hard to see that limbs were connected to the log. She said, "Ike was in the water on the log there, facedown. When I came down the path, I couldn't see the log. I thought he had . . . he had . . ."

"Drowned?" Mrs. Dorrance unfurled her umbrella and punctuated the word with a crisp snap of the mechanism which locked it into the upright position.

Mutely, Libby nodded.

"And then what?"

"Once I reached the water, I realized he was lying on a log. But he didn't stir, not even when I called to him. So I stepped out on the log and . . ."

"Fell in?"

"Something like that, yes," said Libby, uncertain why she felt as if she were picking her way barefooted along a path of broken glass. Unnerved by the skepticism in Mrs. Dorrance's gaze, she skipped the details. "I was afraid to leave him to go for help for fear he'd slide back into the water."

"Do you usually water your horse here, Miss Watson?"

Puzzled by the seemingly unrelated question, Libby shook her head.

"Then please explain to me why you chose to today when there must be easier access any number of places along your route."

"Naomi told me Mr. Galloway was ill. She asked me to see if he needed a doctor."

"So you *did* seek him out?

Guardedly, she said, "Yes, I suppose I did."

"Do you think that wise?"

Libby resented being taken to task for something that was both innocent and unavoidable. "I was only trying to check on Mr. Galloway and see if he needed a doctor," she reiterated.

"A word to a neighbor and someone else would have done it," reasoned Mrs. Dorrance.

The woman was so unyielding, so iron-fisted! Just stubborn enough not to be governed by her critical eye, Libby turned her attention back to Ike, bathing his flushed face with her dripping skirt tail. In so doing, she noticed the teeth marks she'd left on his jaw. Bruising marks. She'd broken the skin. She spoke to him, prodded him gently, trying to rouse him, all without success.

Meanwhile, Mrs. Dorrance refused to be ignored. She rephrased her question. "Couldn't a neighbor have checked on him, Miss Watson?"

"The thought didn't occur to me."

"I guessed as much." She passed Libby her umbrella. "Here, shade his face if you must, but quit fluttering over him and listen to me. My granddaughter came home from the library with your journal yesterday."

Libby's heart crowded up her throat. She swung around to look Mrs. Dorrance full in the face as she continued without pause.

"I don't know how it got on the shelf, but I'm assuming it was in error. It wasn't my intention to pry, rather, as the temporary guardian of Sophronia, to be diligent about what she was reading, particularly as it was an unpublished work. You show promise as a writer, Miss Watson. Though I did not think your writings were age-appropriate for Sophronia."

Libby could only stare. *Did she really think she had put her journal on the shelf for public reading? How obtuse could she be?* "Those were private thoughts, Mrs. Dorrance. Sophronia took the book from my home, not from the library. Without my knowledge. I've been worried over what became of it."

"I'm sorry. I didn't realize she was unauthorized to take it."

Unwilling to have it skimmed over so lightly, Libby said, "I want it back right away."

"Of course. Sophronia will be dealt with appropriately."

Libby ran her tongue along the underside of her bruised lip and forced herself to ask, "Did you read it?"

"Your name is not in it, Miss Watson. Initially, I thought it was a diary someone had donated, and that it might be of interest. In the beginning, the people mentioned were unfamiliar, so as you can understand, I read with no sense of intrusion. However, as the names and situations became those of local people, I began to feel I was invading, so I stopped reading. I had, by then, deduced you were the author."

The length of Mrs. Dorrance's explanation was in itself an admission of wrongdoing. She felt guilty and was anxious to justify her actions. Cringing at having had her personal thoughts browsed through as if they were part of *The Old Farmer's Almanac,* Libby said, "In the future, I'll be more careful."

"There's no need to be embarrassed. Frankly, Miss Watson, I was struck by your tender nature," Mrs. Dorrance went on, dealing yet another surprise. "You show promise, not only as a writer, but as a woman of fine moral character. I'd hate to see that compromised by Mr. Galloway."

"Compromised?" sputtered Libby, heat sweeping up her neck. "Mrs. Dorrance, I assure you, you have nothing to worry about there!"

Unmoved, Mrs. Dorrance said, "If my bluntness offends you, then be advised, I have never learned the art of cushioning hard truths within gentle phrases. Nor am I blind. You're wet and disheveled. Your lip is bruised and unless I'm mistaken, you've left the mark of your teeth in Mr. Galloway's jaw. There is more to this story than you are telling me, and my instinct is that you are protecting Mr. Galloway."

Incredulous, Libby said, "Can't you see that he is gravely ill? Have you looked at him? Touch his face! See how hot he is!"

Mrs. Dorrance declined and waited, her silence an indication that Libby's denial had in no way diminished her suspicion.

"What happened is precisely what I told you. What do you think happened?" The moment she asked, she wanted to call the words back, for she had given Mrs. Dorrance the worst sort of opening, an opening she promptly pressed.

"It looks to me as if he tried to take advantage of your good intentions, Miss Watson. And that you fought his advances. But what I don't understand is why you would protect him."

Deeply offended, Libby leaped to her feet. "He was delirious, Mrs. Dorrance. He thought I intended him harm and he fought. Yes, *fought.* But I assure you it was the fever. He meant me no harm."

Unmoved, Mrs. Dorrance said, "How swiftly you come to his defense."

"That's because he hasn't done anything wrong!"

"Then you aren't attracted to him on some level?"

"You've read my journal. You know my affection for Angus. You saw his name there repeatedly, didn't you?"

"Miss Watson . . ."

"Didn't you? Answer me!" demanded Libby, so enraged that black spots danced before her eyes.

"Yes, I saw his name."

"And did you see Mr. Galloway's?"

"No. But then, as I said, I didn't read the entire journal."

"You didn't see it because it isn't there," Libby broke in. "What does that tell you?"

"I don't know, Miss Watson. Perhaps that you, like Maddie, hide even from yourself the matters closest to your heart."

"That is preposterous!"

The sweet, melodic song of a cardinal from a nearby tree shamed Libby for her shrillness. Ike stirred and opened fever-clouded eyes. She pressed her fingers to her mouth, her heart constricting.

Mrs. Dorrance stood up and brushed off her skirt. "It sounds as if help has arrived."

Libby swung around and looked up to the road. It was Decatur McClure arriving in her mail buggy, driven by Paulette Harding. Libby would never have expected to be glad to see *him,* but in that moment he seemed less malevolent than Mrs. Dorrance.

"He's burning up," Libby told McClure, as he came down the bank on long, skidding strides.

He hunkered down beside Ike and laid a hand on his head. "Malaria, I'm guessin'."

"Malaria?" Libby's hand flew to her throat. "Are you sure?"

"Ain't the first time he's had it." McClure grunted as he came up again, Ike's body draped over his shoulder. "I'll take him to my place and look after him till he's on his feet again."

Mrs. Dorrance forgotten, Libby scrambled up the bank after the tall, raw-boned McClure. "Shouldn't he go to Dr. Harding's?"

"From what Miz Harding said, Doc's on his way. Once Ike gits some medicine in him, 'bout all there is for it is time and rest," replied McClure.

Having crested the bank, he folded Ike's inert body into Libby's mail buggy. Paulette Harding helped ease Ike onto the seat, then climbed out. Decatur took the lines and called back, "You can ride along or you can wait here for Doc."

"We'll wait," Mrs. Dorrance answered.

McClure's gaze sought and held Libby's. "Which is it gonna be?"

Reluctantly, she said, "Go ahead, Mr. McClure."

The buggy rumbled away, Proctor stepping lively in response to the whip in a hand less gentle than Libby's. Paulette, her cheeks flushed from the rapid-fire chain of events, angled Libby a long look, but asked no questions.

"There's a bench in front of Mr. Galloway's sirup shed," Paulette said. "Let's cross the road and sit down while we wait for Melville." With a wry grimace, she added, "I have a notion he may be cross with me. I didn't tell him about our excursion."

"I'm surprised at you, Paulette," chided Mrs. Dorrance with her usual candor. "Why would you fail to be honest with him? He's a reasonable man.

He wouldn't have forbidden you, surely." She turned and called back, "Come along, Miss Watson. You can tidy up a bit while we wait."

Libby scarcely heard her, for her shrill denial was echoing in her head again. *That is preposterous!* Preposterous or not, she had never felt such a wrenching as when Ike's eyes opened and, for one lucid moment, bored into her soul. It was as if someone had turned her inside out, exposing her heart to her own eyes.

"Elizabeth." Mrs. Dorrance employed her given name. "Are you coming?"

How could the woman be so blind about so much where human nature was concerned, and yet be right about this? *Dear God, how could I have fallen in love with the wrong man?*

Mrs. Dorrance and Paulette, so elegantly attired, sat beneath the shade of Ike's sap house and watched the road. Libby, in her muddy clothing, could endure the heat, the flies, the mosquitoes, even the obligatory answers to Paulette's anxious questions. It was the wait itself that was so difficult to tolerate, for while she had never nursed anyone through malaria, she knew it was not a disease to be taken lightly.

Dr. Harding finally arrived. Libby and Paulette climbed into the buggy with him, but Mrs. Dorrance opted to wait where she was. On the ride to Decatur McClure's home, Dr. Harding mentioned that most of the men who had served in the Spanish American War had caught malaria, Ike being no exception.

"Then he's in no danger?" asked Paulette.

"I can't say that until I've seen him," replied her husband. "Now, what is this about you and Mrs. Dorrance and Mrs. Lamb calling at Skiff's Store?"

Paulette averted her gaze. "I was going to tell you about it this evening."

"Tell me now," he urged. When Paulette had done so, he shook his head. "It sounds to me as if Ike's misfortune saved your hide. Skiff would have hauled out that old peashooter of his and picked the feathers right off your hat."

"But Mrs. Dorrance said . . ."

"Turned his dogs on you, too."

". . . it was our civic duty to . . ."

"To what? Get yourself shot?" Patience taxed, the doctor said, "Watch yourself, Paulette, or I'm going to forbid you to keep company with Madeline Dorrance."

Paulette bore the chastisement in a docile silence. After a moment, she peered at her husband from beneath a fringe of lashes, and said in a small voice, "Would you, Melville? To be honest, that woman scares me to death."

Libby was nearly convinced of Paulette's sincerity when Paulette sent her a surreptitious grin. The doctor, unaware he was being hoodwinked, patted his wife's knee, and said, "Very well, then. I guess you've learned your lesson." By the time they reached Decatur McClure's boxcar home in the woods, the couple was chatting amicably.

Dr. Harding's assumption that Libby was anxious to retrieve her buggy and return to town dictated the only reasonable course of action. It would be suspect if she, in wet rags and tangled hair, were to linger for some word of Ike's condition.

Taking his black medical bag from beneath the seat, Harding said to his wife, "Miss Watson's horse looks pretty worn. Why don't you wait and ride back to town with me?"

"You'll take Mrs. Dorrance?" Paulette asked Libby as she climbed into her own buggy. "She could go with us, but Melville seems to think she's a bad influence," she added, arching her husband a coy glance.

Her husband gave no sign of having heard her as he strode to the door of McClure's boxcar home. Decatur opened the door for the doctor, then closed it behind him without a glance in Libby's direction. Hope for some small words concerning Ike faded. Praying for his safekeeping, she shook the lines over Proctor's back and turned the buggy around.

It was a long ride back to Edgewood, made longer by a short detour to the Dorrance dairy farm. White-faced cows and draft horses mingled in roll-ing green pastures skirting the two-story farmhouse. The house was painted white, as were the outbuildings and fences, and even the trim on the stone dairy barns. A grape arbor grew along a garden bordered in flowers and a child's rope swing swayed from the limb of a stately oak tree just yards from the mounting block where Libby stopped the buggy.

Mrs. Dorrance stepped onto the concrete mounting block. She shook the folds from her skirt and the kinks from her limbs before descending to the ground. Peering back at Libby from her sharp black eyes, she invited, "If you'd like to come inside, I'll get your journal."

"I'll wait here," said Libby stiffly.

Mrs. Dorrance was not long in returning. She passed Libby the notebook. "I spoke to Maddie this morning shortly before setting out for the grove. She tells me she spent the night at your house."

"That's right," said Libby, clutching her Memorandum book in one hand and the lines in the other.

"I suppose she also told you it was her husband who died in Dr. Harding's office yesterday?"

"Yes," said Libby.

"She deceived me for months, but she was candid with you." Mrs. Dorrance sighed, then stiffened her spine. "She's having him buried this afternoon. A secretive affair."

"What is to be gained by making it public knowledge?" Libby countered.

"Honesty is at issue here, Miss Watson. I cannot condone what Maddie has done. Nor will I lie for her."

"Did she ask you to?"

Mrs. Dorrance's mouth thinned. "Omissions are lies, too. Nor is it right that she should compromise the honesty of other people, asking them to keep her secret. Mr. Lamb. Dr. Harding. Angus. You and your father."

But not her own mother. Libby almost felt sorry for Mrs. Dorrance. She drew such bold lines in the dirt, making life one long confrontation. Even when she was right, she stirred a passive resistance in others, making adversaries of some who in their hearts might sympathize had she been less rigid.

"I can't speak for the others, but I don't mind keeping silent," said Libby. "From what I understand, life with Mr. Daniels was punishing enough."

Mrs. Dorrance received her words in silence. She started toward the house, then turned back to call, "You have a devoted suitor in Angus Cearlock, Miss Watson. I'd advise you to think of him next time you feel pressed to check on Mr. Galloway's health."

Heat flooded Libby's face. She turned the buggy around, resenting the woman's heavy thumb and how free she was about where she set it. Libby escaped, but not unscathed.

23

That evening Libby's father went once more to Zerilda's to sit with Mrs. Baker. David had run up the street to return one of Mrs. Gruben's kittens. Abigail was in the kitchen. Libby was waiting in the shade of the porch when Angus came up the walk. She gave him an abbreviated account of what had happened at Old Kentucky.

"What were you doing there in the first place?" he asked.

"Delivering the mail."

"I know that," he said with studied patience. "What I don't understand is what you were doing at the creek."

She hesitated, for just as words could not capture the sun shimmering on shocked wheat or a storm breaking across the prairie without diminishing its splendor, so too did words by their limiting nature reduce her entreaty and God's answer. The swing creaked as she sat down.

Angus sat down beside her. At her silence, he asked, "Did you spot him from the road?"

"No. I had a bucket and was on my way to get Proctor a drink when I saw him."

Her nerves leaped as Angus laid his fingertips along her jaw and turned her face his way. His frown darkened. "What happened to your lip?"

Libby flushed and freed her chin without answering.

"Libby?" he prompted.

"I told you he was out of his head with fever. I had trouble getting him out of the water."

"He hit you?" Angus sprang out of the swing.

"No, he didn't hit me. We collided, that's all. I wish you'd sit down and not let this evolve into a quarrel."

"Can I help it if I don't like the picture I'm getting?" he countered.

"So what was I supposed to do—let him drown?"

Angus growled something inaudible. He shoved his hands into his pockets and strode to the other end of the porch. Libby studied her clenched hands. How she had dreaded this conversation, for she could no longer say that her feelings for Ike were those of simple friendship. She didn't want to hurt Angus or injure his pride. *Lord, I feel guilty! Why do I feel so guilty?*

Regretting the impatience shading her last words, Libby drew a shallow breath. "Have you talked to Maddie today?"

"Yes, this morning and again this afternoon. She was anxious about the details concerning Daniels's burial."

"How is she handling it today?"

"She's firmly in control again. Almost, anyway," he amended. "At the last minute, Mr. Lamb convinced her it was indecent not to have a few words and a prayer said over that scoundrel husband of hers. She finally consented to Pastor Shaw coming along, widening the circle of her confidants."

"Maddie attended the burial?"

"Yes, I went along with her. She asked me to."

"It's kind of you to help her," said Libby, wondering why he thought an excuse was needed. "From what I've seen, she isn't getting much emotional support from Mrs. Dorrance."

"No."

Was he thinking about last night? Wishing she hadn't seen him comforting Maddie? Feeling it put him at a disadvantage? Libby touched her toes to the porch floor, put the swing into motion, and sifted through snatches of last night's conversation between Angus and Maddie. Certain phrases begged for clarification, for they were connected with that long-ago night Maddie had spent with Ike at the lake.

Mrs. Dorrance's mistrust of Ike clearly dated back to that incident. *Penchant for swimming with the ladies,* she'd said. *Wouldn't like to see your moral character compromised.* As he had compromised Maddie's. That's what Mrs. Dorrance was intimating, and by all accounts, he had.

It had been reckless of him; reckless of Maddie, too. And though there had never been any hint of impropriety in Ike's behavior toward Libby, if the accounts were accurate, she needed to be realistic about his past and Maddie's part in it. Just because he had turned her own head and her heart had followed didn't mean it was prudent.

He had called her by Maddie's name. Did he entertain feelings for Maddie even yet? Was he no blessing at all, rather a temptation in Libby's path? *Is that what this feeling is, Lord? A temptation I ought to resist?*

The more Libby pondered the question, the less certain she felt of the answer. Standing a few feet away was a wonderful man. Devoted. Ambitious. Clever. Charming. Willing to give her everything she'd ever wanted, including the education she longed for. A man of distinction. Would she let him go for a fellow of questionable principles?

Libby backed away from the thought, for as hard as she tried to be objective, she couldn't make the term "unprincipled" fit what she beheld in Ike's character. His awareness of his Maker showed in the works of his hand, in his manner toward friends and neighbors, even in his hospitality to a sick stranger. Were the accounts accurate? Or had the stories grown, as gossip often did?

Having gathered from last night's conversation between Angus and Maddie that Angus had secondhand knowledge of the incident at the lake, she wondered if she dared ask him what he knew of that night. As she was debating the wisdom of it, Angus sat down in the swing again. Two of David would have fit between them. A comfortable distance, and not just because of the heat. Libby summoned her courage. "If I were to ask you something, would you try not to think too poorly of me?"

Angus emerged from his reverie to smile at her earnestness, his first smile since he'd mounted the porch. "I could never think poorly of you, Libby. What is it you want to know?"

"Last night, when you and Maddie were talking, I heard her lament something that happened at the lake when she was younger. A tryst, I guess you would call it."

Angus's smile vanished. "Libby, please don't ask me about that. I'm not at liberty to discuss it."

Libby folded her hands in her lap, regretting having asked, for clearly, he was uncomfortable. Indeed, only a moment or two passed when Angus remembered paperwork waiting at his office. With a brief apology, he said he had best go.

Libby tensed in expectation as he came to his feet and bid her good night, for he had become increasingly bold about touching her hand and other displays of affection. But he took his leave without touching her. It eased her tattered conscience, though she had yet to identify what she had to feel guilty over. He had declared himself to her, but she had made him no promises. Nor had her heart deliberately strayed.

Ike, Ike, what have you done to me? All day, he'd been in her thoughts. Tangled, worried, fretful thoughts. Wanting reprieve, Libby walked up the street to collect David from the Grubens' yard.

Mr. Gruben's white shirt stood out in the gathering darkness as he labored with a shovel at the south side of the house. Mrs. Gruben called to Libby. "We're digging resurrection lilies. Would you like some bulbs, Libby?"

Remembering the lovely pale pink blooms that took on a hint of blue after they reached their zenith, Libby accepted.

"I'll dig them. Can I, Mr. Gruben?" asked David.

"May I," Libby corrected.

"I asked first," said David, reaching for the shovel.

Mr. Gruben grinned and relinquished the shovel into Davie's hands. He wiped his brow and beckoned for Libby to follow him into the shade of a nearby tree while his wife oversaw David's digging. He lit a cigar, and asked, "How's the obituary on Mrs. Steadman coming along?"

"I plan to write it this evening," said Libby. "I've got all the information."

"Good. While you're at it, better do something on that Robinson fellow."

Libby's pulse quickened. "Do we know enough of him to piece something together?"

"Only what he told Ike the night he showed up at his door. He never regained consciousness to talk to Doc."

Relieved to find nothing in his expression to indicate he suspected there was more to the Robinson story than that of a stranger dying in Edgewood, Libby promised, "I'll turn it in on Monday."

"A paragraph is sufficient. Hopefully, people will weigh the facts against Hascal Caton's prophecy of a dire epidemic, the old troubler."

Mr. Gruben went on to mention the upcoming community dinner, to be held by the New Hope Ladies Aid Society between afternoon and evening performances of the circus. Advising her to see Mrs. Bee for further details, he stepped back up to the hole and retrieved the shovel from David.

David dropped to his knees and reached into the hole. "Wow! Look at them all."

"Bring me the whole clump," said Mrs. Gruben from her yard chair. She separated the bulbs, inadvertently sprinkling dirt over her crutches where they lay on the ground, then gave Libby a handful of bulbs. "Mr. Gruben will get you a paper to wrap them in."

"That isn't necessary, I'll put them in my apron pocket."

"You watch now, and don't let her put those in the cellar, son. You'll be eating them in your vegetable stew," teased Mr. Gruben.

"Don't you listen to him, Davie," said Mrs. Gruben. "They don't look a thing like vegetables."

David peered into Libby's pocket. "They don't look like lilies either. I guess you just can't tell what's inside the skins of things."

It felt good to smile with the Grubens at David's innocent remark. But awhile later, when the mosquitoes had driven them home and into the house, and Libby was skipping through her Memorandum book assessing the damage of its having been read by Sophronia and her grandmother, she found herself applying what David had said to people as well as growing things. Maddie. Abigail. Zerilda Payne. Decatur McClure. Madeline Dorrance. Even Ike. Like a human bouquet, God kept poking his children under her nose, as if to say, *"Take a closer look. See what's inside the skins."* After David had gone to bed and Abigail retired to the room she and Libby shared, Libby lit a lamp at the kitchen table and put pencil to paper.

On Friday past, John Robinson, a stranger to our town, lost his struggle to an illness that had subjected him to severe influenza-like symptoms over the past week. Despite Dr. Harding's and Mrs. Brignadello's conscientious care, he died at two p.m. and was laid to rest on Saturday at the Brock Cemetery northeast of town.

As her tired eyes skipped over the piece, she remembered Mrs. Dorrance's words concerning Maddie involving others in the burden of her secret. *Just the facts,* Mr. Gruben was fond of saying. This fell far short of facts as she knew them. But her conscience would have been a good deal more troubled if she had betrayed Maddie in the interest of journalistic integrity. So thinking, she turned her attention to Gram Steadman's obituary.

24

Angus escorted Libby to church the next morning. They accepted a luncheon invitation from the Brignadellos after services. Angus's parents as well as the Hardings were invited, but Paulette came alone, as Dr. Harding had driven out to the grove to check on Ike.

It was a lovely meal, the table elegantly set, the company cordial, the conversation skipping from the coming circus, to the community dinner, to political strategy, to plans for the group trip to the World's Fair, only weeks away.

"Catherine and Charlie have visited the fair six times since moving to St. Louis," said Mrs. Gentry. "She declares the whole city is captivated by it."

Mrs. Gentry dipped her fingers into the finger bowl and whisked them in the water like a little sparrow splashing in a puddle. Oblivious of the damp spots spreading on her sister's tablecloth, she darted Libby a warm smile. "I'm so glad you'll be going with us, dear. Angus, are you certain you can't come, too?"

"Now, Ida, don't distract the boy. He has an election to win and business in Springfield that week," reminded Mr. Gentry.

The door on politics standing open, the gentlemen excused themselves and went out on the porch to smoke and plot and speculate. The ladies retired to the shade of the backyard. They discussed the upcoming community dinner and their expectations for it as a money-making project for the New Hope Church building fund, exchanged regrets on the passing of Gram Steadman, then turned their thoughts once more to the fall election.

Mrs. Gentry enthused over the farm wagon Mr. Gentry had had customized for their travels. It was to conjure images of the covered wagons that had rumbled westward across Illinois half a century earlier.

"A fitting way of reminding voters that Angus is the seed of pioneer stock," Mrs. Bee chimed in with approval.

"Exactly. People need to know he represents high moral integrity," said Paulette.

Mrs. Gentry bobbed her head and fanned her perspiring face. "We're going to call it the 'gospel wagon.' "

As the afternoon wore on, Libby battled a vague sense of displacement. If it wasn't Ike slipping into her thoughts, it was Abigail and Adam. Obviously, she could discuss neither with Angus. No news, she decided, was good news where Ike was concerned. But Adam? He wrote Abigail. Why didn't he write them? Were there things he couldn't yet bear to share?

Late in the evening when both David and Abigail had gone to bed, Libby joined her father on the porch swing. She sighed, and said, "I wish Adam would write."

"He will, lass, when he's ready."

Envious of his patience, Libby unburdened herself of a secret worry that had taken root when Abigail had questioned Naomi, asking if she'd ever regretted not giving Frankie up at birth, if not for her sake, then for Frankie's.

"There could be only one reason she would ask such a question," she said.

"Abigail, I'm thinkin', is worryin' about this child's future," said Father. "I'm thinkin' she canna conceive of Adam bein' able to be a true faether to the comin' bairn."

Libby picked at the chipped paint on the arm of the swing. "You think she'll give the baby up, then?"

"I know ye've a heart for the bairn already, but it isna a matter of what ye're thinkin' or wantin'," Father said gently.

"I know that."

He smiled at her defensive tone. "Then be knowin', too, that God has lovin'ly fashioned the wee one. He isna a God of neglect."

"Father, you're dodging the question," she objected.

"Lovin'ly fashioned, Lib. Lovin'ly fashioned," he said again.

Lovingly fashioned? Despite Abigail's bad judgment, lovingly fashioned. The careless conception of this child in no way influenced God's meticulous work. Father was right. It was shortsighted to think He would take no fewer pains preparing a home for the baby than He had in the fashioning of it. Whether that home be with Adam and Abigail or elsewhere.

"Sometimes I sense Abigail's trying to find the courage to talk about it, or at least about the baby not being Adam's. But whatever it is she would say, she loses her courage and I, too, lose my courage just to tell her, *'We know, Abigail. We already know.' "*

" 'Twould be meddlesome of us to hasten her unburdenin'. No, lass, dinna force your knowledge upon her."

Wounded, Libby said, "I didn't mean in an accusing way, Father. Just so she'd feel free of that portion of worry and a little less . . . alone in her troubles."

"If she opens her heart to you, Lib, yer peacemakin' concern canna help but ease her torment. But ye canna be the mainstay of her comfort," cautioned Father wisely. "Nor can Adam. 'Tis the work of God to rescue her from the hurt and loneliness and turn her tears to joy."

Joy? *Lord, can there ever be any joy in this?*

Libby's thoughts shifted unexpectedly to Naomi. Her fractured marriage, her many hardships. The whole situation had seemed so bleak not long ago. Yet in these past months, as she leaned on God, there was sunshine in Naomi's face, the sunshine of patience and peace and hope and trust and, yes, even humor. Could joy be far behind?

"Keep prayin', lass," said Father. The swing shifted as he came to his feet and went inside, leaving her to do just that.

Libby ran the mail route again on Monday, the day of Gram Steadman's funeral. On Tuesday, as Maddie's Freethinkers Society convened for their first meeting at the library, Paulette mentioned that Ike's fever had broken.

Libby's heart lifted in gratitude for the answered prayer. Maddie, watching the door, mistook her broad smile for one of encouragement, and returned it as she waited for the arrival of the few who had promised to come.

Mrs. Bee and Naomi came a bit late. Another fifteen minutes went by, and, finally, Maddie closed the door. She joined the four of them and faced what the rest had feared all along.

"It would seem no one else is coming."

Libby exchanged an uneasy glance with Naomi.

"Perhaps Tuesday is a bad night," said Paulette, trying to ease Maddie's disappointment.

"We could try Thursdays," chimed in Mrs. Bee. "No, no. The Berry Sisters meet on Thursday, don't they?"

"Wednesday is church night. What about . . ."

Maddie waived their thinly veiled sympathies. "I appreciate your loyalty, sisters, but the truth is in Edgewood I'm more of a liability to a cause than an asset. You've proved your sisterhood just by coming. So, we can either eat cobbler, drink lemonade, and go home. Or we can eat cobbler, drink lemonade, and start a quilt."

"A quilt?" Mrs. Bee echoed.

"For Abigail's baby," said Maddie.

Libby's heart sank. While she appreciated Maddie's uncharacteristic gracious weathering of disappointment, she couldn't let the ladies go to so much work when Abigail might not even keep the baby. She was searching for a way to explain without betraying Abigail when Naomi spoke up and spared her the need.

"Yer a fine one fer makin' things happen, Miss Maddie. We got the library to show for it, so I ain't tryin' to steal my idea back or nothin' . . ." She grinned at the glances her friends exchanged, and continued. "But I'm thinkin' bigger now."

"Bigger?" echoed Maddie. Naomi's reference to her tendency to capture the ideas of others and most of the credit, too, passed right over her head.

Naomi nodded. "The thing 'bout baby quilts is the young'un's outgrow 'em long b'fore they's wore out. Lib had a clever idea for a full-sized quilt that would be a piece of Edgewood that Abigail could take on home with her after the baby comes. Ya got yer tablet with ya, Lib? Go on an' show 'em."

The concept of a quilt appliquéd to form a rural scene appealed to Paulette's artistic nature. She improved on Libby's drawing while Mrs. Bee ran home to bring her sewing widgets and Libby left to fetch the fabric pieces she'd been accumulating for the project.

Much later, as they were all engrossed in the project, Libby stepped back from the table covered in varied fabric scraps. As she eased the kink from her back, she watched their faces, lit by the gaslight, and listened to their amiable chatter and occasional bursts of laughter. Sisters, Maddie had called them. Maddie, to whom the word was almost a battle cry. Maddie's own life was full of disunity. But here they sat together, harmoniously picking over scraps of cloth, each with her own unique skills and ideas pouring out freely for Abigail, whom two of the four scarcely knew.

The first stitch had yet to be sewn. Yet Libby, looking on, was struck by their unity. *Sisterhood*. This giving, this blending of ages and skills and ideas and heart embodied the word.

The week progressed. News came from the grove that Ike was steadily improving. Children's Hour was going well, as Libby read to a growing group of children the story of runaway Toby Tyler. Frankie began helping his mother at the store. Even less expected, he had confessed his "horse borrowings" and was planning to do odd jobs as compensation to the owners.

A good week. A very good week, and yet, Libby couldn't seem to shake her melancholy. While it lent a wistfulness to her written voice, it dulled the luster of her musical one. Or so Maddie accused as she offered her a lift home following the Berry Sisters practice on Thursday evening.

"You are aware, aren't you, that 'Yankee Doodle' is not a dirge?" she said as they followed Dorene and Chloe out of Paulette's house.

Libby offered fatigue as an excuse and waved to the Berry girls as they went their separate ways. But Maddie was not so easily fooled. She folded the petaled skirt of her colorful dress beneath her, making room on the seat as Libby climbed into the surrey beside her. "The serious campaigning doesn't begin for another month and already you sing as if it's a chore. What's the matter? Have you and Angus quarreled?"

"When would we quarrel? He spends most of his time in court in Bloomington." In an attempt to wiggle out from beneath Maddie's penetrating gaze, Libby indicated Maddie's dress. "That's a pretty gown. Is it new?"

"You don't have to be tactful with me, Libby. If you have something to say about my putting my widow's weeds away, then rest assured I've heard it all from Mother."

Libby was certain she had. The gown of melon and lime couldn't have been more vivid.

The rig lurched forward beneath Maddie's able hand, arcs of dust lifting from the horse's hooves. Maddie snapped at a fly with the buggy whip. Mouth thinning, she confided, "Mother's urging me to drop out of the Berry Sisters. She warned that if the truth about Damon becomes public knowledge, my association with Angus's campaign may prove an embarrassment to him. I won't, though. Not unless Angus himself asks me to."

Libby hoped it wouldn't come to that, for Maddie had a stage presence and an ease that instilled confidence in the rest of them.

Steering the conversation away from Angus, Libby said, "Davie and Opal have been missing Sophronia in their circus games."

"Mother has limited her social activities as a punishment for taking your journal. In other words, no more jumping into the buggy and going to town with Aunt Maddie," Maddie added in a careless way that betrayed more than it hid.

Libby had wondered why Mrs. Dorrance, not Maddie, had been bringing Sophronia to Children's Hour.

Father was on the porch when Libby arrived home. It was the first she had seen of him since breakfast, for he hadn't yet come home from work when Libby left for practice. She smiled and flung up a hand in greeting, then stopped short, momentarily paralyzed by the sight of Dr. Harding's buggy parked at the side of the house.

Abigail's complaints of indigestion at lunchtime and her disinterest in supper suddenly took on new meaning. Her heart pounding, Libby hastened up the porch steps.

"Aye, lass," Father answered from the top step. "The bairn has come."

"Come?" Incredulous, Libby's hand flew to her throat. "You mean, she's had it? It's all over?"

Father nodded, and his smile fell short of lighting his eyes. "The lass, I'm thinkin', is uncommonly brave. Not at all like yer mither, God love her. My sweet Annie terrified the everlastin' wits oot of me with her lusty wails when her time was upon her. But not the leddy Abigail. She endured it silent as a lamb. I was knockin' at the door, offerin' to go fetch you from yer sing-song when Mrs. Baker, whom I'd met on me way to the station to wire Adam—she kindly consented to come along home wi' me to help with the birthin' as Mrs. Bee was not to be found—stepped oot with the wee one in her arms. The next thing I knew, there was Doc shakin' me hand and congratulatin' me on bein' a grandfaether."

"Well, what is it?" cried Libby on her way to the door.

"A bonny lass, with a face as sweet as a flower." Father's smile retreated into careworn lines as he added, "B'fore ye rush in, I would ha'e ye to know a letter came from yer brither today."

"In a moment, Father," said Libby, intent on squeezing past him.

"Just a glimpsie, lass." He pressed the letter into her hand and went inside, leaving Libby alone on the porch. Hurriedly, she read the opening paragraph:

Dear Father:

Forgive me for being so long in writing this letter, but as you will understand it is painful for me. I'd give anything if Jacob hadn't meddled in it. The whole matter should have remained between Abigail and me. But what is done is done. I would be lying if I said forgiveness came easily. But I have forgiven her—at least I think I have, and we were doing all right. Then Jacob thrashed Weasel Brooks and people started putting two and two together, as I knew they would. It was that which kept me from pounding Brooks myself. As you can imagine, the situation became unbearable for Abigail.

Weasel. A nickname, no doubt. And a fitting one, too, though Libby couldn't place it. Men came and went in Thistle Down, drinkers and brawlers and womanizers mixed in with a lot of decent hardworking family men. She read on, more slowly.

I've told Abigail that I'll raise this child as my own, if that's what she wants. I want to, Father, but only God knows if I can do the job justice. If I can't, then it would be better to face it now, for Abigail's talked about making other arrangements. She realizes to do so will mean explanations to you and Libby, explanations she'd like to avoid as she is so far unaware that Jacob has passed the truth along. She's feeling so ashamed and fearful of your opinions toward her shifting that I haven't told her you already know that the child isn't mine. This whole matter has taken a toll and I'm worried about her emotional state. I want you to know, though, that she mentions your kind treatment in every letter. I can't thank you and Libby enough.

I'm sorry about all of this and hope I haven't made you hang your head. Pray we can put it behind us soon and get on with our lives. Give Libby and David my love.

Adam

Eyes misting, Libby folded the letter back into the envelope. *Other arrangements.* That's what Father had wanted her to see. Adam, preparing the way, should Abigail give the baby up.

Libby tried to remember what Father had said that had brought comfort over this very issue just a few days ago. Tried, and when memory failed, reasoned that after all, the baby *would* be a hardship, not just emotionally but economically. In Thistle Down, there was only a thin line between "just getting by" and poverty.

At length, Libby dried her tears and went inside. Father hadn't mentioned that Mrs. Baker was still there. She smiled and beckoned Libby toward the rocking chair. Wrapped in a soft blanket and cradled in her arms was the tiny niece who wasn't a niece at all. Libby's eyes filled afresh as she knelt beside the chair and caressed the tiny dimpled fist.

"Oh my," she said with a breathless rush. Was there ever a face so pink and perfect? Libby kissed her finger and touched the baby's tiny rosebud mouth and whispered, "Hello, little one. Hello."

At length, she got to her feet again and made her way to the room she had been sharing with Abigail. Abigail lay in bed, unaware of Libby standing in the doorway. Scattered around her on the sheet were Adam's letters. Face pale, eyes heavy, Abigail picked through them as a child would treasured possessions. Smoothing the creases made by frequent handling, turning them over as if to search out some small phrase of special significance. A tremulous smile on her lips, she traced what must have been Adam's signature, then buried her face in the letters. *To what? Catch the scent of him?* One hand fell to her empty womb as the other clung to the letters.

Libby turned away, eyes filling once more.

Dear God, what a mess!

It wasn't an eloquent prayer. Eloquence was hard. Praying itself was difficult, as her compassion clashed with the hoarse whisper of less kindly emotions. Libby turned away without a word. She let herself out the front door, walked to the edge of town, and started out Tile Factory Road before letting the tears come.

It did no good to cry. Nothing did any good.

A quiet Presence told her that wasn't so. That God loved her, flaws and all. It was an unsettling reminder, for she hadn't been thinking of God, nor of her own flaws. Defensively, she reasoned that at least she, like Adam, had done nothing to make her family hang their heads.

God didn't quarrel, simply strengthened the message that she was loved.

But His love placed expectations upon her, forgiveness among them.

She *had* forgiven. Hadn't she? Libby stood at the edge of the road for a moment, watching the summer breeze ripple the green corn leaves to the east and swallows dip and dive over the fragrant meadow to the west.

"As far as east is from the west, so far has he removed our transgressions from us." The words of the familar Psalm came to mind, as quiet as a grain of pollen fluttering from the tassel to the silk of the corn. Pollinating forgiveness. The kind that made love grow. Divine forgiveness. The kind only God could produce in her, if she was willing to be His vessel. *Was* she willing?

25

On Friday, Ike caught a slow train into town to get his medicine refilled at Doc Harding's. As luck would have it, the doctor was at the station, picking up some supplies that had come into the express office. He gave Ike a ride to his office and mentioned, as he passed along the recent news, that Thomas Watson's daughter-in-law had given birth to a baby girl last evening.

Doc left his buggy in the alley and led the way in the back door to find Mrs. Bee waiting with the news that there was another baby ready to be born. Sheriff Conklin's wife was in labor.

Dr. Harding tossed his hat on the horsehair sofa. "How far apart are her pains?"

"Five minutes," said Mrs. Bee.

"I'll have a look at Ike first, then," said the doctor.

Mrs. Bee collected his hat and caught his jacket, airborne toward the same sofa, and hung them on pegs by the door, all the while quizzing Ike as to how his recovery was proceeding. Ike told her that he was feeling much better.

"That's a relief. You had us worried. You're still staying at Decatur's?" asked Mrs. Bee, and at Ike's nod, said, "Have you seen anything of Mr. Caton?"

"No, ma'am. Not a thing."

"If you do, give him a piece of my mind." She snatched a medical book off the end of the sofa and returned it to the shelf. "That old busybody has been agitating the bench brigade over at Willie Blue's all week, telling them you caught influenza from Mr. Robinson and that Melville didn't know what he was treating and all sorts of rot."

"Sarah Jane!" objected the doctor. He slanted his sister a reproving glance. "Ike didn't come in here to catch up on the gossip."

"Very well, then." Mrs. Bee tilted her chin, raked her fingers through her hair, and warned, "But mark my words, someone had better put a stopper in old Hascal's gullet before folks start biting on these rumors of his." She poured water from a pitcher into a basin at the washstand, placed a clean towel beside it, then excused herself and left them alone.

Ike took off his shirt at the doctor's bidding, and asked, "Hascal had me laid out, did he?"

"Preached over and buried," said Dr. Harding.

"That's old Hack for ya. Never lets sentiment get in the way of a good epidemic."

Dr. Harding chuckled as he rolled up his sleeves, washed his hands, and methodically went about the business of checking Ike over. He expressed relief at finding no indication of a swollen spleen or signs of jaundice and was cautioning Ike to give himself a good long rest when Mrs. Bee returned to remind him of Mrs. Conklin. She folded and tucked a fresh white apron under her arm and prodded her brother with a look that fell just short of a physical shove.

"Go on over and tell them I'll be right there," said the doctor.

"All right, but don't dawdle, you hear?" Mrs. Bee took the doctor's black bag and scurried down the corridor.

Hearing children's voices coming from the lobby, Ike paused in stuffing in his shirttail. "What's going on out front?"

"Children's Hour. Haven't you heard? The ladies have turned my lobby into a public library."

"Reckon I *did* read somethin' about that in the paper."

"Paulette and Sarah Jane talked me into sharing my building. They're looking on it as a stopgap measure until something more permanent can be done. But I don't mind telling you it's a nuisance. The only thing keeping me from putting my foot down is all the work the ladies have put into it." Dr. Harding shoved his arms into his black suit jacket, and added, "For two weeks, I tripped over ladies dusting, ladies scrubbing, ladies unloading boxes of books until I stopped coming through the lobby altogether. Now the place is overrun with children."

With a tilt of his head Ike indicated the symphony of giggles coming from the lobby. "Must be gettin' a good turnout."

Dr. Harding nodded. "Miss Watson's been reading a circus story to them all week. She's got them hanging on her words."

Libby. He should have guessed she'd take an interest. Listening hard, Ike picked Libby's reading voice out over the snickers of the children, then lost it again as the doctor said, "I mean what I said about taking it easy, Ike."

"I got a wheat crop to get in."

"Best hire some help, then. Relapses are common with malaria. You know that as well as I do."

"It'll be a trick to find any help, what with nigh every man in these parts in the field."

"I can't tell you how to tend your farming, Ike, but I can tell you if you don't take it easy, you're going to be right back in a cycle of chills and fever. You aren't to do any heavy work. You understand?"

What he understood was that the grain wasn't going to harvest itself. It wasn't just farmwork, either. There was wood to be cut and equipment to be installed and a hundred other chores remaining to be done before he would be ready to make sirup in the spring. Dodging the issue, he changed the subject, saying, "Thought I'd thank Miss Libby for the trouble she took haulin' me out of the water. Don't want to interrupt the story, though. How long do you suppose she'll be?"

"Awhile yet," said Dr. Harding. "You're welcome to wait here if you like. Your medicine is there on the desk. If you leave before I return, lock the back door."

"Thanks, Doc."

"Sofa's comfortable. Make yourself at home."

The children had quieted up front. Ike could hear the animation in Libby's voice and sense the spell she was weaving with her story reading. He stretched out on the sofa, sloped his hat over his eyes, linked his hands on his chest, and let his thoughts drift to the day he had fallen ill. He remembered feeling bad and Frankie coming out to see him in the night. But after that, it got vague. He didn't recall leaving Naomi's cabin or walking to the creek or anything about Libby. Decatur said she was wet from head to foot when he arrived on the scene. Muddy and sporting a bloody lip.

Visualizing the scene Decatur's words painted, Ike wondered, as he waited to see her, what he'd put her through that day. His pulse quickened as the sounds shifted. Libby's voice was crowded out by the clamor of chairs scraping the floor and children's voices chiming as they picked out books to take home. Hearing their chorus of good-byes and the front door banging after them, he came to his feet, put his medicine in his pocket, started out the back office and down the dim corridor just as Libby came toward him from the other end.

She carried a book, her finger marking the place. The light streaming through the front window was behind her, filtering through her hair like sparks flying off a smithy's anvil. She turned, a silhouette in sunshine, and spoke to a child out of Ike's range of vision, her slender curves and cinched waist gilt-edged in light.

"Your grandmother isn't here yet? Better wait right here, then," she entreated the unseen child.

"But it's hot in here. Can't I wait across the street?"

"All right," said Libby, her patience accentuating the child's petulance. "But don't stray any further. I've got to check the back door, then I'll be right with you."

The front door slammed before Libby got her words out. She sighed, her gaze lingering on something behind her even as her feet were moving toward him. Finally, her head came around, too. All at once, she stopped short. "Ike!" Her free hand flew to her midriff. "You startled me."

"Sorry." Ike closed the distance between them, meeting her in the middle of the hallway. "If yer lookin' for Doc, him and Miz Bee went out on a call."

"Mrs. Conklin's time. Mrs. Bee told me on her way out."

"I hear you're an aunt now."

She nodded, but offered no further information. "I was just going to lock up."

"I took care of it," he said. He saw her gaze dart over him and away as if she was trying to recover from her shock and realized he must not look like much. Truth was, he hadn't looked in a mirror since he fell sick. But he remembered the postwar trip home, a war in which tropical disease had proved more costly than the marksmanship of the Spanish. On the way home, he saw his own gauntness reflected in comrades, some of whom were still fighting the disease as they crossed the waters.

"You look like you could use a good meal," she was saying over the rush of his thoughts. "What did Dr. Harding have to say?"

"Seems to think I'll make it if I take it easy a spell."

"You'd better listen to him, Ike. You're looking pretty puny."

"Decatur's cookin'." He made light of it. "Takes a good constitution to survive a steady diet of grits and gravy and black-eyed peas."

Her mouth curved into a smile. There was no swelling in her lip that he could see. No sign of injury. But there was something different about her. A hush fell between them as he tried to figure it out. Was it her hands? Hugging that book like it'd come apart if she was to let go. Or her eyes? Right next to skittish. Like a shy pup, that gaze. Making runs at him, but never standing still long enough for him to fathom what had her so tongue-tied.

He tucked his hands under his arms and rocked back on his heels. "What's this about you takin' me swimming?"

"*Me* takin' *you?* Ike Galloway, you nearly drowned us both! You leaped up off that log like a crazy man and sent me flying backwards into the water. Ruined my clothes and sank my hat and shrank my shoes two sizes. Not to mention taking ten years off my life."

Relieved she'd found her stride, Ike grinned. "You're lookin' pretty lively to me."

"No thanks to you."

He chuckled. "Think you could work your way around to forgivin' me if I took you down the street and replaced your shoes and hat and dress?" Seeing the pink steal to her cheeks and her lashes come down, he took the high road and added, "You can bring your little brother along if yer worryin' what Angus will think."

"Angus is in Bloomington."

"Then how about an early supper over at Baker's while we're at it?" he said.

She frowned and pointed out, "It was my favorite skirt, too."

"Blue-and-white pin-striped?"

Her chin dropped. "You remember?"

"No. Just a guess." He never saw her in it, but he didn't think of the Spanish soldiers. Good riddance as far as he was concerned.

A small pucker formed just over her eyebrows. Another pursed her lips. "Are you sure you don't remember anything?"

"Don't seem to. Why don't you fill me in? I'll stop ya if anything sounds familiar."

Her color deepened. Wrists crossed, both hands clutching the book to her chest, she said, "There's not much to tell, really. You were out of your head with fever and of the opinion I intended you harm. I must say, for a sick man, you defended yourself superbly."

War dreams. He wanted to explain, but he had no words to make her understand. And if he tried . . . she really *would* think he was crazy. Seemed safer, keeping his nightmares to himself and letting her wonder.

"You called me Maddie," she said into his thoughts. "Did I mention that?"

He saw something stir in her gaze and knew she was asking with a purpose. Yet he was so relieved to have her wonder about Maddie instead of the madness that compelled him to fight a phantom enemy, he didn't think ahead to possible ramifications, just shrugged and said, "Must have been the water."

She crooked one eyebrow. "Water makes you think of Maddie?"

"Not if it's in a glass," he said, and smiled.

"Why is that?"

Close enough to see the book rise and fall with each breath she took, he didn't risk having another joke fall flat. Which only left the truth. Part of it, anyway. The other was up to Angus. "Once, when we weren't much more than kids, Hascal Caton caught Maddie and me out by the lake fishin'. Like to give Mrs. Dorrance a conniption."

"Just fishing?"

He blinked, for something in her tone reminded him of ice cracking on a winter creek, schooling him to caution. He realized she had already heard this story, and not the straight version of it either. How could she? He had never told it, and back then Maddie was too busy protecting Angus when she should have been protecting herself.

Belatedly he saw the danger. Even if he managed to find words that painted the picture and were still polite enough for mixed company, there was no reason for her to believe him. Worse, she might dismiss the truth as an attempt on his part to discredit Angus. "Swimmin', too," he said, then added on sudden inspiration, "Have Maddie tell you about it sometime."

"Perhaps I will."

The look that accompanied her words made his nerves jump. He didn't mean to reach for her, but there his hand was, stretching out to check her retreat as she dropped her gaze and turned away, murmuring something about having to see about Sophronia.

"Lib? Before you go, I want to say thanks and tell you I'm sorry for throwin' you in the water."

"Even if you don't remember it?" she said softly, and to his wonder, did not withdraw from his touch on her arm.

"Even if I don't remember it," he echoed.

"All right, then. You're welcome," she said with a little quirk at the corner of her mouth.

"About that shopping spree . . ."

"I can't let you, Ike," she said gently. "Father wouldn't like it."

Nor would Angus. She didn't say it, though. Probably guessed her father's opinion carried more weight with him. Reluctant to let her heroics go unrewarded, he asked again, "Dinner, then?"

"I can't tonight. My brother Adam is coming on the evening train."

"One more thing, and then I'll stop botherin' ya."

"You're not."

It was almost a whisper, those two words. He noticed a faint blue vein beneath the skin of the milky column of her throat. A tiny crease, too, that reminded him of baby skin, it was that white and delicate. He saw her swallow, and swallowed, too. Shifted closer. "Decatur says your lip was bleeding. I was worried I'd hurt ya."

"It's fine," she said. "Healed nicely."

"So I see." He couldn't stop looking at her mouth.

Color swept up her throat until her face was almost as red as her hair. It seemed as if that millisecond between wanting to touch his mouth to hers and see if it was as soft and supple as it looked and the next, where he caught her looking at the bruise she had left on his jaw, lasted forever. But that third millisecond when Mrs. Dorrance's voice rang from the unseen door and Libby jumped back like she'd been hit by lightning was the one that brought reason flooding in.

He'd lost all respect for Angus Cearlock years ago, but durned if he'd try and kiss his girl behind his back. He would make her his girl first, God willing. And when he did, he didn't want to have to worry about Angus coming along and taking her back like a stolen kiss.

"She must be looking for Sophronia. I've got to go." Libby's voice dropped. "And Ike?"

Her face ripened like a sunset spilling over the sky. He saw her pulse beating at her temple and her lashes come up to reveal cloudless blue eyes. Mrs. Dorrance's second call went unheeded as she brushed a strand of hair behind her ear and finished in a whisper, "About dinner . . . ask me again sometime."

And then she was gone, leaving Ike wondering if he'd heard her right. He thought about it awhile and when the dampness had dried from his palms and his pulse was steady again, he walked down the street to the millinery shop and bought a hat that would adorn her hair, not hide it like so many of the hats women were wearing these days. Ike had the box wrapped up in colored paper, then found Teddy Baker and paid him to take it to her.

26

Father had gone to meet Adam's train. Dinner was ready, and Libby was sitting on the swing polishing an article for the *Gazette* when Teddy Baker brought her a telegram from Angus saying that he had been delayed and would not be returning home from Bloomington in time to come to her house for dinner.

Had her feelings run deep, Libby would have been hurt over such a brief and inadequate explanation. As it was, she folded the telegram into her new Memorandum book and found a coin for Teddy, who lingered unobtrusively at the base of the steps with Sugar panting at his feet.

"I'm sorry, I didn't mean to keep you waiting," she said, for it was obvious by the wrapped package dangling from one hand that he had other errands to run.

"Aw n-o-o-w, don't get in a hurry." He drew the words out in that drawling way of his. "Here's something else for you."

"The package is for me, too?" asked Libby, surprised.

"I was s'posed to bring it by earlier," Teddy confessed with a flash of large white teeth. "But this one wanting this and that one wanting that . . ." He lifted his shoulders and let them fall, finishing, "Awe-e-l-l, I can't be everywhere."

Libby patted Sugar on the head, then waved to Teddy as he and the dog went on their way. She sat down on the swing and unwrapped what turned out to be a stylish navy blue hat. Not one of those ostentatious ones, but a pert flat-crowned hat with a narrow brim and a matching blue band. There was no card, but it had to be a guilt offering from Angus for canceling at such short notice.

Repenting of her critical attitude toward his brief telegram, she thought with a pang, *You shouldn't have!* She could not in good conscience keep it. Not after yesterday, for her moments with Ike in Dr. Harding's corridor had clarified her growing discontentment in her relationship with Angus.

From the start, Angus had been attentive. Chivalrous. The model suitor, courtly and courteous. Skilled at pitching woo, even in the midst of a quarrel. And a good sport when his amorous advances met with gentle rebuffs. But the answering spark was missing, relegating their courtship to a pleasant pastime marked by occasional voids of loneliness. Loneliness which in telltale fashion struck even while she was with him. Ike had yet to court her or speak a single term of endearment. And yet with a look he had ignited what Angus, for all his courting, could not.

Sorting through her emotions, Libby flipped her book open to a fresh page and spilled her thoughts onto the page:

> *Even now I vacillate about speaking with Angus over my shifting feelings. A future with him seems so perfectly fit to my ambitions that it's hard to let go. With him, in time, I feel certain I could eventually secure more education. His political ambitions promise a life so different from the one I have known. There would be new places and faces and experiences and adventures to fill many a book! Understandably, my head cautions me not to be too swift closing doors, nor to close them with too firm a hand. But my heart, for better or worse, has a mind all its own.*

Libby sighed, took another admiring look at the hat, and regretfully returned it to the box.

It was wonderful to see Adam again. Libby was reassured by his tenderness toward Abigail that he was not wavering in his determination to keep his word concerning the child. But a single moment in his two-day stay defined the obstacles that lay ahead. Adam was sitting at Abigail's bedside, holding the baby and remarking over her beauty, when Libby inadvertently drew his attention to the baby's unusually tiny ears. Suddenly, his face was no longer the beloved face of her brother, but an impassive mask.

Father noticed his reaction as well. Later, when Libby questioned him, she learned that Brooks real name was Lester, and that the men on his shift called him Weasel because of his exceptionally small ears. It was an innocent mistake, and hardly one Libby should or could apologize for. But she felt bad all the same.

Abigail loathed the idea of returning to Thistle Down. Knowing as much, Adam spent part of Saturday in Bloomington at the Chicago and Alton Railway Shops, checking out the possibility of employment there. While the situation was hopeful, there were no immediate openings, so he filled out some papers to put him on a list for future openings.

Planning to return when Abigail and the baby were strong enough to travel, Adam went to the station on Sunday evening to catch the train back to Thistle Down. Father went along to see him off. In their brief time alone, Adam told Father that Abigail was still unaware that his family knew the baby wasn't his. That was the way he wanted it if they were to keep the child.

"If?" Father reported echoing back at him.

The final decision, Adam told him, was up to Abigail. Which was the same as saying it had yet to be made.

In the following days Abigail regained her strength fairly quickly, and occupied herself with the demands of motherhood, though it worried Libby that she lacked the cheery sparkle evident in most young mothers. Father confided his concern, too, and redoubled his kind and caring efforts.

It was a week and two days after little Rose's birth before Abigail could be talked into getting out of the house and away from the baby for a while. Naomi, who had come daily to fetch Opal and visit, offered to stay with Rose while Libby took Abigail and the children out to the lake for an early Saturday morning picnic breakfast.

"A circus breakfast picnic," David and Opal called it, for the circus was due in town that day.

They wouldn't be able to stay long, as Libby had baking to do for the community dinner and Abigail would have to return to nurse the baby. Libby had also promised to help Mrs. Gruben pick and arrange the flowers for the tables and help serve the dinner before going to the circus.

The day dawned with a glorious sunrise. Libby, Abigail, David, and Opal watched the colors ripen, then strengthen to daylight as Proctor drew them along Tile Factory Road toward Spring Lake. The short trip was made without incident, the breakfast of biscuits and honey and fresh peaches from Mrs. Gruben's tree disappearing quickly.

Libby fed the crumbs to the ducks, while Abigail went for a walk. The birds were singing overhead as Proctor, behind her, had his own picnic. His placid ripping at the grass blended with David's gentle coaxing, "Here, fishie fishie. Here, fishie fishie."

He lay on a finger of land jutting into the lake, arms outstretched, hands in the water. Opal sat beside him, gazing into the trees to the north.

"You're awfully quiet," Libby called to her with a smile. "Wishing you'd brought some fishing line?"

"Daddy fishes here sometimes," Opal said, without taking her eyes off the trees.

So did Ike. Or he had, anyway. As a youth.

A cloud drifted over Libby's contentment as she thought of Ike calling her by Maddie's name and of Maddie's reference to the lake incident. *Water under the bridge,* she reasoned. Minor, too, when measured against Maddie's elopement with a man who had subsequently exploited and abandoned her. And yet it was like a splinter in some hard-to-reach spot: difficult to remove, yet impossible to dismiss. The truth was, she was more confused than ever about that long-ago and still-gossiped-about incident.

Would Ike urge her to ask Maddie about it if there were shame attached? Tuesday, as she met with Maddie, Paulette, Naomi, and Mrs. Bee to work on Abigial's quilt, she had thought about doing just that. But thinking and doing were poles apart, and there was little opportunity, anyway.

Libby returned to the picnic quilt and stretched out on her stomach, her thoughts once again tracking over her encounter with Ike a week ago at Dr. Harding's office. A faded bruise on his jaw was the only evidence of their underwater struggle, but he was thin. Too thin, and pale beneath his fading tan. She skipped over his frail appearance, heart leaping at the remembrance of him studying her mouth as if deciding just where to land the first kiss. Forward of her, maybe, but she would have welcomed the kiss, had Mrs. Dorrance not come in.

Libby gazed across the lake to where Abigail was picking her way along a path between trees and water, and decided maybe it had been a fortuitous interruption after all. What had possessed her, being so willing to throw caution to the wind where Ike was concerned?

Knees bent, ankles crossed, elbows cocked, chin resting between her palms, Libby looked from the ducks to Abigail as she returned from her walk and dropped down on the quilt beside her. The exertion had painted roses on her pale cheeks.

She opened her hand. "See what I found?"

Libby rolled the robin's egg over in Abigail's outstretched palm. "Pretty."

"Um." Abigail's attention strayed to David's hookless, lineless fishing technique. "He and Opal get along better without Frankie and Sophronia."

"Frankie and Phronky. What a pair." Libby giggled. "Wouldn't it be funny if they grew up, fell in love, and got married?"

Abigail flashed a rare smile. "Not only do you have a wild imagination, you're a hopeless romantic. I guess I used to be, too."

"You've got a sweet baby girl and a fine husband, if I do say so myself. That's romantic, isn't it?"

Abigail sighed, a sigh too heavy, too old for her years.

Libby sat up as Opal came trotting over. She dropped between them and leaned her face against Libby's arm, her expression nearly as forlorn as Abigail's. Libby wrapped her arm around the child, and said to Abigail, "Show Opal what you found on your walk."

"Reckon it'll never hatch now," said Opal, rolling the robin's egg over in the palm of Abigail's hand.

"Did it blow out of the nest?" asked David, joining them.

"Maybe. Or maybe the mother bird pushed it out," Abigail replied.

"That's mean," said Opal.

"Maybe she couldn't care for it," reasoned Abigail.

"Why not?" asked Opal.

"I don't know. But God knows," said Abigail. She wrapped the robin's egg in her handkerchief, then turned to look back over her shoulder. "Hear that?"

Libby heard it too. It was a rumbling commotion. Like distant thunder, only more hollow-sounding and resonant. It distracted her from Abigail's contemplations concerning orphan eggs. Opal and David jumped up. They squinted into the eastern sun glossing the trees that screened the railroad tracks and Tile Factory Road.

"Is it a train, Lib?" called David.

"Dray wagons, I think. I hear animals." Libby scrambled to her feet just as a circus wagon rattled over the railroad crossing and into the clearing.

"It's the circus!" cried David.

Opal was thunderstruck. She stood as still as a fence post, gazing in wonder as wagon after wagon poured into the lake pasture pulled by two, four, six, even eight span of horses. Harness and trappings rubbed and clanked. Wagons creaked on colorful webbed wheels, the grass muting that peerless hollow musical whine the heavy hubs made as they turned on greased axle shafts. Carts and gilly wagons hauling the trappings followed float wagons, tableau wagons, cage wagons carting wild animals, and a wagon made for the band. Interspersed were the elephants shuffling along swinging their trunks. Camels, zebras, mules, and ponies, all of them hitched to conveyances of varying sizes and purposes. The animals had caught scent of the water. They advanced on the lake, their pace checked by the steady hands of the able teamsters.

"We'd better get out of the way." Hastily, Libby gathered the remains of their picnic and moved Proctor, who was unnerved by the spectacle, to the south end of the pasture near the freshly cut wheat field. She retraced her steps back to Abigail and the children just as a shiny black surrey pulled into the midst of the melee.

A mustachioed man in a straw skimmer leaped out and began shouting orders to those who were pouring off the horses and out of the wagons. A second portly fellow in a tall black hat, a frock coat, and black trousers that disappeared just below the knee into the tops of shining black boots, climbed out of the buggy and strode over to introduce himself as Samuel Bigelow, owner of the circus.

"I apologize for the intrusion, but our twenty-four-hour man sent word that this was the last watering hole before town."

"Twenty-four-hour man?" echoed Libby.

"Advance agent. He was in Edgewood yesterday, checking on final arrangements with Mr. Gentry. What are we, about a mile from Edgewood?"

"Closer to two, sir," said Libby. "You can take the road you were just on straight into town. Or you can follow the wagon track through the field there and take the back way into town."

"I believe we'll stick to the route our man marked."

"We saw the arrows on the telegraph poles," Opal spoke up.

The portly gentleman crouched forward, propping his hands just over his knees, and solemnly asked, "You didn't move any of them, did you, little miss?"

"Oh, no sir!" cried Opal, shocked at the very idea. "What if ya was to miss us?"

He laughed. "Now that *would* be a tragedy."

"Cain't think of a worse un'," Opal said. "I got a ticket for the afternoon show and the evenin' one, too. Ain't I, Miss Lib?"

"Yes, indeed. This is Opal," said Libby, resting a hand on the little girl's shoulder. "She's been looking forward to the circus for weeks."

"David, too," said Opal, kindly including him.

David scarcely noticed, so enraptured was he with the spectacle unfolding around them. Following his gaze, Libby saw the trainers beginning to wash the dusty wagons as well as the magnificent menagerie of animals, both domestic and exotic.

"Can I help give the elephants a bath?" asked David.

"May I," Libby corrected.

The man chortled. "You would both get a bath."

"Ain't there somethin' we kin do?" pleaded Opal.

Mr. Bigelow stroked his lip as he considered her request. "Tell you what. You see that pretty lady walking along there by herself? Why don't you pick her a handful of flowers and see if you can coax a smile out of her? If you do, you come back and tell me, and I'll let you ride into town in the telegraph wagon. How would you like that?"

Opal let out a squeal of delight and fell straightaway to plucking yellow flowers that grew like patches of sunshine in the pasture bordering the east side of the lake. But David delayed, asking, "What's a telegraph wagon?"

"Lead wagon," said the man. "The job of keeping us on the route into town falls to them."

"Can we ride with him, Lib?" asked David.

Libby exchanged glances with Abigail. Seeing her hesitation, Mr. Bigelow said kindly, "We run a Sunday School Show, ma'am. No harm will come to them, you have my word on it."

"Please, Libby? Please, please?" begged Opal.

"I suppose it would be all right," Libby decided. "But you have to do what Mr. Bigelow tells you and not get in the way."

The children missed the last half of Libby's warning, so intent were they on their lightning flower picking. Libby saw that Mr. Bigelow wasn't listening, either. His eyes had strayed to the lady standing idle in the midst of that giant anthill of activity. Libby saw a muscle tighten along his jaw line as the woman received the children's gift of flowers and thanked them with a fleeting smile. David came running back, but Opal lingered a moment, shyly digging her toe in the grass as the woman talked to her.

"Who is she?" Abigail asked.

"My wife," said the man. "The best acrobat in the company until a year ago."

"She got hurt?" asked Libby with a pang.

"In a manner of speaking. Though not in the ring." He removed his hat, and, looking toward his wife, said, "We lost our little girl."

Seeing him blink back a glint of tears as his wife's gaze lifted to his, Libby murmured, "I'm sorry."

Abigail asked, "Does she perform?"

"No. Not anymore." Stubby lashes coming down, he brushed dust from his hat. "If there were little ones to pass her skills on to, the desire in her might awaken. But we had only the one." Catching himself up, he said with a squaring of shoulders, "Forgive me, ladies. I didn't intend to burden you with our sorrows. You've been most kind. The children, too. They have earned their reward."

"Which one is the telegraph wagon?" asked David, round-eyed and eager, as Opal came back to his side.

Mr. Bigelow smiled over his quick adoption of the circus term, and clapped him on the shoulder. "Come with me, I'll introduce you to some of the kinkers."

"Kinkers is performers. Miz Bee told me so," Opal whispered to Libby, then raced off to catch up with Mr. Bigelow and David.

Libby, watching them go, was struck by the irony of a man in the depths of his sorrow traveling with a circus that brought such joy to others. She observed Mr. Bigelow's manner as he moved among his employees. A pat here, a word there bringing order out of chaos. She could see that he cared for these people. That they, in turn, cared for him. The children, she decided, were in good hands. She hoped she hadn't overstepped her bounds, granting

Opal permission to ride in the lead wagon, but she couldn't conceive of Naomi denying her the thrill of parading through town with the circus.

"What is a Sunday School Show?" asked Abigail.

Libby chuckled. "I don't know. I'll ask Mrs. Bee. She's our circus expert." She paused a moment, then asked, "Are you sure you won't come with me tonight? Angus isn't going to make it home, and Father has already made plans to see the show with Teddy and Davie and Frankie. We could take Rose with us."

"Thanks, Lib, but no," Abigail declined.

It was intoxicating, watching the dusty, road-weary group of travelers primp and polish and shine themselves into a gleaming, glorious troupe. When the parade call was blown, clean-shaven men in knee-high blackened boots and vests and smart hats climbed aboard tall wagon seats. Women in tights and glittering costumes and gauntlet gloves with feathers in their hair found their places aboard horses, floats, even pony carts. The musicians in full uniform clambered aboard the bandwagon to put a last-minute shine on their instruments.

They lined up, high-stepping steeds and powerful draft horses alike wearing plumes atop their bridles and brass medallions on their harnesses. As did the elephants. The zebras and mules and ponies wore feathers, too. Even a little dog pulling a cart pricked up his ears, appearing to listen as Mr. Bigelow bellowed, "On your best behavior now! Gentlemen, no smoking, spitting, or chewing. Ladies, lots of smiles when we hit town. And don't stop waving until we pull into the grounds."

Libby blew a kiss to David and Opal, already aboard the lead wagon, then looked around for Abigail and spotted her at Mrs. Bigelow's side, making a gift of her robin's egg memento.

27

🌹 "What is a Sunday School Show?" Libby asked Mrs. Bee later that evening at the Columbian. With Angus out of town, she had made herself available not only for the preparations, but also for the serving of the New Hope Ladies Aid Society's community dinner.

"A reputable circus. No pickpockets, no cheats, no coarse talk. Clean enough for Sunday School." Enjoying being singled out for her circus knowledge, Mrs. Bee lifted her chin, slid the last piece of raspberry pie onto the last clean plate, and sailed it out to the only remaining customer.

It wasn't quite six-thirty, but it had been a full day, preparations for the dinner having required the better part of it. Libby's cakes were not as moist as she would have liked, but Mrs. Gruben's floral centerpieces were a hit. She was disappointed Mrs. Gruben could not be coaxed into attending, but she was looking forward to telling her how people had raved over her flowers. And that the profit on the project had surpassed all expectations. All in all, it had been a smashing success, largely because of all the volunteer help with the dinner, Sophronia among them. Mrs. Dorrance, who had come for the cleanup, had brought her along.

Returning to the kitchen, Mrs. Bee confided, "A lot of folks laughed up their sleeves at Chester Gentry for thinking of a circus as a campaign fundraiser. But it looks to me as if he's going to come out smelling like a rose. I never saw such a mob of people. If the dinner crowd was any indication, it'll be a straw house again tonight."

"Straw house?"

"Overflow crowd. You'll be sitting on the straw yourself, if you don't get going.'' She nudged Libby and pointed, adding, "There's Naomi and Opal now.''

Libby turned to see Naomi in the doorway. Failing to get Abigail to accompany her, Libby had asked Naomi and Opal if she might tag along with them. Naomi's green eyes glowed, her anticipation nearly as keen as Opal's. Wearing the pretty red dress Mrs. Bee had made her for the church social earlier that month, Opal beckoned for Libby to hurry.

"Goodness sakes, don't keep the child waiting. Give me that,'' said Mrs. Bee, pulling at Libby's apron string.

Glad to have all the work of the dinner behind her, Libby laughed and peeled off her apron and called to Naomi and Opal, "I'll be right there.''

Sophronia paused in clanking and clattering dirty dishes together to tug at Libby's skirt as she passed. "Are you going to the circus now?''

Libby smiled and nodded. "How about you, Sophronia?''

"Maddie was going to take me this afternoon, but Grandmother said we'd go tonight instead.'' Sliding the stack of dishes back onto the table, Sophronia wiped her hands on the apron shrouding her dress. Careless of the richly embroidered collar, she gave the lace swathing her throat an impatient jerk and fell in step with Libby. "Then the cream separator blew up and we were late getting here and there's all these dishes to wash.''

"Blew up?'' exclaimed Libby. "Mercy!''

Opal, coming to join them, talked right over her. "You mean you can't go to the show until these are done?'' She swept the tables of dirty dishes with a crestfallen glance, and said with painful honesty, "That'll take all night, Phronky.''

"She said, 'Duty before pleasure,' so here I am in this awful itchy dress and I can't even go to the circus!'' Sophronia glowered and batted her lashes, fighting back tears. "I'll be glad when school starts and I can go stay with my other grandmother until Mama and Papa come home.''

Opal turned a soulful face from her mother to Libby, and entreated, "Can we ask her granny if she can come with us?''

Libby wasn't mean-spirited enough to want to see the child deprived. But neither was she asking Mrs. Dorrance for anything that might be construed as a favor. Sensing her hesitation, Naomi murmured in Libby's ear, "I ain't got nothin' agi'n a child washin' a few dishes, but it don't seem right she ort to miss out on a circus whilst she's doin' it.''

"I know. But . . .''

"Reckon there'd be no harm in askin','' said Naomi. Tugging self-consciously at her skirt and smoothing her faded shirtwaist, she strode over to Mrs. Dorrance, spoke briefly to her, and to Libby's astonishment came back with two dimes in her hand and Mrs. Dorrance's permission for Sophronia to accompany them.

The circus had set up on the vacant lot at the edge of town where the members of the New Hope Church hoped to build soon. The huge tent with folks crowding beneath its canvas made Libby think of a ship jammed with travelers, all anxious for their first glimpse of a magical shore.

She and Naomi were fortunate enough to find seats for themselves and the girls on the top row where a breeze stirred at their backs. The sky behind the ponytail clouds was still blue as the evening began with a gala parade of clowns and dog and pony acts and mules trained to waltz, roll barrels, jump hurdles, and even pick up handkerchiefs.

Opal, who had seen the afternoon performance with Mrs. Bee, narrated each act as ladies in glittering costumes, feathers, and spangles performed daring stunts from ropes and bicycles and the bare backs of galloping steeds. Naomi exclaimed over the revolving ladder acts and juggling acts and feats of strength and dexterity. But it took a muscular tumbler in tights to impress Sophronia. She studied the precision of his race down a long ramp, caught her breath as he bounded on a springboard and catapulted high in the air and turned two somersaults before being dragged back to earth by gravity's force.

Naomi gave the girls permission to go for a lemonade during intermission, while she and Libby held their seats. With their fans they stirred air heavy with the scents of circus animals and dusty straw and too many sweaty bodies crowded together. It was almost time for the second half of the show to begin when Opal came racing back with the news that she had just seen her father.

"Here? At the circus?" Naomi's jaw slackened. "Are you sure?"

"Yes, Mama. He's across the way, sittin' with Mr. Watson and Frankie and Davie and Teddy Baker and some others."

"I don't know anything about it," said Libby, in response to Naomi's questioning glance. "I can't think it was planned. Father would have mentioned it."

"Ain't like Decatur. Cain't hardly drag him to town, not even on business," said Naomi.

"Kin I go sit with him and Frankie? Kin I, Mama, please?"

"You got Sophronia with ya, and I promised her granny I'd look after her. Where is she, anyway?"

"In line for lemonade. Please, Mama?" Opal tried one more time. "I ain't seen him in a long time."

Swayed by her daughter's pleas, Naomi relented a little. "Go say howdy if yer of a mind to, but then you come right back, ya hear? I mean it now, Opal. Don't make me come fetch ya."

Opal hugged her mother's neck. "I won't, Mama. Thank you, Mama."

Naomi patted Opal with a rough hand and watched her clatter away, but there was a distressed look in her eye that hadn't been there a moment ago. "Don't know what got into him, comin' to a circus," she muttered. "Used to be, gettin' him to town was rougher'n pullin' teeth. Fine time to go and change his ways.''

Naomi fidgeted and chattered as she was prone to do, and flapped at the sweltering air with her fan. When five minutes had stretched to ten, she searched the crowd that had swallowed Opal without a trace. ''Where is that gal? Kin ya see her, Libby?''

''She'll be along shortly.'' Libby lifted her eyes from the printed program and tried to distract her. ''It says here the comic mule is valued at over a thousand dollars, can you imagine?''

Naomi sat back, unusually silent, and didn't take her eyes off the printed program until Sophronia and Opal returned sipping lemonade.

The second half of the circus was no less spectacular than the first. The lion trainer thrilled the children, as did the rolling-globe act. But it was the family team in the double-trapeze act that delighted Libby the most. Three brothers and one sister performed acrobatic turns on the bars and then, in the most astounding feat of courage she had ever witnessed, the girl was hurled from the hands of one brother a distance of thirty feet or more to lock hands with the second brother. It was an image forever emblazoned on her mind.

Opal was no less impressed. ''I'm going to be a swing girl,'' Libby heard her tell Sophronia as they started home.

''Not me. I'm going to be leaper,'' Sophronia replied.

''There aren't any girl leapers.''

''There is now.'' Sophronia thumped her chest with her thumb, her eyes diamond-bright.

They angled toward the center of town, the streetlamps lighting the way. The girls strolled ahead of them, whispering and sending back glances.

Naomi, having recovered from the shock of Decatur acting so out of character, paid them little heed. Savoring the rare evening out, she said, ''Cain't say when I ever had sech a treat. 'Cept maybe when Mr. James Whitcomb Riley done a reading at the Columbian, and Decatur bought me a book of his poems. Shoulda thought to pack it when I come to town.'' She shrugged off her regret. ''Don't matter, railly. I got most of them words in my head anyways.''

At Libby's coaxing she recited a poem, then another. Admiring her resilience, Libby smiled, and said, ''I can see where Frankie got his talent for memorizing.''

Naomi acknowledged the compliment with a modest tuck of her chin. ''Ginerally speaking, when it comes to mistakes folks make and the hurtin' it brings, I ain't so shore but what the real talent is in the art of forgettin'.''

The Columbian was dark, everyone gone home except for Mrs. Dorrance. Libby spotted her buggy parked alongside the building. She was sitting ramrod-straight on the seat, watching for them. Sophronia whispered to Opal, thanked Naomi and Libby for taking her with them, then plodded on to meet her grandmother.

Libby said good-bye to Naomi and Opal and left them at the alley leading to Willie Blue's back door. She continued alone past the Columbian, turned left, and passed the south-facing entrance to the same building. She was passing the jail when she saw a fellow at the end of the block standing beneath the streetlamp that lighted the pedestrian railroad crossing. Dressed in dark trousers, a pin-striped shirt, and a vest, he had Ike's height and his stance, but was so thin, she wasn't certain it was he until he took his hat off and the streetlamp bathed his face in light.

"Evenin', Libby," he said when the distance between them had narrowed to a few feet. "What'd ya think of the circus?"

"It was grand," said Libby, her heart leaping at the realization that he had been waiting for her. "You made a trip in for it?"

He nodded, one hand in the pocket of his dark flannel trousers, the other tapping his hat against his leg. "Decatur talked me into it. Ran into your father and them."

"You sat with Father? Opal didn't mention seeing you."

"She had her eyes fixed on her daddy. They get together, did they?"

"Who?"

"Decatur and Opal. Opal said her mama told her to come back to her own seat once she'd said howdy, but that Decatur could stop by the store if he wanted to visit for a spell."

Libby jerked her head up and declared, "Naomi said no such thing!"

Tiny lines crinkled the outer corners of his eyes. "Wondered myself if Opal made it up."

"If you saw through it, then Decatur certainly should have."

"Don't think he was wantin' to too hard."

"No wonder Opal and Sophronia had their heads together all the way home. The scamps!"

"Naomi's plain-spoken," he reasoned. "If she don't want Decatur there, she won't be long in sayin' so."

"Of course she doesn't want him. Why would she want him?"

"I don't know, Lib." He put his hat on again, canted it low, and added amicably, "He cain't cook, he doesn't clean up after hisself, and he's broody as a coon dog left under the porch when the moon's shining high."

"Now there's a picture."

They traded smiles and as if by mutual consent left the McClures to the McClures. Ike didn't ask if he could walk her home, but then neither did he presume to take her arm as they crossed the railroad tracks side by side. It was a gorgeous night, the magic of the circus receding to the mystique of two hearts taking silent measure. Seized by a childlike exhilaration, Libby trapped a lightning bug, admired the soft glow it made between her cupped palms, then let it go again. It flitted past her ear and landed in her hair.

Ike plucked it out, a chuckle rumbling from his throat. "See what ya git for goin' bare-headed. Where's your hat?"

"Circus is no place for a hat. I didn't want to block the v . . ." Distracted by the fleeting brush of his fingers in her hair and the intoxicating warmth of his gaze, Libby was a sentence and a half down the wrong track when she realized what he meant. She stopped short. "Was it you who sent the hat?"

"Sure it was me. What'd ya think?"

"I thought it was Angus. I assumed he was apologizing for staying in Bloomington last weekend instead of . . . he sent a telegram saying . . . oh, never mind. I *do* like it, I like it very much. But there was no card. So I didn't realize . . ." Watching his face, she stopped prattling and suffered a pang. "Now I've gone and hurt your feelings."

"No ya ain't, Lib," he said, a boyish pluck to his smile. "I was just wondering . . . I've seen every which kind of holiday card, but where do ya suppose a fella'd find one that says thanks for saving my life?"

Relieved, Libby willed her hammering heart to hush, and protested, "I didn't save your life."

"Didn't ya? And here I've been tellin' everyone you did."

Libby answered his bid for a smile. They passed the Grubens' home in companionable silence. Ike's pace slowed a bit as they left the last streetlamp behind. "I been studyin' what you said," he ventured, his voice dipping low as his eyes settled on her again. "About asking you again sometime. For dinner, I mean. I'd like that, Lib."

"Me, too."

"Are you about ready for that buggy ride, too?"

"The one where you're going to show me you're really not such a bad fellow with horses?"

"That's the one."

"I might be coaxed into it. Though I don't believe I care to go anywhere near the creek."

He laughed. "Sounds fair enough."

Between the lines of gentle bantering, they were drawing ever nearer to the completion of what had begun a week ago in Dr. Harding's dim corridor. It brought to sharp awareness the way her immediate future was linked to Angus's. Libby hadn't considered it an encumbrance before. Suddenly, it was.

Averting her face, she said, "I suppose I should speak to Angus first before

. . . before I accept your invitations. As you know, I've been practicing to sing for his campaign circuit."

"De monk, de monk, de monk," he sang softly. "Ya got a rare talent."

Libby flushed and laughed at the memory of him walking in on that dress fitting and catching her playing the monkey in her inside-out dress with the pinned hem and the arms missing. "And you, a talent for sneaking up on people."

He denied it with a soft chuckle, and stopped at the edge of her yard in a patch of clover that grew between the street and the beaten path. The conversation stopped, too. Libby breathed the light, sweet bouquet of crushed clover blooms and tipped her face to the velvet sky and the silver sheen of stars.

Ike's gaze moved over her face, his voice rumbling out of his throat rich and low. "Are ya gonna let me come courtin', Lib?"

His directness triggered gooseflesh. "I'd like that. So long as my obligations to Angus's campaign aren't a problem."

He stirred the clover again, shifting his feet. His demeanor shifted too, an ever-so-slight flattening of his mouth and a sharper definition of his eyes as his lashes swept down and up again.

Gingerly, she added, "It isn't just the singing. I'm to cover his campaign stops for the *Gazette* as well."

"You told Mr. Gruben you'd do it?"

"Yes."

"You want to go, don't ya?"

"Yes," she said, and made no excuses.

"Then you should do it, I guess."

"You don't mind?"

"It ain't up to me to mind. Though I wouldn't feel right about courtin' somebody else's girl."

"I won't be going as his girl," reasoned Libby. "He'll understand that, as soon as we've had a chance to talk. After that, I'm just another Berry Sister." Seeing no change in his expression, she added, "My gown is made. We've practiced and practiced, and as I said, Mr. Gruben's counting on me. I wouldn't feel right pulling out now."

"I ain't askin' you to, Lib."

But he *was* asking her to make a choice. She saw with a sinking heart that he didn't want her singing for another man's cause. Saw, too, that he wouldn't claim what he wasn't sure he could keep.

She wavered, torn between her heart's impatient clamor and the wish to follow through on her plans. It was a hard decision. A chancy one, too. Praying she wouldn't be sorry, she said quietly, "I can't go back on my word, Ike."

He mulled that over a long moment and finally nodded. "All right."

"All right, *what?*"

He drew a deep breath and looked her in the eye. "I got obligations, too. Crops to get out and work around the sirup camp. Seems like we'll both have more time, come November."

After the election. Her fingers twisted the corded handle of her pocketbook. "It sounds like a long wait."

"Yep," he said, drawing himself up to go. "But then, when you think of it, the sturdiest trees in the forest is them that grow slow."

It was a thoughtful reply, seasoned in wisdom. It was irrational of her to feel let down and impatient with it. And with him. But she did, for hearts were not ruled by the calendar. She drew a deep breath and let it go slowly. If he could wait, then so could she. And she wasn't going to make herself miserable doing it.

28

Ike sat in front of Naomi's woodworking shop, listening to a heavy train clack over the night rails and thinking maybe he was as much a buffoon as that critter he'd seen in the circus sideshow. The only understanding he and Libby had come to was that come November, maybe they'd come to an understanding. What kind of romancin' was that? But what else could he do?

Her obligations were legitimate ones, in *her* mind anyway. It wasn't her fault that there was in *his* mind that long-ago lakeside image: *Maddie coming out of the tall grass, dandelion wool in her hair. Angus slipping off in the dusk, bootlaces dragging and his shirttail hanging loose.* The same Angus who was stumping for votes on a Prohibition platform claiming it was a matter of moral conscience. Had he lied so often about that tryst until he'd forgotten the truth himself?

Ike hadn't. He wasn't voting for a man with no more honesty than that, and he'd be a bigger hypocrite than Angus if he pretended it didn't bother him that Libby would soon be trekking over the countryside with him.

Libby isn't Maddie.

God impressed the thought upon him so firmly, Ike lifted his face to the star-studded sky. "I know. But if I say she's my girl and she goes anyway, then where am I?"

There came no affirmation of being right or wrong. He leaned back, hands linked behind his head. What was done was done. He'd committed himself to waiting, and he'd stand by that decision. If it was God who had opened the door, it wasn't going to swing back in his face.

Distracted by the sound of a wagon coming along the road, Ike came to his feet. With only distant stars to light the night, he recognized the horse and wagon before he recognized Billy Young. The wagon creaked in harmony with the leather trappings as Billy stopped the team.

Ike walked out to the road to meet him. "Wasn't expectin' to see you by here tonight."

"I gave Chloe Berry a ride home from the circus. No more than pulled up to her gate than she hit the ground moving," he said from the wagon seat.

"And she didn't invite you in to say hello to her folks?" said Ike. "You aren't makin' much headway with that girl."

"I'm in no danger of getting tied down anytime soon," said Billy with unflagging good humor. He jumped to the ground. "Glad to find you still up. We could play some cards if Decatur's willing."

"I don't know as he's home. He stayed behind to visit with the young'uns awhile."

"Thinking about inviting Naomi home, is he?" Billy guessed shrewdly.

Ike leaned forward and looked toward the tracks. The sound of the train was fading in the night. He spotted a dark shape moving their way. "Reckon that's him now. Ask him yerself."

"Just wondering about you, Decatur," Billy called. "Thought maybe you were sparking one of those circus gals."

Decatur flung himself down on the ground, propped his back against the hitching post, and hooked long arms around a bent knee. "Been lookin' fer that rib I misplaced. But durned if she ain't set on keepin' it."

"Rib?" echoed Billy, puzzled.

"That's right, rib. The one what God got so free and easy with. Tell him, Ike."

"Adam and Eve," said Ike.

"Oh!" Enlightened, Billy chuckled. "Shucks, Decatur. If you want the rib, you've got to take the woman, too."

"What do you know about it, you ain't even dry behind the ears? You or Ike, neither one." Decatur spit toward the road. "Ya seen that bruise on Ike's jaw? Don't s'pose he told ya how he come by it. Miss Libby, that's how. She took a hunk out of his jaw and was fixin' to use him for fish bait when I come along."

"Rescued him, did you? You're a better man than me, McClure," said Billy, egging him on. "I wouldn't risk Miss Libby's disfavor that way. Not with hair that red."

Judging by Decatur's mood, it must not have gone too badly with Naomi. Ike said, "You two goin' ta talk, or are we goin' ta play cards?"

They went inside, lit a lamp, and played a few hands. But Ike was tired. It had been a long day, and as much as he hated to admit it, Doc Harding was right. His strength wasn't near what it had been before he fell ill. Or was it disappointment taking its toll?

"You fellas go on with yer game without me. I'm turnin' in," he said with a yawn, and pulled off his boots.

Billy had lost every hand and was ready to call it quits. He stretched and made for the door, then delayed his departure long enough to wheedle at Ike, trying to get him to reconsider about going down to St. Louis to parade with the other members of the First Volunteer Cavalry. Ike told him to go home, just like he always did when Billy got pesky.

"Never saw a man so set against being honored," grumbled Billy. "You might even surprise yourself and have a good time."

"If he don't wanna go, he don't wanna go. What ya pesterin' him for?" groused Decatur.

"Habit," said Billy, and let himself out.

Billy was right, in part, Ike thought. He might have a good time. Knowing that Libby was going to be at the fair overseeing Frankie, Ike was thinking for the first time that maybe he *should* take advantage of the opportunity to see the fair, even if it meant marching in a parade or two.

Decatur, uninterested in walking home, sprawled out to sleep on the floor a few yards a way. Too tired to fall easily to sleep, Ike thought about Chester Gentry funding Libby's trip to the fair. No secret as to why that went against the grain. He had only to look back over the years to the grovel-in-the-dirt feeling of standing before his father's half brother with his head hanging and his heart pounding and his mother's nervous hand kneading his bony shoulder as she asked for food and shelter.

In recent years he had worked at not holding Chester's tight-fisted response against him. Sometimes, he thought he'd gotten over it altogether. Then God would show him he hadn't, and that that was pretty poor pay for the rescue He had provided in the unlikely form of Willie Blue.

"You recollect that story you was readin' to me the other night?" Decatur spoke in the darkness, stirring Ike from his reverie.

"Which one?" asked Ike, for he'd taken to reading the Bible out loud to Decatur in hopes of helping him over rough ground the same as Willie Blue had done for him. Decatur favored the Old Testament stories. He was taken with all that blood and gore and rods turning to snakes and back again. Or so Ike thought anyway.

"The one about the old widder-woman and the young widder-woman," Decatur said, proving him wrong.

"Naomi and Ruth?"

"Yep, that's the one. What was the meanin' ya fixed to her name?"

"Naomi? My stepdaddy says it means *pleasant,*" replied Ike.

"I mean the other one. The one she gived herself when her menfolk was all dead."

"Mara. Means her life become bitter." Ike waited, and when Decatur said nothing further, asked, "Why were you wantin' to know?"

"Jest thinkin' about Opal's mama. May take to callin' her Mara, too. Seems like she's turned bitter."

Maybe it hadn't gone so well after all. Ike inserted into the silence, "The story didn't end there. Things got better."

"On account of Mara's next of kin helping her out by marryin' the young widder-woman. That was some purty bold plannin' they done."

"It was hard times," Ike pointed out. "Woman needed a man to look after her."

"Don't seem like Naomi does."

Helpmeet. The word dropped to mind. Naomi was no weak sister. Looking after wasn't what she needed so much as to be appreciated as a helper. Looked to Ike like Decatur should have figured that out by now. Or maybe he had. Maybe he was just too stout-headed to admit he wanted to be needed and appreciated, too. Ike sighed and closed his eyes and thought what a complicated work God had made when he breathed life into man.

Though it had been a late night, Ike awakened at dawn, pulled on his boots, splashed some water on his face, and was crossing the bridge on his way to take care of his team when Naomi came along on Libby's horse Proctor. Her hair was loose and tangled about her shoulders, her mouth taut, strain showing in her green eyes. There was no reason to think her distraught condition had anything to do with Libby, yet Ike's mind made that leap. His heart slammed against his chest.

"Opal and Sophronia run off with the circus!" Naomi cried as she drew even with him.

Air found its way to his lungs again. Ashamed he should be so weak with relief when she was so anxious, he caught the reins with one hand and steadied her with the other as she slid to the ground. "You sure that's where they've gone?"

"Yep. It's in this here note."

"Where's the circus's next engagement?"

"I don't know, jest that it's north. See there?" Naomi pointed out the animal dung and the multitude of tracks littering the north–south road just beyond the bridge. "What sort of folks take off with two young'uns what don't belong to 'em?"

"Maybe they don't know. Wouldn't be hard to stow away in an outfit that size." Ike took a closer look at the trail they'd left and judged them to be only an hour or so down the road. He told her so, and added, "I don't think

ya need to fret over any harm comin' to them, Naomi. They seemed like
decent folks.

"I talked to the man who owned the whole outfit," he went on, "and
asked him about that feller who died. Told him he said he'd worked for the
circus. He told me the man was as good a ringmaster as he'd ever seen, but
he let him go on account he bedeviled the ladies in the troupe. Still, he was
sorry to hear he was dead. Now that don't seem like the sort of feller you'd
have to worry about trustin'." Having done his best to reassure her, Ike
added, "Why don't you go on back to town and let me fetch 'em home for
you?"

"Much obliged, Ike, but it ain't yer place. I'm goin' after Decatur. He had
a hand in Opal actin' up like this."

"How's that?"

"She coaxed him into comin' by Willie Blue's last night after the circus.
Reckon she thought if she could jest get us together, we'd patch things up.
It didn't work out that way, and she got all tore up." Naomi blinked hard,
her throat working over emotions she was trying to hold in check. "Maddie
come beatin' on the door awhile ago, sayin' Sophronia was missin', and sure
enuf, Opal was gone, too. Said in her note she was goin' away ta be a swing
girl. Ya see, don't ya, why Decatur or me should be the one to fetch her
home?"

Ike accompanied her back to the shop. He led Proctor along, then tied the
horse to the hitching post and went around back to get him a bucket of water
while Naomi went inside. When he came back, the door was standing open,
their quarrel spilling out.

". . . yer wantin' to see me, then come see me," he heard Naomi light into
Decatur. "But don't come scootin' in on the skirt tail of that girl. You hear
me, Decatur? These kids is havin' a hard time of it, and it ain't their fault.
It's yers and mine."

"Now hold on there a minute," Decatur growled like a bear stirred out of
hibernation. "She said you was wantin' me to stop by."

"Yer a grown man and yer gonna stand there and tell me ya cain't see
through a child's wishful thinkin'? I ain't fooled, not fer a minute. In all the
years we been married, ya ain't done nothin' ya didn't feel like doin', so
don't try and say ya came for any reason except ya wanted to. I ain't faultin'
ya for it. I'll talk to ya till ya give me a reason not to. But it's gonna be
honest talk."

"Honest talk? What do you know about honest talk? It wasn't me who
brung all the trouble on us by holdin' back on it bein' Willie Blue fathered
Frankie, like his name was somethin' worth protectin'."

"Don't start that up again! I cain't take ya standin' with yer foot on my
neck, tellin' me it's all my fault, and it all goes back to Willie. I been faithful

to you since the day we took our vows, and if that don't count for nothin', then we got nothin' to say. Now are you gonna fetch our girl home or do I do it myself?''

"Sure you got time, what with a store to run and all?"

Ike winced at Decatur's sarcasm, slid the bucket down where Proctor could reach it, and moved off a few yards.

Naomi's voice carried to him. "I wouldn't be runnin' that store if you didn't tell me to get out and take the boy with me. So don't be actin' like it's that store that's got betwixt us.''

"Maybe I didn't mean for ya to go.''

"Then maybe you shouldn'tna said it. I ain't no mind reader. Somebody says for me to go, I go.''

"Then go on up the lane where ya belong, and I'll go get our girl.''

"Yer forgettin' Frankie.''

"I ain't forgettin' him. He's got a home here same as Opal.''

"But does he have a father? You think about that, and when ya got an answer, we'll talk some more." Naomi bolted out the door, her skin stretched tautly over her chin and cheekbones She grabbed the reins from the hitching post and flung a leg over Proctor. "But ya best remember I ain't buildin' on rotted floorboards,'' she called back. "I want a fresh start or no start at all.''

Naomi's face darkened as she spotted Ike standing there. But she lifted her chin and called to Decatur one last time, saying, "While yer getting Opal, fetch Miz Dorrance's granddaughter home, too. She's gonna have a conniption when she finds that girl gone.''

Decatur appeared in the doorway, boots in hand. He looked like it was his gut, not Proctor's sides, feeling the spur of Naomi's heels. Eyes blazing, he watched her ride off, then yanked his hat down hard on his head, sat down to pull on his boots, and laced them up in a stillness as ominous as the eye of a storm. Ike was about to slip around back and make himself scarce when Decatur came to his feet.

"I got ta walk up the lane and git the team. Opal's run off with the circus and Naomi's wantin' me to fetch her home.''

"Take mine. They've been fed.''

"Save me some time." Decatur pulled up his suspenders, struggled with his emotions a long moment, and finally said, "No way to start the mornin'.''

"Depends on how you look at it.''

Decatur glowered at him from beneath beetled brows. "Ain't no way *to* see it 'cept troublesome.''

"Helpmeets can be that way, I reckon.''

"Helpmeets?'' echoed Decatur scathingly.

"That's why He took that rib for, ya know. To make ya a helpmeet.''

"Who, Naomi?'' Decatur snorted. "She been a heap of help, ain't she?''

"Then what're you wantin' her to come home for? Or isn't that what ya meant when ya told her to go on up the lane?"

Decatur dragged a hand over one bristled jowl. "Galloway, ya got awful keen hearin' for a man with one ear."

Ike shifted his weight and tugged at his bad ear.

"If a man don't stand up to a woman when she chews him over like soup bone, why he may just as well let her have the other eleven ribs, too."

"You ain't wearin' 'em right, anyway," said Ike on sudden inspiration. "Ya got 'em turned upright, lookin' through 'em jest like a jail cell. That's what fear does to a man. Shuts him up tight inside himself."

Decatur swore and started down the road and was almost to the railroad tracks when he called back, "I ain't much in the mood to argue. But if I was, I'd say ya might try out yer own advice b'fore you go foistin' it off on me."

Ike cupped his hand to his bad ear like he hadn't heard. Decatur snarled something about a man minding his own business and strode away, stirring dust with his stamping feet.

Grin fading, Ike circled around back again, pumped himself a cup of water, and sat down on the well surround. A familiar weakness lapped over him in waves. Good thing it was Sunday. Felt a mite feverish, too. *Make it go away. I got to be stronger tomorrow. I got wheat to cut, Lord. Make it go away.* He went back inside and took his medicine, then gathered up his belongings and took them back over to the sirup camp. If Naomi did decide to come home, she'd be needing her shop back, and he didn't want to be in her way.

Ike rested the remainder of the morning. It was getting close to noon when Decatur passed by, taking the girls back to Edgewood. Opal was slumped over with her head on Decatur's knee. Sophronia had made a pillow of Opal's back, the pair of them swaying on the seat as the horses drew the wagon along. Circus adventure must have taken its toll.

"They all right?" Ike called from the door of the sap house.

"So far," Decatur called back. "Ask me again, once Naomi and Miz Dorrance git aholt of 'em."

Ike waved and watched the wagon until the trees had swallowed it up. Feeling better for his rest, he went on down to the creek to see if the fish were biting. He was setting bank poles when he came across a battered hat of plaited straw and water-stained ribbons and recognized it as Libby's.

Must be the one she had lost the day she'd pulled him out of the creek. He got his boots wet retrieving it, and wondered, even as he took it back to the sap house with him, what it was good for. It was too far gone for refurbishing. She wouldn't want it back. But somehow, Ike couldn't bring himself to throw it away. At length, he got a hammer and nail and fixed it to the sap-house door, then stood back and eyed it awhile. It sure enough looked like it belonged there. Though if she was to ride by and see it . . .

He deliberated awhile, but didn't take it down.

29

  The *Gazette* office smelled of ink and stale cigar smoke, the live ashes of which were being scattered by Mr. Gruben's small spring-loaded desktop fan. It wasn't even noon yet, and it was sweltering in the office. Earl Morefield whistled off-key and worked at the typesetting machine while Mr. Gruben scanned the articles Libby had presented him for Friday's paper. The newsprint from Earl's folded paper hat had turned the beads of perspiration on his brow to a gray sheen. Libby fanned herself with her notebook as she waited.

"Very nice," said Mr. Gruben of Libby's article on the circus. He snubbed out his cigar, leaned back in his chair, and locked his hands behind his head. "I especially like the glimpse of the circus folk washing their stock and their wagons out at the lake. How about a personal touch on the wrap-up, too?"

"I'm sorry, sir, I don't quite understand," said Libby.

"What? No quote from the two little girls who ran away to be kinkers?"

Seeing his mouth twitch, Libby confided, "I'm in enough trouble as it is. Mrs. Dorrance came by my house this morning and took me to task for reading *Toby Tyler* to the children."

"So I heard." Mr. Gruben leaned toward his desk again and leafed through an untidy assortment of papers on his desk. "She was by here awhile ago and left an open letter to the editor for Friday's paper."

Libby could make a fair guess as to the contents. The trauma of Opal and Sophronia's having run away with the circus, only to be safely retrieved yesterday morning by Decatur McClure, had caused quite a ripple. The girls were fine, but Libby was still smarting from Mrs. Dorrance's stinging rebuke over the irresponsibility of reading the children a story that made heroes of rebellious youngsters who ran away from home. She braced herself and asked, "Does her letter recommend the closing of our library?"

"Something like that."

Libby cringed. "It never occurred to me that the children might get ideas from the story. Still, she has no right to punish the whole town over my poor judgment. I've already apologized. What else can I do?"

"Come now, Miss Watson," said Mr. Gruben, as if disappointed in her lack of pluck. "You're taking too dismal a view of this. Controversy may turn out to be the making of a library that has so far attracted little attention beyond that of the children."

"The making of it?" Incredulous, Libby begged to differ. "Forgive me, Mr. Gruben, but I don't see how Mrs. Dorrance's overreaction can spell anything but disaster."

"Then you haven't thought this through. Get out into the community and talk to people. Ask for opinions on what they expect from a library and whether or not they are committed to seeing it succeed."

"But Mr. Gruben . . ."

He flung his hands out in a shooing motion, a wordless dismissal.

Doubtfully, Libby picked up her Memorandum notebook and let herself out. Mrs. Dorrance was on her high horse, and he thought that could somehow be used for the *good* of the library? Such optimism required a better imagination than hers!

But it wasn't her place to second-guess, just to write what he requested. If he wanted opinions, Willie Blue's was a good place to start. Libby walked next door and strolled to the back, to find Hascal Caton lolling back in Captain Boyd's rocking chair expounding his pet view of late.

"Didn't I tell ya Doc wasn't bein' cautious enuf about makin' sure whatever that Robinson feller had wasn't catchy? Gram Steadman dies, then Ike sickens nigh unto death and now old Ebenezer Jones and his woman are tremblin' over the grave and still, Doc is treatin' it like business as usual."

"Mr. Jones has been nine weeks with the liver complaint, Hack," Captain Boyd said, "and Doc gave Mrs. Jones only a month to live six months ago. There's no mystery sickness where either one of them is concerned." Seeing Libby, he came to his feet with a welcoming smile and touched his fingers to his pillbox cap. " 'Morning, Miss Willie."

Libby returned the captain's greeting and greeted the other gentlemen as well. Mr. Lamb and Major Minor responded, but Hascal Caton was bent on holding the floor and couldn't be bothered with pleasantries.

"Old Skiff out at the grove, he's sicker'n a dog. What about that?" he demanded, wheeling back on his rockers.

"I'll wager Miz Dorrance put a curse on 'im on account of his moonshinin'," ventured Major.

"And the feller stayin' overt' Mrs. Baker's?" demanded Mr. Caton. "He ain't worked since last Thursday."

"If you mean the lineman for Home Telephone Company, it isn't sickness keeping him off the job," said Captain Boyd. "Doc said he slipped climbing a pole, came down on the ring where he'd tied his horses, and nearly tore off his middle finger."

"Tarnation! I ain't gonna name 'em one by one, but thar's sixteen folk I can count right this minute took to their beds, and yer tellin' me we ain't got an epidemic on our hands?"

Minor arched forward on his cracker barrel, spit toward the coal bucket, and drawled, "Hack, ya go countin' noses in other folks' bedchambers, Mr. Lamb'll soon be plantin' *you.*"

The other gents slapped their knees and chortled.

"Tell me, Mr. Caton, how is the wheat harvest comin' along oot your way?" asked Father in a good-hearted effort to lead the conversation down a less contentious avenue.

"Farmers out Old Kentucky way are gettin' good yields, though it's a mite hot for the horses. Man pushes 'em too hard, they'll drop dead in their . . ." Spotting Frankie coming down the stairs with the slop jar, Hascal Caton stopped dead in *his* conversational traces. "What's got into you, boy? That's woman's work."

Waiting for a break in the conversation into which she could insert her library questions, Libby swung around to see Maddie coming down the stairs on Frankie's heels. She was carrying a graniteware basin of water. Her hair was piled upon her head like a glistening black cloud and dressed in a white pearl netting. Her white layered skirt and shirtwaist were shiny with starch and crisp from pressing. Angelic was too soft and too serene a word for her, yet Libby had never seen her look lovelier.

Her only blemish was the frown she wore as she singled Mr. Caton out of the circle of gents and blasted away at him, saying, "Woman's work? And what exactly is man's work?"

"Why, seein' that woman don't slack off none. And that, Miz Daniels, is a full-time job," declared Hascal. Gratified by Major Minor's salty chuckle, he thrust out his chest and added with a narrowed eye, "Handsome young widder-woman like yerself might make a lesson on that iffen she's bent on findin' a feller to replace the one she's jest buried."

"Hush now, Hack, that's going too far," murmured Captain Boyd in his velvet voice.

Libby's heart bolted to her throat, preoccupation with the library suddenly secondary to the realization that Maddie's secret was out. Her gaze skipped from Mr. Caton's face to Maddie's.

"There, there, Captain. Don't you worry about me. I can fend for myself," she claimed, her proud chin in the air. Her walking-length skirt, layered and adorned with tatted lace and embroidery-fringed scallops, snapped as she followed Frankie around the counter and out the back door with a basin of wash water in hand.

Libby sidled behind the counter and past her father to where Naomi was knocking the dust off the spice jars with studied deliberation. "What's going on?" she whispered.

Naomi kept her voice low. "Miss Maddie's had a fallin' out with her ma. Plannin' on goin' down to Mr. Cearlock's sister's to stay fer a spell."

The news was unexpected. "What did she and her mother quarrel over this time?" Libby asked.

"She ain't said exactly, but she's been over to Mr. Cearlock's and back a couple of times this mornin', so I'm guessin' it's somethin' to do with word gettin' out it was Dr. Daniels who died overt' Doc's," confided Naomi in a hush.

"Who told?"

"Cain't say. Pa picked it up somewheres. It's all over town." Naomi ended the roundelay of whispers as Maddie returned with the empty basin in hand.

She greeted Libby, but her gaze, usually so direct, fell quickly away. Addressing Naomi, she said in the same low tone Naomi and Libby had been using, "I'm going out to Mother's to pick up a few things I forgot."

"Yer gonna git yerself all hot and dusty, walkin' back out," observed Naomi.

"I won't be walking. Thank you, Naomi, for letting me freshen up here. I'll get my things and be out of your way."

"What the devil was ya whisperin' 'bout?" demanded Hascal as Maddie retreated up the stairs.

"Nothin' that concerns you, Pa." Naomi took a silver dollar from the cash register and slid it onto the counter. "Why don't ya walk on overt' the bank and git me some nickels? I'm clear out."

"Send one of the young'uns," Hascal said, dodging her ploy to get him out of the store.

Maddie came back downstairs, a dainty pearl-covered purse dangling from one gloved hand, a parasol in the other.

Mr. Caton eyed her, and ventured, "Mr. Lamb, I been meanin' to ask, what's a body hafta pay to git one of them thar secret burials?"

Mr. Lamb blanched and ceased swatting flies with a rolled-up newspaper. "Mrs. Daniels, I assure you it wasn't me who divulged that information."

Maddie's gaze flicked over him as if he were the fly instead of the swatter. Her demeanor chilled another dozen degrees as she addressed Hascal Caton. "Here's an epidemic for you, Mr. Caton. An epidemic of busybodies. A highly contractible disease of small minds and niggardly spirits and idle hands, and you, sir, exhibit all the symptoms.''

"Now hold up there jest a minute . . ." blustered Hascal.

"Picking over people's lives like they were jigsaw puzzles!" Maddie shook her head. "And our leaders think women are too fiddle-headed to vote!''

Mr. Lamb, Captain Boyd, and even Major Minor, sharing the edge of her blistering stare, had the good grace to take it in silence. But not Hascal. Florid above his salt-and-pepper whiskers, he shot back, "What the devil did ya expect, comin' home makin' out like you was a widder when ya wasn't?''

"That would be my business, not yours," said Maddie haughtily. "Though I would be interested in knowing how you came by your information.''

Hascal sniffed. "I ain't got nothin' ta say 'bout that.''

"Congratulations, Mr. Caton. You're learning." Maddie swung around the counter and disappeared out the back door again, white boots clicking smartly.

"If she ain't a piece of work. Kickin' up her heels since she was in short skirts and no-account as all get out. Where's she get off unloadin' on us like we was some kinda . . . What she doin' upstairs, anyways?''

"Let it go, Pa," warned Naomi. "Ain't gittin' any cooler in here with tempers sparking. Now about that change . . .''

"Tarnation! Give me the dollar, then, and I'll go," flared Hascal, coming to his feet. "Never heard the like of sech jawin' over needin' a few nickels.''

Captain Boyd, Mr. Lamb, and Major Minor stirred to their feet as well. The door opened just as they reached it, and in walked Decatur McClure. Libby saw Naomi's chin drop. Saw her hands jerk and swift color sweep up her neck and crowd over her face.

Decatur nodded to the men, removed his hat, and continued on toward the back of the store. The old ones turned and followed his progress. Hascal, standing in the door letting in flies, was the first to recover his surprise. He greeted his son-in-law in a tone far more cordial than he'd used on his daughter. "What brings ya to town, Decatur?" he asked.

"Come to see 'bout the young'uns." McClure stopped and turned back to ask, "Say, you boys know who's ailin' overt' Doc's? Seen a quarantine sign on his front door.''

"Quarantine?" Mr. Lamb and Major Minor echoed in unison.

"I tried to tell ya! Didn't I try to tell ya?" Hascal nearly fell out the door in his eagerness to get to the bottom of it. Mr. Lamb, Major Minor, and Captain Boyd weren't far behind him.

Her library article all but forgotten, Libby was torn between escaping on their heels and staying put in the event Naomi would appreciate more than Father as a buffer between herself and her estranged husband, for Billy

Young and Zerilda had already left on their mail routes and there wasn't a single customer in the store. By the time the clatter of feet and the banging of the door faded, Naomi had her head down. The spice jars glistened from her vigorous buffing.

Father filled the silence with a warm greeting to Decatur and made the decision for Libby, saying, " 'Tis a mortal hot day, laddie. A flamin' hot day. Libby, lass, skip oot the back door and fetch Mr. McClure a cold drink from the pump. And will ye be so kind as to carry Abigail's letters home with ye as ye go?"

"Father, I'm not going home this minute," said Libby, uncertain whether it was a good idea to abandon Naomi so completely.

"Then tuck them into yer pocket, lass. They'll keep well enough there. I canna help thinkin' I could do with a cold cuppie as well."

Libby glanced at the letters, one from Adam, the other bearing the logo of the Roth–Bigelow Circus in the left-hand corner. The circus? Now that was odd.

"Come along with ye, lass." Father gave her a nudge.

Libby slipped the letters in her pocket and fended off Father's rushing so as to catch the first rumble of words between Decatur and Naomi.

"The young'uns here?"

Evenly, Naomi replied, "Opal's playin' at Libby's."

"What about Frankie?"

"Out back washin' the slop jar."

"You got anything agin' him comin' on out to the grove with me, helpin' cut Ike's wheat? Doc's jest dared Ike to try runnin' the binder hisself, an' the crop ain't goin' to wait."

"Take him, then," said Naomi. "If he's cantankerous about it, remind him of the times Ike's give us a hand."

"Reckon I will, if it comes to that. A man's got to teach his son to be neighborly." Decatur paused, leaving plenty of dead air between those words and the next: "Ya whop Opal fer runnin' off?"

Libby slipped out behind her father just as Frankie was coming in with the slop jar. Father stretched out a hand and pointed him toward the pump. " 'Tis a dust-choked gentleman just beyond the door. Ye'd be doin' a guid deed if ye were to take him a cuppie. There's a guid laddie," he added when Frankie returned from the pump with a cup of water.

"Father, you should have warned him," Libby reproved as Frankie trekked inside.

"And hae him bolt on our poor Mr. McClure? God bless him, contrivin' to mend what he hae rent asunder."

"I'm not sure mending is possible. You should have heard Naomi when Decatur came to the circus. She fumed and fretted, not at all pleased. I have no idea what she said when he showed up at her door, but I don't think he lingered long."

"I winna doubt the man's errand is genuine," said Father. "Ike is fair overloaded wi' work, and not so mortal sturdy by the look of it. 'Tis a verra temperamental sickness, malaria. Bruisin' to a man's strength and a long while in mendin'."

Grudgingly Libby relented a bit. "I'm glad McClure has a conscience toward Ike, anyway." Abruptly, she asked, "What is going on with Maddie?"

The light in Father's eyes dimmed. He shook his head and murmured in sad reflection, "The lass's secret is all a'tatter and Hascal, the rogue, should be hangin' his head for his bedevilin'."

"Any idea who told?"

" 'Twould seem the leak came from the doctor's office."

"Dr. Harding?" asked Libby in surprise.

"No, lass. I canna say for certain, but 'twould seem it was Mrs. Brignadello. Such verra large ears for a small leddy to be wearin'."

Mrs. Bee. She should have guessed. For all of her good points, the woman had a lively interest in the affairs of others that made a real risk where any secret was concerned.

"Ye would not be contemplatin' revealin' the leddy's runaway tongue, would ye, lass?"

At Father's straying glance, Libby turned to see Maddie exit Angus's side office door and come up the alley toward them. "No, no. Of course not," Libby rushed to assure him, for what purpose would it serve to hurt Maddie further with the knowledge that one of her own "sisterhood" had leaked the news about Mr. Robinson being her husband?

As Maddie came toward her, Libby glimpsed something akin to guilt in her expression. There was a falter in her step that seemed out of character as well.

Maddie dropped her gaze from Libby's inquiring glance, then lifted it again and like one drawing a deep breath for an uphill climb, set her chin, and said without ceremony, "I'm borrowing Angus's rig for the ride out to Mother's. I'm pressed for time, but there's a matter I'd like to discuss. Could I coax you into riding out to the farm with me?"

Attributing Maddie's discomfort to the tempest Mrs. Dorrance was raising concerning the library, Libby said, "If this involves your mother, we've already talked. She came to see me early this morning."

"Indeed!" said Maddie, her eyebrow crooking. "And you're not upset?"

"Of course I'm upset," said Libby, puzzled by Maddie's uncharacteristic solicitousness. "I apologized, hoping she could be—"

"*You* apologized?" Maddie's well-shaped brows arched, confusion rippling her brow. Suddenly, her face cleared. "You're talking about the library. Yes, well that sign of hers on the doctor's door was unfortunate. But that wasn't what I wished to take up with you." Stopping, darting Libby's father a glance, Maddie asked a second time, "If you would ride along, we could talk."

Her curiosity stirred, Libby nonetheless had to decline. "I'd like to, Maddie, but I can't right this minute. I'm under a noon deadline, and Mr. Gruben has asked me to interview some people concerning what is to become of the library."

Seeming more herself, Maddie exclaimed with a spark of impatience, "I can sum it up for you. Mother's set her face against the library, not because it was a bad idea, but because it was an idea I supported, and she thinks me incapable of supporting a *good* idea."

Kindly, Father inserted, "I canna help thinkin' if the two of ye would not fall so quickly to bickerin' and fault-findin', ye might discover how verra much ye have in common."

Maddie drew herself up and looked at him as if he had fallen to earth from some distant star. "In common? Mr. Watson, we are as different as night and day! I've made my last effort at mending fences with that woman!"

"Be wary, lass," cautioned Father.

"You mentioned a sign. What sort of sign?" asked Libby, her thoughts backtracking over Maddie's words.

" 'Quarantine—Contagion of the Mind.' Which sums up Mother's diagnosis as to what is ailing me," said Maddie. She thrust out her proud chin. "You needn't look so sorry for me; she made the same essential assessment when I eloped with Damon. Now are you coming with me or not?"

Libby scarcely heard, so struck was she with sudden realization. "When Decatur was talking about the sign in Dr. Harding's door, he meant the library. There's no epidemic."

"Of course not," said Maddie. "Don't tell me you thought there was?"

"I canna help thinkin' Mr. Caton was taken with the notion, as well," inserted Father.

Like a swift-changing sky, Maddie gave a short laugh. "In that case, there's no telling how far *that* rumor will travel." Dismissing the whole matter as quickly as she had taken it up, Maddie issued Libby one last invitation. "You're sure you won't come?"

"I can't, Maddie."

"All right, then. But if you should bump into Angus, tell him we haven't had a chance to talk yet."

"What does Angus have to do with—?"

"I'll try to catch up with you when I come back from Mother's and explain everything," said Maddie. "If not, I'll write from Catherine's. Take care of yourself, Libby." She unfurled her parasol and hurried down the alley.

Libby stood looking after her, for her good-bye seemed eerily final. Had her mother turned her out? Was that why she was going to Catherine's?

Beside her, Father mused, "I canna help thinkin' the Leddy Dorrance and her wee sign will be visitin' trouble upon us."

Libby dragged her troubled thoughts away from Maddie, fixed them on Mrs. Dorrance and the stir she was causing over one innocent children's book, and set her chin. "Two can play at word games. An unbiased article on the library, says Mr. Gruben. Fair enough!" She snapped her Memorandum book open. "I'm taking direct quotes. Do you have an opinion you'd care to express on the threat Mrs. Dorrance represents to our library, Father?"

Father sighed. "Only that ye can not in fairness blame it all on the leddy."

"Why, Father? She is making a mountain out of an anthill and you know it! What does she want from me, anyway? You were standing right there in the door when I apologized to her!"

Father nodded and gently concluded, "And havin' done so in private, 'twould be verra proud and sinful to attack her wi' yer smokin' pen in Mr. Gruben's verra public *Gazette.*"

His words acted like a pin on Libby's ballooning indignation. Public apology? He thought she should write Mrs. Dorrance a public apology? *Lord, why did I even ask?*

30

By the time Libby got to the library, the sign was gone from the door. She let herself in to find Paulette and Mrs. Bee on their knees, pulling books off the shelves and packing them into crates while Dr. Harding, in rare form, expounded over all the grief this "flea-brained" idea had brought him.

"But, dear, it was an innocent mistake," said Paulette in a conciliatory tone.

"I am endeavoring to run a business here, Paulette. From the beginning I didn't relish having my front office turned into a library," declared the doctor, plowing both hands through his hair. The floor creaked beneath his frenzied pacing. "It was distracting to my patients and trying on my patience, but I endured it because you and Sarah Jane coaxed and pleaded and pouted and bullied. But great guns, if it didn't turn into an afternoon child-watching service. And now this. I refuse to suffer the indignity of being the center of a controversy with Mrs. Dorrance nailing quarantine signs to my door and the town clamoring over the rumor of some deadly disease originating in my very office. I won't have it! Now you pack up those books and get them out of here."

"We're packing as quickly as we can, Melville. Please, dear, lower your voice. You're scaring Libby," said Paulette, dashing Libby a glance.

Watching books meant to be shared and enjoyed being packed into crates, Libby stood torn between despair over the loss and guilt over Dr. Harding's undeserved trials.

Mrs. Bee finally had enough of her brother's sparking and spouting. She shook her finger under his nose. "Melville, kindly get a grip on your temper.

All this hysteria isn't healthy for a man your age. Take a deep breath now and stop stamping about and shouting like a madman.''

Dr. Harding turned on his heel, bolted down the inner corridor, and closed himself into his office with a bang that brought a wall hanging crashing to the floor.

"Ordinarily, I would say he will come around," said Paulette. "But this time I'm afraid he has put his foot down and intends to keep it there."

"He does," agreed Mrs. Bee. "He has a right to do what he chooses with his office, I suppose. But confounded if I'll stand here and let him storm all over me!''

Libby picked up the crumpled sign from the floor, her resentment mounting as she beheld the word *'Quarantine'* formed in big bold letters. Beneath it, riddled in bullet-sized letters, *'Careless Books Cause Contagion of the Mind.'*

Dr. Harding had finished what Mrs. Dorrance had started. But that wasn't to say they had to go down in the pages of Edgewood history as the library that folded without a fight. So thinking, Libby disregarded Father's counsel, opened her Memorandum book, and, with pencil poised, asked, "In your opinion, ladies, should reading to the town children be a function of the library? What role do you think a library should play in a town?''

Libby spent an hour traveling the village square, asking similar questions. When she had collected enough opinions, she crossed over to the park and sat in the shade of the bandstand, piecing the quotes together in what became less an unbiased article than a rebuttal to Mrs. Dorrance's strong-arm tactics. She left her article at the *Gazette* office and started home, only to cross the street and see Angus coming toward her from the far end of the block.

For a fraction of a second, she toyed with the idea of retreating in the opposite direction, for the whole morning had been one battering wave of trouble after another. She wanted to be calm when she talked to him, careful and sensitive, so as not to say anything that might injure him. A tough assignment, considering wounds were all but unavoidable in matters of the heart.

"Libby! I was hoping that was you.'' Impeccably groomed, he cut a smart figure in his white summer flannels, white suit jacket, and straw boater.

"Hello, Angus," Libby greeted him. "You missed a good dinner Saturday night, and the circus was first-rate.''

"So I heard. I was sorry I couldn't make it back to town in time, not only on your account, but Chester's, too. He'd gone to a lot of trouble making all the arrangements and touting it as a campaign fund-raiser. Of course, nobody goes to the circus to hear a campaign speech, anyway.''

"I wasn't aware you were planning to make one.''

"I wasn't. But Chester would have liked me to have been there. A presence, so to speak," he said distractedly.

"I hope it proved profitable for your campaign fund."

"Modestly so." With a look back over his shoulder that took into consideration the sheriff's open windows, Angus said, "Let's continue as far as the railway tracks, shall we?"

Libby moved with him and, when they were a safe distance from the sheriff's office, lifted her face in silent inquiry.

Angus cleared his throat. "You've seen Maddie?"

Libby nodded.

"I want to apologize," he said quietly.

Apologize? Uncertain of his meaning, Libby noted the way his gaze fell away at her questioning glance. He took off his eyeglasses, dropped them into his pocket, and held the fabric wide as if he might find the words he was searching for tucked inside.

"There was an incident in our past, Maddie's and mine, that . . . resurfaced recently," he said, piecing his words like fragments. "I was unaware of its impact on Maddie until Robinson . . . rather, Daniels . . . died . . . and she came to me in such . . . upheaval."

Libby caught a flicker of an idea as to what this was about. Maddie's look of guilt, Angus's matching expression. Like mirror images. Noting the perspiration beading his upper lip, she felt the flicker explode into blinding realization. He was searching for words to break it off with her! Why hadn't she seen it coming? His distraction of late, the broken dates. The interests he and Maddie shared. Their easy manner with each other, and something less definable, something that had sparked jealousy in Libby at the church social and even before.

Angus's mouth was still moving, his hands, too. ". . . we find that we still care for each other . . . I'm sorry, Libby. I hope I haven't hurt you."

Moments ago, she'd been practicing those very words. The irony of it was lost in a wave of humiliation. How could she have been so slow to catch on! It had already been discussed and decided between them. Behind her back! *Isn't this what you wanted? To be free of entanglements? But to be dropped for Maddie . . .*

The half-formed thought was so flagrantly self-centered, Libby was ashamed. Her tense grip was crimping her notebook. She tried to relax her hands and, as if from a distance, heard herself say, "We talked only briefly, Maddie and I. She was in a hurry to drive out to her mother's and collect a few things."

"She didn't tell you we're getting married?"

"*Married?*" The word rocketed out of Libby.

Angus shot an anxious glance over his shoulder. Lowering his own voice as if in hopes she would modify hers, he said, "I've asked her to be my wife, and she has accepted."

"I see," said Libby, her nerve endings twitching in aftershock. It sounded ridiculous, her thundering question followed by those two meek words. Embarrassed by his scrutiny, by the whole situation, scarcely knowing what to say, she forced a pleasant note into her voice. "Am I to be invited to the wedding?"

"That's sweet of you, Libby, but no. We're going to Bloomington today to speak our vows in a private ceremony with only my parents attending. I tell you that in confidence," he hastened to add. "Maddie's mother was quite taken aback by the news. She urged us to wait until . . ."

"After the election?"

He flushed at the swiftness with which she grasped the political implications of his marrying a woman whose husband had not been under the sod long enough for grass to blanket the grave.

"The marriage was over," he said, as if perceiving her thoughts. "Long before Daniels died. Maddie feels it ludicrous of her mother to expect her to observe mourning traditions. However, as Chester was quick to point out, we want to avoid any hint of impropriety. So we'll wed quietly and honeymoon in St. Louis. I have professional obligations and will be dividing my time between Springfield and Bloomington, so I won't be able to spend more than a few days there. But Catherine has invited Maddie to stay on until after the election."

"She won't return to sing with the Berry Sisters?" asked Libby.

"It seems unwise," said Angus. "Under the circumstances, I imagine it would be uncomfortable for you as well. Rest assured, I readily release you of the obligation."

He was bumping her out of the Berry Sisters! And after she had laid it all on the line for him where Ike was concerned!

"You can keep the dress, of course," he added.

"That's generous of you, Angus, but no thank you." Writhing in the ungainly silence that followed, she couldn't keep the nip from her voice as she added, "I'm surprised, naturally. About your marrying, I mean. But I'm not upset. Or hurt. Really, I'm not."

His sad smile refuted her denial in a way that brought fresh heat to her face. But to protest further would only strengthen his myopic view of her as the jilted one. She bit her lip to curtail her rattling tongue.

"As I started to say, our lives are linked by the past, Maddie's and mine. I don't feel at liberty to disclose any more than Maddie herself is willing to confide, so I'll leave that to her. Except to say that if I continue to shrug aside the responsibility that begged to be shouldered a long time ago, then there is on my character an indelible blemish that makes me unfit for political leadership of any sort."

He had gotten beyond the awkwardness and found his stride. The orator,

couching rejection in handsome phrases. Assuming the blame and handling
it with such mastery that "Why?" and "Do you love her?" and "Have you
always loved her?" seemed like an intrusion. Or was it? Didn't Libby have
a right to know? Checking her retreat, she tilted her chin and took the offensive.

"Tell me, Angus, have your political aspirations made you so cautious
that you're afraid to be honest with me?"

Taken aback, he said, "You can't believe that, surely. I confided our wedding plans, a secret known only to our families."

"Your plans, perhaps, but not your reasons. I'd like to know what
prompted this sudden decision."

"I just told you . . ."

"You told me nothing, Angus. You phrased it well, but it was still nothing."

"I've hurt you," he said softly.

"I'm not hurt. But anything less than the truth is shabby treatment."

Angus tugged at his collar and hedged, "It's difficult to speak candidly
lest I offend your sensibilities."

"Never mind my sensibilities."

He winced at her tartness. "Very well then. Last week you troubled my
conscience by asking me about Maddie and a long-ago tryst at the lake."

"Troubled *your* conscience?" Libby's heart quickened. "But it was Ike
who . . ."

"No, Libby, it wasn't. It was me."

The words dropped as quietly as the first raindrops of a summer shower,
but the impact was as if the whole skies had opened. How hard she had
struggled, weighing her heart leanings against her feelings about Ike's sup-
posedly tarnished past! And now to learn that what she had reluctantly accepted to be true might not be true at all! Careful, lest she misunderstand,
Libby said, "It wasn't Ike? You're sure?"

The obscure movement of his lips fell just short of a smile. "Yes, I'm
sure. Hascal Caton, meddlesome old reprobate, saw Galloway and Maddie
there together and drew his own conclusions."

"But why would Ike shoulder the blame if he had no part in it?"

"He didn't assume blame. All he said was that he and Maddie were fishing
or swimming or some such thing. And I guess that's true."

"You guess?" echoed Libby.

Angus dropped his gaze. "I left when Galloway showed up. If only Maddie had left, too, it might have been long since forgotten. No, that isn't so."
A shadow passed over his face as he corrected himself. "Maddie brought
that home to me the other night in my office, speaking of how men like me
so carelessly take a girl's virtue, callous to the cost of her good name."

Maddie's words, heard from beneath Angus's office window, were still vivid in Libby's mind. Embarrassed, she dropped her gaze. "She didn't say men like you."

"No, she didn't. The significance of her *not* naming me is what opened my eyes to how keenly she felt the wounding and yet didn't strike back. *Maddie,* who always strikes back. She had every reason to, but she didn't. Not in all these years. She took her punishment and mine, too."

He that covereth a transgression seeketh love . . . Maddie, of all people, living that ancient proverb. Maddie, who so outspokenly resented the inequality of the sexes. She, of all women, had to abhor sexual dalliances being viewed as morally reprehensible in women, yet tolerable in men. What woman didn't? That she would hold her tongue for Angus's sake could mean only one thing.

"It was a youthful mistake, and a long time ago," Angus said over Libby's rushing thoughts. "But aspiring politicians have come to ruin over smaller indiscretions. Knowing as much, I can only think how poorly I've recompensed her for her loyalty of all these years. The shelter of my name is all I have to offer her."

Marriage, symbolic of reciprocated love, was an occasion for rejoicing. Why then did Libby feel sad for both of them, and at the same time, cognitive of her own naïveté? She had trusted Angus. Felt safe with him. Now she found herself wondering where their relationship might have strayed had he stirred the passions in her that he had apparently stirred in Maddie. Unable to look at him in the same way, Libby said, "I wish you and Maddie much happiness. If I don't see her before you leave, give her my love."

He nodded and searched her face. "One more thing, Libby. May you find someone who brings you as much joy as our association has brought me."

Libby resisted the urge to pull her hand free as he kissed it. She walked away, thinking, *Be watchful of her pride, Angus. Don't ever let her suspect you view your proposal as sacrificial.*

And yet, in her heart Libby knew that he did. She supposed that made his gesture noble. It was sad to think he couldn't erase the blemish from Maddie's reputation, despite his best intentions. Not even if he publicly admitted his own part in it.

Not as long as people peered around the beam in their own eye to behold the mote in their neighbor's.

Not just forgiveness but forgetfulness. An east-to-west cleaning of the slate. God never withheld it from repentant hearts. Libby wondered as she started home, *Why then do we?*

31

Libby carried the thought home. She took a blanket into the backyard and spread it beneath the apple tree. Opal and David were playing in the branches above her. Their voices blended into the afternoon haze as she opened her old Memorandum book.

Thank You for being that covering, and for Your tender nurturing of what You have created.

Libby dropped her pencil, rolled onto her back, and used the old Memorandum booklet into which she had emptied so many of her personal thoughts as a shade for her eyes. She had filled the last page. The names of those who had become part of her life in Edgewood were sprinkled throughout the booklet. Except for Ike.

She had yet to scrawl his name over a single line. Mrs. Dorrance had been right about that. Her thoughts of Ike, even her hurts, she hugged close to her heart. Just as he stubbornly clung to the ideal of all things in their proper season when the obstacle between them had melted away. She couldn't even tell him, for she had given her word to Angus to hold his marriage in confidence.

The thought of Ike eased the scrapes and scratches of the day and gave Libby a more circumspect outlook. Admittedly, dissolution of the library was harder to take than Angus's marriage. She took pride in having sown the first seed, even if it was Maddie who had caused it to sprout so swiftly into a library, a library that was brought down in a day by Mrs. Dorrance's displeasure.

Recalling Ike's words about the sturdiest trees in the forest being those that grew slowly, Libby reasoned that in the garden, only the weeds sprang up overnight. Seed crops and flowers took time. Was the article she had turned in to Mr. Gruben a seed or a weed? Libby knew the answer. It had been hidden in her heart, overshadowed by her anger.

She went inside for fresh paper and sat down in the kitchen as Abigail finished feeding the baby. Remembering the two letters Father had handed her earlier that morning, Libby took them from her pocket and passed them to Abigail in the rocking chair.

"You've got mail."

"From Adam?" Abigail's face lit up at the sight of his bold handwriting on the top envelope. She stopped rocking to open the letter.

The baby whimpered in protest and waved her little fists. Libby chuckled and reached for her. "Give her to me, Abigail. I'll rock the wee bairn." She took Abigail's place in the rocking chair and shifted the baby to her shoulder. "Yes, you fussy little Rosebud, you. Listen to you, bleating like a lamb. And on a full stomach, too."

"I'll slip out back a minute," said Abigail over Libby's gentle cooing.

Libby was accustomed to Abigail's guarding her privacy where Adam's letters were concerned. She waved her away, then thought of the second letter she'd given her and called after her, "Say, Abigail! Who's writing you from the circus?"

Abigail's reply was lost to the noise of the back screen door slamming.

With little Rose so sweetly nestled in her arms, Libby's mild curiosity over the letter was soon forgotten. She touched her lips to the baby's dark downy head, sang and rocked and gently stroked her tiny back until little Rose fell asleep. Mrs. Baker had loaned Abigail the cradle she kept for hotel guests. Libby lowered Rose into it.

Brushing at the damp spot on her shoulder left by Rose's Cupid's bow mouth, she sat down at the kitchen table to rewrite her library article. Absorbed in the process, she scarcely noticed when Abigail returned. But after a while, she glanced toward the stove to see her drawing hot water from the stove reservoir. In the sink was a basin lined with outing flannel. Abigail poured hot water into it, added cool water and tested the temperature with her elbow before crossing to the cradle.

Discerning her intentions, Libby smiled. "Is it sleeping dogs or sleeping babies you're supposed to let lie?"

"Both, I think," said Abigail as she bent over the cradle to undress her little daughter.

Libby finished her article and joined Abigail at the sink just as Rose came awake with a wail. She chuckled at her thrashing fists and feet.

"Rose, Rose! Your face is as red as your name. Don't you like your bath? My, what a great, tragic face you're wearing."

Abigail, hands full, lifted one shoulder and rubbed at her eye.

Libby giggled. "What's the matter? Is she winning this water fight?"

"A little soap in my eye. No, no, it's all right," Abigail said, when Libby moved to take over while she tended her eye. "Stings a little, is all. Don't you have a deadline or something?"

"The article!" Libby caressed the baby's dimpled chin. "You're a distraction, little Rose. Yes you are, with your face all puckered up. Aunt Libby's off to see Mr. Gruben. I hope he won't storm like our wild rose of a bairn."

Leaving Abigail to her mothering, Libby returned to the *Gazette* office with her revised article and tried to explain her change of heart to Mr. Gruben. At length, they came to an agreement. He would use the second article just as it was written. The first, he would divide into individual quotes, naming each source, and use them as short fillers throughout the pages of Friday's paper. At Libby's insistence, he agreed to discard her editorializing on the subject of one individual closing down what belonged to the whole community.

Libby was on her way home once again when Opal and David hailed her from the edge of Mrs. Gruben's garden. They sat in the grass, watermelon juice dripping off their chins. The sun shone off Mrs. Gruben's gray head where she sat enthroned on an upturned washtub, dripping juice on her crutches as she enjoyed the fruit of her gardening labors. Beckoning, she said, "Have some melon with us, Libby."

Libby walked across the grass to join them, saying, "Just a small piece."

"Nonsense. There's plenty. She has that lean and hungry look, doesn't she, children?" Mrs. Gruben lapsed into an eloquent Shakespearean quote that soon had the children giggling. Pleased with her responsive audience, she sliced off a generous chunk of melon, shifted her crutches out of the way with her foot, and made room on the upended washtub.

The melon was a wonderful treat after having missed lunch. At Mrs. Gruben's urging, Libby helped herself to a second piece and joined their seed-spitting contest until Marmalade, one of Mrs. Gruben's many cats, emerged from the garden with a watermelon seed stuck to his head. He flattened his yellow ears and looked annoyed at having his nap interrupted by a shower of seeds. David laughed, but tender-hearted Opal peeled the seed off his head, then raced David to the pump to wash.

"You had better be washing the juice off, too. It's nearly time for Children's Hour," Mrs. Gruben told Libby.

Deducing that Mr. Gruben hadn't yet carried home the news about the library, Libby told her what had happened. Mrs. Gruben looked aghast.

"And what of Children's Hour? You don't mean to say the children are to be deprived of hearing the end of the story?"

"It looks that way," said Libby.

"Why, that's a crime!"

Arching a rueful smile, Libby said, "Dr. Harding is disenchanted with the whole thing, and without his lobby, we're out of options."

"You say it was the story of Toby Tyler that caused Mrs. Dorrance so much distress?" asked Mrs. Gruben. At Libby's nod, she asked, "Has she read the book?"

"She knew it was a circus story. And that Toby ran away from home. Beyond that, I have no idea."

"But don't you see? The moral of the story is in the closing chapters. Toby repents of running away and is glad to be home again. Judging a story that's only half-read is like judging a cake before it's baked! What have you done with the book?"

"It's packed away."

"Find it, then, and bring it to me. And Libby? There *will* be Children's Hour today."

"There will?" asked Libby, hope freshening.

"Yes, there will. For any child who cares to come to my house, I'll be reading from *Toby Tyler* this afternoon at three o'clock. Post a sign to the effect on Dr. Harding's door while you fetch that book. Oh! One more thing. Stop by my husband's office on the way. Tell him to come home, please, that I must have a word with him."

Libby made yet another trip uptown. To her relief, Mr. Gruben bore the order to come home in good humor. She continued on to Dr. Harding's office. Mrs. Bee helped her locate *Toby Tyler* amidst the crated books and promised not only to post a notice concerning the rescheduled Children's Hour, but to personally walk the children down to Mrs. Gruben's house. She also offered her own home as a meeting place for Maddie's Freethinkers Society the following evening.

"Freethinking Quilters," said Mrs. Bee. "There's no reason for us to quit, just because the library is closed."

Libby hadn't thought that far ahead. Mrs. Bee was obviously unaware that Maddie had left town. But it would hardly be a tribute to Maddie's vision of "sisterhood" to discontinue work on the quilt they had only just begun simply because Maddie was leaving.

"At seven?" she asked, and Mrs. Bee nodded and waved her out the door. "See you then."

Libby's thoughts lingered on Maddie and sisterhood as she started across the park. And on her own relationship with Angus. Suppose her heart had been engaged? She would have entertained a far different view of Maddie stealing him away right from beneath her nose. When it came to matters of the heart, Maddie hadn't allowed herself to be governed by the noble ideals she so passionately espoused. But could Angus succeed where past relationships had failed? Could he love her enough to fill that void in her soul?

"Enough," Libby realized, was a relative term. But there was a Love that knew no boundaries, that east-to-west love she'd learned about at her father's knee. Libby pondered what that meant in her own life in relation to Ike in particular as she paused at the edge of the park and waited for a Woodmancy's livery buggy to pass. Her thoughts shifting from Maddie to Ike to her own voids, she would have given the occupants of the buggy no more than a glance had Major Minor, who was driving for the livery, not waved to her from the seat.

His passengers were both attractive women dressed in flamboyant colors and feathered hats. One woman cradled a baby while the other one leaned near, her features animated as she admired the little one.

Just as the buggy began making the turn south, the woman holding the baby raised her face. Such joy! It lifted Libby's heart just to look at her. Though she was a stranger, standing out like a tropical bird, there was a nagging sense of familiarity about her.

Libby tried unsuccessfully to dismiss it as the buggy rattled over the railroad tracks and on to the station half a block away, where a passenger train waited. All at once, her heart jumped with delayed recognition. Of course! It was Mrs. Bigelow, the circus owner's wife! Just as quickly, an ugly suspicion slammed into her head-on.

The letter that had come for Abigail from the circus. The infant, cradled so lovingly in the woman's arms. Soap in your eyes? *Oh, Abigail. No, Abigail, no! Surely, you didn't.*

Libby clutched her book and ran, only to be stopped as the flagman closed the crossing for the northbound train. Tears of frustration filled her eyes as she turned up the alley and sped north toward the next crossing. But the slowly accelerating train beat her to it and shut off that crossing, too. Libby looked up and saw in the train window the woman's profile as the train rumbled past. The clacking wheels spit sand and dust. Eyes stinging, she was transported for a fleeting moment to another day and another train that had nearly carried Davie away. Except this time it was no childish prank gone awry.

Anguish filled Libby's throat as she raced alongside the train, knowing it was futile. Rose wasn't hers. Even if by some miracle the train stopped, the baby wouldn't be safely restored to her as Davie had been. Libby stumbled to a halt, her fist pressed to her mouth.

Father had forewarned her. Adam too, through his letter. Even Abigail, in a wordless way. Why had she lowered her emotional guard, only to be caught defenseless? Libby retraced her steps to the shadow of the grain elevator, buried her face in her hands, and sobbed.

At length, she thought of Abigail, of David and little Opal, too. She prayed they had stayed at Mrs. Gruben's for Children's Hour and hadn't seen Mrs. Bigelow come for little Rose. *I just held her in my arms! There's a milk stain on my shoulder from her little rosebud mouth.*

Libby hunkered down and dried her eyes on the hem of her dress. Struggling to hold back the tears that kept welling up, she followed the railroad tracks home and descended the steep bank. From the board the children used to bridge the ditch, she saw Abigail in the backyard on the laundry bench, sobbing into her apron.

Carefully so as not to startle her, Libby joined her on the bench. As Abigail lifted her tear-ravaged face she saw that the robin's egg she had so recently given Mrs. Bigelow was now cradled in her hand.

Fresh tears stung Libby's eyes as Abigail began a stammering, tearful explanation about Lester Brooks, about her tortured fears of little Rose being a thorn in Adam's heart, about sending him into those wretched mines to support a child that wasn't his.

Libby slipped her arm around Abigail's shoulder and whispered, "I know, Abigail. I know all about it. I have known for weeks."

Legitimate fears, all, for she, too, hated those mines, where poverty was measured in the number of mouths a man had to feed, where accidents and sickness and gut-wrenching labor claimed men before their time. She, too, knew that Adam, for all his good intentions, might not be able to cradle little Rose with her tiny shell-like ears and not think of Brooks. What she couldn't know was the unbearable loss of motherhood that Abigail was feeling. A loss born of her own excruciating choice. All she could do was hold her and let her cry. Compassion stirred and poured from Libby in a gentle, monosyllabic crooning not unlike that with which she had crooned baby Rose to sleep such a short while ago. It was balm not only for Abigail but for her own pain, too.

As the storm of tears at great length subsided, Abigail spoke haltingly of the woman who had taken little Rose to raise as her own.

"Sh-she's very kind. Sh-she came to see me the n-night of the circus. We t-t-talked for a long time and s-she s-said she would c-come for the b-baby j-just as soon as I l-let her know. I w-wasn't s-sure then I c-could do it."

"When, Abigail?" Libby asked gently. "When did you decide?"

"The d-day Adam left." Brushing away tears from eyes that had spilled them by buckets, Abigail whimpered, "Please don't hate me, Lib."

Tears stung Libby's eyes. She thought of Naomi, once in a position not unlike Abigail's. Remembered her saying not long ago *Cain't ya do for kin what ya did for me?* Of east-to-west forgiveness. Of Father saying, *If ye haven't the feelin' for it, then do it in faith and the feelin' will follow.* But the feeling was there, welling up from a weary, battered heart passed over by the wheels of that train, yet still intact.

She drew Abigail to her feet and embraced her. "Hate you? When Adam loves you so? Never, Abigail. Not ever."

Later, much later, while Abigail was off to the station wiring Adam as to when he could expect her home, and Father was in the parlor talking to David of Abigail's decision, Libby curled up on a quilt beneath the apple tree with her journal and wrote a prayer by the fading light of day:

What a lot of nurturing we need, so anxious to be loved and under-stood, and yet so careless that we end up hurting ourselves and those we love, too. Angus and Maddie. Adam and Abigail and little Rose. Decatur and Naomi and Opal and Frankie. Even poor little Sophronia. Fragile flowers, needing the Gardener's protection from life's blasts. Even when those blasts are of our own making.

32

It had been a long week, made longer for Ike by the frustration of lacking the strength and endurance to bring in his own wheat crop. Decatur had cut it with the binder on Monday. Billy had come out two afternoons at the end of his mail run and helped Decatur and Frankie shock the wheat. And the threshing crew had threshed it out yesterday. Decatur and Billy would have pitched the straw up in the loft for him, too, but Ike had told them to leave it; he would work at it in spurts till he got the job done. Decatur would have done it anyway, but Billy, seeing Ike had taken about all the sitting on his hands and watching others do his work that he could stand, had coaxed Decatur into riding back into town with him and Frankie.

There weren't words to say what it meant to have friends who would step in and do what those men had done for him. If ever there was the opportunity to return the favor, he wouldn't disappoint them.

Miss Maudie Morefield, who owned the land Ike was farming, had been by that afternoon. Eighty if she was a day and still driving her own buggy. She had collected from the elevator for the sale of the wheat and was pleased with the yield and the price it had brought. They had a tenant arrangement, a fifty-fifty split. Thanks to his friends, Ike had made enough profit to keep his farm equipment patched up and pay off the evaporator, which was to be shipped from Leader Evaporator Company in October.

Ike asked Miss Maudie, as he had the year before and the year before that, if she'd ever consider selling him the forty acres. She had said not at this time. Truth of the matter was, he wasn't sure he could get a loan for it, anyway. Once he got the sirup camp up and running, he would be in a better position to judge where he stood. There were ideas in his mind, dreams that made him wish he had someone to share them with. And not just anyone.

Helpmeet, that spirit-breathed word he had passed on to Decatur, settled over him, bringing with it such sweet longing for Libby, it took all of his self-control to keep from heading into town and tell her he was wrong, that he didn't want to wait until November, that he didn't even want to wait until next week, that he wanted her at his side now, today and every day.

"What would ya have to say to that, Lib?"

That he was awful impatient for a fella who'd just a week ago remarked upon the sturdiness of slow-growing things?

Ike rolled off his cot in the gloom of the sap house and walked out to the mailbox to collect the *Gazette*. He settled on the tree-shadowed bench in front and searched first for the articles with Libby's by-line. Her piece on the circus made him smile. When he'd walked her home last Saturday night, she hadn't mentioned having met up with those circus folks even before the circus hit town. Farther down the page, he caught her by-line on a piece about the New Hope ladies earning $78.90 on their community dinner that same evening and that groundbreaking for the church was scheduled for spring.

But the article that brought her closest was the one about the library closing. Ike knew she was proud of the way the ladies had pulled together and brought to pass in a week what the village board had not accomplished in years of talk, so it wasn't hard to guess the disappointment the library's closure must have caused her. And yet, there was no evidence of anger or blame or self-pity in the short piece, which began in the spirit of petition, with a verse from the Book of Psalms:

As far as the east is from the west, so far hath he removed our transgressions from us." In the spirit of that verse, may I convey my hope that anyone who was disturbed over the novel I read to the children at Children's Hour the week preceding the arrival of the circus will forgive my error of judgment. I regret having lacked the wisdom to preface the story with an explanation that the story was to be enjoyed, not pressed into action. I wish to thank Dr. Harding, who kindly loaned his lobby that we might conduct our "library experiment." Having brought the experiment to a conclusion, whether or not our town is to have a real library is in the hands of our village fathers.

Ike tracked on through the paper, then came back to Libby's piece. More than once, he had seen that temper of hers flare up. But she had a contrite way of getting those fires banked that went beyond simple conscience. It wasn't a lesson learned by rote or even by example. Rather, it came from heeding that still, quiet Voice within.

Love for others, for life itself, shone in her face and glowed in her eyes and gave her laugh a sweet lilt. Had she any idea just how endearing it made her to him?

33

"What do you think so far, Mrs. Bee?" asked Libby as she modeled the gown she was making for the trip to the World's Fair. The group from Edgewood, which had swelled to twenty-six, was leaving for St. Louis on the Monday morning train. Much to Libby's relief, Angus's marriage to Maddie had not strained her association with Angus's mother. Mrs. Gentry had made a special trip into town the previous week just to be certain Libby still intended to go with them to St. Louis and oversee Frankie.

"Quite dressy," said Mrs. Bee. "The fit is excellent. But it is just a little . . ."

"Plain?" Libby supplied the word. She moved out of the intense sunlight pouring through Dr. Harding's lobby window.

"Yes!" said Mrs. Bee. She laid a finger along her nose, her gaze moving over Libby again. "I like the hat, too. It was made for that dress."

Ike's gift hat. *The dress was made for the hat.* Libby had taken the hat with her when she chose the navy blue challis. Mrs. Bee, generous with her advice, had schooled Libby in piecing the dress together. The smocking ornamentation on the high collar and yoke were Libby's handiwork. The bodice fell in gentle folds from a yoke to the fitted waist, where it was gathered into a wide band that fitted snugly through the waist and hips. The skirt of the dress flared from the hipline and ended in an eight-inch flounce.

"I don't believe lace embellishments would be overdoing it. Would you like me to add the decorative touches?"

It was a tempting offer, but courtesy demanded a token protest at the very least. Libby remonstrated, saying, "I can't ask you to do that. You have your own sewing and ironing and packing."

"Nonsense! I have everything laid out and ready. It's been slow here at the doctor's all week."

"But what about little Martha Berry's sing-song gown?" Libby asked, borrowing an expression from her father.

"I finished altering your dress for Martha two days ago and dropped it by Paulette's where they were rehearsing last night."

"In that case, enough arm-twisting. I accept. If I can do something for you in return, you need only ask."

Mrs. Bee smiled. "I'll remember that. Turn around now, and I'll help you with the buttons."

Libby presented her back and the row of tiny buttons. "How is Martha doing? Does she fit in well with the group?"

"She has a strong voice and is thrilled about being part of it. Though Dorie hasn't quite forgiven you and Maddie for abandoning ship."

"So I noticed," said Libby, feeling a pang of regret over the loss of an adventure she'd been looking forward to since early summer. "Dorie came out of Baker's yesterday with her nose so high she would have drowned had it been raining."

Mrs. Bee chuckled and swept her white lock of hair back into the fold of dark waves. "She'll come around. Though I wonder about Angus. He must be very disappointed."

Libby colored at her probing glance. Though Mrs. Bee was Angus's favorite aunt, he had left her in the dark concerning his marriage to Maddie. By necessity, Libby supposed. The only thing the woman couldn't seam up was a secret. The whole town was still humming over the information she had overheard, then leaked, concerning Mr. Robinson's relationship to Maddie. Careful not to give away anything that might tip her off concerning Maddie and Angus's marriage, Libby said hesitantly, "Angus and I have agreed to . . . see other people."

Genuine regret crossed Mrs. Bee's pert features. "So that's why you dropped out of the singing group. Angus said you made some excuse about all the practices cutting so sharply into your other obligations. Paulette and the girls accepted it at face value, but I wondered then if there wasn't more to the story."

"You'll still do the trimmings for me, won't you, Mrs. Bee?"

Mrs. Bee flung her arms around Libby in a motherly gesture. "Of course I will. Dear, dear. I hope he hasn't broken your heart."

"Just a tiny rent. Nothing your magic needle can't sew up," said Libby, for Mrs. Bee, contrary to her words, would be offended if Libby failed to exhibit a little hurt over the loss of her nephew.

Mrs. Bee hugged her again. "I'll have this ready for you tomorrow if you want to drop back by about this time."

"It will have to be after the mail run. I'm carrying the mail for Billy tomorrow. He leaves for the fair today."

Mrs. Bee paused in snipping a thread from the gathered sleeve of Libby's dress to chide, "You're taking his route with only three days left to prepare for the trip? Libby! Why are you crowding yourself so? Can't Captain Boyd do it? He's coming out of retirement to fill in for Billy all next week, isn't he?"

"Yes, as a favor to Father, for which we're both grateful. With Billy and me gone and all the men in the fields, Father would have had a hard time finding someone to do it. That being the case, he doesn't want to overimpose on the captain."

"Harvesttime, the only man who can't find a job is the fellow who doesn't want one," Mrs. Bee called from the corridor as Libby changed out of her dress.

"Billy was teasing Father yesterday, saying he'd had some offers from farmers that sounded pretty good compared to his mail check."

"Hinting for a raise and asking for time off all in the same breath. That sounds like Billy." Mrs. Bee laughed. "I hear he's trying to coax Ike to go down and parade with the Rough Riders."

Libby's heart quickened. "Is he having any luck?"

"Obviously, you've never bucked up against Ike's hard head."

"I haven't seen Ike in town in a while. How's he doing?"

"I'm assuming he's improving. He hasn't been in to see Doctor, anyway."

Libby had thought that by now he would have heard she had dropped out of the Berry Sisters. But maybe the singing group was beneath the notice of Hascal Caton, the chief purveyor of gossip out Old Kentucky way. *Did Ike's thoughts stray to her? Did he miss her as she missed him? Or was he so busy, she scarcely came to mind at all?* Despite her firm resolve not to be unhappy over the wait, it hurt Libby's feelings that he hadn't been to town at all.

Libby stopped at the store for the mail. There was a letter from Abigail. She poked it into her pocket unread and started home, passing the Grubens' house on her way. Mrs. Gruben was sitting in the shade, conducting Children's Hour amidst kids and cats and a backdrop of lovely flower beds. Seizing a momentary reprieve from all the washing and ironing and packing she had to do, Libby dropped down on the Grubens' lawn in the midst of the children and waved to Mr. Gruben, who came out on the porch with a writing tablet in his hands.

Libby had worried about telling Mr. Gruben she wouldn't be going on the campaign trail after all, as she was no longer a part of the Berry Sisters. But as matters now stood, he planned to send Earl Morefield instead. He insisted that Earl, with his above-average writing skills, was equal to the job. Privately

Libby suspected Earl and Dorene Berry's courtship had as much as anything to do with Earl's willingness to accompany the group. But Mr. Gruben had a replacement, that was the important thing.

Zerilda's granddaughter, clutching a kitten, smiled shyly at Libby. Little Opal slid close, and told her, "Sophronia's nanny come and fetched her today. She's goin' back East to her other granny so's she can be ready for school. She stopped by the store and said good-bye."

"You're missing her?" asked Libby.

Opal nodded.

"School's starting Monday. You'll make lots of friends." Though Opal was seven and too big for lap-sitting, Libby pulled her onto her lap and kissed the top of her head. Opal settled against her as if she could use the comfort and, when the story hour was over, accompanied Libby and David home.

With the children playing in the backyard, Libby sat down in the kitchen and read her letter from Abigail, which proved to be a thank-you note:

Dear Libby:

Adam and I are overwhelmed by the beautiful quilt that you and your friends stitched for us. I can't thank you enough except to say that as much as I admire it for its beauty and warmth, it can in no way compare to the gift of hospitality that was mine throughout my stay.

Adam is still hopeful of receiving word of a job opening at the Chicago and Alton Shops in Bloomington. It would be an answered prayer, not just because of the difficulties here in Thistle Down, but because we would be so much closer to you and your father and David. Adam, Jacob, and I send our love to everyone.

Affectionately,
Abigail

No mention of how her own family had received the news that she hadn't kept the baby or how she was feeling. The lack of mention came as no surprise; they were getting on with their lives. Under the circumstances, what else could they do?

Libby reread Abigail's words concerning the quilt. She smiled, for no one but God could have foreseen Maddie's Freethinkers Society turning into a quilting club! In the two weeks since Maddie had left Edgewood, the group, now calling themselves the Free Thimblers, had grown to eight. In a marathon of quilting last Tuesday night, they had finished Abigail's quilt. It was even lovelier than Libby had envisioned, thanks to Paulette's artistic flare and Mrs. Bee's skill with a needle.

The scene depicted a narrow dirt road winding between fields of gold and green. There was a crooked fence row, some barns, and off on the horizon, the trees of Old Kentucky. But best of all, Paulette had fashioned a mail buggy out of some dark fabrics. There was even a tiny spark-sized impression of a red-haired mail carrier! The ladies had embroidered their given names on the lower left-hand corner of the quilt. Like artists signing their canvas!

Ike saw Libby pass by in her mail buggy on Saturday. He knew Billy had gone to the fair, but he had expected Captain Boyd to be carrying the mail. He was up in the haymow of the barn when he caught a glimpse of her buggy crossing the bridge. Between the trees and the distance, it wasn't much of a sighting, yet it was enough to get his heart pumping.

He stood in the door of the loft gazing beyond the barn lot through the screen of trees, hoping for another glimpse, and thinking of a verse that wondered over the way of a man with a maid. Blamed if the sight of her didn't fill him with wonder, too, and put a foolish grin on his face. Beneath the grin was an ache and an urge to throw down his hay fork, clean up, and head straight into town.

If he hadn't promised Decatur he'd be up that evening to help work on the porch, he might have given in to it. Years ago, Naomi had tried to get Decatur to put a porch on their boxcar home, and he wouldn't do it. Now here he was, wanting one. Said it'd make a nice view for a feller if he was of a notion to sit out of an evening and give the skeeters somethin' to chaw on. It was a sizable porch, plenty roomy for a fellow living all by himself. Later that evening, when dusk caught them putting the nails in the floor, Ike said as much to Decatur.

"What'd ya think, I'm fixin' on sittin' here by myself?" Decatur flung his hammer into a pile of tools and his hat after it. He dropped down on a stack of boards they had yet to nail. "Truth is, I'm tired of my cookin'. Tired of missin' Opal and Frankie. Tarnation, Ike! Ya know I don't like carpenterin'. I didn't put these here fresh floorboards down jest fer somethin' to fill my time."

Ike dragged his arm across his brow. "So what are ya goin' to do?"

Decatur squared his shoulders. "I'm fixin' to talk to her. She been a lot of things, but she ain't never been bitter b'fore. It ain't comely on her."

"Don't look any worse on her than it looks on you."

"What're ya gittin' at?"

"A fresh start needs a foundation if it's goin' to last."

"Better last, 'cause I ain't goin' through this agin."

"Then anchor it in bedrock. Don't let it get away from you again."

At length Decatur nodded. He squared his shoulders in the deepening twilight and turned Ike's way. "That rock you bin jawin' 'bout? Git yer book and go over't with me agin'."

"It's gettin' too dark to read. How 'bout I just tell it to ya?" asked Ike, for the story Decatur was asking for was the same one he asked for every time Ike read to him from the Bible. The story wasn't just about the devotion between a mother-in-law and a daughter-in-law, nor was it simply a love story between Ruth and Boaz. Woven into it was God's redeeming love for man.

Ike felt a peace come over him as he told it. The words came as if they'd grown right there in his head, for he knew that tonight Decatur was hungry to hear with more than just his ears.

The next morning, when Ike came across the railway tracks and waited for Pastor Shaw to come along in his handcar so he could give him a ride over to the Timber Creek Church where he preached early services, there was Decatur, waiting to go too.

The Pastor seemed to know he had a receptive audience in Decatur. He seemed to be talkin' right to him all through the service and when the altar call came, a team of oxen couldn't have held Decatur back.

After services, as they were taking the minister back to his handcar, Hascal Caton was sitting out on the porch of Skiff's Store when they passed. He got his eyes filled up and poked an elbow at Skiff and called, "Tarnation, Decatur! Ain't seen ya shined up in a coon's age. Somebody die and I miss it?"

Decatur took the bull by the horns, and hollered back, "Go on in ta town, old man, and tell yer girl they buried the old Decatur McClure."

It was no exaggeration. The man beside Ike that day was not the same man who had driven his family away a few months earlier in pain and fear and fury. There was hope in Decatur, fresh hope and a glow and an eagerness to have restored to him what he had so blindly pushed away.

Ike could only trust that God had just as painstakingly prepared Naomi.

34

The long-awaited trip to the fair had arrived at last. With quick, deft fingers Libby donned Ike's gift hat for the ride to the station while David helped Father load her luggage in the buggy. The breeze was cool and smelled of autumn. Birds trilled the joy of morning song. The pink blush of sunrise caught and kindled and flamed across the sky, lighting their way to the station where the switch targets and the lanterns of trainmen still burned.

Milling on the platform were friends and neighbors and well-wishers, some of whom were going on the trip, others who had come to see them off. Libby left the loading of her baggage to Father and paused to drink in the exhilaration of tramping feet, shuffling baggage, chorusing good-byes, and the chuff of the southbound train coming into the station. She closed her eyes and breathed in the intoxicating travel smells of burning coal and hot oil and dissipating steam and shared her joy for this long-awaited trip with the Giver of every good and perfect gift.

The engine popped off steam with a whoosh that opened her eyes and sent Uncle Willie's old beagle leaping back out of harm's way. Laughing at her own tweaking nerves, Libby returned Captain Boyd's smart salute, then caught the eye of gangly Teddy Baker and waved good-bye. He gave his cap a shy tug and stooped to calm Sugar with a reassuring pat on the head.

"Good-bye, Father. Good-bye, good-bye! Davie, you have a good first week at school. I'll bring you a souvenir from the fair." Thwarting David's efforts to wriggle out of her grasp, Libby kissed him hurriedly and Father, too.

Naomi and Opal were there to see Frankie off. He was tugging at the tie Naomi had insisted he wear.

"He looks like a scholar, jest smart as a whip, don't he, Miss Lib?" Opal expressed her pride in her brother in words Libby was fairly certain she'd heard from Naomi.

"An apt description!" Libby cocked her head to one side, assessing Frankie's new knickers and jacket and billed cap.

"Yer wearin' yer breakfast, son. Stand still, now," said Naomi, licking her finger.

"Quit yer spit-bathin', Ma. Yer rubbin' the hide off me." Frankie grimaced.

"Cain't send ya off lookin' like ya ain't cared for," said Naomi.

Frankie endured Naomi's hug and kiss with the same good grace Davie had shown Libby. He winced at Opal's treading on his toes as she collected a hug, too. "Are you ready?" he asked.

Libby nodded. Together, they started across the platform toward the waiting train, Father, David, and Naomi pressing through the crowd with them, while Opal trailed far behind. They were only feet from the boarding steps when Decatur McClure stepped out of the shadows to intercept them.

"Frankie. Glad I ketched ya," he said, and tipped his hat to Libby and Naomi.

Naomi, openly flustered, averted her gaze. The train whistle blasted over Decatur's opening words, but it was apparent he hadn't come as a last-minute spoiler, for he dropped a fistful of coins into Frankie's hand. Frankie looked at the coins, then at Decatur, a question flickering in his eyes.

"Ya worked hard learnin' them verses, son," said Decatur by way of explanation. "Ya have a good time now, and mind Miss Libby."

Frankie's ears turned as red as his hair, his facade of toughness slipping. He opened his hand and picked through the silver dollars, five of them in all, then fixed his eyes on Decatur again, measuring more than the weight of the coins.

A muscle flexed along McClure's seamed cheek. He thumped his hat against his thigh and looked from Naomi, who had backed away, to Frankie. Libby caught her breath, for to look into the man's eyes was to recognize that he wanted nothing so much as to mend his broken family. What had happened to him? Where was that hard, impenetrable mask? That bitter expression she had come to think was part and parcel of him?

Opal suddenly spotted her tall father beyond the human wall of well-wishers, broke through, and flung herself at Decatur. "Daddy! What brung *you* to town?"

"Come to see Frankie off."

She wrapped her spindly arms around his waist and tilted her face. "Was ya gonna see me, too?"

McClure's jaw slackened. The crevice in his whiskered chin twitched. He lifted his fair-haired child off the ground and answered her question with a question. "Opal, ya love yer daddy?"

"Yep." She cut her eyes her brother's way. "So long as ya don't talk mean to Mama. Ain't that right, Frankie?"

Frankie didn't utter a sound, but the words had hit their mark. Throat working, the big man hugged Opal closer. "Didn't yer grandpa tell ya? They buried them mean words with yer old daddy. This un' here, he's learnin' a better way."

He said some more words. Words lost to the second, longer wail of the whistle and the conductor's "All aboard!"

Her heart in her throat, Libby bade her family one last good-bye, hastened on a few steps, then glanced back to see Frankie put the money in his pocket and shake the hand Decatur thrust at him.

Averting her gaze, Libby noted dew glistening on the fading perennials that skirted the platform. Could the McClures' marriage, like a spent perennial, weather the wintry blasts of separation and hurt to send up a brave new shoot? *Had Ike been right all along?* It would seem so, for her last glimpse of Edgewood as the train pulled away was of Naomi coming through the crowd to join her husband and daughter.

Beneath that ray of hope, and heartening thoughts of Ike's goodness, Libby set her face toward St. Louis. They were no sooner under way than Kersey Brignadello uncased his banjo. Mrs. Bee clapped time while Angus's parents and the Lambs and the Shaws and twenty-odd travelers, Libby included, joined in singing that much-favored tune, "Meet Me in St. Louis, Louis."

Once in St. Louis, the Gentrys, anxious to see Catherine and baby Tess, departed for Catherine's home from the train station, taking the luggage of their daughter's houseguests with them. Armed with directions to Catherine's home by streetcar, Libby and Frankie followed the rest of the group onto a train that would take them to the fair. Once there, Libby, Frankie, and the Brignadellos splintered off from the rest of the group, most of whom would be staying at the Inside Inn Hotel on the southeast corner of the grounds.

Having eagerly devoured each newspaper article, listened attentively to the firsthand accounts of those who had attended the fair, and read the programs they brought back, Libby was still in no way prepared for the spectacle waiting at the end of their journey.

The Exposition celebrating the one hundred and first birthday of the Louisiana Purchase featured America poised upon a worldwide stage, proudly displaying what hard work, noble values, and a progressive attitude had accomplished in such a brief span of time. The displays of the other nations, their art, their music, their technology and industry and education, even their parading military, was a cultural extravaganza to titillate the senses. Equally enlightening were the living displays of people from tribal villages in native garb encamped upon the grounds, going about their daily activities as they would in their homeland.

The gently rolling grounds were magnificently landscaped to befit the graceful ivory-tinted buildings, the grandness of which made Libby think of pictures of the ancient Roman Empire. Formal gardens flanked these stately edifices and plazas and thoroughfares with pools and fountains and beautiful cascades glistening like liquid jewels in ivory settings. Boats of every description floated on the lagoons, the waters of which reflected the palatial splendor of domes and columns and arches and statuary of every shape and size, some of the human forms as scantily clad as Adam and Eve in the Garden of Eden.

Libby and Frankie meandered along with the Brignadellos until the middle of the afternoon, when Frankie began clamoring for a ride on the Observation Wheel. The revolving wheel towered over everything else on the grounds. Libby remembered reading that the monstrosity, also known as the Ferris Wheel, would carry as many as two thousand people and that the gondolas on the revolving framework of steel were the size of streetcars. Others who had been to the fair said the ride easily afforded the best view of the entire exhibition.

But when Frankie spotted the ticket price, he had a change of heart and decided to see first how well his money held out and how else he might wish to spend it. Much of the same mind, Libby said, "We have the rest of the week to decide."

They strolled the Pike, notable for its amusements. Some of the entertainment there was educational, some sensational, some purely recreational. Concessions and restaurants abounded along the strip. They saw clowns, musicians, acrobats, exotic animals prodded along by their trainers, and much, much, more as they wandered past the vendors where barkers promoted their shows. Many of the shows required tickets. Others were free. It was to these that Libby and Frankie gravitated, and even then there was not enough time for more than the briefest whetting of their appetites.

By the time they met the Brignadellos and boarded the streetcar for Catherine's house, Libby despaired of ever seeing all the fair offered on the short visit. Eventually they found seats on the crowded car and exchanged news of what they had seen.

"The Philippines Exposition was an eye-opener," said Mrs. Bee, who was sporting a braided palm-leaf hat made by the natives. "Not just the walled city of Manila, but the villages of the different tribes. Some live in houses on bamboo poles. Why, you'd think a strong wind would bring them down! I saw a fellow shoot a sparrow out of a tree with an arrow and traded my hat to a Bontoc Igorot. They are hat hunters, you know,'' she added with a sniff that implied she'd done her homework.

"Headhunters," corrected her husband, who was seated behind them.

"Headhunters?" Mrs. Bee whirled around. "I thought you said he was admiring my hat!''

Kersey turned and winked at Libby. "No, dear. It was that swath of white hair in your raven black locks he had his eye on.''

"My stars! Headhunters? What were they thinking, bringing them here?''

"I wouldn't worry too much, Mrs. Bee. The Igorots have agreed to settle for dog meat while on St. Louis soil. Started a regular run on dogs, according to Chester.'' Kersey nudged Frankie, and added, "Do you suppose Catherine has a dog?''

"Shame on you, Kersey, for even thinking such a thing!'' scolded Mrs. Bee.

"My feet are killing me,'' declared Libby, the tremor of the streetcar massaging her numb soles. "Tomorrow I'm going to figure out how to use the intramural.''

Frankie lifted his eyes from the fair program. "Costs a dime.''

Libby laughed. "Cheaper than new shoes.''

"What do you think a fellow has to pay for one of those roller cars?'' ventured Kersey.

"With or without the guide?'' asked Frankie.

Mrs. Bee exchanged a smiling glance with Libby, and whispered, "Bless my soul, a few dollars in his pocket, and the boy turns into a banker!''

Catherine's home was located in a lovely old neighborhood at the corner of two quiet streets. The lot it occupied was deep and well shaded by towering hardwoods that put Libby in mind of Old Kentucky. There were twin Gothic windows on the second-story front-facing side of the house, a turret crowned in a high witch's hat, and serpentine columns supporting a front veranda.

"I'm pleased with everything about it, except the mustard color,'' said Catherine. Diminutive like her mother and aunt, blond and dimpled and fun-loving, she tried to hug the Brignadellos and Libby all at the same time.

"It's a lovely color. Like autumn leaves,'' said Libby.

"Indeed,'' agreed Mrs. Bee.

Catherine wrinkled her nose. "I think it's hideous. It bruises my eye just to look at it. Charlie has promised to hire someone to repaint it before winter sets in.'' She laughed, and added, "Maddie offered to save Charlie the money and paint it for us. He declined her invitation, fearful that Maddie on a high ladder is an invitation for disaster. Though he is letting her have a go at

Tess's playhouse." Flicking a careful glance Libby's way she added, "It's wonderful, having her here."

Wishing to reassure her, Libby smiled. "It's been quiet in Edgewood without Maddie. Where is she, anyway?"

"She's out back, putting a little cream on the gingerbread. Trim, that is, not dessert. Poor Uncle Kersey, aren't they feeding you?" Catherine added at her uncle's crestfallen expression.

"No, and your aunt has walked my limbs down to stumps," he replied.

"Then don't let me keep you standing. Come in, come in! Dinner, come back here with that!" Catherine leaped at a medium-sized mongrel with a dish towel in his mouth, then sighed in exasperation as the dog darted away with his prize. "Charlie bought the mutt off a couple of little scoundrels down the street who were bent on selling him to the Igorots."

"Not the headhunters?" cried Mrs. Bee.

Catherine nodded. "President Roosevelt insists they are our guests and that we are to cater to their tastes."

"I wouldn't want to see that carried to an extreme," Mrs. Bee said, fingering her lock of white hair.

Kersey patted her arm. "You just stick with me and mind your own beesness, Mrs. Bee, and you'll be safe enough."

Catherine laughed. "They've been model guests, if you can believe what you read in the papers. You look gorgeous, Aunt Sarah. You too, Libby. Where did you get that precious hat?"

Libby linked arms with Catherine on the way in and replied, "It was a gift from Ike Galloway."

"Gift?" chorused Mrs. Bee and Catherine in unison, eyebrows arching.

"Replacing the one lost at sea," Libby added, though in truth, her old straw hat was no longer lost. On Saturday, she had spotted it hanging from Ike's sap house door. Almost like a welcome mat. Something tangible to evoke a sense of her presence. What a priceless gesture!

"Catherine, did Maddie tell you about Libby pulling Ike out of the foamy brine?" asked Mrs. Bee.

Libby could tell by Catherine's expression that she had. But Catherine had a little fun with it, saying, "Fell in the pickle barrel, did he?"

"Wasn't no pickle barrel," Frankie said, his first words since leaving the street car. "It was the creek he fell into, Miz Catherine, on account of he was sick. He ain't feelin' real pert yet. Pa cut his wheat, and I helped shock it."

"Is that so? That's hard work, Frankie." Catherine smiled and asked after his mother's health and Opal's, too. She confided that she had been frightfully homesick, and couldn't say enough how good it was to see people from Edgewood. Her graciously phrased welcome put Libby at ease as they toured the house with its spacious rooms, luxuriously draped floor-to-ceiling windows and handsome furnishings.

The second-floor room Libby was to share with Maddie was well fitted to Maddie's personality. The embossed wall coverings were dramatic, the carpet deep-hued, and the decorative touches sparse, but vivid. Libby found her luggage and warm water waiting there.

She took off her jacket and hat, washed her face and hands, and patted her hair into place before retracing her steps to join the Gentrys, the Brignadellos, and Catherine downstairs. Little Tess, who had learned to walk since leaving Edgewood, was enjoying the attention lavished upon her by her doting grandmother and aunt, while Mr. Gentry questioned Kersey about the fair.

Frankie, in the meantime, had disappeared. Upon inquiring of Catherine, Libby learned he had gone outside to explore the yard. Excusing herself, Libby went in search of him and found Maddie instead.

Dressed in men's trousers, an old shirtwaist, and a painter's cap, Maddie was applying cream-colored paint to the gingerbread trim on the playhouse in the backyard. Hearing Libby's approach, she swung around to exchange greetings. "What do you think of St. Louis, Libby? Are you enjoying the fair?"

"Very much so. Though it makes me feel like a snail in the woods. I can't possibly move fast enough to see it all. How have you been, Maddie?"

"Just fine, though I'm missing Sophronia, if you can believe it. I got a letter from her saying she was going home to stay with her other grandmother until her parents return from their trip."

"Yes, she left last week," said Libby. "Opal misses her."

"An unlikely pair, those two." Maddie put down her brush and held up her hands for Libby to admire her blisters. "See here? Catherine has imposed upon my good nature in an effort to get everything ready for her company. I've scarcely seen anything of the fair. But now that you're here, maybe I'll tag along with you and Frankie."

"What's this you're grumbling about all work and no play?" Catherine called, coming across the yard, her lightsome laughter ringing. "Don't listen to her, Libby. Angus was here for three days, and I scarcely saw a thing of him, so enamored were they with the fair."

"That simply isn't true!" exclaimed Maddie. "Angus and I spent hours and hours getting a start on this carpenter's lace. Washings and sandings. What an awful waste of gingerbread. And paint, I might add."

"It's lovely, and you're doing a masterful job of refurbishing it," said Catherine.

Maddie reached for a paint rag, only to have it jerked away by the dog. "Dinner!" she grumbled. "You're a menace."

Catherine laughed, and warned Libby, "Don't leave anything you value where he can get it. I've lost count of the cushions and baby toys he's chewed up. I keep threatening to take him to the Igorots and pay them to take him."

Libby laughed. "So *that's* how he came by his name!"

"Charlie's dry wit," said Catherine, dimpling at her appreciation. "Maddie, we'll be eating in about an hour, if you'd like to come in and clean up."

Maddie thanked Catherine for the summons, then forestalled her when she tried to take Libby back to the house with her, saying, "If you don't mind, I'd like a word with Libby before you spirit her away."

"Of course. I'll see you both at the table in an hour." Catherine retreated across the shaded lawn, the dog at her heels, Maddie's rag in his mouth.

The westering sun had enough strength left to filter through the leaves and dapple Maddie's face. The lights and shadows shifted with the breeze. Fixing her eye on Libby, she said with customary bluntness, "I suppose you were surprised when Angus told you we were getting married."

"Stunned," conceded Libby.

"Be honest with me, now. What are you thinking?"

"I'm thinking that Angus did well by himself."

"Libby, the diplomat."

Responding to an internal nudge, Libby slipped an arm around her. "So now I'm a diplomat, am I? What happened to sisterhood?"

"As usual, you're much too kind. I should be shot for treason to the cause, and we both know it," said Maddie. But she accepted the hug in the spirit it was given.

"And you're too hard on yourself."

The stiffness left Maddie's chin. She searched Libby's face for a long moment. "I hope I haven't hurt you."

"My pride was stung, but not my heart."

"Is that so?" The corner of Maddie's mouth tipped. "My, but you know how to strip victory of its sweet savor, don't you?"

Realizing how much she had come to value what had long seemed more like an uneasy truce than a friendship, Libby replied, "We're very different, you and I, yet very much the same. I've learned a lot from you, Maddie. I hope to go on learning."

"Now that *is* encouraging." Maddie smiled, picked up her brush, and trekked to the house.

Remembering what had brought her out to the yard, Libby was about to go in search of Frankie when a small sound drew her attention. The creaking wasn't repeated, but her pulse quickened. Holding her skirts close so as not to brush the paint, Libby ducked into the playhouse.

It was a cozy space, eight feet long and almost that wide. She had to bend her knees to keep from hitting her head on the ceiling. Sidestepping a small table and chairs and a doll bed, Libby crossed to the other end, where rungs nailed to the wall and a trapdoor gave access to the second story. She folded the door back and found Frankie stretched out on the floor, sound asleep.

Or was he? Thinking of the conversation she and Maddie had shared, alarm stirred in Libby. She watched his face for a moment or two, listening to his even breathing, and was about to give him a shake when one eye popped open.

"Frankie McClure! Have you been eavesdropping?"

"Not me, Lib." He looked affronted that she could think it of him. "I was jest havin' a look around and thinkin' what Opal'd make of sech a place for playin' and countin' my money and wonderin' jest how far I could stretch it so's I can take some presents home. They'd like that, don't ya think?"

Her heart softening, Libby nodded. "Yes, and I think it's nice of you to want to. Now, about what you heard . . ."

"I don't give much notice ta weddin' talk, Miss Lib. Honest."

So he *had* heard. If he repeated a fraction of their conversation to his grandfather, Hascal Caton, there was no way Maddie and Angus's marriage was going to stay secret until after the election. Libby thought it over for a long moment, then said, "This is a wonderful place. Not nearly so crowded as the house, either."

"I was thinkin' that, too," said Frankie. "I ain't much for crowds. I ain't much for Mr. Gentry neither, if ya want ta know the truth."

"That's rude, Frankie," said Libby, though in truth she wasn't much for Mr. Gentry, either. He might be a good husband and stepfather, but the fact that he had never sought to restore family ties with Ike, his own half brother's son, didn't endear him to her.

Frankie tucked his chin, and said, "A couple of blankets and a feller could sleep out here purty good."

"Now there's an idea. Would you like me to ask Catherine if you could camp out here?"

"Would ya?"

"I would if you'd make me a promise."

"Name it," said Frankie.

"I want you to promise me you won't repeat a word of what you just heard."

" 'Bout Miss Maddie and Mr. Cearlock gettin' married? Ya want I should swear it?" he asked, his face somber.

"A man of his word doesn't have to swear it. And you, Frankie, have become a man of your word. If you say you won't, your handshake is good enough for me."

"I promise, then." Looking pleased, he shook Libby's hand.

35

Frankie had been gone three days when Decatur went to town and came home with Naomi on the seat beside him, little Opal bouncing around in the back of the wagon. Ike rose from the bench in front of his sap house and walked out to the road to meet them.

Awkward as a schoolboy trying not to boast when he'd done well and knew it, Decatur stopped the team, and said, "Naomi's wantin' to have a look at the new porch."

"Hope ya can look with a kindly eye, Naomi," said Ike.

"It don't have to be fancy," she said, her shoulders thrown back and a blush upon her cheeks. "Jest a spot to sit in the evenin' and rest for a spell."

"Stone pillars under it and new floorboards tacked down real tight," Decatur told her. "Even got a railin' so's Opal kin practice her circus rope walkin'."

"Don't ya get her started, she jest about talked herself outa bein' a circus gal." Naomi turned and smiled at Opal.

"Brung yer laundry. Widder Harpster fussin' over it lyin' about in her way." Decatur swung down off the wagon seat and reached into the back of the wagon for Ike's laundry just as Opal clambered over the tailgate and started pestering to race on up ahead.

"My limbs could use a stretchin', too," said Naomi. She climbed down and ambled on toward the bridge, hand in hand with Opal, both of them drinking in the view as if their eyes had grown parched for it.

Ike unleashed the grin he'd been holding back and clapped Decatur on the shoulder. "Looks like ya got back that rib you've been stewin' over."

"Yep, sure enuf."

"Close up the store, did she?"

"Nope. Mr. Watson's goin' ta share the keepin' of it with her for a while. It'll mean her goin' ta town three days a week, but it wouldn't be right, keepin' her from it. She feels duty-bound on account of the little redhead givin' it to Frankie. And besides, ain't nothin' but trees and critters out here, and I reckon that's lonesome for a body likes jawin' at people." Decatur slapped his hat against his leg, and added, "Speakin' of Miss Libby, Opal says she ain't singin' with the Berry girls no more."

Ike's pulse quickened at the surprise of it. "How come?"

A slow grin stole over Decatur's lined face. "I dunno. But iffin I was you, and I had my ribs on straight, I'd be findin' out."

"Reckon I could ask."

"Yep." Decatur climbed back up on the wagon seat. Taking up the lines in his hard, knotty hands, he looked down at Ike from his lofty height, and added, "Lessen yer scairt."

Ike wouldn't give him the satisfaction of responding. But when Decatur had gone along, he stood with his laundry in his arms, his eye on Libby's battered hat, his mouth gone dry, and his heart beating too fast. Had Libby given up the singing for him?

If so, why hadn't she told him? It wasn't for lack of opportunity. She'd gone by on the mail route on Saturday.

Pride, he thought. She could quit the group for him, but she stopped short of letting him know it was for him. *If it was for him.* But why else would she quit? *Why hadn't she told him?*

He stood for a long while, trying to come up with an answer to settle the edgy feeling rising within him. Knowing what he knew about Angus, he had felt his concern was justified. Was it? Or was he guarding his own pride? Even if she had to sacrifice something important to her just to make it right with him?

Scairt. Decatur's accusation echoed over him. Scared he'd poked a pinhole in a dam and that it needed attention. He went over it again in his head and came up with the same answer.

What was to keep him from taking the evening train south and going after her? He weighed the idea and nearly dismissed it, not because it wasn't plausible, but because he had told her he would wait until November, and it was hard to admit how difficult he was finding the wait. He stood there a moment longer, thinking how he'd smarted off to Decatur, telling him fear was a jail cell and that a man locked his own self in and could let his own self out if he had the courage. If that was the case, then Decatur had thus far proved himself a braver man than Ike Galloway.

Ike, who thought he'd been cured of impetuous ideas years ago, seized hold of this one and straightaway acted upon it.

* * *

Libby wouldn't have believed time could fly so swiftly. Monday, Tuesday, Wednesday gone, Thursday now under way, and so much yet to see. The wonders of the fair defied description, even for a writer's vocabulary. She had fallen into bed the last two nights, too exhausted to put pencil to page. But today, she had brought her journal along to capture glimpses of the Exposition while she waited for the parade in which Billy Young was to take part.

Maddie had come with her today, but had left her to her journal keeping while she and Frankie climbed the DeForest Wireless Tower for a lesson on wireless telegraphy and an elevated view of the grounds. On a bench looking across the Grand Basin and up the cascading waterfalls toward Festival Hall and the Colonnade of States, Libby sat with her open Memorandum booklet on her lap and skimmed what she had written thus far:

There is an ethereal aura about the fair, as if a master illusionist had spread a magic fan over the hills. And indeed the layout of the 'main picture' as they call the heart of the fair, is fan-shaped, with Art Hill acting as the handle of the fan and the palatial exhibit halls spreading outward over the sloping landscape. Everywhere I look, there is beauty. But if I were pressed to pick only one view to store in my mind forever, it would be Festival Hall. It makes me think of a fancy wedding cake on the king's banqueting table.

The grounds are breathtaking at night when the lights come on, illuminating buildings and statuary and gardens and bridges and fountains and the cascading waterfalls with their silvery rushing music as they spill from fall to fall and finally into the Grand Basin.

Yesterday at sunset as Frankie and I sat with Mr. and Mrs. Brignadello waiting for the lights to come on, I lifted eyes weary from trying to capture it all to the sky and caught my breath. Such a sky! Pinks and blues and purples melting into one another and gently fusing behind a network of dimpled clouds. I looked with fresh eyes at this splendid Exposition, thinking how all the sweat and toil and creative energies expended in putting it together are but a dim reflection of our Maker's great, inexhaustible imagination. His sun and moon and stars will shine on, spectacular light shows long after the brilliance of this fair is but a memory. I was reminded that our lives are but a vapor that appears for a while and then vanishes and that I would like not to waste it.

Rereading the last passage, Libby thought of Ike, for he had been on her mind the previous evening, as she gazed into the sky and wondered if he was looking on the same stars in Old Kentucky.

Feeling restive of a sudden, she was glad to see Maddie and Frankie coming back. They hiked to the Illinois Building, located on a hill a stone's throw from the Observation Wheel. Flowers were being distributed in honor of Illinois Day, but the line was long, and Libby didn't want to wait.

She and Maddie and Frankie wrote their names in the Illinois registry and made a tour of the pavilion while waiting for the parade of which Billy Young was to be a part. It was an impressive building, with its large dome and mosaic floor, but Frankie soon lost interest. He went outside, then returned to tell Libby and Maddie they had better hurry if they wanted to see the parade.

With pomp and pageantry, the parade was led by a general, some fair dignitaries, and a number of Illinois officials, all in handsome carriages. Libby looked for Governor Yates among the men. She was certain she'd recognize him, for he had spoken at a Republican rally out at Spring Lake earlier in the summer.

Maddie nudged Frankie, who was standing in front of them. "Wave to the governor, Frankie."

"Where?" Libby and Frankie echoed together.

Maddie indicated a man on horseback. She cupped her hands to her mouth and called, "It would be a privilege to vote for you, Governor Yates."

"Maddie!" Libby's face flamed at the stares they were garnering from the crowd.

"If you can't take the heat, skedaddle!" Maddie gave fair warning, then cupped her hands again and chanted, "The vote, the vote, the vote!"

The governor smiled benignly and waved. Oblivious to the disparaging glances, Maddie kept up the chant until a band came along the parade route and drowned her out.

"Merciful patience!" cried Libby. "Next time I see a politician coming *your* way, I'm running the *other* way!"

Maddie tossed her head, and countered, "You'll thank me someday."

Several military bands followed and on their heels, one military company after another. Libby was rethinking just how much of an asset Maddie was going to be to Angus's political aspirations when a cheer moved through the spectators in a wave.

The sound grew as the First Volunteer Cavalry was announced. Roosevelt's Rough Riders. Veterans of the Cuban conflict. They had offered their keen shooting and riding skills, even their very lives, to liberate Cuba from Spain. Volunteers all, they had since resumed their lives as plainsmen and mountainmen and farmers and cowboys, but the indelible impression they had left on their countrymen could be heard in the patriotic pride that grew to a deafening roar, drowning out the sound of hoofbeats and creaking leather and even Libby's embarrassment with Maddie's shenanigans. She joined the

show of appreciation as the motley sun-baked crew of men rode on toward
the review stand, boots shining, sunlight glinting off their spurs and pistols,
distinctive blue polka-dot bandannas fluttering in the breeze.

Frankie tugged at her sleeve. ''Ain't that Billy?''

Libby followed the direction of his pointing finger, but the gaze that tangled with hers didn't belong to Billy Young. The mouths of the crowd were
still moving, but the resounding din faded as if some internal pressure had
sucked away all sound except that of her own pounding heart. For it was
Ike's gray eyes that smiled at her from beneath the brim of a Cavalry hat.
He had come!

He motioned for her to wait. She nodded, and without uttering a sound, it
was arranged. Amazingly, Frankie hadn't seen him. But sharp-eyed Maddie
had.

''What was *that* all about?'' she asked straight out.

''What was what all about?'' Libby said, feigning innocence.

Maddie's gaze skipped over Frankie, then came back to Libby. Initial
surprise gave way to a throaty laugh. ''No *wonder* you've handled my breach
of sisterhood so masterfully. Catherine mentioned he'd given you the hat that
hasn't left your head for three days, but somehow the significance of it escaped me.''

''Maddie! I only brought the one,'' Libby protested. ''You're making too
much of a hat and a wave.''

''That was no wave, that was a signal. It couldn't have been any clearer
if it had flashed from a lighthouse. To which your face bears a striking
resemblance.'' Ignoring Libby's sputtering objections, Maddie swung around
and entreated Frankie. ''Let's head for the Pike and Shoot the Chutes. We'll
go to the North Pole, too, my treat. And then we'll see if we can't make the
U. S. Life Saving demonstration.''

''Isn't Libby coming?'' asked Frankie, looking back.

''What for? She knows the routine. Ike can attest to that,'' said Maddie.
She got a loose grip on Frankie's shoulder, and called back to Libby, ''I'm
stealing Frankie for the day. Can you find your own way home?'' At Libby's
nod, she added with a tilt of the mouth, ''You'll forgive me if I don't wait
up?''

Libby gripped her handbag and Memorandum book tightly and pretended
not to hear.

There was no pretending when it came to the brief speech made by the
president of the Exposition or the governor's response—both were lost on
her as she watched for Ike. The ceremony was over, the crowd gone by the
time he returned on foot. He had changed into gray flannel trousers, a white
shirt, a dark suit jacket, and he came to her bringing a lily. He offered it
with a wordless smile that plucked at Libby's heartstrings.

It was hard to breathe, even harder to think. "The flower patrol isn't after you, are they?" she asked.

He grinned. "I didn't pick it off the floral clock, if that's what yer thinkin'."

Libby buried her smile in the lily and inhaled its sweet perfume. "It's lovely."

"Yep," he said, but his eyes were fixed on her, fixed so firmly, she flushed and averted her gaze and dropped the fragrant petal. His fingers brushed hers as they stooped as one to retrieve it from the ground. Suspended in that squatted position, facing him, she was keenly aware of their left thighs nearly touching, their fingers brushing as they both held the lily. Oblivious to the pounding feet of passing people, the whirring mechanics of the nearby Observation Wheel, the whip of the flags hanging from masts atop the Illinois Building, she lifted her eyes to his and saw at this close range that his eyes were not simply gray. They were a meshing of slate and pewter and shades of deep blue. The sun had etched squint lines at the outer corners. Gilded lashes, sun-browned face. As he returned her silent scrutiny, she fancied that the undulating beat of the pulse at his temple matched the toccata of her own. Moistening her lips, she asked, "What're you doing here?"

"Lookin' for you."

"It isn't November."

"I got lonesome for ya, Lib."

His honesty wrapped around her heart like the tendrils of some sweet wild vine. The breeze teased her hair and the air smelled fresh and the bark on the nearby maple tree, so nicked and knotted and scarred, was to her eyes ruggedly beautiful. As was his ear. Flushing at the strong desire to reach out and cover his old war wound with her hand, she dropped her gaze, and admitted, "Me, too."

He gripped her hand and came to his feet, bringing her up with him. "I wanted to talk to ya about the Berry Sisters. When I heard you'd quit, I got to thinking it was selfish of me to want ya to, and that's no way to be."

"I didn't quit," said Libby.

"Then you're still singin'."

"No. But I didn't quit. Angus . . . well, he . . ."

Suddenly, Ike seemed to get the picture. Confusion gave way to relief. "It was him, then, and not me put a stop to it?"

She caught her breath, for it was clear that he had come thinking she had sacrificed the singing for him. Would the fact that she *hadn't* weaken the impulse that had brought him to her? Hesitantly, she said, "He thought it might be awkward for me, since we . . . since he . . ."

"Ya told him you'd go politickin' but not courtin'?" he said, helping her out.

Libby flushed. "I was going to, but he beat me to it. Part of it, anyway. The courting part."

Ike's mouth flattened, his expression moving from surprise to something harder to define. At length, he lapped his arms across his chest, rocked back on his heels, and declared, "He broke it off with you and booted you out of the singin' group? That wasn't very sportin'. Not after all the practicin' and dressmakin'."

"He offered to let me keep the dress," she pointed out lamely, for it was clear that Ike, knowing only half of the story, was thinking poorly of Angus. What else could she say with Angus and Maddie wanting to keep their marriage a secret until after the election? Anxious he not misunderstand, she said with a quick smile, "It worked out for everyone, actually. An amicable parting of the ways."

"Ya haven't changed yer mind then?"

"About us?" she asked. He nodded. The look in his eye fractured her thoughts. Velvet wings beat at her rib cage. She shook her head. "No. What about you?"

His mouth twitched at one corner in a boyish, lopsided grin. "It wasn't Billy's naggin' or a hankerin' to parade that brought me here. Funny thing is, I did enjoy myself, seein' the boys and listenin' to them run on, their stories growin' with the tellin'."

"And the parading?"

"Had to pay the piper for room and board," he said, and smiled. "Billy was all mornin' pokin' me and sayin' 'Yer having fun, now aren't ya! Didn't I tell ya?' "

Libby smiled and looked, half-expecting to see Billy hovering somewhere in the background. He wasn't, but she did see Angus's parents and the Brignadellos coming along the avenue toward the Illinois Building. "Let's walk, shall we?"

"What about Frankie?" Ike asked, belatedly noticing his absence.

"He's with Maddie for the rest of the day." Shamefaced, Libby added, "I'm shirking my duty, so to speak. And about to get caught at it, too. Are they following?"

"Who?"

"Mr. and Mrs. Gentry and the Brignadellos. Didn't you see them?"

"To be honest Lib, I wasn't lookin'," he said, tailoring his stride to hers. "I was thinkin' what a fine hat that is yer wearin'."

Libby laughed. "It is, isn't it? The fellow who gave it to me has impeccable taste, wouldn't you say?"

"If yer fishin' for a compliment, I'll jest save you the trouble and tell ya straight out, you suit my taste jest fine."

He laughed at her flustered protest that she hadn't been fishing at all and pointed at the Observation Wheel. "You been up on that yet? Then how about goin' with me?"

"Past experience in your company warns against it," said Libby, sweeping his face with a sidelong glance. "But never let it be said I'm not a good sport."

He laughed and paid the fare and led the way. As they waited for other passengers to board one of the trolley-sized cars that made the revolution on that massive wheel, Ike answered her inquiries concerning the harvesting out at Old Kentucky. He in turn asked her about the fair. Just as she began a brief overview of the sights she and Frankie had seen, the mechanical engine whirred, and the gondola began to climb.

Libby stopped mid-sentence, her stomach lurching, the blood rushing to her head. She stifled a squeal, closed her eyes, and sucked in air through her teeth.

"Aw, now you ain't goin' ta see nothin' thataway." Ike nudged her with his shoulder, and chided, "Why, we're creeping along like a turtle."

Hesitantly, Libby opened her eyes and saw that he was right. Thunderstruck by the view, she exclaimed, "Why, it's positively dizzying!"

"See there? Didn't I tell ya?"

"There's the main picture! It looks just like the postcard I sent Father and Davie!"

"There's the falls and the lagoons. Ain't that somethin'?"

They took turns pointing out sights as the gondola car whirred to the top and stopped. The view of the exhibition grounds and city beyond was so exhilarating, Libby laughed out loud. "Look at the trees. They look like broccoli from here. And the people! Imagine that! They're no bigger than mice." Encouraged by Ike's soft chuckle, she exclaimed, "Look very hard, Ike. Way, way, way off to the south—isn't that Edgewood?"

He slid one arm along the back of the seat. Leaning forward, squinting as he pointed past her toward the distant north, he played along, saying, "And ain't that Old Kentucky? Yessir, I see Naomi's shop and there's old Hack, humpin' along growling to hisself 'cause everybody's feelin' fine and nary an epidemic to be found."

Feeling fine. Libby's heart echoed his words as she answered the laughter in his eyes. Wonder of wonders, with the world on display in the ivory city below, he and he alone filled her senses. She looked from the gracious lines of the flawless architecture below to the line of his jaw, from the opalescence of the buildings to the gray of his eyes, breathed the varied bouquet of the fair and relished the scent of him. His gaze was on the view, as if he were set on memorizing it, unaware that she, at the same moment, was memorizing him.

Abruptly, the motion of the wheel shook her out of her reverie. Libby lapped her arms over her midriff. "Hang on to your stomach!"

Ike smiled and moved his hand off the back of the seat to cup her shoulder in a bracing motion as their gondola dropped over the edge and began the descent. Libby's nerves leaped again, a leaping that had little to do with the ride.

All too soon, they were earthbound again. But Libby was walking on clouds for the rest of the day, for at her side was the one attraction the world exhibition had been lacking all week.

They walked and took in some shows and rode the intramural and visited as many pavilions as they could squeeze in before a delicious aroma drew them into the Irish village. Over dinner Ike mentioned that Naomi and Opal had returned home to Old Kentucky.

A month ago, the news would have filled Libby with misgivings. But she had gained some insights from the situation with Abigail and Adam and was ready to acknowledge that her view of Decatur had not been entirely right. Her gaze settled on the lily, a symbol of resurrection. She had carried it with her all day. It adorned their table now, its trumpet-shaped bloom filling the mouth of the water glass. Stretching a hand toward it, Libby said, "I suppose you knew he came to the station to see Frankie off? He gave Frankie five silver dollars." Reflecting on that moment, Libby met Ike's gaze. "There was something different about him that day. I can't put my finger on it, except to say I looked at him and didn't feel the urge to run the other way."

A trace of a smile graced Ike's mouth. "He's made his peace with God, Lib. Makes a difference in a man."

Libby blinked back unbidden tears as Ike, in simple words, told her of the changes in Decatur and how he had decided to work with God and not against Him. It wasn't just the hope represented in Decatur rebuilding his family, the foundation on the rock; it was the thought of Ike's faithfulness, of his caring enough about Decatur to stick by him when nearly everyone else, herself included, had condemned him.

"Are you going to tell Frankie his family is back together again?"

"It ain't my place to. Anyway, Opal'll be cross with me if I go giving away the good news b'fore she gets a chance to."

Libby smiled and agreed he was right.

After dinner, they watched the lights come on all over the grounds like tiny sparks catching, growing stronger until they glowed unwaveringly. It was a sight to dazzle the eyes, those millions of lights outlining the buildings and statues and bridges and avenues and cascading falls. Like gazing at fireworks that held their place in the sky, steadily burning without being consumed.

They strolled the Pike where the lights burned even brighter. Ragtime

music and a playful mood prevailed. The throngs pressed so close, Ike kept
hold of her hand, lest they lose one another in the crowds. She savored the
warm, firm pressure of his callused palm melding with hers.

When the noise became wearing, they found their way to the gondola
landing where the music of a five-piece Italian band floated on the cool
autumn breeze and a harvest moon spun of red gold shone on the waters,
gilding Ike's strong face. Libby's fingers tightened on his hand. He returned
the pressure and smiled down at her. Heat swept up her throat and with it,
a heightened awareness of his lean body and squared shoulders and straight
carriage. He returned her gaze with an easy grace born not of vanity or pride,
but honesty. *Ya suit my taste jest fine,* he'd told her earlier, and wonder of
wonders, she could see in his eyes that she did. All the lights of the ivory
city seemed reflected in their depths.

An older couple came along, the woman in a roller chair. Ike stepped
behind Libby to make room for them to pass. He freed her hand only long
enough to enfold it again with his own left hand. ''Ya want to go for a boat
ride?''

The coiling of nerves surpassed the over-the-top feeling on the Ferris
Wheel. Libby nodded and shifted away from his feather-light whisper tickling
her neck.

They settled in a gondola and moved away from the landing. The tender
music and the foreign words sung by the musicians mingled with the liquid
caress of water washing at the gondola and spilling off the boatman's oar.
But no sweeter was it than the rhapsody of her own heart as Ike slipped his
arm around her.

With the orange moon over his right shoulder and stardust on the water,
Libby felt the million twinkling lights and the sights and sounds of a once-
in-a-lifetime Exposition slip away. She leaned her shoulder into his, lifted
her face to the sky, and wondered wistfully if water still made him think of
Maddie.

At her sigh, he teased and coaxed until she finally told him. He laughed
and landed the kiss she'd been waiting for since that day in Dr. Harding's
dim corridor.

''Maddie *who?''* he whispered.

Her lips tingled with the reverberations of his kiss. Fading softer, softer.
His mouth hovered close. So close, she was aware of its warmth though their
lips were not touching. She lowered her lashes for fear he could see stirrings
she had until today thought existed only in dime novels.

''Lib?''

It was only a word, but the tender resonance of it was as eloquent an
invitation as any she had ever heard. Entrusting her heart to him, she met
his waiting lips, closed her eyes, and found some answers to life she hadn't
even known she'd been seeking.

36

𝕷 Libby awoke early on Friday, her last day at the fair. Enjoying the luxury of indoor plumbing, she bathed and dressed in the gown she had made to match Ike's gift hat and thanked Maddie for seeing after Frankie the previous day.

"We had a good time together," said Maddie, who was just climbing out of bed. "Frankie's full of beans, of course, but he's still a better fellow than his grandpa will ever be."

In too sunny a mood to endure an enumeration of Hascal Caton's flaws, Libby said, "Ike's going roaming with Billy this morning, so I guess you and Catherine are stuck with me. You'd better get dressed. We're leaving in an hour." She moved to the mirror and noted, as she swept her hair into a chignon, that Maddie was still immobile. "You *are* still going, aren't you?"

"I have nothing else to do. The painting is done, and Angus is in Springfield." Maddie met Libby's gaze in the mirror and ventured, "About this flirtation you're having with Ike . . ."

"Flirtation?" Libby paused in shaping loose curls to frame her face. "That sounds like something out of Dorene Berry's mouth."

"In other words, mind my own *bees-ness, Mrs. Bee,*" Maddie said, borrowing a line from Kersey Brignadello.

Libby reached for her hat. "Did I mention that Ike is meeting me after lunch today? If we have time, we're going to ramble through the display of horseless carriages."

"The automobiles, is it? I'd like one of those myself. May I come along?"

"There's a silly question. I'm not taking all this trouble making myself lovely just to be upstaged by you."

"A *serious* flirtation, by the sound of it," said Maddie.

Serious had such a staid connotation. She was soaring! Shining from the inside out! She caught herself humming the "Animal Fair," giggled, and when Maddie strode down the hall to bathe, sang it, then quieted to a smile at some deep, hidden certainty that there were more sweet discoveries in store for her. And that they, too, would be revealed in due season.

Catherine left Tess at home with the housekeeper. She and Maddie, Libby and Frankie, the Brignadellos and the Gentrys stopped on the Plaza of St. Louis to watch some troops drill to the music of a military band. The couples made arrangements to meet the girls back at the Lindell Entrance to catch the Delmar streetcar at five. Catherine was planning a special dinner for her guests on this, their last night in St. Louis.

Libby and her friends, with Frankie in tow, visited the Manufactures Pavilion, where industrial arts from numerous countries were on display. She felt a little less anxious as to how Frankie was going to receive the news of his family's reunification when Frankie pored over a display of playing cards made by American Indians and broke a silver dollar to buy a deck for Decatur. He tagged along as they explored the textiles display, and bought a colorful scarf for Opal.

Libby had never imagined that such a wide variety of apparel existed, or that French gowns could be so exquisite. She bought a souvenir teacup for Abigail and another for Mrs. Baker at the Japanese Garden, where they stopped for green tea and Japanese cakes. Frankie bought a similar one for Naomi and entrusted the fragile purchase to Libby as they tramped on to visit Jim Key, the educated horse. The amazing animal did simple mathematics and spelled words by picking up letter blocks in his mouth. His stunts provided some lively conversation over lunch at the German Tyrolean Alps on the east end of the Pike.

Angus came along unexpectedly as they were finishing their lunch. A warning finger to his lips forestalled Catherine from being a spoiler. He slipped up behind Maddie's chair, put his hands over her eyes, and laughed as she whirled around in her seat.

"I thought you had to be in Springfield all week," Maddie cried.

"Now, what kind of welcome is that?" said Angus, feigning injured feelings.

Maddie, unaware Frankie knew the truth, recovered her surprise and put on a sham, saying, "We're nearly finished eating, but there's a chair between Libby and Catherine if you'd care to join us, Mr. Cearlock. Catherine was just telling us about the Temple of Mirth and how the mirrors distort the human form."

"How much did it cost, Miz Catherine?" asked Frankie, his hand going to his pocket.

"I don't recall. But finish your lemonade, and I'll take you there before I go home. My treat," Catherine added, for Frankie's frugality was by now notorious.

Angus slipped into a chair between Catherine and Libby. Libby saw him glance at Frankie, who was engrossed in stacking and counting his dwindling coins. He whispered to Libby, asking her for a piece of paper. She took one from her notebook and watched as he dashed a line across it and folded it in quarters, then she forgot it again as Catherine regaled Angus with a tale of that "wretched black dog," as she called Dinner, and his penchant for collecting newspapers off the neighbors' doorsteps.

Libby started at Angus's nudge.

"To Maddie," he whispered, and slipped her the note beneath the table where it was out of view of Frankie.

Libby did his bidding and dropped the note into Maddie's lap. After all, Angus had no way of knowing that there were no secrets at this table, at least not where keeping his marriage to Maddie from Frankie was concerned. The notepassing was rather romantic, actually.

Frankie looked up to see Maddie scanning the note. "What's that?" he asked.

"It's a game I learned on the Pike," said Angus. "I pass you each a note. More paper, if you please, Miss Watson."

Libby supplied another page from her notebook and sat by watching Angus's superfluous attempt to bamboozle Frankie.

"What're ya doing that for?" asked Frankie, as Angus tore the paper into four pieces.

"Patience, lad. Patience." Angus scribbled messages on each paper scrap and dropped his pencil. "There now!"

Frankie reached across the table and read them one by one: "Time heals all wounds. Time waits for no man. Time for lunch." Frankie frowned over the last one and held it up for all of them to see. "Ain't nothing but a picture of a thumb."

"A thumbnail sketch of a thumb, my boy, and the very note you want least to draw," corrected Angus. "Now mix them all up. Each of you draw one, and whoever draws the thumb must thumb through his purse and buy lunch."

Frankie's hand shot out to cover his pile of coins. "Where'd ya learn sech a game—the Foolish House?"

Seeing Frankie blush at their laughter, Libby patted his hand. "I'm with you, Frankie. A fool and his money are soon parted."

Looking vindicated, Frankie finished his lemonade in one long swallow,

pocketed his coins, and went with Catherine to visit the highly acclaimed
Temple of Mirth.

If Ike had had his druthers, he would have spent the morning with Libby.
She had a supper obligation at Catherine's that evening, so they weren't going
to have the time together that they had had yesterday. But Billy was wanting
to show him the high spots of what he'd seen over the past week. Billy had
gone out on a limb for him, getting him a bunk in the overcrowded barracks
when he had shown up unexpectedly. Billy had been there to help harvest
his wheat. Billy had been there in Cuba. Except for Willie Blue, Ike had had
no better friend than Billy. So he had tramped at Billy's side from one exhibit
hall to another, his concentration steadily dwindling as the morning wore on
and his thoughts turned increasingly to Libby. But at last the morning had
passed.

He ate at the mess hall with Billy, then rushed to the Pike to meet Libby,
who had told him in advance that she would be eating lunch with her friends
at the German Tyrolean Alps. Now, he nearly broke stride at the sight of
Angus Cearlock seated beside her at the table.

A waiter with a group of ladies at his heels trooped past him, then stopped
to wait while a second group abandoned a nearby table. By the time the
traffic cleared, Libby was on her feet, waiting for him. Her smile, as warm
as a physical touch, crowded out his misgivings.

Ike greeted Maddie and shook Cearlock's hand. Cearlock kept his gaze
away from Libby, yet his surprise that Ike was here to meet her was apparent.
He overcompensated with a hearty, "What do you make of the fair? Quite
an extravaganza, isn't it?"

"Took some agile minds to put it together," Ike agreed. He reached for
one of Libby's bundles. "Ya ready to go?"

Nodding, Libby explained, "Angus took the train down from Springfield
to surprise Ma . . . Catherine, that is. And his parents, of course." She gathered her pocketbook and her parcels and warmed him with another smile.
"Frankie and Catherine just left for the Temple of Mirth. If we hurry, we
can catch up with them."

They had excused themselves and were turning away when Cearlock called
after Libby, saying, "You're forgetting your note, Miss Watson!"

Libby chuckled and, with a random reach, grabbed one of a half dozen
wrinkled scraps of paper from the table. She stuffed it into her pocketbook
without looking at it, smiled and waved to Maddie, who was grabbing the
other notes up.

"What was that all about?" Ike asked.

"Oh, some nonsensical game Angus made up to tease Frankie. Strikingly similar to the game of Old Maid, come to think of it," she said. "Whoever drew the thumb note was supposed to buy lunch."

Ike missed the point of it all, but he smiled because just looking at her made him feel like smiling. They had no more collected Frankie than Billy came along and spirited the boy away with plans to visit the Aeronautic Concourse.

They made their way through some of the state buildings and were within shouting distance of Inside Inn Hotel when Dr. Harding and his wife Paulette came along.

Doc shook Ike's hand and asked him how he was feeling while his wife visited with Libby. Before parting company, Paulette kindly offered to take the souvenirs Libby had bought up to her room so they wouldn't have to cart them around all day. It was obvious she was surprised to see Ike with Libby, and just as obvious that the doctor was anxious to whisk her away before she started asking questions.

Libby must have noticed, too. As they walked on, liberated of parcels, she said, "I don't think Angus has told his aunts and uncles we're no longer courting."

"Reckon they're figurin' it out for themselves." Ike reached for her hand and pulled her to a stop. As he looked into her upturned face, the fancy trimmings and trappings of the fair seemed garish and tiresome. "What would you think of gettin' away from here for a while?"

Surprise flickered in her eyes. "Where would we go?"

"I don't care. Jest somewhere quiet where we can be alone."

Color washed out the pale freckles that the sun had sprinkled over her cheeks. She averted her blue gaze. For a moment, he was afraid she'd misunderstood him. But, no. Her red-gold lashes swept up, and a smile tipped the corner of her mouth. She said, "A little enchantment goes a long way, I guess."

Truth was, she was all the enchantment he wanted. By mutual agreement, they exited the grounds and walked along a country road that skirted the high-board fair fence as far as the eye could see.

It was lovely open country, untouched as yet by city developers. His eye drawn by the blaze of fall color, Ike tucked Libby's hand in his and started for some trees standing amidst the waving grasslands.

"Hear the birds?" Libby paused in the whispering grass to listen, then jumped back as a rabbit darted across their path. She laughed at herself and looked back toward the road, but offered no objections when he continued on toward the trees.

Willows and sumacs and young hardwoods grew along the banks of a little stream. Ike stopped beside it and lifted his eyes to the leaf cover. "Second-growth trees."

"How can you tell?"

"Scrappy-looking. No real size to 'em. Not like those back home."

She smiled. "Ike Galloway! You're homesick."

He chuckled. "Not so's you'd notice. Though there was a time, back in Cuba, when I told God I'd seen all of distant shores I cared to see, and if He could be so kind as to git me home, my feet weren't likely to stray far off Old Kentucky soil."

"Tell me about the war, Ike. How'd you get hurt?" she asked.

He saw her gaze stray to his ear. Funny, he didn't think about his tattered ear much, except when he missed what was being said. "Ain't much to it. We was trying to git up a hill, and the Spanish was trying to hold us down. I got hit by flying fragments, that's all."

There was a cadence to autumn that got in a man's blood—the breeze stirring, rattling dry leaves, and insects chirping a shriller note as if they knew time was running out. The season itself could make him melancholy without thinking of that war. He gestured across the stream toward a fallen log. "I reckon yer feet could use a rest. Let's cross the stream and sit down."

"Think we can jump it?"

He smiled at the fetching way she cocked her head to one side, measuring the width of the stream. "It ain't that wide, Lib. Git a runnin' start, and ya'll make it easy."

"If I don't, I'll spend the rest of the day in wet shoes."

"Quit yer fussin' then, and I'll carry you across."

She narrowed her eye at him. "If it's all the same to you, I'll stay right where I am."

He overrode her token protest with a broad grin and swung her into his arms. "Hang on now, this first step's a big 'un, and if I miss it, well, we'll both get wet."

"Wouldn't be the first time."

"You're awful sassy. Might just drop ya on purpose," he teased.

"I'm not that easy to drop," she said, and laced her hands firmly behind his neck.

His heart was pumping pretty good by the time he leaped over the stream to the other shore. But he overshot the mark and plowed right into a cobweb spun between low-hanging branches.

Libby squealed and nearly lost her footing as he set her down, so intent was she on brushing the sticky gossamer strands from her face and arms and hair.

"Ya ain't scared of spiders, are ya?"

"No, but I don't want them crawling on me! And don't you dare laugh!"

"I ain't," he said, but he was. All that brushing and jerking at her clothes and the color sweeping over her flushed face tickled him.

"Is there anything crawling on me?" she demanded.

"No."

"How would you know? You aren't looking!"

"Yes, I am, Lib. I been looking at you ever since you came down the steps there at the Columbian and knocked the wind right out of my lungs."

"The buggy accident again! That wasn't my fault."

"I was talkin' about before the accident when I first laid eyes on you, and I said, 'Watch yer step, miss.' I shoulda added, 'Yer standing on my heart.' "

"Oh, Ike!" Her hands went still.

He reached out and framed her cheeks between his hands and thought of summer skies over Old Kentucky as he looked into her eyes. Her skin was soft to his calloused fingertips. Her lips were slightly parted. He closed his eyes, touched his lips to her forehead, her nose, her mouth. He heard her breath catch in her throat. Felt her hands close around his wrists, but didn't pull his mouth away until the pressure of her fingers on his wrists tightened, an unspoken restraint.

"I know," he whispered. "I want to hold you, that's all."

She let go of his wrists, let his arms close around her. He kissed away her reserve. Her hands encircled his neck and she nestled sweetly against him, kissing him back. At length, he kissed her forehead again, cradled her head against her shoulder, and whispered, "This courtship's perkin' along, ain't it?"

He felt her smile against him. "A little too briskly, perhaps," she murmured.

"I know. Ya ain't to worry about it, though."

She pressed against his chest with her hands, arched her head back to look into his face, and replied with trust in her eyes, "I know that."

"Good. Then all ya got left to worry over is that spider crawling up yer back."

He laughed as she paused in the act of spinning around, then pushed at him with her open palms. "Very funny."

He caught her hand in his and pulled her over to the log and told her about farming for Miss Maudie Morefield and how well it had gone this year. Told her, too, of his wish to buy the land sometime in the future, and shared his vision of the sirup camp growing a little bigger and better year by year.

She sat quiet for the longest time, her fingers laced around one knee. Talked out, he thought, though he'd done most of the talking, something he didn't often do.

Something on the ground caught her eye. She reminded him of a little leaf, fluttering to the earth to pick up the broken shell of a robin's egg, then going so still, he assumed she saw something else on the ground. Spider, maybe? A grin tweaked at his mouth.

"What's the matter, Lib?"

"Just thinking," she said.

"About what?"

"Abigail." She returned to him on the log, the broken shell in her hand. Without looking at him, she said, "I suppose it's all over town that she gave her baby away."

He had heard rumors. Curious to know if what he had heard was true, yet reluctant to pry, he said, "Heard something about it from Minor."

"I'm not surprised. He drove Mrs. Bigelow to our house to pick up the baby, then back to the station. What'd you hear?"

"Nothin' worth repeating. You know how he is. Major source of minor information, that's how he come by his name." With a pang, Ike saw her eyes fill with tears.

"In this case, it wasn't so minor. A child's whole future weighed into the decision."

"How come she gave her up?" Ike asked.

"Several reasons, the deciding one being that the baby didn't belong to Adam." With a seeking glance, she added, "I'm not sure why I'm telling you this."

"You can trust me."

"I know that. I just don't want you to think we're the kind of people who give children up at random."

Seemed like she took on everybody's hurts. Ike reached an arm around her. "Folks make some hard mistakes. It ain't yers ta fix, Lib. Only to care."

She looked at him from tear-washed eyes, then away again. "Abigail was wanting to get married, and Adam was putting her off. They broke up for a while. But I never once guessed she was seeing someone else. Or that she would . . . would let him take such liberties. I don't want to think she loved the fellow. But maybe she did. Or at least thought she did. And that she could trust him to stand by her. But he didn't. Then she and Adam got back together."

"Adam knew it wasn't his?"

Libby nodded, the leaves rustling beneath her feet.

It sounded like Naomi and Decatur all over again. Libby must have perceived his thoughts, for she tucked her chin and dried her eyes and said the whole situation had given her a new perspective on Decatur McClure.

"I was pretty set against him for a long time," she admitted. "But not you, Ike. What was it you saw in him that no one else saw?"

Ike shrugged. "What matters is that they're back together."

"I guess you're right." She sighed and dropped the shell and dusted her hands. "I can't help thinking Adam could have worked through his feelings and raised the baby as his own if Abigail had just trusted him enough to let him try."

"Sounds to me like they still got their work cut out for them," said Ike.

Libby nodded, her expression so dismal, Ike pulled her head onto his shoulder, and added, "There ain't nothing wrong with second-growth forest, Lib. Or third-growth either. God gives lots of chances."

They returned to the fairgrounds a short while later, but once they had collected Libby's parcels, they had time for little more than a cold drink. Ike walked her to the gate, where Frankie was already waiting, along with Billy, the Brignadellos, and the Gentrys.

Catching sight of Ike and Libby, Mrs. Bee left the others and rushed to meet them. "Ike Galloway! Maddie told us you were here. When did you arrive?"

"Yesterday," said Ike. Wondering how long it would take her to work out her curiosity, he asked, "You and Kersey enjoyin' yerselves?"

"Oh my, yes! It's the experience of a lifetime." Mrs. Bee shuffled her parcels and tipped her head to one side. "So you came to march, did you?"

Ike grinned, and told her straight out, "Truth is, I came down hopin' I could talk Libby into takin' in the sights with me."

"You did, did you?" Mrs. Bee measured the distance between herself and her husband and aimed a behind-the-hand whisper in Libby's direction. "See there, Libby? And you thought it would take a magic needle to stitch up your h-e-a-r-t."

Ike had his bad ear to her, but what he didn't catch, he read on her lips, right down to the spelling. Libby turned red, but lifted her face to his and smiled as if to say that, of course, Mrs. Bee would think Angus had done some heart damage. She was his aunt, after all, and the doting sort.

Kersey came along. Looking askance at his wife, he said, "Mrs. Bee? Are you minding your—"

"Business? Why yes, of course, dear," said Mrs. Bee sweetly. "I was just about to invite Ike to join us at Catherine's for dinner. What do you say, Ike?"

"That's nice of ya, but Billy and me are plannin' to tour the Transportation Building," said Ike, glad for a ready excuse. He took the hand Kersey thrust toward him, talked a minute, and would have gone on his way, but Ida Gentry joined them and echoed Mrs. Bee's invitation.

Mr. Gentry, Ike noted, stayed by the gate gazing off in the distance, aloof as always. *Or was it that even after all these years, he still couldn't look his half brother's son in the eye?* Gentry needn't have worried. Ike had no intention of joining them. He repeated his excuse concerning Billy, to which Frankie piped up and asked if he could stay at the fair, too.

Sensing Frankie wasn't entirely comfortable with the Gentrys, Ike said, "Be all right with me if it's all right with Lib."

Libby left the decision to Ida Gentry, who acquiesced once Ike had promised to see that Frankie got home safely by bedtime. Frankie claimed he knew what streetcar to take and what way to walk and what turns to make when they disembarked, but Libby pulled a scrap of paper from her pocketbook anyway and wrote down Catherine's street address and some directions just in case.

Ike shoved the note into his pocket without taking his eyes off her. He wished their time together hadn't melted away so fast, wished for a less public good-bye, wished for the first time in his life that he'd learned to take a girl's hand and kiss it the way he had seen Angus do a time or two. The gesture was so unsuited to him, he couldn't help thinking that if the road to love was long enough, a fella would surely manage to make a fool of himself. He overcompensated for his weakness for her with a good-bye that was just short of abrupt and trooped back to the Transportation Building with Frankie and Billy.

But for Ike, the appeal of the World Exposition had long since paled. Entertaining some loose idea about talking Frankie into calling it quits when the building closed at six, he pulled the note out of his pocket. The penciled handwriting puzzled him. As did the message.

"Under the carpenter's lace." *Carpenter's lace?*

Ike flipped the note over and found Catherine's address written in Libby's hand. But the words on the other side . . . Must be the note from the lunch table. *Was it Angus's hand?*

Ike talked himself out of it. He had watched Libby pick it up off the table. She'd plucked it from the others and hadn't even looked at it. She had laughed over the note. It was a bit of fun, was all. One of those things where a fella just had to be there to understand. Anyway, if it had been intended for her, if there was any significance to the message, she wouldn't have been so careless as to let it fall into his hands.

37

It had been a wonderful week and Catherine the perfect hostess. But after dinner when Catherine's guests decided to stroll to a nearby park where a band of local musicians was giving an open-air concert, Libby politely declined to join them.

Maddie, pleading weariness, followed Libby upstairs to their room. Once there, she changed into her Berry Sister gown, and when Catherine and the remaining guests had gone, slipped down the back staircase for a rendezvous with Angus.

Taking advantage of the quiet evening alone, Libby tried to write in her journal. But already the magic of the fair had faded. She couldn't bring it into sharp enough focus to do it justice with her words.

Putting out the light, Libby wandered to the window, raised the sash, and lifted her face to the sky.

When I consider Thy heavens, the work of Thy fingers, the moon and the stars, which Thou hast ordained, what is man that Thou art mindful of him? And yet He was, there was the wonder. He was swift to hear and eager to unfold His plan for the good of His children. He had a plan for her, a plan for Ike. Did their lives blend as one in His perfect plan?

Distracted by movement below, Libby looked beyond the stretch of open yard and tall bushes toward the freshly painted playhouse. From the ground floor, the bushes screened the playhouse from view. But the lavishly gingerbread-trimmed structure—*carpenter's lace,* Maddie had called it—was plainly visible from Libby's vantage point, a fact that must have escaped Maddie and Angus's attention. They stood in the open door of the playhouse, wrapped in each other's arms. The dog Dinner slipped past them and into the playhouse.

The moon was not as orange and round as it had seemed from the water last night, but it shed a silver light on everything it touched. Even on Dinner as he darted out of the playhouse with something in his mouth. Libby couldn't tell what he had, but whatever it was, Maddie and Angus wanted it back. They looked like children, dashing around the bushes after the silly dog. Libby smiled at the laughter on their faces. In short order, they abandoned the chase for more pleasurable pursuits. As the embrace lengthened, Libby turned her eyes away, partly discretion, partly because it stirred a yearning for Ike and conjured all sorts of memories of her afternoon with him.

She wasn't sure how she had come to tell him about Abigail, but she was glad that she had. He could be trusted with what she had told him. Further, it served as a stark example of just how tangled life could become, should they grow careless in guarding their feelings for each other.

Libby pushed the window down and closed the curtains, appreciating for the first time those messages of restraint taught at home and from pulpits and whispered from lips of those who had learned the hard way. Untested herself, she hadn't understood how easily the lines between lust and love could blur. In fact, she hadn't understood lust at all. Yet her growing attraction to Ike and the stirrings he had awakened gave her a new empathy for Naomi and Maddie and Abigial. Empathy, and a realization that she was as vulnerable as any other woman in love. That the difference had to rest not in her feelings for Ike, but in her faith.

It was almost nine when Ike returned Frankie to Catherine's house. He was tired, but Frankie wanted to show him where he had been sleeping out. "Fairy hut," Frankie called it, mentioning fancy woodwork. Ike had thought he meant the inside woodwork, but as it turned out, it wasn't the inside that had so captivated Frankie. It was the gingerbread on the outside of the child's playhouse. Ike could see how it might conjure images of pixies and fairies.

"I made a picture of it for Opal, but I ain't shore she'll believe it," said Frankie, as if he needed Ike's eyes for confirmation. "Ain't it queer folks would build somethin' so fancy jest for young'uns ta play . . ."

"You hear something, Frankie?" Ike interrupted. He tilted his head, listening hard.

"Probably jest Dinner diggin' a hole," said Frankie.

"Dinner?" questioned Ike.

"He's the dog Miz Catherine's husband Charlie bought off of them boys I was tellin' you about. You know, ketchin' dogs for the Igorots."

Ike shushed him with the wave of hand. Voices, sure enough. Folks talking quiet over by the bushes. Frankie heard them, too. "Angus," he whispered.

Ike nodded, for by then he had recognized Cearlock's silhouette. There was a woman with him. She had her back to Cearlock and Cearlock had his back to them. The breeze stirred through the bushes, reshaping the branches, making a fleeting window. Everything in Ike went numb.

He knew that dress. He pictured Lib standing childlike on a footstool in Doc's lobby, swinging her arms and singing that nonsense song. De monk, de monk, de monk. *Who* was the monkey? He stood within yards of that fairy hut, thinking maybe *he* was, and praying he was wrong. He wasn't conscious of having spoken, yet Frankie looked at him with sudden misgivings. There was wisdom beyond the boy's years in his eyes.

He whispered, "Whatcha gonna do, Ike?"

What could he do? He'd told Libby plain enough he wasn't courtin' another man's girl. But if she had set her cap for Angus, why had she spent so much of the past two days with him? Why had she let him kiss her, hold her, share his dreams with her? *Or had he just been too quick to believe that what he felt for her was mutual?* Mrs. Bee talkin' about stitching broken hearts. Angus sitting next to her at the table. Passing her that note. As if to say *I can take her any time I want her.* To say, *Git on down the road.* As Gentry had said to his mother and his sister and him a dozen years ago. Ike tried to shake off that embedded memory, reasoning one had nothing to do with the other. But somehow, the hard edges overlapped.

"Go on to the house, Frankie. Go on!" he urged. His voice was sharp enough to make Frankie turn and go.

De monk, de monk, de monk, ringing in his head, Ike was turning, too, when a dog darted toward the hut, a corset in his mouth. *Not Lib's, surely not Lib's!* After all those words about her sister-in-law? What were they? Empty smoke?

Ike swung around and with his world caving in around him, strode back toward Cearlock and the girl. He saw then why the girl was facing away, saw Cearlock's hands fumbling with her buttons. He couldn't have felt the pain more keenly if the bone stays in that corset had slashed through his heart. Anger fogged over reason until he was buried beneath the weight of it. He wasn't conscious of crossing the clearing, but there he was, catching the flutter of that familiar moon-washed gown as he spun Cearlock around. Blood roiling, he launched his fist just as the woman behind Cearlock turned his way. *Maddie!*

Paralyzed by the magnitude of his error, Ike pulled up on the punch, but too late to stop it altogether. The timing was such, Cearlock saw it coming and ducked to one side, leaving Maddie in the line of fire. The blow, having lost most of its momentum, glanced off her shoulder. She let out the startled cry a mouse makes when caught by the tail. Mortified, Ike grabbed her quick, his anger dead in an instant. "Maddie!"

"Take your hands off my wife!" Angus jerked Ike up by the shirtfront.

Half-sick at how near he'd come to hurting Maddie, Ike submitted to Cearlock's manhandling, all the while looking past him and apologizing. "Are ya all right, Maddie? I never meant to . . . ya know I didn't mean to . . . durn it all, what're ya lettin' him . . . yer *wife?*" He halted, the explanation for Cearlock's murderous rage becoming clear.

Cearlock seemed torn between strangling him and battering him into the bushes when Maddie intervened. Hooking her arms around Cearlock from behind, she said, "Angus, this isn't accomplishing anything. Let go of him before you both get hurt."

"I will not! He hit you!"

"Only because you ducked," said Maddie. Swiftly collecting her wits, she added, "Anyway, I'm not hurt. Come on, now. Enough of this foolishness. You're going to have Catherine's neighbors out here if you don't stop this nonsense."

Dropping his hands from Ike's shirtfront, Cearlock rolled his shoulders back as if to shake off his anger. "Speak up, man. Why are you here, and what do you mean by swinging at me?"

"I was seein' Frankie home," said Ike, wishing he'd listened to that voice in his head which had told him earlier today that a man in love could make a fool of himself if he wasn't careful. He had done a bang-up job of it. Knowing he deserved whatever Angus dished out, he asked, "Libby know you're married?"

"Libby? What's Libby got to do with it?" It was Maddie who had spoken. She stopped short. "For pity sake! You mistook me for Libby. That's what this is all about!"

"It's dark, and in that dress . . ." Ike shifted his weight, trying to find a way out and seeing that there was none. "I suppose you're goin' ta tell her."

"I might," said Maddie. Cheerful of a sudden, she added, "Of course, if you were to give me your word not to mention our marriage to anyone until after the election, I might be persuaded to forget it."

"The election? Yer married, and ya ain't tellin' anybody until after the election?" Warily, Ike asked, "How come?"

"You know how it is in Edgewood." Maddie tilted her chin. "With me so recently widowed, it seems wise to wait."

"Confound it, Maddie," said Angus. "We don't have to explain ourselves to him."

Reading between the lines, Ike felt a fresh spurt of indignation, this one solely for Maddie. "Beggin' yer pardon, Maddie, but if I could talk to Angus alone . . ."

Maddie split a doubtful glance between them. "I don't know if that's such a good idea."

Haughtily, Angus said, "I'd welcome the conversation."

"No more fighting? You promise?"

"Why don't you go on inside, Maddie?" said Angus evasively. "And see if you can catch that blasted dog on your way."

Maddie retreated a few paces and jerked her corset away from the dog. Though Angus had intended her to return to the house, she ducked inside the playhouse instead.

"Make it short," said Angus, as the door closed behind her.

"I cain't see why yer ashamed of her. She's pretty. She's smart. She thinks yer worth havin'."

"Ashamed of her? I'm not ashamed of her!" Angus called a bitter imprecation down on his head. "I'm not a violent man, Galloway, but if you keep testing me, I won't be responsible for my actions."

"If it ain't that yer ashamed, then what is it? Why would ya keep yer marriage a secret?"

"Chester thinks that under the circumstances it would be better to wait."

"It ain't up to Chester to think."

"He's taken me in and raised me as if I were his own son. His advice ought to count for something."

"And to think I used to envy you," Ike countered. "But I'll be durned if that daddy of yers ain't weakened yer spine."

"Now wait just a minute . . ."

"Cearlock, that ain't the first punch you've ducked. Eight years ago, ya took that girl's virtue and you slunk off leavin' her reputation in tatters and the whole town yippin'. She got her chin in the air and she's got it there again. Now why do you think that is?"

Cearlock was quiet for so long, Ike got disgusted. "What's the use? It ain't nothin' to do with me, anyway. The Maddie I used to know wasn't slow about stickin' up for herself, so I reckon when she gets enough of dodging blows for you, she'll do somethin' about it." He started away and had almost reached the street when Cearlock called after him. He turned to find the man struggling with himself.

Closing the distance between them, Angus said, "About that time at the lake . . . You're right. It never should have happened, and when it did, I shouldn't have abandoned Maddie." He bit his lip, but kept his eyes level as he added, "Even worse was not speaking up when your name got attached to it."

The apology caught Ike off guard. He started to tell Angus that it was a long time ago and that it didn't matter. But it did. He hadn't seen it then, but the lie he had let stand had reached out and caused other people pain. "Maybe I was wrong. Maybe ya do have some backbone after all."

"Yes, and if you ever jump me again . . ."

Ike shrugged off the implied threat. "I shouldn'tna swung at ya, Angus. Ain't no way to settle things."

"No, and you ought to be shot for what you were thinking."

Ike shuffled his feet and shoved his fingertips into his pockets. "I may be yet, if Lib catches on."

"You're wondering is Maddie going to tell her? I can't help thinking she will."

"Thinkin'? Or hopin'?"

Angus replied with a ghost of a smile, "Both."

Libby answered the knock at her door and found Frankie standing in the dimly lit corridor. She swung the door wider. He strode past her to the window and threw back the curtain.

"Frankie? What're you doing?"

"Jest lookin'."

"At what? Is something wrong?"

"Ike and me come up on Miss Maddie and Mr. Cearlock. Ike didn't know they was married and he saw Angus kissing on her and—"

"Didn't you tell him?" Libby broke in.

"Well, no. Ya made me promise not to."

For two people who didn't mind asking others to keep their secret, Angus and Maddie sure were careless about it themselves! Irritated, Libby said, "Get away from the window, Frankie."

"They's walkin' to the street."

"Who?"

"Ike and Mr. Cearlock."

Libby strode across the floor and joined him. There was no sign of Maddie, and nothing in the men's posture to betray what they were finding to say to one another. But the fact that they were talking was surprising. Today, when they'd exchanged greetings at the restaurant, it had been perfunctory on Ike's part. The handshake, too. And though Angus had been cordial, Libby knew his sentiments where Ike was concerned.

"I'm goin' back down and ask Ike if I can go to the barracks and stay the night with him and Billy," said Frankie.

"I'm sure he'd let you if he could, Frankie, but it isn't up to him. Maybe you can sit with him on the train ride home," said Libby.

"Where're you going ta sit?"

Libby chuckled. "Let's worry about that in the morning, shall we?"

38

Libby accompanied Frankie to the little room off the nursery which Catherine had prepared for him prior to their arrival, made him promise not to return to the playhouse where he had spent the previous four nights, then returned to her own room and undressed for bed. Leaving her black traveling suit and hat out for the trip home, she packed her bags and was asleep when Maddie came in and bumped around in the darkness, getting ready for bed.

"Libby?" she whispered.

Libby stirred, and mumbled a groggy response.

Maddie sighed. "I guess you aren't interested in hearing about the wedding reception Angus's parents are having for us a week from Sunday."

Wedding reception? Libby rose up on one elbow. "Reception, did you say?"

"Angus and I decided to announce our marriage and let the chips fall where they may. Chester tried to talk us out of it, but Ida understood. She and Mrs. Bee are downstairs right now, making plans."

Libby could hear the lilting smile in Maddie's voice. Maddie didn't often lilt. She was more inclined to spike words than make a melody of them.

Libby asked the obvious question first—why the change of heart? The answer brought her feet to the floor. She made a light and delved a little deeper to be sure she hadn't misinterpreted what Maddie meant by "a case of mistaken identity."

She hadn't. Ike had thought it was she. That Angus was buttoning *her* dress. *How could he think that of her?* Libby didn't betray her hurt to Maddie lest it dampen her joy, for Maddie had been waiting a long time to be put first in Angus's life.

But it felt to Libby as if Ike had put her dead last. She could understand how he might mistake the dress. But that he could see Angus's hands work the buttons in the moonlight and still think it was her was incomprehensible. After revealing her pain over Abigail's carelessness, did he really think she would be so reckless herself?

She put the moral question to one side and looked at the issue of honesty. Did he believe she had misled him concerning her feelings for him? That she welcomed his wooing and Angus's, too? Libby wanted to be angry. Instead, she was hurt, for what did all his tender words mean when he held her in so little esteem?

The pale moon shone through the trees, casting shadows on the wall. Dinner barked. Off in the distance, Libby heard a train rumble and wished she was on it, heading home to Edgewood to people who loved and trusted her.

How could Ike? How could he, God? How could he steal my heart and think it of so little worth?

Libby dressed hurriedly the next morning and reached for her hat, only to draw her hand back, the associations too painful. Leaving her hair loose, she tucked the hat into her valise and went downstairs to join the Brignadellos and Catherine's parents in thanking Catherine and Charlie for their hospitality.

Mr. Gentry saw to her baggage while Frankie wrestled Dinner for his shoe, and she and Mrs. Gentry and Mrs. Bee took turns hugging Catherine goodbye.

And then there was Ike. He was waiting for her on a bench in the station. His grip was on the floor, his feet spread to accommodate it. He sat with his forearms on his knees, ticket in one hand. His head came up, as if he sensed her presence, and for a moment, their eyes met.

He hadn't slept well. He'd crimped his boarding pass, folding and unfolding it, and he'd cut himself shaving. Her throat tightened at the flood of involuntary observations. Eyes stinging, she turned and walked the other way. He overtook her and stopped her with the sound of her name.

She held back her tears and lifted her face to his. "Frankie's wanting to share a seat with you on the ride home. You don't mind, do you?"

" 'Course not. Are ya wantin' the window seat? Or shall we let him have it?" he asked, testing the waters.

"That's between you and Frankie."

"Maddie told you, didn't she?" His brow furrowed as he leaned forward and rubbed the back of his neck. "I got no excuse. Best I can do is say I'm sorry."

"I'm sorry too," she said stiffly. "I thought we understood each other better than that. Apparently, I was wrong."

"Don't say it like that. Ya weren't wrong." He reached for her, then let his hand fall away as she retreated a step. Color swept up his face. Seeing Frankie coming, he lowered his voice. "Sit with me, Lib. I been waiting for ya, hoping we could talk."

It was irrational, thinking her name sounded different on his tongue. Sounded treasured. He had some way of showing it. She shifted her valise to the other hand, thwarting his reach for it. "I believe my time would be better spent writing, so long as you're looking after Frankie."

He stood looking down at her, expression disarmed, doubling his boarding pass between the fingers of his restless right hand. "I haven't changed my mind about anything, Lib."

There was no escaping his meaning. But last night's actions outsounded this morning's quiet words. Her emotions as frayed as the pass in his hand, she turned and walked away. This time, he didn't follow. Responding to the final boarding call, Libby made her way to the last car on the train and crowded in among strangers.

The ride began uneventfully. Catherine had tucked an orange and some date bread into her bag. Libby ate it, then tried to sleep and couldn't. At length, she took out her tablet and wrote instead. It wasn't inspired writing, just elements of the fair she planned later to develop into a series of articles for the *Gazette*.

It was in mentioning the Grand Basin and the lagoons that Libby thought of Maddie and Ike, and of that night at Spring Lake. She had believed him guilty of all that was whispered of them. Or at least she had feared he was guilty.

It wasn't the same. It was a long time ago. She didn't know him then. He knew her. Or at least he should, and if he didn't by now, he never would.

He's only human.

Human enough to react hastily, blindly, badly.

Which justifies you in refusing his apology?

Libby closed her eyes and rubbed her throbbing temples. *So what now? Do you nurse your hurt or straighten this out?* She knew the answer, but it took a few miles for her to swallow her pride and make up her mind to find him. She hadn't watched to see which car he boarded, and it was a very long train. Crowded, too.

Libby tried to get around her dozing seatmate, but the woman sat there like a human gate, her legs blocking access to the aisle.

"Excuse me," said Libby, leaning closer. "Ma'am? If you could let me pass, please." Failing to rouse the woman verbally, she stretched out a hand and timidly tapped her on the shoulder.

The woman bolted upright, blinking and blurting, "Are we there?"

"I'm sorry to wake you, but I have to get . . . ouch!" Libby flinched and cupped her eye.

"A cinder?" asked the woman.

Nodding, squinting, rubbing her watering eye, Libby tried unsuccessfully to reach the aisle.

"Still in there, is it?" The woman winced in sympathy. "Sit down, I'll get it."

"That's very kind, but I can do it."

"Nonsense. Sit down!"

Left with little choice, Libby settled back into her seat and tried not to hiss in pain as the woman probed her watering eye with the corner of a handkerchief.

"Easy, easy. There now. Isn't that better?" said the woman at length. "A sharp one, too. No wonder it hurt."

Libby thanked her, grabbed her valise, and was on her way. The Edgewood crowd was in the next car. The hometown folks, having just as good a time as they did on the trip down, delayed her, inviting her to sit with them and sing with them and asking after Frankie. She told them that she was on her way to check on him, and no, she didn't know all the words to the "fair song" and yes, Catherine and Charlie *did* have an absolutely adorable house.

Libby ducked past a frowning conductor in the next car and was making her way through a fourth car when the lurching train sent her tumbling into a silver-haired gentleman who was coming from the other direction. He had button-bright eyes, a handlebar moustache, and amazingly quick hands for an old fellow.

"That's quite all right, dear, no harm done. I say, it's a rocky ride, isn't it though? Sit down, sit down!" He handed her into the inside seat as slick as a seasoned fisherman reeling in the catch of the day, then sat down next to her, slapped his traveling case onto his knees, and beamed at her. "Peterson Hadley Hinkley, at your service, miss . . ."

"Watson. Elizabeth Watson. Now if you'll excuse me . . ."

"You look like a young lady of discriminating taste, Miss Watson. And a crackerjack cook unless I'm mistaken. Yes?" So saying, he opened the case on his knees and flashed an ingratiating smile. "Now, now, don't be modest. I can always spot a young lady who knows her way around a kitchen. But isn't it annoying when those crusts won't brown?"

"I beg your pardon, sir?"

"Pie crusts, Miss Watson. Pie crusts. The Hinkley Tin Company, of which I am owner, president of the board, and head salesman, is proud to introduce a line of pie tins guaranteed to put a flaky golden brown crust on your pie

that will make any mother-in-law weep. Yes, indeed! And it is your good
fortune . . .''

It was her *bad* fortune to have fallen into the trap of this tenacious tinware
salesman, who held her captive with his windy spiel and his bottomless sam-
ple case until the Springfield Station, which was his stop, and her *only* bit
of good fortune so far today.

With the train in the station, Libby made some headway, but they were
moving again by the time she finally spotted Ike. The breath went out of her
at the glumness of his expression as he stared out at the passing countryside
while Frankie slept with his head against his shoulder.

Libby transferred her valise to the other hand. Mechanically, she reached
as if to straighten her hat, only to remember she wasn't wearing it. She strode
on and was within yards of Ike when a tall, lanky conductor who smelled of
garlic and onions blocked her path.

"This car is full, miss."

Libby resisted the urge to hold her finger under her nose and pointed out
Ike instead. "I'm going to slip in between the young man and the boy ahead
there on the right."

The man looked at Ike, then back to her again with a dubious glance.
"There isn't room, miss. Now you go on back to your seat."

Libby suspected her diminutive size had misled him in judging her age.
Wearing her hair loose subtracted years, too. "It's all right, sir," she assured
him. "We are acquaintances."

"Is the gentleman a relative?"

"No, sir. Just a friend. And the boy with him is in my charge," she added
for good measure.

"Young lady, you are scarcely old enough to be in charge of yourself,"
he said, openly disapproving. "Now go back to your seat."

"But I'm telling you, I *know* them."

The brim of his pillbox hat threw a long shadow on his even longer face
as he drew himself to his full, intimidating height. "I'll not have you blocking
the aisle, trying to make an argument, miss."

"But if you would just let me speak with him a moment . . ." Libby protested.

The officious conductor took her by the arm and turned her around. "The
best way a lady traveling alone can keep from inviting unwanted attention is
to stay in her seat. You can't trust every man to be a gentleman. Didn't your
folks teach you anything before turning you loose in the world?"

Embarrassed to the point of tears, Libby gave up and returned to her seat.
Her fellow passenger had debarked, leaving the seat next to her empty. Libby
flung her valise into it and cast a longing glance toward the platform at the
end of the train. It was just feet away and promised a bit of privacy in which

to mop up her tears and overcome her frustration. Praying that awful conductor was busy elsewhere, she ventured into the aisle once more and made her way to the platform.

The breeze was bracing. It cooled her flushed face and blew autumn's scent through her hair. She filled her lungs and exhaled slowly and noted the ripening of the prairie. Brushstrokes of browns and golds and mustard yellows merged with summer's fading greens, creating variegated pastures and tree lines and fields. Corn dried on fading stalks, the leaves rattling in the breeze of the train's passing.

Libby squinted into the deep cloudless sky where a flock of geese winged southward. Did the straggling one there at the end feel as discouraged as she did? So discouraged he could fly over the earth's shifting tapestry and go right on beating his wings with no sense of joy? Fresh tears pooled in her eyes.

You silly thing, you're just feeling sorry for yourself. Now stop it, she scolded herself. *Since when do you let a stuffy old conductor reduce you to tears?* But it wasn't the conductor, and she knew it.

Libby stiffened at the sound of the door opening behind her. *Caught out of her seat again!* Dreading a second confrontation, she flinched and turned and promptly swallowed the meek apology on her lips, for it wasn't the despotic conductor, but Ike. Ashamed of her childish tears, she turned away and made a furtive one-fingered swipe at her cheek.

"Lib?"

How did he do that? Melt her, just saying her name? Fresh tears pooled. "Cinder in my eye," she said.

"Let me see." He turned her around to catch her chin between his thumb and forefinger. "Look up."

"It's out," she said, retreating from his touch.

"What were ya doin'?"

"Just sitting there." She gestured toward the train car as he moved beside her. "It blew in through the window."

"What I meant was, what were you doin' when ya come to my car?"

"If you saw me, why didn't you rescue me from that overbearing conductor?"

"I got here as fast as I could. Anyway, ya told me back at the station you were goin' ta write and not to be wastin' yer time. Or somethin' of the kind."

Libby moistened her lips and struggled with herself. "I'm sorry, I was rude, wasn't I? But you hurt my feelings."

"I was wrong thinkin' it was you." Jacketless, he hunched his shoulders and tucked his fingertips into his pockets. "I didn't want ta think it. It was the dress."

"I know that." She slid him a sidelong glance and, as if to shoulder her own portion of blame, said, "Chloe Berry says you shouldn't let a fellow kiss you until you're engaged. If you'd asked me a week ago, I would have said the same thing. I should have stuck to it, I guess, because I sure seem to have given *you* the wrong idea."

"That ain't true at all." He covered her hand with his own.

"That goes for hand-holding, too," she said, and pulled her hand free.

His color deepened. He wrapped the hand she had rebuffed around the railing. "Lib, ya surely don't think that mix-up last night had anything to do with ya lettin' me kiss ya?"

"Didn't it?"

" 'Course it didn't."

"Then would you explain to me how you could have possibly thought I would be out strolling in the moonlight with Angus Cearlock?"

"It was a muddled piece of thinkin', I reckon. But there was the dress. And the note. And Mrs. Bee sayin' something about stitchin' up your heart like he'd broke it or somethin'.

"I'm telling you he didn't, and I guess I ought to know. What's this about a note?"

His jaw tightened at her flinty tone. Uneasily he said, "Somethin' about meetin' under the carpenter's lace. You gave it to me, Lib. With Catherine's address on it so I could see Frankie home."

"Oh, that!" Suddenly, Libby remembered where she'd gotten the piece of paper. And the way Maddie had been plowing through the remaining paper scraps on the table as she and Ike turned away. "It must have been *Maddie's* note."

He lifted his shoulder and let it fall as if to say he'd figured that out. The sunshine picked out the paler highlights shading his hair as he looked out over the passing countryside. "I been watching the leaves on the trees as we sail by and thinkin' how the autumn rains are goin' to come and wash out the roads and by the time the mud freezes over, it'll be snow keepin' me from seein' you. Then comes sirup season and muddy roads again. I guess what I'm sayin' is we ought to be spendin' our time better'n this, Lib."

"Better than what?"

"Than fussin' over my actin' the fool last night, " he said. "I know I hurt ya, and I'm sorry. I reckon we're both goin' to make some mistakes now and then. But I can't help thinkin' we could get along, so long as being right don't ever become more important than being together."

His tender-sweet words made her ashamed of her childish whim to punish him for a heart wound and a sleepless night and a wretched morning. She slid her hand over his on the railing. "You're right. I'm sorry, too." Her pulse pattering in tune with the clacking iron wheels, she slid him a sidelong glance. "You like being together?"

"More than anything." His fingers curled around hers. His eyes were the dusky shade of gray the sky turns when sudden weather moves in but the sun refuses to give way. "The more I'm with ya, the dearer ya grow. I love ya, Lib. Have since I don't know when."

She was looking through spangles again. Ikes in triplicate. The slow-growing feeling that had been begun the day of the box social at the lake, when he'd tugged at her skirt and told her she had a "shine," was a well-spring bubbling over.

"Fall rains and winter storms and rough roads and crops to get out and in and in and out," he said. "Most generally, I'm a patient man. But I don't feel so patient when I think of the weeks and months ahead and of all there is to keep us apart if we let it. I don't want ta go along us being *two* when we'd make a good *one*. What do you say, Lib? Would ya marry me?"

"Ike." The breath went out of her. She touched her fingers to his lips, as if she could physically capture his words and savor each sweet syllable.

The creases deepened in his sun-browned cheeks as he caught her fingers and held them. "For a wordy woman, ya sure have got quiet."

Laughter and tears mixing, she cried, "I love you, too. And yes, I'd be pleased to be your wife."

"Pleased?" He cocked an eyebrow. "Just *pleased?*"

She kissed his lips and walked into his arms.

It was a gentle kiss, with overtures of a deeper passion. She breathed his scent and kissed him back and caught a glimpse of the years that stretched ahead of them—a patched-up affair of joys and hurts and pain and passion, a quilt of sorts, the raw edges bound by love and stitched with forgiveness and sanctified by God.

Epilogue

Libby, her brothers, and Abigail joined hands in the parlor on an Indian summer afternoon in October. Father's serene gaze swept the ensemble of faces, a smile of paternal pride tipping his mouth. When they had stilled their chatter, he led them in prayer, asking God's blessin' on the marriage of his bonny lass and her laddie, who was, he noted, swift and tireless and mortal persistent in his wooin'.

Jacob laughed at Libby's flushing protest, while Adam slipped his arm around Abigail, and Davie jerked at his crisply starched collar, complaining that he was choking.

"Oot the door wi' ye, laddie, and off to the Grubens' hoose. I winna have ye pesterin' yer sister on her weddin' day!" said Father, sending him to join their friends and neighbors gathered a block away on the Grubens' lawn to share in the occasion.

Jacob hugged Libby and trailed out after Davie. Adam, rarely demonstrative, surprised her by kissing her cheek.

"Be happy, Lib. You deserve it," he said.

Touched, Libby laughed to keep from crying, and told him with a cheeky grin that she intended to be happy, and that if she wasn't, he would be the first to hear about it as he was the one who had started this string of weddings in the Watson family. Her father and Mrs. Baker were planning a quiet ceremony of their own soon, though they had as yet to announce the date.

"She looks like a storybook princess, doesn't she, Adam?" Abigail paused in adorning Libby's soft mass of curls with a cluster of lilies and smiled at her husband.

"As Opal would say, Mrs. Bee has a magic needle," Libby said, and plucked a stray thread from the handsome gown Mrs. Brignadello had made as a wedding gift. Trimmed in silk, it was of shadow-printed cream wool grenadine with leg-o'-mutton sleeves and a trim-fitting bodice.

"Could I steal just a moment to give you your present?" asked Abigail.

"But I told Father to tell you no presents!"

"I'll be thankin' ye to leave me oot of it." Father stepped out of Abigail's way as she scurried off to get her gift.

Adam had just last week been hired at the railroad shops in Bloomington. Between the move and the rent on a tiny house, Libby was sure they had little money to spare for gift-giving. Gently, she said, "Really, Adam. You weren't supposed to get me anything."

"That's good, because I didn't." He chuckled when she wrinkled her nose at him.

Abigail sailed into the parlor with an elegantly wrapped package. "I love it, Libby, but I want you to have it."

Libby caught her breath as the wrappings gave way. It was the quilt she and the "needlers," as Maddie now called them, had made and given to Abigail only a month ago.

"But I can't accept this! It's yours."

"Yes, you can and you will," said Abigail, looking pleased.

Adam pulled out his watch. "You two keep this up, and Lib's going to be late for her own wedding."

"Come along to the porch wi' me, lad. I would have ye to gi'e the signal to the doctor's wife to start the musickin'," said Father. "I will be waitin' on the porch for ye, lass."

"Be right there, Father."

Abigail's doe-soft eyes lifted at the corners as she shook the folds from the quilt. "I wanted you to have it back because it's beautiful and because it depicts your life, not mine. It does, Libby. See here?" She smiled and pointed out the mail buggy and the tiny splash of red showing through the back window that Paulette had said was Libby's hair. "Oh, and I made an addition. See the book I fashioned into the corner here?"

"To represent the proposed library!" Libby made the connection at once. She had written Abigail a week ago and told her the exciting news about Lester Morefield's family making a generous donation toward a public library, and of nearly a dozen other residents matching the amount. "Are you sure you want to give this up?"

Abigail thrust it into her arms without reservation. "I know you meant it as a comfort. But the kindness that I received in this house was the real comfort. More than you'll ever know."

Libby's eyes filled as she embraced Abigail, the quilt caught between them. As welcome as the gift was the assurance that healing was coming to Adam and Abigail, and that she and Father and Davie had in some small way been a part of that healing.

Father and Libby waited until Adam and Abigail had joined the other wedding guests, then they stepped out on the newly poured village sidewalk and began strolling arm in arm toward those gathered in the yard a block away. She could hear Paulette on the accordion. Trees lined the walk like autumn torches. Leaves quaked in the breeze, falling along the path that carried her ever closer to Ike.

" 'Tis a long weddin' march," observed Father. "If ye would be gettin' second thoughts, noo is the time. I hear the doon and oot a-comin'."

Libby braced her fluttering stomach with a gloved hand and smiled at his gentle teasing. "Down and out" was her brothers' name for any train that moved slowly enough that their uncle, Willie Blue, could swing aboard. But that was back in his drinking and tramping days. For all of that, his final years had been a tribute to what God could do with a yielded life. It was Uncle Willie's bequest of the store that had brought her to Edgewood. She had viewed the store and the town as a stepping-stone. But her vision of the town had shifted; she was putting down roots, anchoring her life to Ike's. How meticulously and with what infinite detail God worked at braiding their lives together.

The train chuffed along, blowing its whistle for the crossing and drowning out Paulette's accordion music with a throaty *choo, choo, choo* that hung in the air. Libby slowed her steps, determined not to let the unforeseen disturbance interfere with her outdoor wedding.

Originally she had planned to hold the wedding in the parlor at home. But the room was too small to accommodate their guests. When Mrs. Gruben had graciously offered her yard, it had seemed the perfect solution. Not only was it a lovely lawn, vibrant with flowers, but it guaranteed that this would be one social affair Mr. Gruben wouldn't be forced to attend without his wife.

The twin shocks of dried sweet corn in the Grubens' garden partially blocked Libby's view of the guests as they stopped to wait until the train had passed. She saw the McClures' wagon parked along the street. Naomi had closed the store for a couple of hours so that she could see them exchange their vows.

Generous friends, Decatur and Naomi, lending the woodworking cabin to her and Ike as a home as long as they needed it. In a few hours, she and Ike would cross the threshold as husband and wife.

The train continued on its way. Libby's coiled nerves tweaked as Paulette pealed out the opening chords to the "Wedding March," and the guests, spread over the Grubens' lawn, rose from their benches and chairs and turned of one accord. She and Father started across the path between flower beds that God had so lovingly spared from Jack Frost. An assorted variety of flowers ran together like paints on an artist's palette. In much the same way, friends and neighbors blended into a sea of faces, a heartscape of a place she called home.

Mrs. Baker. Teddy with his familiar stance, one hand behind his back, holding his elbow. Sugar at his side. Zerilda, wearing her habitual scowl and her man-sized shoes. Captain Boyd, tipping his cap and moving his lips in an audible, "Miss Willie," as she passed on Father's arm. Kersey Brignadello and Mrs. Bee, who couldn't resist reaching out and smoothing the skirt of Libby's gown. Mr. Gruben, her writing mentor. Mrs. Gruben, her friend. Dr. Harding. Major Minor, who shifted the wad of tobacco in his jaw and winked at Libby. The McClures, with their shoulders touching, flanked by their children. Hascal Caton, scratching his grizzled jowl and nudging Mr. Lamb, who, along with his wife, stood to Hascal's left.

"Weddin's is cheerier than buryin's, Mr. Lamb, iffin' ya could only figur' out how to make a livin' from 'em," Libby heard Hascal reflect as she passed, eyes fixed straight ahead.

Dorene, Chloe, and Maddie, dressed in their Berry Sisters gowns, stood with the grape arbor to their backs, ready to sing. Pastor Shaw waited in front of the arched rose trellis, the light breeze fluttering the pages of his Bible. Billy was there, too. And Ike.

His shoulders were back, his feet spread, his arms hanging loose, his hands clasped in front of him. Sunlight spilled through the rose trellis, gilding his hair. He was watching her, waiting, reverent and still. His eyes were the color of smoke, and like smoke, his expression was invasive, seeping through her, touching all the secret places: body, mind, and spirit. Heat swept up her neck as light broke across his face, for his smile *was* light to her. It crowded out flowers and family and friends and thoughts of the impending ceremony and the wedding dinner to follow.

With an answering smile, Libby relinquished her dear father's arm and took Ike's. She returned the tender pressure of his callused fingers covering hers and, with heart in hand, stepped from one chapter of life joyously into the next.